COUNTY OF BRANE
PU

P9-DNU-399

1 2017

BEYOND THE SEA

ALSO BY DAVID L. GOLEMON

BEYOND THE SEA

An Event Group Thriller

DAVID L. GOLEMON

THOMAS DUNNE BOOKS

ST. MARTIN'S PRESS ⚏ NEW YORK

This is a work of fiction. All of the characters, organizations, and events portrayed in this novel are either products of the author's imagination or are used fictitiously.

THOMAS DUNNE BOOKS.
An imprint of St. Martin's Press.

BEYOND THE SEA. Copyright © 2017 by David L. Golemon. All rights reserved. Printed in the United States of America. For information, address St. Martin's Press, 175 Fifth Avenue, New York, N.Y. 10010.

www.thomasdunnebooks.com
www.stmartins.com

The Library of Congress Cataloging-in-Publication Data is available upon request.

ISBN 978-1-250-10307-9 (hardcover)
ISBN 978-1-250-10309-3 (e-book)

Our books may be purchased in bulk for promotional, educational, or business use. Please contact your local bookseller or the Macmillan Corporate and Premium Sales Department at 1-800-221-7945, extension 5442, or by e-mail at MacmillanSpecialMarkets@macmillan.com.

First Edition: June 2017

10 9 8 7 6 5 4 3 2 1

For my mother and father, two children of the Depression
who were saved by a war and lived through it to love forever in peace

ACKNOWLEDGMENTS

To the civilian personnel at the Old Philadelphia Navy Yard, thank you for the great tour and explanation. Also a big shout-out to certain shadowy men and women at M.I.T.—your theories scare the hell out of me.

PROLOGUE

COLD SEAS

Truth uncompromisingly told will always
have its ragged edges.

—Herman Melville, *Billy Budd*

The large man with the brown fedora sitting at its usual jaunty angle on his head sipped his coffee and watched the passersby on Flores Street. He sat beneath a green awning with the gold-scripted name of the business emblazoned across its front—*Trans American Fruit and Grain*. The lanky, broad-shouldered man removed the fedora and used the brim to fan his tanned face. He decided to forgo the hot coffee on this warm September morning and simply slid the cup and saucer away from him. His sunglasses hid the dark pupils that never wavered from the onlookers whose wandering eyes strayed his way as they passed by on the sidewalk fronting the shop. His white shirt was already starting to be saturated by his sweat even at this early hour. As much as he hated the climate, he was ever grateful not to be posted to Iceland or even, God forbid, Alaska. The man was here as a punishment for disagreeing with one of the more powerful men in government service. So, the sweat he would have to suffer with silently along with his banishment. His letter of resignation was written out and sitting upon his desk, ready for the military attaché's signature and forwarding to Washington, D.C. The man was thinking that it may be past time to serve the war in a more direct way.

A morning cloud eased its way past the city and gave a moment's respite from the early morning sun, allowing the American to look up into the otherwise empty sky. He felt, or rather sensed, the man pull up a chair next to him.

"Good morning, Colonel. You're here early," the younger man said as Colonel

Garrison Lee, former senator from Maine, lowered his head and fixed the man with a curious look. He remained silent, content not to comment on such an obvious deduction.

He was amazed at the youthful team he had been given for the job they had to do in South America. He had been lucky thus far in not losing one of these kids of his to enemy activity but knew with their "just out of college" arrogant, can-do attitudes, that blessing would not last long. His dark brows rose over the heavy sunglasses.

"Sir, we finished that job last night."

Finally, Garrison Lee removed the sunglasses from his face and fixed the younger man with his deep and very disturbing blue eyes. He waited without saying a word. He could see the boy was nervous about something. It was usually best for these kids if they broached the subject of their nervousness on their own without being pushed to do so by him.

"We planted the recorder on the professor's phone with no problem and even fixed his car with a tracking broadcaster."

Lee had to shake his head in dismay at the term *tracking broadcaster*. That meant they had been successful at placing a ten-pound electrical tracker that was equivalent in size to a Motorola home radio.

"Well, I see that old Wild Bill picked the right tenth-grade class to join the team down here."

The young officer flinched at the comment. He had graduated top of his class at the United States Naval Academy last year and had been one of the few handpicked by William "Wild Bill" Donovan, the head of the American OSS, the Office of Strategic Services, the country's foremost intelligence gathering apparatus in wartime service. While not up to British intelligence in capability, the OSS was well on its way to becoming pretty good at their jobs, if he could keep these college campus all-stars alive long enough.

"From the look on your face, Mr. Hamilton, I think I sense a *but* coming. A word of advice, young sir: with that terrible poker face of yours, stay out of gambling halls and never, ever try to bluff that new bride of yours with that hidden talent of giving away your poker hand. What's the girl's name again?"

"Alice, sir." The young naval ensign on duty in Argentina on detached assignment to the OSS swallowed and tried to look away from Lee's eyes as they bored into him. "As I said, sir, we placed all listening devices and thought we were away clean, but—"

"Hamilton, are you going to tell me before or after the damn Nazis finish their work in Europe?"

"I guess we didn't get away as cleanly as I thought, sir."

"Look, Hamilton—"

Lee stopped in midsentence when he saw the small gray-bearded man with wire-rimmed glasses holding a leather satchel to his chest like it was armor plate. Garrison recognized the man immediately, and his eyes shot to young Hamilton, who found he couldn't hold the colonel's accusing gaze. The small man was thirty feet away and was looking toward the street nervously before his eyes again settled on the two men beneath the awning. Every time a passing vehicle moved by their location, the man would ease back into shadow. The experienced colonel caught all of this with one glance.

"I guess you'll have an excellent reason why one of the foremost Nazi climatologists is standing right over there and not currently being tracked by your tracking devices." He held up a strong and brutal-looking hand before Hamilton could speak. "Don't tell me. He bugged you and your men at the same time you were tagging him, right? I'm beginning to think that possibly old J. Edgar Hoover trained you himself."

"We were followed, Colonel. I take full responsibility for blowing our cover."

Lee tilted his hat back on his head and unfolded his long legs from beneath the table and stood. His six-foot-five-inch frame was intimidating to all, including the young field agent. He simply patted young Hamilton on the shoulder and faced the Nazi climatologist the OSS had tagged as worth keeping an eye on. The small scientist was the last on their list of three hundred suspected or proven German nationals in Buenos Aires to be "tagged," or bugged to keep track of their whereabouts.

"Anything else I should know, son?" he asked as he rolled the sleeves of his white shirt up as he continued looking at the man from Dortmund, Germany, his hometown according to his OSS dossier.

"He came in just a few minutes ago and asked to speak with the station chief."

This time Lee did look down at Hamilton. "In those words?"

"Exact words, Colonel."

Lee smiled and then approached the smallish man, slightly overdressed in a tweed jacket. He noticed the good professor's raggedy shoes and the motheaten material of his coat. *The Nazis must not place too high a priority on what they pay their scientists these days*, Lee thought.

"Sir," he said as he approached the man. "I'm—"

"Don't bother with an alias, Colonel Lee. We really do not have time for it," the man said as his eyes flicked to the street beyond, as if he suspected the devil would drive up at any minute. The man's beady eyes behind his glasses moved around, examining the faces of the people passing by. He still held his leather valise protectively in front of him.

Garrison Lee tried to hide his astonishment at the smaller man's abruptness and his general knowledge of just who it was he was speaking to. It was obvious that the front of Trans American Fruit and Grain wasn't playing well to German intelligence. The Gestapo was getting ever better at these things.

"I suspect we can converse someplace more private?" the professor asked.

Lee kept his curiosity quiet for the moment. This man already had too much information going in; no need to give him any more. He gestured to the door of the offices and the quieter and much cooler spaces beyond.

"Mr. Hamilton, will you join us, please? Right this way," Lee said as he held the door open.

As they walked in, several women typing at their desks looked up as their machines went silent. Colonel Lee knew that every one of them had a free hand soothing the handle of a Colt .45 in a holder just below the level of their desks. The two men standing by a watercooler looked shocked as one of them even allowed the water in his conical paper cup to spill from his hands. Lee knew these two men were also on the highly secret detail to bug the scientist's car and phone. Lee looked at them until the better part of valor made them shy away. The large American escorted his guest into his office and was followed by young Hamilton, who rolled his eyes at the secretaries, who weren't secretaries at all, and the two men he had been assigned with the night before. He knew they were all probably going to end up in the Pacific Ocean after the colonel was finished with them. The old man took a seat, and Lee noticed the satchel was still pinned to his chest.

"Coffee, or something a little stronger, Mr. . . . . ?"

"*Colonel*—you know very well who I am. After all"—he looked up at Hamilton, who saw himself and his ineptitude reflect off the man's glasses—"your men here practically informed me of your interest. By the way, young man, always check the door for tape across the door's jamb, a simple trick for sure, but one that informs very well that your private property has been entered . . . how do you Americans put it? Oh yes, 'on the sly.'"

"All right, I'll bite. Yes, we do know who you are, sir. You were being watched as an enemy agent of not only the United States but of the people of Argentina. You are Professor Arnold Wentz, climatologist and oceanographer. You're sixty-one years old, from Dortmund, Germany. Fell out of favor with certain elements within the Reich and was sent into what amounts to permanent exile in South America. In the United States' economic parlance, you make forty-seven dollars and fifty-two cents a week in salary. Not very appreciative of a man with so many letters following his name."

The Nazi remained silent. His guess as to who these Americans were was now confirmed. He also knew that since this Colonel Lee exposed everything to him, he would either be able to convince him of his sincerity or he would be found floating facedown in the River Platte. German agents within these borders had confirmed beyond doubt the large man knew his business.

"Now, we seem to know each other, Professor. What can I help you with?" Garrison asked as he placed his size 15 shoes up on the desk and waited.

Finally, the old man lowered his satchel and took a deep breath. Treason was not a thing to be taken lightly, especially against the Gestapo and the death dealers of the Third Reich. He opened the case and removed an item, and then, with untrusting eyes at both Lee and Hamilton, he opened a map and spread it out.

"Six years ago, in the spring of 1937, I was employed by the Reich's Marine." He looked back at the tall and thin Hamilton. "That's the German Navy."

Hamilton rolled his eyes and was about to say something when Lee's raised left eyebrow stopped his retort.

"The project was called"—Wentz smiled embarrassingly—"of all things, Operation Necromancer. This was a joint effort by the Luftwaffe, the Wehrmacht, and the navy to find a feasible way to cloak machines of war from enemy radar, which was mostly theory at the time and not a practical application. Most of us thought it was pure speculative theory at the time. Now all the world powers have embraced radar as a tried-and-true science. Operation Necromancer was an attempt at a new science called the unified field theory. It combines the sciences of electromagnetic radiation and gravity. To put it more simply"—again, the look back at an already irritated Hamilton—"uniting the fields of electromagnetism and gravity into a single sustainable blanket field."

Lee removed his fedora and tossed it on his desk. He placed his hands behind his head and fixed the Nazi weatherman with a glare as if the man were wasting his time. "Invisibility." Lee had read an article from the London *Times* about the theory, and the article was distributed to all station chiefs across the world. Lee thought the theory had far too many holes in it to make it work. But then again, he was a former politician with no mind toward the sciences. The ceiling-high bookcases filled with science periodicals in his office attested to the fact that Lee was trying to change his ineptitude in that regard.

"Correct, Colonel. I can see you have heard of this theory before."

Lee didn't respond; he just waited.

Wentz cleared his throat, unable to gauge the temperament of the giant American before him. The younger agent was easy; he was an *eager beaver* as the Americans called it. But this man was one of experience and something perhaps a little darker than any man he had ever met.

"Our first attempt at this science was using field generators the size of which were unheard of before this. The test would take place on board the obsolete battle cruiser *Schoenfeld*. A vessel chosen for its size and space. Of course, these generators were the most powerful German science could obtain and implement at sea. The final product of this attempt would be that these field generators would make it possible to bend light around an object via refraction so that the object became completely invisible to the naked eye. It also could achieve the desired effect of rendering the ship in question completely invulnerable to radar systems. This was gained through the use of capacitors arranged around the steel hull of said ship. In essence, gentlemen, it allowed the radar waves to pass harmlessly around the object."

"Comic book stuff," Hamilton mumbled, drawing a look and raised brow from Lee.

"Young man, I believe I explained the process is attained through built-in transducers disbursed throughout the ship's exterior hull, designed so that it wasn't noticeable to the casual observer. Basic science."

Hamilton again rolled his eyes, and Lee caught it but said nothing, simply because he was also inwardly doing the same thing as the kid: not believing a word the professor was saying. Maybe an obvious ploy to get American sympathy and a free pass to the States for his own personal protection. But, of course, the young Hamilton couldn't hold his tongue.

"Buck Rogers crap if ever I heard."

Professor Wentz turned and once more looked at Hamilton. "Buck Rogers, yes, exactly. Your disbelief was and is to our main advantage in developing this science. So fantastic that no intelligence agency or military in the world would ever commit resources to stopping it."

"Okay, so you were working on a cloaking device that would, if it were successful, make ships invisible to visual detection and defeats radar. What happened, Professor?" Lee asked.

"The project was stopped in its tracks by the party and Adolf Hitler personally."

"This is going to take one hell of a long time, Professor, if you don't stop with your dramatic pauses."

"The ship, the battle cruiser *Schoenfeld*, was lost with all hands. Five hundred and thirty-seven men just vanished, never to be seen again, or so we thought." The professor looked down at his worn shoes and then removed his glasses, which Lee noted were cracked in the left-side lens.

"Continue."

"The experiment not only rendered the *Schoenfeld* invisible to our primitive radar systems of the time. It physically vanished from the view of over a thousand eyewitnesses. Just vanished." Wentz reached down and brought six black-and-white photographs out of his satchel. Each was stamped in German in big red letters that Lee was educated in—TOP SECRET. "The reason I accepted this so-called banishment to this hot and miserable country was the fact that this experiment has to be stopped at all costs. One of the flaws in our system was in sustaining the energy needed from the power generators. They just weren't powerful enough—that is, until a very distinguished man came up with the novel application in using what we now know as industrial-grade blue diamonds, found only here and in South Africa. Very rare and very valuable. I was sent here not because I fell out of favor but because I am tasked with finding these very elusive diamonds."

"Now those little gems I have heard of. The University of Chicago has placed feelers out to all diamond and mineral companies around the globe." He looked at Hamilton. "Now we know why—power generation applications."

The professor spread the six photos out on the desk, and after a second of hesitation, Lee sat up and looked.

"The *Schoenfeld* abruptly returned two years later in the fall of 1939 just out-side of Le Havre. She was found and towed in by the German navy. This is the *Schoenfeld* as she looks today."

Lee, with a curious Hamilton, looked at the black-and-white photos. The *Schoenfeld* was clearly shown. She had been dry-docked somewhere in Germany. As Lee looked closer, he reached for a magnifying glass on his desk and then reexamined the first photo. His mouth fell partially open—emotion the experienced intelligence man never allowed to show openly.

"My God," Hamilton said, disappointing Lee in the fact that he expressed surprise in front of the German scientist. He had been told to always act as if you are never surprised. But this time even Garrison Lee was at the very least uncomfortable looking at the photo.

Men, sailors—at least three hundred of them—were burned and buried in the battle cruiser's superstructure. Contorted in agony and frozen into many misshapen forms and all burned beyond recognition, everywhere. Parts of the ship were melted, others pristine. Men were melted into her decking as if nothing more than long-dead candles. The teak deck had been burned away in most areas, leaving charred steel plating, but held firm in other parts of the ship. The stern of the large vessel was scorched and actually bent ten degrees lower than the rest of her hull. Lee ran his fingers through his hair and then looked up at Wentz.

"That is not all of it, Colonel," the German said as he pushed a second picture into Lee's view.

Vegetation of some sort permeated the ship. Small trees, vines, flowers, unimaginable vegetation of varying variety.

"The plant life on board, as you can see, is not burned as the rest of the ship. The material is very much alive."

"How?" Hamilton asked as he looked at the amazing photo.

"That's not the question here, young man. The right question is why. Why is this material not burned like the rest? And why did the ship that vanished in front of a thousand eyewitnesses return at all? And how, since there was no one left alive to initiate that return?"

"Well?" Lee asked.

"Even those points are not the real story, Colonel."

Lee was becoming frustrated and showed it with his glare.

"Many renowned botanists in Germany have come to the same conclusion—none of this plant life is found anywhere on this planet."

Lee continued to stare at the man who had clearly seen better days in the sanity department. "You mean to tell me that while attempting to electromagnetically hide a vessel with rather dubious science, you made that ship vanish into another world?"

"That is precisely what I am saying. Perhaps *another world* is not the proper term that should be applied here, Colonel Lee. Maybe another plane of existence is a better theory."

Lee examined the other photos. "This one?" he asked as he turned the photo around for Wentz's viewing.

"Wherever the *Schoenfeld* disappeared to, it happened in no more than three minutes. To us, it was two years; to the ship, only three minutes. That is a picture of the captain's cabin. You can see the date on the calendar as circled by her captain as the exact date of the experiment, and this is a close-up of one of the disfigured and burned crewmen. Not very appealing, I admit, but crucial. See the time on his wristwatch? That and the date on the calendar coupled with the time specified on the sailor's watch proves that the *Schoenfeld* was only gone for three minutes."

The other German intelligence photos were close-ups of the damage done to the bodies of the sailors. Broken, bent, and charred, mouths open in agony. Lee pushed the photos away.

"I can get these photos to my superiors, Professor. But before I do, I want to ask how a climatologist is privy to this type of top-secret information outside of the fact they sent you to corner the market on hard-to-find blue diamonds."

"Ah, the gist." Wentz removed the photos and handed them to Hamilton. He again indicated the map he had previously placed on the desktop. "My duties were to study the seas surrounding the vessel during the experiment. Water temperatures, impact of electromagnetism on seagoing animal life, things such as that. During the run-up to zero hour, we conducted generator testing on the electromagnetic field. We started noticing certain disturbances when the generators were turned on. Small, hurricane-like formations started to pop up in the vicinity of the test site. Hurricanes, as you know, just don't suddenly appear. They build up, usually around Africa, and then move west and north. We counted no less than six of these small, deadly storms appear every time the field generators ramped up. Never before or since did these storms arise in that area. It is suspected that because of power fluctuations without the steadiness of flow the blue diamonds could deliver, our current system brings together pressure variants from two differing planes of existence."

"Your point, Professor?" Lee asked, beginning to lose what patience he had but mostly because the German was speaking in scientific terms so far beyond him it became frustrating trying to keep up.

"Here," he said, pointing to a map of the North American eastern seaboard. This made Lee somewhat nervous. "The same storms have appeared here off Norfolk, Virginia." His finger moved to another circled location. "And here, off Newport News, and here, just outside New York. Three different hurricanes of a weak nature and very brief in duration, and also two of which occurred during the off-season for storms such as this. They appeared in minutes and vanished just as fast."

"Your people are testing this device in American waters?" Lee asked as he straightened with a look of apprehension on his tanned face.

"No, Colonel Lee. The German government has curtailed all experiments in the area of bending light for stealth purposes."

"Are you saying American theorists are possibly following the same science?" Hamilton asked incredulously.

"That is exactly what it is I am saying, young man. This experiment must be stopped. We also have information that the Russians may also be experimenting with the same technology in the Black Sea. As a matter of fact, my government has recently discovered they may have already achieved success to a certain degree. If this is true, and if you Americans are trying the same thing, we could see a major catastrophe in the next year. We could lose everything, or anything that is close to the experimental platform—that includes entire cities."

Lee sat back into his chair.

"Our intelligence says that the probable location for the testing of the unified field theory is happening somewhere in and around your Philadelphia Naval Shipyard. Colonel, you must warn your superiors that this cannot happen. We have agents in the Soviet Union attempting to explain this in a roundabout way to the Russians through diplomatic channels, but as you may know, the Russians don't particularly like Germans that much. This must stop. Even our fair-minded Herr Hitler has seen the dangers this scientific path may lead us down."

The professor pushed the last photo over so Lee could see it clearly.

"Another German ship?" he asked.

"No, this is the *Simbirsk*. This is the vessel believed used in the Russian experiment. Our agents now report she cannot be located anywhere in the world."

Without warning, Hamilton, with just an acknowledgment through the dip of Garrison Lee's head, reached over and pulled the map and the photos from the desktop.

"I believe, at least, that you believe this is a viable threat. So I hope you have your bags packed, Professor. I'll get you to Washington, and once there, you can explain your theory to my boss. If you're lying to us in any way, you'll soon learn that we backward Americans aren't as backward as you might think. Now if you'll—"

The bullets smashed through the closed window and sprayed the far wall. Lee immediately dove over his desk and knocked Wentz from his chair. Hamilton slammed his body against the far wall and allowed the map depicting the sudden storm positions and the black-and-white photos of the two warships to fall to the floor. He pulled a Colt .45 from the back of his trousers and went into a prone position.

In the main office area, an explosion sounded as a grenade detonated. The interior windows exploded outward and into Lee's private office, showering them with tinted glass. He heard the reports of several .45s explode as the team inside the office laid down a covering fire. Lee had his full weight on the professor as he kicked out to get Hamilton's attention.

"It's time to move operations; I think our secret is out!" Just as the words came out of his mouth, another potato-masher-style hand grenade burst through the already shattered window. Lee ducked his head as the grenade went off, the concussive force sending his body off the professor to slam into the far wall. Then another detonation went off, and then all went silent.

Thirty minutes later, Lee's eyes fluttered open, and he realized he was in a cool place. He automatically reached for his hat but found his head bare as he sat up. The cot was hard and far too short for his body. He rubbed his head and felt the bandage that partially covered his left ear. But all he knew or cared about at that moment was the fact that he was missing his hat. He looked around the bare room and saw young Hamilton getting treated by a man in a filthy white lab coat.

"What in the hell happened?"

Hamilton looked over as the doctor applied the last piece of tape to the gauze that was wrapped around his left forearm.

"Well, Colonel, let's just say we got evicted in no uncertain terms. We're at the safe house in Santiago."

"You all right?" Lee asked as he placed his bare feet on the cool floor. Again, he reached for his fedora before he remembered he didn't have it.

"The hat didn't survive. Neither did the good Professor Wentz. That second grenade landed right on top of him. What's left was on the shirt you were wearing."

"Who'd we lose?"

"Three. Nancy Chalmers, Peggy Grace, and Will Nelson. The new kid from Rhode Island." Hamilton lowered his eyes as Lee stood on shaky feet.

"Potato mashers. Goddamn Germans. Should have seen it coming."

Hamilton nodded that the doctor should leave. When they were alone, young Hamilton tossed Lee a new, clean shirt after securing the door. "Potato mashers, yes; Germans, no. The professor covered his tracks pretty well. No one knew his intentions. I went through his valise and found maps and communication supplements. He had dates and times of where we were. He had been planning on approaching us for quite some time, Colonel."

"Then who?" Lee asked as he buttoned up his new shirt. His countenance was troublesome to Hamilton as he turned and opened the thick door.

"Bring the bastard in, Jerry," Hamilton said as he stepped aside as Lee tucked in his shirt.

The man was small, gruff, and hadn't shaved in weeks. The heavy flannel shirt he wore was stained in blood, and the dark-haired man looked as if his treatment by Lee's team hadn't been too gentle. This man had only met the soft side of the OSS. Lee's eyes fixed threateningly on the man who was being held upright by Jerry Lester, a second lieutenant from the army also on detached service. Lee sat and slipped on socks and shoes as the small man struggled arrogantly against the larger man holding him. Hamilton tossed a folder onto the bunk where Lee sat tying his shoes.

"We have more on this guy than *Photoplay* has on Rita Hayworth. This is Ivan Nevalov, Stalin's number-two man in Argentina, also number one on our elimination list."

The small, filthy-looking man looked up at the mention of his name and then spit blood onto the floor, which elicited a nice slap on the side of his head from the angry agent holding him. "He and his hit team tried to make it look like German agents by using their equipment. Even the bullets and weapons were German made."

Lee didn't have to look at the folder containing the intelligence on Nevalov. The KGB operative was quite well known in these parts and had been suspected in the disappearances of at least three Americans operating in South America. Allies or not, Lee hated the Russians.

"Why eliminate the good professor, Ivan?" Lee asked as he tied off the last shoestring.

The man smiled through bloody teeth but said nothing.

"We know you're concerned about the spread of certain technology about this theory on the bending of light. Do you want to discuss it?" Lee finished and then stood. He walked over to a chair and removed a Colt .45 from a holster and charged it. He turned and he wasn't smiling.

"I think we can make a deal here, I mean being allied nations such as we are," Nevalov said in very good English, and then the man spit blood once more from his mouth.

"Actually, Ivan, I just wanted to know if that was the reason for your assault on my place of business. Unlike my superiors, I don't deal well with cold-blooded murderers. And I am sure as hell not sitting down to talk with a man who killed three of my people. Step away, Lester."

"You Americans and your bluffing. This is not your Wild West and the RKO Corral. This is not a poker game; this is not—"

The .45-caliber bullet caught Nevalov in the top of his forehead, and his brains went all over the wall. Jerry Lester and young Hamilton only stared at the body of the Russian agent as his limp frame finally slid to the floor. Lee tossed the still-smoking weapon on the bunk and then fastened his belt buckle. He looked up and saw his two men staring at him in shock.

"We didn't have time to deal with this guy. We already know what he knows." Lee grimaced as he stepped toward his two men. "And I am sure as hell not into the habit of sitting down and exchanging pleasantries with a man who just killed three of my people." Garrison tore off the bandage covering his right ear. "Write it up in your reports if you see fault in my actions. Now gather up what work we have from Wentz."

"What are we going to do, Colonel?" Hamilton asked as he watched Lee nonchalantly step over Nevalov's unmoving body.

"You, Mr. Hamilton, are going to establish another cover inside Buenos Aires and set up a new shop. As for me, I'm flying out to go have a talk with our boss and the Department of the Navy."

Hamilton and Lester watched as Lee left. They exchanged looks of unease.

"Jesus, have you ever seen anything like that?" Lester asked.

"The man really does not like Nazis or Commies, does he?"

WASHINGTON, D.C.

Lee sat and fumed inside the office of William "Wild Bill" Donovan, the head of the Office of Strategic Services. The large and burly former attorney slammed his phone back down into the cradle. He cursed as he fixed Lee with a stern look.

"The goddamn Department of the Navy insists that we don't know what we are talking about. Three weeks and all we get is the runaround, even with President Roosevelt screaming bloody murder about what his navy is doing behind his back."

"Did we get verification from the National Weather Service on any freak storms in the Atlantic?"

"They tracked two of them just three days ago. One minute, a full-blown hurricane; the next, calm seas. The damn phenomenon was witnessed by half of the damn eastern seaboard. We brought that evidence from that Nazzy bastard Wentz to the navy brass, and all they did was stare at us like we were insane. My boys in weather say another is now forming around Atlantic City, New Jersey, and spreading to Philadelphia."

"Look, Bill, I lost three good people on this. I would like an answer as to why. Let me go to the navy and ask questions my way. It sounds like they are going to attempt this crazy experiment. They may not have this information from naval intelligence."

"Or they have just chosen to ignore it." Donovan looked at Lee and shook his head. "The people you lost were my people, Lee, not yours. And as much as I would like to set you loose on the damn navy brass, I have another way of doing things. You need to curb that famous temper of yours."

The phone rang. Donovan held eye contact with Garrison and then snatched the phone up. "Donovan," he answered harshly. Lee saw Wild Bill straighten just a little as he listened to the voice on the other end.

"Are you kidding me?" he screamed into the phone. Garrison saw Donovan's shoulders sag momentarily. "Yes, I am sorry, Mr. President. It's just a little frustrating not knowing what it is your other damn hand is doing. When is this supposed to happen?" The room went quiet as Donovan listened. "Can you order it stopped?"

Lee stood and paced. From Wild Bill's tone, they may have been too late. Or delayed enough that the testing had already commenced.

"Can you get me and Colonel Lee inside?" Again, he listened. "Can we expect full cooperation from the navy and Chicago University?" Another frown. "Thank you, Mr. President," he answered and then placed the phone down.

William H. Donovan stood and grabbed his coat. "Come on, Lee. We have some people to meet."

PHILADELPHIA NAVAL SHIPYARD
PHILADELPHIA, PENNSYLVANIA

It had taken Donovan and Lee an hour and fifty-five minutes by small plane to get from Washington to the shipyard in Philadelphia. The official naval car that met them had ensconced in the backseat no less than the former chief of naval operations, Harold R. Stark, a man Wild Bill Donovan had no love for. It was the portly Harold Stark who had been in charge the night of December 6, 1941. He could have changed history, if, as in Donovan's biased opinion, "he had been up to the task." The former naval chief was dressed in a black suit and was not at all happy to see Lee *or* Donovan.

"I should have known, Harold. This was your project, wasn't it?" Donovan said as he took the seat next to Stark while Garrison Lee folded his long frame into the front seat with the driver.

"I am not here to answer your questions, Donovan. You are here to observe the experiment firsthand. You are not to report on what it is you witness nor comment on the same." Stark smiled at Donovan, and it was meant as an insult to the man. "You understand the penalties involved. Both you and your watchdog up there."

Donovan smirked and then saw the back of Lee's shoulders tense.

The rest of the ride went in silence. They passed through no less than six more security checkpoints. With each stop, Garrison noticed the weaponry of the attending shore patrolmen became far more serious. The last checkpoint was manned by a fire team that included one .30-caliber machine gun with a crew of six.

The Chevrolet pulled up to a small sandbagged bunker fronting an area of dock that was ringed with large tarps spreading around the dock area like the sides of a great circus tent. The bunker was placed dead center and all blocked the view of the small bay in front of them.

A naval lieutenant commander stepped forward and pulled Stark's door open with a salute, and the same was done for Donovan and Lee without the military greeting that they both had earned.

One more time, Lee and Wild Bill Donovan had to show their identification, which was matched against a set of orders just received from Washington. Each man was allowed to pass into the darkness of the bunker.

Lee was quicker than Donovan to examine the inside of the bunker and its many occupants. Each naval technician sat at a console with scopes and electronic instruments that failed to be familiar to Garrison. Armed shore patrolmen were stationed along the far wall and watched all personnel with a wary eye. Lee shook his head and then stepped to the front. Leaning close to a radar tech, he saw outside, through a thick pane of glass, the bay. All shipping had been moved, and all viewing access to the water had been blocked by large cranes hoisting tent-sized tarps into the sky. In the middle of all of this was a brand-new destroyer escort. It was one Lee recognized immediately, as it was just featured in one of last year's *Look* magazine articles. The USS *Eldridge*, a new breed of fast destroyer, sat majestically in the closed and calm waters of the navy yard. Lee stiffened when he noticed the crew of the *Eldridge* was placed along the railings of her deck. Her proud five-inch gun turrets looked as if they were manned and ready. Lee turned to Donovan.

"She's fully crewed," he said as if in astonishment.

Donovan turned to Harold Stark, who had sat down in a large chair toward the back of the bunker with two of his assistants.

"Didn't you read the report we sent you in regard to the suspected German casualties?"

Stark gestured to a man in a white lab coat. "Professor Williston says what you described in your report was not feasible. *Impossible* is the word I believed he used. Isn't that right, Professor?"

The short man turned and removed his glasses. He gestured toward Lee and Donovan. "These are the men?"

Stark smiled and nodded. The professor placed his hands on his hips and glared at the two civilian-dressed security men.

"I'll have you know I had to answer questions for a solid three days after your report was sent to us. You made many people around here nervous with your propaganda."

"Propaganda? Why, you little—" Lee reached out and took Donovan by the arm to calm him. The burly man relaxed and then shot Stark a look.

"It was my report, boss," Garrison said as he calmly looked at the much smaller professor, who saw that maybe he shouldn't be too accusatory.

"Needless to say, your fears are groundless, gentlemen. Our preliminary tests have shown us nothing but promise."

"Why the full crew? Why not just the staff you need to make the attempt?" Lee asked.

"Because we have other readings we have to assess. Can the crew be hidden as well as the vessel? What are the initial effects of light bending on the human body? They are all volunteers, Colonel Lee. Not one man is on board that ship that does not wish to be."

Lee and Donovan remained silent.

"Thirty seconds to generator start-up, Professor."

The man turned with excitement and went to the machinist mate who had just informed him it was now time to commence what the world would come to know as the Philadelphia Experiment.

The USS *Eldridge* sat silently as her crew heard the warning siren sound. Men went to railings, and others vanished belowdecks to witness one of the great scientific achievements in world history.

Again, the blare of the siren sounded. Once, twice, and finally a third time. Four men had gathered at the fantail and watched as the men and scientists lining the quay disappeared into other bunkers for protection. The men felt the generators far below in the engine spaces start up. The hair on their arms rose straight up. The hair under the caps also pushed against the resistance of being held in place. The current of air smelled of thick ozone. Electricity sparked against steel bulkheads and railings.

Above the *Eldridge*, the skies darkened as suddenly as if a curtain had been pulled down upon a stage. Rain started to fall, and the wind increased by thirty miles per hour.

"We have a very serious formation of rain clouds slamming the coastal areas. The center of the storm is calculated to be right there!" The technician was pointing out of the thick glass at the now bobbing USS *Eldridge*.

"You still think this is a natural phenomenon, Dr. Frankenstein?" Lee asked as he, too, pointed at the weather developing outside.

"Commence power pulse!"

An acknowledgment came back from the destroyer. Before anyone could protect themselves, a loud, eardrum-piercing scream sounded, which brought those standing to their knees in pain.

"Damn!" Donovan shouted, and even Admiral Stark yelped and covered his ears.

A pressure wave of air expanded outward from the now heavily rocking *Eldridge*. Rain started to slant as the wind speed increased to eighty-five miles per hour. Men were shouting out readings, trying desperately to be heard above the din. Bolts of lightning shot from the forward superstructure of the *Eldridge*. Men were tossed about as if the ship were in a heavy sea.

"Start the generators!" the professor yelled into the radio. Try as they might, they could not hear the response from the ship.

A bright, electric-blue circle of light surrounded the *Eldridge* and then went outward like the spokes of a wheel. The light slammed into the dock area so hard that sandbags were dislodged. Dust and dirt fell from the plywood ceiling, and men ducked as the light and pressure wave struck the thickened reinforced glass of the bunker. Lee tackled Donovan as the world went bright with white light as the glass exploded inward.

It was a man screaming words Lee couldn't understand that made him move. Garrison helped Donovan to his feet as the scene quickly faded down to a dull light.

"My God, she's gone!" a voice called out as rain soon found its way into the damaged bunker.

Men scrambled to their feet as technicians who had been terrified only a moment before were now pointing and shouting with glee. Lee looked at Harold Stark as he was assisted to the now empty window frame.

"You did it, Professor. She's actually vanished!" Stark exclaimed.

Lee and Wild Bill watched as the harbor waters settled. There was a wide circle of white foam that filled the area where the *Eldridge* had lain at anchor. She was gone. Lee looked at Donovan and both men were speechless.

"Radar?"

"No contact!" came the reply filled with glee.

"Sonar?"

"All clear. Just the usual harbor floor clutter."

The professor finally allowed Stark to turn him, and the two men shook hands. Other technicians joined in as the revelry was a charging tool for the men who had been frightened beyond measure only a minute before.

Lee slapped a console in front of him. The loud bang stopped the revelry as all eyes turned to the large man.

"Congratulations. Now do you have a way to get them back?"

The professor looked at Lee as if he were addressing a child of limited learning abilities.

"The generators will automatically shut down after a one-minute duration."

Before anyone could comment, the weather once more turned ugly, and this time, it hit with a vengeance. More sandbags lining the bunker caved in, and these took several of the shore patrolmen down.

The electrical pulse shorted everything out. Lights, radar systems, sonar, all went down. Rain was horizontal as all was inundated with water from the hurricane-force winds that lashed the navy yard.

A tremendous *pop* sounded and made the men and women inside the bunker bend over. Most were nauseated beyond endurance, and most gave up their breakfasts.

Garrison Lee was first to raise his head up and see the outside world as the winds lashed the harbor. Waves washed over the empty dock areas, and many men were pulled back into the sea. Then he saw the impossible. The USS *Eldridge* reappeared.

The world had now opened a door that might not be able to be closed again.

"Recorder!" the professor yelled as the storm outside began to diminish in strength.

"Recorders are nonfunctional!"

"Then write this down," the professor called out angrily as Harold Stark was looking beyond him at the most amazing sight he had ever seen in his life. "On this date, October 28, 1943, the United States destroyer escort USS *Eldridge*, DE-173, was successfully hidden from radar and visual detection. Mission, success!"

Everyone inside started clapping and cheering as they all proudly looked on. The *Eldridge* was steaming hot in the cold waters of the harbor. She was blanketed in a thickening fog that almost completely hid her from sight. Again, it was Garrison Lee who saw the first signs of trouble.

"What have you done?" he asked no one as his thick fingers grasped the broken window seal as the full image of the *Eldridge* came into clear view.

"My God. I guess this answers the question of *Can we go too far?*, doesn't it, Slim?" Donovan said as he joined Garrison at the window. He turned and his eyes fixed on Admiral Stark.

Garrison examined the smoking, steaming hulk of the *Eldridge* and found he couldn't breathe.

"Is this what you imagined your phase shift would look like, you maniacs?" Donovan asked angrily as he turned to the visibly shaken professor.

"Yes, sir. The bending of light by electromagnetic fields, rendering massive interference to any radar in the world, essentially blinding them, is now a fact, even if . . . if . . ." The words trailed off. His statement was like he was rendering it by rote without his usual enthusiasm.

"But something has obviously gone very wrong," Lee said as if to finish the professor's weak statement.

"No, no, no," Stark said as he tried not to look at the smoldering *Eldridge*. "It went right, better than anyone could ever have imagined. It did vanish from every radar within three miles of the shipyard. You saw it yourself, Donovan. It just disappeared. Went away. It came back seventy-five seconds later. From my viewpoint, it was a rousing success that just may win this war for us."

Donovan stepped forward but was stopped by two naval shore patrolmen before he could throttle the admiral.

"Look at that! You call that a success?"

Below, men were seen half in, half out of steel bulkheads. Sailors had died in agony as they had been exposed to the phase shift's power, the exact same outcome Donovan and Lee had warned the navy of. Now it was there for all to see. All sailors abovedecks had been fried to death by men of their own nation.

As they watched, men were rushing aboard without regard to their own safety. Security, shipmates who had been left ashore for the testing, and other naval personnel crowded the decks as they rushed to help those men hideously killed by the power of the experiment.

Stark couldn't help it any longer, his argument about the success of the experiment no longer viable as he bent at the waist and vomited.

Lee swallowed hard as he watched men below trying to remove several bodies from the *Eldridge*'s superstructure. Sailors were buried half in, half out of her decks and her bulkheads, and all were burned to a crisp. This last observation was causing several of the men attempting at cutting the bodies free to lean over and vomit. This was happening the entire 306 feet of the brand-new destroyer.

Colonel Lee pushed several security personnel away from the collapsed opening. Many were assisting Admiral Stark as he also tried to get out. Lee felt Wild Bill Donovan grabbing his suit jacket as the two men made it out into the hazy light of day. The weather had magically cleared, and with just the exception of the heavy ozone smell of electricity, all was seemingly normal.

Lee grabbed one of the shore patrolmen by the arm as he ran by and directed him to assist several sailors who had been washed over the pier railing by the tremendous backwash of seawater as the *Eldridge* returned from its maiden voyage to somewhere. His eyes fell on the destroyer sitting three hundred yards away. Steam was still rising from her superstructure, and even as he watched, the strong anchor chain on her bow crashed down into the sea. The large ship swayed both to the starboard and then port as she settled into her watery placement. Boats of all sizes were rushing to her now settling hulk. Lee saw one of these whaleboats as they cast off with a slew of medical personnel aboard.

"Don't go out there!" Donovan ordered as he adjusted his eyesight to the scene before him. Wild Bill had taken Lee's arm in his to try to stay him from boarding the whaleboat.

Garrison removed Donovan's hand and then ran toward the accelerating boat. He jumped the six feet from the pier to the now moving boat. He crashed down inside and was helped to a sitting position by two navy medics. Lee's eyes settled on the fast approaching *Eldridge*. The ship was hissing steam jets. The capacitors lining the sides of her hull were so hot that the gray paint covering her hull plates sizzled and then burst into small flames, and then as the capacitors burned out, they went dead of power. This was happening the entire length of the destroyer.

"What in the hell happened?" one of the naval medics said. The closer they got to the *Eldridge*, the more of the horrors became visible.

"The price of being gods," Lee mumbled, confusing those aboard who heard the obscure comment.

Garrison saw many of the rescuers who had already boarded were in the process of throwing up. Many were on their knees. Some even wept as they came across their fellow seamen scorched and charred. The whaleboat slowed, and then Lee, not waiting, jumped to the boarding ramp that fronted her starboard side.

Gaining the deck, Lee couldn't help it. He also bent over as his stomach threatened to disgorge the breakfast he had eaten three hours earlier. He allowed his stomach to settle. The smell of scorched flesh kept that little maneuver in check until he gradually became used to the smell. The man's eyes were wide as he was being spoken to by a kid no older than nineteen. The sailor was holding the man's hand and talking calmly to him.

"We need men over here!" came a shout not far away. Garrison looked up and saw medics running toward the stairs that led to the bridge wing of the destroyer. "Cutting torches! We need cutting torches over here!"

Lee scrambled and turned the corner on the charred decking. He came to a screeching halt when he saw one of the *Eldridge*'s crewmen. The man was buried up to his chest in burned teakwood. The deck sectioned the man completely in two—one part below and one above the deck. Lee had to get closer to learn all he could about what had gone wrong. He knelt as close as he could without interfering with the rescue attempt. Lee swallowed when he saw the blood soaking into the burned wood of the decking. It spread in a wide arc around the sailor who was obviously in shock. The boy's lips moved, and Lee thought he heard him say, "What took them so long?"

"The duration of the event was only one minute," came a shocked voice from behind them. Lee straightened and saw Stark and the professor as they watched with wide eyes the attempt at freeing the man buried in the deck. Lee knew that the situation was helpless, and he knew the men who had caused this guessed the same. He angrily tried to hear what the boy was saying.

"I didn't get that, son. What did he just say?" he asked.

The medic, who was talking softly to the sailor, answered without turning away from those frightened eyes. "He's in shock; I wouldn't take anything he has to say seriously."

Lee got closer. "What did you see, son?" he asked, drawing a severe look backward by the medic.

"We . . . were . . . boarded. They took the ship . . . in less than five . . . minutes," came the slow, pain-filled words.

As the men around him prepared to start cutting the deck away from around
the boy, the hairless and scarred head slowly sank forward as the boy died from
being severed in two. Lee stood and faced the professor and Admiral Stark. He
then silently turned to Wild Bill Donovan, who had just joined them.

"We need to get a marine detail up here," he said as he turned and ran to
the gangway, where a security force of four boatloads of marines started to
board. Garrison confronted the lieutenant leading the four separate teams.

"We may have an intruder force aboard this ship," he said as the young marine officer was staring wide-eyed at the carnage around him. Lee reached
out and took the marine by the shoulders and shook him. "Get a fire team together, son."

Donovan joined them and then, with his terrifying and booming voice, got
the marines to react. They shook off their initial terror.

"Belay that order! We have men to help here!" Admiral Stark shouted as he
saw what Lee was attempting to do. Both Lee and Donovan knew that Stark
felt the control he wielded over the project starting to slip away.

"Marine, we may have men trapped inside that ship, do you understand?
Do your duty," Lee said as he tried to get the officer to ignore Stark and his concerns for controlling the situation.

"Right. I want one squad forward of section three, another to the aft hatches.
The other, come with me."

Lee, without thinking, reached out and quickly unsnapped the marine's
shoulder holster and pulled out the lieutenant's Colt .45. The boy looked but
said nothing. He noted the size of the man directing him and decided not to
reference any provenance toward command. He nodded and then bounded up
the steel stairs toward the bridge section high above them.

The thirteen men plus Lee passed several bodies that had succumbed to
their injuries. Garrison knew then that any personnel caught abovedecks were
already dead. He knew this from the German reports on their failure five years
before. Lee swallowed and followed the marines to the open bridge wing. The
first of the squad to reach the hatch was a gruff sergeant. He gestured for two
men to open the large hatchway. One turned and shook his head.

"Hatch has been dogged," the sergeant said as he stood and went in another
direction. They traveled around the bridge wing to the opposite side. They met
the second fire team as they started to breach the hatchway on the opposite side.
The marine sergeant saw the explosive being placed just to the left of the dogged
hinges of the steel barrier. Lee bent low as the word was given and the explosive
charge was detonated. The boat rocked the men as the hatchway blew inward.

Several of the marines took up station to the front, and with their combined strength, they pulled the thick steel outward where one of the strong hinges had held. They finally freed the hatch, and the first two men vanished inside the darkened bridge.

Lee waited until the far younger and better-armed marines entered, and then he cautiously followed with the .45 at the ready. The bridge was empty. It was also a wreck. Papers flew around, and the bridge windows had been smashed, and by the way of the glass patterns on the steel deck, Lee knew they had been broken from the outside. Someone entered the bridge uninvited.

"This is not how I envisioned my day going, Lee," came the voice from behind him.

Donovan was there and had somehow gotten ahold of a Thompson sub-machine gun. Lee's eyes went from the tommy gun to the frightened face of his boss.

"Have you ever shot one of those before?" Lee asked with concern.

"Of course, Lee," Donovan said.

Garrison knew the man was lying, but whether it was to him or himself, he wasn't sure. He did know he was just as frightened about what they would find as the head of the OSS was.

"I'll tell you what," he said as he allowed Donovan to step up beside him. "I'll trade you. How about that?"

Donovan looked insulted at first but saw Lee's sense of it and exchanged weaponry.

"These things are rather touchy," Lee said as he once more started moving forward as the marines advanced into the interior of the *Eldridge*.

Suddenly, the line of marines stopped as they entered the main companionway from the bridge section to the command area that was filled with the radio room and the officers' quarters. All flashlights were turned to the far end of the companionway. Lee's eyes widened when he saw what was waiting for them.

"What in the hell . . ." Donovan's words trailed off just as the same statement started to come from the lips of every man in the marine fire team.

At the far end of the corridor, barely visible in the lights of no less than four powerful flashlights, were what had boarded the *Eldridge*.

"Can someone explain to me just what in the hell those things are?" a young corporal asked as he raised his M14 to his shoulder.

"Hold fire," Lee said as he stepped to the front of the stalled squad. Donovan tried to stop Lee from taking the lead but failed, and he cursed Garrison's take-charge persona.

The bipedal creatures were standing over two of the downed crewmen of the *Eldridge*. The crewmen were dead. The eyes of the creatures took in the new element. Garrison charged the Thompson as he took these strange beings in.

The creatures were wearing some form of breeches that only traveled the length of their legs to the knee. Their shoes looked as if they were made of some form of seagoing life. The same for their partial pants. They were bare-chested. They weren't frightened or shocked; they just stared as if they had been interrupted and it hadn't been appreciated. It was the tentacles that curled around their necks and moved as if of their own free will, up and down, circling their thick necks. Lee saw the scales of the creatures as they gleamed inside the lights being cast by the flashlights. Lee saw the dark, fishlike eyes as they took in the marine intruders. The heads were scarce of hair, and their hands looked to be webbed. They wore brightly colored ribbons, and they all had extremely lethal-looking swords on their hips. These were slowly withdrawn as the intruders aboard the *Eldridge* took offense at the newcomers. As the men watched, one of the strange creatures stepped forward of the other two. Its feet hit several expended rounds that had been fired during the boarding of the destroyer. Lee knew then that the crew of *Eldridge* had at least fought for their ship before losing it.

As the creature stepped to the forefront, Lee did the same.

"We must take them alive," said a voice from the rear of the group.

Lee knew it was Admiral Stark.

"Harold, I think you are done giving orders here. In case you didn't know it, you have just killed an entire crew of men over this madness," Donovan said as he also pushed forward of the marines.

Stark huffed up his chest but said nothing as the young marines looked at him with wonder in their eyes over his callousness.

The thing hissed loudly as it took in the large human standing defiantly before it. Lee watched as the back eyes settled upon him.

Before Lee knew what was happening, the sound of gunfire erupted throughout the large ship. Distant shots were heard, first sporadic, and then they increased in volume until they could feel the vibration of the gunfire through the steel of the deck.

The thing before them screamed something, and then its rather large sword was raised above its head, and the large animal charged Garrison. Lee stood his ground, and then he opened fire with the Thompson just as the other two creatures charged with swords in hand. Every marine was glad to open fire. Bullets struck the marine animals and tore into their scaly bodies, sending shards of bright fluorescent scales into the air and the lighting. The small battle was soon over as Lee stepped forward. The lead creature moved, but it was Wild

Bill who placed a round into the creature's head. The body went still as did the others.

"We have reports of fighting throughout the ship, same opposition. Thus far, there are no signs of the crew."

Lee turned to face the lieutenant. "Drag these bastards out into the light."

Garrison watched as Stark was shoved unceremoniously out of the way as the marine detail dragged the creature that Lee had just dispatched into the bridge area, where they could get a good look at it.

"What have you done, Harold?" Donovan asked as he nervously looked behind into the long and dark companionway.

"We have much to learn from this experiment."

"Yes, we have learned that we discovered another way to kill ourselves," Lee said as he knelt down to examine the species of beast before him.

He could see that there was intelligence behind those dead and open eyes. Garrison reached out and touched the large sword that was still clutched in the creature's web-fingered hand. The teeth, which were stained in the reddish blood, were clear and sharp. The rags it wore had been hand sewn and stitched. The weapon itself was wood. The blade was fashioned out of some mineral Lee couldn't place. It was a see-through bluish color and had an edge like no other weapon he had ever seen before. He reached out and touched it and then pulled his bleeding finger back, as the blade that had barely touched his skin cut deeply into his flesh. He winced as he looked at the scabbard, which held a knife. This Lee pulled free, and he examined it. It was also made of wood but was fashioned with a clear edge of some form of diamond-like material. Then Lee saw the pouch wrapped around the creature's waist. He reached for it.

"Everything here is navy property, Lee. We want it all." Stark was still being held at bay by his own fright, and the order was basically ignored by the OSS officer.

Garrison felt Donovan kneel beside him as he opened the leatherlike pouch and pulled something out. It was folded. The paper itself looked aged and waterlogged. Garrison unfolded the paper and looked at it. Donovan was confused as he also took it in.

"What is that?" he asked as several of the young marines also joined the two men as they studied what it was this creature had carried into battle.

The page was wide, as if from a magazine or book. It was a painted picture of pirates and of wooden ships. It seemed familiar to Lee, but he just couldn't place it. The writing was what he did recognize. It was written in Cyrillic. Russian.

"This is strange," Donovan said.

"No, sir. It's a page from *Treasure Island*."

Both Lee and Donovan looked up into the baby-faced marine who was look-ing at the full-page picture and words.

"How do you know that?" Lee asked.

"I have the same book on a shelf back at the barracks, sir. Only it isn't writ-ten in no Russian."

Lee looked back at the colorful and exciting picture of who had to have been Long John Silver with a broadsword waving above his head. "The kid's right. This is a Russian-language version of that book."

Lee compared the picture to the clothing the creature wore. If he didn't feel as if he were losing his mind, he would have sworn there was a resemblance to the clothing worn by the pirates depicted in the page from the book—the swords, the strange breeches the beasts wore, even down to the tentacles that had been wrapped in brightly colored ribbons. Garrison quickly folded the paper and placed it in his pocket. He eyed Donovan, and the look said, *Let's get the hell out of here.*

Hours after the event, Lee was ordered back to South America and to his station. Donovan met with the president of the United States three days later and, through his report, which did not jibe well at all with Admiral Stark's ver-sion, talked the president into not funding any more experiments in the phase shift field—ever again.

Garrison Lee had kept the page from *Treasure Island*. The depiction of Long John Silver remained with him for the rest of his life. His dreams were always filled with the same memory of that day during the war years. While men of other areas of endeavor were consumed by actions against their fellow men at a time of war, Lee's were centered around a little-known incident that occurred in home waters during that same conflict.

Yes, he remembered the creature that had scale-covered arms and legs, and what was most disturbing were the tentacles, his memory recalled. The skin had been clear in his mind—like that of a jellyfish, with dull, colored highlights of green, blue, and clear white. The face had been that of a human, with the exception of the clear, large, and very pointed teeth and even larger black, lid-less eyes. The braided hair was almost seaweed-like in appearance. Lee remem-bered the *Eldridge*'s superstructure and the men who had lost their lives upon it. He swore he would never allow technology like that to ever exist again.

Years later, Garrison Lee would go to his grave without ever fully under-standing just what it was that happened in the world's oceans in the 1930s and '40s and to tell the truth, he was quite content to go to his final resting place willingly without that information.

On that day in October of 1943, Garrison Lee, future director of Department 5656, secretly known as the Event Group, became a witness to the results of a little-known scientific incident officially labeled as Fleet Action 129871.

Legend would later label it the Philadelphia Experiment.

PART ONE

SHOW OF FORCE

I have seen enough of one war never to wish to see another.

—Thomas Jefferson
Letter to John Adams,
25 April 1794

1

Rear Admiral Jon Andersson, the Dutch commander of the immense NATO operation Reforger IV, sat in his command chair aboard the aircraft carrier USS *Nimitz* and pursed his lips as the mighty warship sank deep into a trough and then fought her way back to the surface. His eyes watched the northern seas as the storm increased in size and ferocity.

Andersson was extremely proud to have been chosen as task force commander for the largest seagoing war games in the history of the NATO alliance. The task: escort a living lifeline of over two hundred transport ships from Norfolk, Virginia, to the NATO base at Scapa Flow in Scotland. The Games and Theory Department and NATO intelligence were concerned that in the ever-increasing standoff with Russia and her new aggressive posture around the world, NATO could not act fast enough to a wartime crisis by getting vital supplies and war matériel to Europe in a rapid enough response time, which would ensure the fall of NATO forces before the full might of America's military could come into play. This Reforger mission was to prove that no matter the timing, the NATO navies of the world could meet the challenge.

His thoughts about the increasing size and suddenness of the storm were interrupted by the captain of the USS *Nimitz*, Charles McAvoy. He handed the admiral a flimsy from communications. Andersson read the communiqué and frowned.

"My reaction exactly," said McAvoy as he reached out to steady himself as the *Nimitz* once more went on an elevator ride to the bottom of an immense trough.

Both men quietly sweated their anxieties until the forward flight deck finally rose from the sea.

"Orders?" McAvoy asked as he watched the concerned look on the tanned face of Admiral Andersson. He liked the Dutch task force commander. The man was no-nonsense and understood his duties and responsibilities of guiding the most powerful battle group in the history of the North Atlantic. He knew the man would make the right decision.

"Okay, Chuck. That does it. Let's get the civilian transports turned around and order them back to the coast. Get a coded message off to NATO Maritime Command—Operation Reforger IV has been scrubbed due to heavy and dangerous weather concerns."

"Aye," McAvoy said. "You're doing the right thing, Admiral." The captain of the *Nimitz* was about to leave the command wing but hesitated when he saw the admiral was still mulling something over as he watched the heavy seas continue to batter the giant carrier.

"We'll give the transports thirty minutes to start for home and then get our boys out of here also. Have the *Houston* hold station until all command ships are clear of these seas. Also, have the frigate *De Zeven* and the cruisers *Shiloh* and *Bunker Hill* standing by with the *Houston*. All will hold station until the fleet's egress maneuver is complete."

McAvoy noted the admiral's orders. They were in essence leaving a rear guard of the Dutch Provinciën-class frigate *De Zeven*, the US Navy's Ticonderoga-class cruisers USS *Shiloh* and *Bunker Hill*, and as a guard to the smaller asset, the navy's Los Angeles–class attack submarine USS *Houston*. All would form up together to keep an eye on the Russian Red Banner Northern Fleet steaming only two hundred miles to the northeast. The rest of the battle group, consisting of German, Dutch, American, and many other ships of the NATO northern command, would make a slow turn in the heavy seas and follow the transports back to Virginia. McAvoy saw the angst in the admiral's face. He dreaded seeing the final portion of script on the fleet action report of Operation Reforger IV: *Mission Failed*.

The admiral remained silent as the seas rose and fell once more. The weathermen under his command had been surprised when the strange storm suddenly turned without warning. Even Norfolk was taken by surprise. He knew he was acting prudently, but that did not make the mission failure any more palpable. He knew the Reforger battle group would have, could have, fulfilled their mission in a time of actual war, but this fact would still be lost on NATO command, and even the Russian Navy would declare NATO assets in the North Atlantic weak in comparison to their mighty Red Banner Group. The humiliation and second-guessing would be silent, of course, but his career would still take a hit. Ridicule, and crap, to put it mildly in his estimation, rolled downhill.

LOS ANGELES—CLASS ATTACK SUBMARINE USS *HOUSTON*

"Lord, look at those seas. I would hate to be those boys on the frigate and cruisers. I don't think they're going to be too enthusiastic about chow tonight," Captain Roger Thorne said as he removed his eyes from the periscope and then turned the sail cameras and monitors on throughout the ship for his crew to see what the surface navy was currently battling. "One MC, please," he said as the chief of the boat, MCPO Harry Hadland, handed the microphone over to his commander. "All hands, this is the captain. We'll be holding station for the next eight hours. We'll keep *Houston* as shallow as possible during that time, so we're still going to get some roll. During this time, there will be no hot meals, so saddle up to the salad bar, ladies and gentlemen; it's going to be a long ride." He was getting ready to hand the chief of the boat back the mic and then clicked the button once more. "It could be worse; you could be up top with the surface boys. So let's keep the bitching to a minimum, and don't eat all the ice cream."

The young sailors around the control center chuckled, relieving the tension of the impending hurricane they found themselves surrounded by. The captain, satisfied that his crew was up to the task, went to the navigation console and leaned over the projected map.

"Captain, the latest plot shows the surface fleet and transports are clearing the storm just to the south of Greenland; they will soon slow and take shelter in shallow seas. The *Nimitz* and her group are only an hour from getting to calmer waters. Only one fire and four injuries reported from the fleet. The task force got off lucky. Why didn't anyone pick up on this weather? We could have had some serious issues here."

Captain Thorne looked up from the navigation plot and rubbed his eyes, and then he winked at his second in command, Lieutenant Commander Gary Devers. "According to CINCLANT, there's hell to be had with the meteorologists about storm predictions. I suspect a few boys will be reassigned soon to Iceland, or at the very least Alaska."

Both men laughed but soon became serious as the huge attack sub took a sudden pressure dip from the waves above them.

"Feels like the entire Atlantic is knocking on our door," Devers said as he grabbed for the console until their stomach-churning roll was stopped.

"I'd take her deeper, but with a frigate and two battle cruisers in harm's way, I want to be able to go to rescue stations at a moment's notice."

"Understood, Captain."

"Well, I think I'll get some of that salad," the captain said as he stretched. "First officer has the deck."

"Aye, first officer has the deck."

"*Conn, sonar.*"

Lieutenant Commander Devers took the mic so the captain could go eat. Thorne hesitated anyway. "Sonar, conn."

"*We have an unknown signature bearing three-two-seven degrees, north, eighty miles out. We missed it because of the high swells, but we have a solid fix now.*"

"Roger," Devers said as he and Thorne simultaneously leaned over the plot board. "Okay, three-two-seven degrees. Those aren't our boys up there," Devers said as the captain increased his frown.

"With the Russian battle group here"—Thorne pointed to an area three hundred nautical miles from the *Houston*—"and with us, the two cruisers, and the frigate here." His finger moved to another spot on the chart. "That leaves us an unknown in our vicinity."

"Sonar, course and speed of target?" Devers asked into the mic.

"*Speed is, well, she's not moving as far as we can tell, sir. Still hard to get a good fix because of the high seas, but her course is erratic. Sir, she looks dead in the water.*"

"It has to be Russian," Devers said as he watched the captain use his grease pen to trace a course to the target area.

"Gary, get to sonar and get me a precise fix. Also, get off an extremely low-frequency message to *Nimitz* and explain the tactical situation. Tell command we will attempt to investigate."

"What about the frigate and cruisers?" Devers asked.

"Tell them to stand by and not to sink until we return."

Devers chuckled and then left control. Thorne took the mic and then faced the men in control who were watching with concern. "Sonar, size estimate of target?"

"*Undetermined at this time, Captain. Best guess is possible heavy cruiser displacement.*"

"Civilian traffic?" he asked.

"*Nothing but the Ruskies—excuse me, Russians, sir, just to the north.*"

"Mr. Cartwright, let's bring her about. Take her down to two hundred, all ahead flank."

"Aye, Captain. Steering three-two-seven degrees, all ahead flank. Give me two hundred feet in depth."

The USS *Houston* turned her massive, blackened, sound-baffling bulk toward the unknown target eighty miles away that was braving one of the worst storms in North Atlantic history. The *Houston*'s crew felt the sharp angle of the bow dip low in the sea, and the increased reactor noise tripled as the huge warship started to speed her way into the unknown.

EVENT GROUP COMPLEX
NELLIS AIR FORCE BASE, NEVADA

For what seemed like the first time in years, the director of America's securest and blackest operational group in federal service toured the expansive facility situated 1.5 miles beneath the sands of Nellis Air Force Base just outside of Las Vegas, Nevada.

Dr. Niles Compton had come a long way from the days when he had been recruited from MIT and Harvard by a man who, if the country had known existed, would be one of the most beloved and celebrated Americans in the history of the country. For fifteen years since taking over for that very man, Dr. Niles Compton had tried to live up to former senator and onetime general Garrison Lee. After years of trying, it had been Garrison Lee's longtime assistant and close confidante, Alice Hamilton, who set him straight—"Be you, Niles," she once told him. "Garrison recruited you for your talent, not because he needed talents like his own." Niles smiled in remembering her talk. "Garrison was a military man, but he always believed this group needed civilian control and oversight, and civilian freedom to maneuver, not a man bound by military correctness and order. He needs you, Niles."

As Compton limped through the curved plastic-lined hallways of the underground complex, the men and women of the Group nodded and greeted him. They still had not become used to seeing this man out of his offices on level seven. Lately, to the surprise of the six hundred–plus men and women on the Group's roster, the director was found at all hours visiting and greeting his people in their laboratories, engineering departments, and the many classrooms, where the continuing education of all members of the Group was a major priority.

The Group had come to be more comfortable around the brilliant man from MIT—even the black eye patch covering his damaged and now useless right eye or the limp he now suffered with because of the attacks from deep space during the Overlord operation were now a commonplace sight among the halls and vaults of the Group. Most—behind his back, of course—now compared his infirmities to those suffered by Compton's mentor, Senator Garrison Lee, right down to the eye patch and scarring on the right side of his face and his limp.

Compton strolled into the immense cafeteria at 3:30 A.M. and went directly to the kitchen and the men and women doing the day's baking. He sat with them and had coffee and talked about their routine. After he left, the bakers and cooks exchanged looks of disbelief that the director had sat and spoken with them.

Niles sat at a corner table as one of the night bakers brought him a fresh cup of coffee. Niles thanked her and then contentedly looked around him. Five people, from the looks of them all engineers, were speaking in soft tones as they ate an early breakfast. These people looked over, and they nodded at the director. Niles noticed Master Chief Jenks at the head of that table acting like he was holding court. He stood and, with his white lab coat floating behind his ample bulk, made his way to the table where Niles sat.

"Mr. Director, mind if I have a seat?" the gruff lifetime navy man asked.

Niles eased a chair out with his foot and nodded.

Harold R. Jenks, master chief petty officer, and one of the more brilliant mechanical engineers Niles Compton had ever met, seemed to be settling into his duties well at the Group. He had completely reorganized the Group's engineering departments into far more effective subgroups. He accomplished this by convincing Assistant Director Virginia Pollock to allow her Nuclear Sciences Division to accept men and women from his department and integrate his mechanical engineers into hers. The move was paying off nicely as the cooperation between the two competing sciences settled into a comfortable and affable routine.

"Master Chief, up late with your people, I see."

Jenks looked at the four men and women as they stood with their breakfast trays and moved off. "Nah, busy moving quantum theory out of engineering and placing it where it belongs, with those eggheads in nuclear sciences. It makes Ginny happy, I guess."

"I imagine Virginia is indeed happy. She's getting thirty-two new bodies." Niles smiled. "You seem to be accepting of your personnel losses with dignified grace."

Jenks finally sat. "Dignified grace? Yeah, have you ever really sat down and tried to argue with that woman? Surrender was the better part of valor, I assure you. My people were acceptable casualties in an ongoing war Dr. Virginia Pollock always seems to be winning."

"*Surrender with honor* is one of my favorite sayings around here when arguing with either Virginia or Alice. Welcome to the surrender club, Master Chief." Niles smiled and sipped his coffee.

Jenks looked around. At three thirty in the morning, there was now no one in the cafeteria. Niles watched the stubborn man, frightening to all, squirm, adjust his lab coat, and then squirm again. Once more he looked behind the serving line at the front and the open kitchens beyond. Niles sat patiently waiting. He folded his fingers on the tabletop and smiled once more with a raised and scarred brow over the eye patch.

"Maybe just start at the beginning, Master Chief."

"I guess surrender is what I want to talk about."

Niles just sat and continued smiling, waiting patiently. Last year at this time, he would have grown frustrated and unhappy with someone wasting valuable time in sitting and stuttering in meaningless conversation. Now Compton relished these moments. After the loss of so many personnel the past few years, he had learned a valuable lesson—the job was never more important than *his* people.

"Oh, hell, Sparky." He saw Niles didn't even flinch at the nickname he had heard Jenks was using behind his back. But he remained silent. "Sorry, Niles. I didn't mean that. In my short time here, I have learned one immutable fact of life; I have seen why you command so much respect around here. To lead with honor and by example is the quality more leaders need in today's messed-up world." He looked away guiltily. "Myself included."

"Master Chief, this particular biscuit doesn't need the buttering as much as you think." Niles sipped his coffee and then fixed Jenks with his good left eye. "Is this about Virginia?"

The color in Jenks's face dropped out so fast that it looked to Niles as if the lights had suddenly been turned off.

"You know?" Jenks asked, incredulous that the director knew the small details of life at the complex. "Ginny said she's told no one."

Niles laughed. "And she has told no one. Do you think anyone in this group can ever get anything past the security department? Since Will Mendenhall and Jason Ryan have been filling in for Jack and Carl, they have become rather good at dealing with secrets, even those involving relationships between active Group members." Niles exhaled. "Pardon the pun here, but I tend to turn a blind eye toward these rules about fraternization. My people lead lives most in this country could never fathom. They are lonely people involved in work they cannot discuss even with their closest relatives. Sometimes I suspect they need each other. You and Virginia are no different."

"Then you don't have a problem with me and . . . Slim?"

"Go get some sleep, Master Chief."

"Yes, sir." Jenks started to stand and then stopped and faced Niles. "I don't say this as often as I should, Mr. Director, but in the short time I have known you, well, hell, you're a good man."

"Thank you," was all Compton said as Jenks huffed and then tossed a dead cigar into the side of his mouth, cleared his throat, and then abruptly left.

Niles watched him go and shook his head. Regardless of his lack of tact, he liked the master chief as much as he liked anyone. You would never get a hesitant answer from him, that was for sure.

Niles decided he had had enough and pushed his coffee cup away and was starting to leave for his quarters when he saw the new deputy director of Computer Sciences, Xavier Morales, wheel himself into the cafeteria. Niles pursed his lips and then slowly sank back into his seat. Xavier saw Niles and sped over in his old-fashioned wheelchair, which the boy clearly refused to part with even though Master Chief Jenks and Virginia offered him a model that would have shocked most of the known world in its sophistication. But then, that's one of the reasons Xavier had become so likable so fast. He was truly grounded in computer sciences, and that was all he ever concentrated on. Without really knowing it, Niles had placed all his confidence in the young genius far faster than he had intended.

"Europa said you were here and not in your quarters," Xavier said as he wheeled up, accidentally bumping the table and spilling what remained of Compton's coffee. "Sorry."

Niles only smiled as he used a napkin to clean up the spill. "Doesn't anyone get any sleep around here anymore? I have Master Chief Jenks and Virginia acting like star-crossed lovers in a soap opera and a computer genius who has never been caught sleeping in his room." Compton placed the cup farther away and tossed the wet napkin into the saucer. "Now, before I order you to your quarters for some sleep, what's up?"

Xavier removed a large boxlike device from his lap and placed it on the table. "It's finished."

Niles's eyebrows rose. "Ah, the Europa link laptop," Niles said as he sat up to look at the stainless steel box. He opened it, and his lips made an *O* as he looked over the new system.

"Of course, junior here doesn't have 99.99 percent of Europa's computing power, but this link can outthink anything in commercial or private use as far as memory. A field team no longer has to link directly with Europa's mainframe to get answers. Odds are this little baby can answer anything they need. The only thing the user cannot do is tie into the mainframe. It is secure and Group-member-voice activated. If anyone tries to use this closed-looped system by voice command or even keypad use, the system will blow up in their faces." Xavier patted the laptop, which was about ten inches thicker than a normal system.

"Good job," Niles said. "This will lessen the need for direct contact with Europa by field teams."

Xavier liked to see a pleased director. He smiled and then looked around the empty cafeteria.

"Uh, the real reason I stopped in is not for telling you something you probably already knew about Europa Jr. here." He closed the top and then moved the system away. "Europa received one of those burst transmissions at 0220 hours. The transmissions are clouded in code for your eyes only."

"Thank you, Xavier."

Morales lingered and was tapping his fingers on the tabletop.

"Something else?"

Xavier didn't know how to continue without invoking the director's wrath.

"The transmissions are coded for a reason, Doctor. I am not a spy and would never circumvent policy in regard to sending illegal communications."

"I would never even think that," Xavier started to say in protest.

Niles held up his hand to stop the computer man from continuing.

"Xavier, maybe it's time I brought you in on this since you're good enough to see a pattern in these classified transmissions. My assistant director doesn't even know, and I would like to keep it that way. Understand?"

"You want to keep Dr. Pollock out of the loop?"

"For now, yes. In case I . . . well . . . die or something, Europa has been programmed to deliver all this information to Virginia, only if it becomes necessary."

"Sounds mysterious," Xavier said politely with raised brows.

"It sounds treasonous is what you mean."

Xavier only smiled, knowing that the outward appearance of impropriety was a mask used by Compton.

"Is the new laptop link capable of red-one communications?"

"Of course. She wouldn't be much good if we couldn't get new orders out to field teams."

"Of course," Niles said as he pulled the large box over to him and then used his voice to activate the ghost of Europa's mainframe. "Europa, Compton 22361. Initiate contact with Farmer John, please. Clearance code, Lion in the Dale."

"Contact cleared and initiated," came the Marilyn Monroe voice pattern from the laptop.

Xavier winced and looked around as Europa's voice echoed off the empty cafeteria walls. He reached out and lowered the volume. "Sorry."

"Hey, at least it works," Niles said with a smile.

As they watched, a series of lines appeared, and then the picture on the screen went to snow and then cleared, and then a series of bright flashes started flowing through.

"This is by far a communications standard I am not aware of," Morales said as he watched the strange series of flashes.

"It's communicating with a not-well-known satellite system. Instead of code names and voice security, some friends designed this system to make use of light patterns to initiate contact. Secure beyond belief."

"I thought that was only a theory."

"Well, it was a theory until the Overlord mission, then it became apparent that cooperation between mirror agencies in other governments, in this case only one other, dictated we have a form of communication that professional politicians have no clue exists." Niles smiled. "Politicians come and go, but real-world problems will always remain. Excuse me. This may get a little touchy." The light patterns on the screen started to rotate and then steadied, and as both men watched, a face appeared on the screen.

"Did I catch you sleeping, old boy?" came the accented voice from the man on the screen. He was balding like Niles and wore a tweed suit with a large and very bright bow tie. His half-moon glasses were perched jauntily on his nose.

"Hello, James. No, not sleeping."

"Niles, old man, do you have someone there with you?"

Niles saw concern etch the face of the most brilliant intelligence officer Compton had ever heard of. They had known each other since being introduced by their mutual friend Garrison Lee back in 2001. With Durnsford, himself, and their little green alien friend, Matchstick Tilly, they had devised the Overlord plan years in advance. The two men trusted each other far more than their governments would care to hear about.

Niles cleared his throat. "Yes, I am afraid our little game has been discovered."

"Don't tell me, that little wheelchair-bound boy you got off the street? I should have known, and you should have, too, old man. Our dossier on Dr. Xavier Morales is far more extensive than even I was led to believe."

"Thus, there are now three of us."

Xavier started to say something, but a quickly placed guided missile of warning stopped him. There would be no discussion between Durnsford and Xavier Morales.

"It's close to be morning teatime over there, so what concerns you enough to delay that?"

"Niles, old boy, you won't believe this, but our little suspicion about our friends in Eastern Europe has now been confirmed. We here at MI6 have received word of our man being placed on some form of alert for movement into the North Atlantic—what for remains to be answered. Is there any word on your end of anything out of the normal happening there?"

Niles pursed his lips and thought a moment. "From my security brief this morning, all I know is that NATO is currently conducting Operation Reforger IV in that area, but that's it."

"Yes, we have the same data. Why would our hidden group put their best man on alert for the North Atlantic? It can't be to observe a war game that has been scheduled for three years. It has to be something else."

"I agree. I'll start checking on this end."

"Good show. Now, if we do find a reason for this man of theirs to show himself for the first time since the Ukraine, it has to be for something that scares them or would lead to their hidden agenda."

"What do you propose?" Niles asked as Xavier became more confused as the two powerful men spoke.

"Since we have verified that it is indeed our suspected man leading the mission there, we will need someone to verify his identity."

"There is only one man who can do that on a purely visual basis, and he's on another assignment at the moment."

"Niles, old chap, we need that murderous man identified. Can you divert your asset in case we discover the reasoning behind this sudden Russian interest in the North Atlantic? I just don't like the smell of it."

"I'll see what can be done without blowing more than just his cover on an ongoing operation in the Middle East."

"With that man, I would love to hear about his adventures, I really would," Durnsford said.

"Yes, I bet you would, James, but even friends must keep some secrets from each other."

Durnsford laughed. "Indeed, old boy, indeed. Secrets must be kept."

"Go have your tea; I'll see what can be done for here. But if it is necessary, James, you have to handle it on your end. I don't like dealing with our asset on any level. He has yet to earn my full trust."

"I understand completely. I have never met a man who I couldn't understand like that gentleman. Talk soon, Niles."

The screen went blank, and then the Europa laptop made a squelching noise, and then she shut down.

Xavier wanted to say something, but Niles again held up his hand to stop the query from being voiced.

"Suffice it to say we have a new relationship with a friend after Overlord, and we and that new friend have worries about who is really in control inside Russia. It's suspected that they have an agenda we have yet to figure out, and both of our governments have yet to catch on. All our combined intelligence services are drawing a blank on this mysterious group. Now we may have a lead that can change all of that if we can prove this man who was just placed on alert for action in the North Atlantic works for this mysterious entity without President Putin's knowledge."

"I don't understand."

"Good."

Xavier watched as Niles stood up and, without a look back, left the empty cafeteria. He took up the new laptop and then smiled.

"I love a mystery." Xavier left the room and decided that he would know what needed to be known by the end of the day. "Come on, Europa. We have some digging to do."

LOS ANGELES—CLASS ATTACK SUBMARINE USS *HOUSTON* NORTH ATLANTIC

The crewmen inside the large control center felt the heavy roll as *Houston* came shallow. She was in a trough, and the view through the periscope was swamped momentarily. Captain Thorne rubbed his eyes as he switched the scope to night vision, an ambient-light-viewing system that utilized existing light from stars, the moon, and sometimes just stored heat energy to illuminate the darkness of the world without sun. There it was—Thorne just caught a brief glimpse of the raised portion of the target's large upper pagoda-style superstructure.

"Damn, she's a big bitch." He slammed the scope's handles to the up position. "Gary, take a look at this," he said as the *Houston* rolled slightly to port. The storm was increasing in size and volume.

The first officer stepped up and brought the stainless-steel handles down and then gazed into the scope. He waited as the high seas broke over the sub's sail tower and then peered into the scope again.

"Jesus." He turned and looked at Thorne. "Captain, she has two massive barreled gun turrets, one forward and one aft."

Thorne slapped a sailor on the back. "Get into the computer library and match that silhouette against existing warships. Gary, send his station a picture, will you?"

At the scope, the first officer clicked a button with his thumb and snapped several pictures as the sea rode low enough to get good shots. He then relinquished the periscope back to the captain.

A specialist at his station started typing into the computer keyboard while the pictures were fed into the system for identification comparison. It was a program that not only matched existing silhouettes of warships all over the world but also had their power-plant noise recordings and screw-propeller signatures for the newer ships.

"Okay, that thing's moving too damn much. Take us down to one hundred and hold station as best you can. We don't need her rolling over on top of us."

"Aye, Captain. Okay, gentlemen, let's get out of this surface clutter. Give me thirty degrees down bubble. Take her to six knots and come parallel to target and hold station."

"Communications, anything on VHF?"

"Conn, radio, there's nothing, Captain. Target is cold black on electronic or voice communications."

"Sonar, conn, anything else out there besides our phantom?"

"Conn, sonar, negative. We're clear at this time."

"Damn, this is strange." Thorne saw the technician running the silhouette program stop typing and then turn white-faced to his captain. "What is it?" he asked.

"Sir, we have a hit on the silhouette index. But it was identified through historical records, not from active naval rolls."

"Well?" he asked impatiently. He was disappointed that his crew may have been affected by this unknown. Their reactions in the past were fast and to the point.

"She's Russian, Captain."

"Gary, bring *Houston* to general quarters, please," he said with an angry look at the technician. "Battle stations—submerged."

"Aye, Captain."

As the warning tone and announcement by the chief of the boat sounded throughout the cavernous interior, men ran to their battle stations.

Thorne stepped up to the technician but stopped by his first officer. "Gary, let's get two fish into tubes one and two. I don't want to take any chances with this lone wolf."

"Aye."

"Now, what else have you got from the historical records?" he asked as he leaned over and examined the technician's computer screen.

"The nomenclature is coming up now, Captain."

The screen started flashing with the silhouettes of hundreds of surface combatants around the world. Every ship was identifiable through this trusted system detailing any vessel that sailed the world's oceans.

"Oh, man!" the young blond-haired tech said, exhaling. "Sorry, Captain," he said after his nonprofessional exclamation.

The captain read and the words scrolled across Thorne's glasses, and then the captain straightened. He had to read it again and leaned over the station once more. He was feeling a fluttering in his stomach over the strangest situation he had ever encountered at sea. The captain picked up the 1 MC mic and addressed his crew.

"Crewmen of the *Houston*, here is what we're tracking. We have a Russian warship seven hundred yards to our starboard beam. She is an original Soviet Kirov-class battle cruiser. Not the modern Kirov class. I repeat, she is not part of their modern Kirov class."

The men in the control room exchanged uneasy looks. The captain saw this and decided to let them in on the whole story. The technician already knew, so there would be scuttlebutt ringing throughout the boat if he didn't address the situation now.

"She's a fat one," he said, trying to ease their minds with humor. "Forty-three thousand displaced tons. This monster is also packing six sixteen-inch rifled guns situated inside two turrets you could fit the Lincoln Memorial into."

Again, the men and women inside the control center looked uneasy. Sixteen-inch *guns* was what caught their attention. What ship in the world carried that size armament anymore?

"Okay, I want scuttlebutt kept to a minimum, and maybe, just maybe, you'll have a great ghost story to tell your grandkids someday." He was smiling but saw that his crew was not. He again spoke into the 1 MC mic. "She's the *Simbirsk*, a battle cruiser. Launched, 24 November"—he paused as his eyes met those of his first officer and then roamed to the men and women under his command—"1939."

The crew in other spaces of the giant sub stopped what they were doing. Even the forward torpedo room came to a momentary halt before being harangued back to work by their weapons supervisor in loading the expensive and delicate Mark 48 torpedoes.

"She was reported sunk in 1944 by German U-boat *U-521*. Now, until we know what's happening here, we will remain at battle stations—submerged. More information as we get it. That is all." The captain clicked off and then looked pointedly at his first officer. "Gary, bring us shallow. We need to get off a coded ELF message to *Nimitz*. We'll let them pass this one up the line." Thorne placed the mic back into its holder and then faced Devers once more. "I don't care to be explaining to the chief of naval operations just how and why we are tracking a ghost ship reportedly sunk over seventy-five years ago."

"I guess you're right about one thing, Skipper: this will be something to tell the grandkids."

"Let's hope. Weapons, I want a rolling fire solution. Be ready for any target aspect change. Set safeties on both fish to seven hundred yards. I want to be able to respond quickly enough if that phantom is more alive than what she's showing."

"Aye, safeties set at seven hundred yards," came the response.

As if to say *that's not all you have to worry about*, the seas started to scream, and the wind picked up by forty-five miles per hour in just the past three minutes. What they thought was a tropical depression became officially known as Hurricane Tildy, at 0435 hours.

The ghost ship was bringing the dark and stormy night along with her.

2

KIROV-CLASS BATTLE CRUISER *PETER THE GREAT*
FOUR HUNDRED NAUTICAL MILES NORTH OF HURRICANE TILDY

One of the largest warships in the world, and also a class of vessel named after the mysterious phantom the Americans were now tracking, the modern Kirov-class battle cruiser *Peter the Great* made her way north and home after receiving word from Red Banner Northern Fleet headquarters that the NATO Reforger IV exercise had been canceled, much to the relief of giant missile cruiser's captain, Viktor Kreshenko. He sat high on the raised chair just inside the enclosed bridge wing. He was a proud captain whose brother was recently lost on board *Peter the Great*'s sister ship, the *Pyotr Velikiy*, lost to enemy alien fire off the coast of Antarctica during the Operation Overlord campaign.

Peter the Great was now exiting the storm-tossed seas west of Scotland with her two escort vessels, the Slava-class missile cruiser *Marshal Ustinov* and the smaller Udaloy-class destroyer *Admiral Levchenko*. The two fleet Akula-class attack submarines had exited the area five hours ahead of the smaller section of the battle group. The rest of the fleet had disbursed when it was confirmed that NATO command authority had called a halt to their aggressive war games.

Peter the Great slammed her heavily raked and aerodynamic bow into the last of the deeper troughs caused by the storm that had now been reclassified as a hurricane and named Tildy by the American National Oceanic and Atmospheric Administration. The giant warship eased her beautiful bow up and out of the water, shedding the sea like a mythical giant whale. The new warship was one of the more respected missile cruisers in the world, and NATO had the highest regard for her prowess at destroying other surface ships. Yes, she was the mightiest ship the rebuilding Russian Navy had on her books.

First Captain Viktor Kreshenko smiled as his men held on to stanchions and rigging as they happily made their way out of the storm area.

"Captain, a message from Red Banner Northern Command, sir," a young communications runner said as he stood at attention.

Kreshenko held out his hand without removing his eyes from the seas ahead. He again smiled when he saw the sailor weave and then almost stumble as he came onto the enclosed bridge wing.

"If you can speak, son, read it to me," the burly, bearded captain said without moving.

"Sir, it's for captain's eyes only."

His hand shot out, exasperated that he would be contacted at all. He knew the pencil pushers in Moscow had never tried to maneuver one of the largest warships in the world out of the path of a hurricane. Now, what did they have to tell him that only he could understand? The runner placed the yellow flimsy in the captain's hand and then made a hasty retreat. Kreshenko read. Then he read the communiqué again, and then again. He hissed a curse and then slammed his hand down on the intercom. "Second Captain Dishlakov, come to the bridge wing, please."

The captain waited. While he did, he reread the orders again, and he felt his stomach turn over. Now, the young sailors he was laughing at earlier for being seasick and for not having sea legs weren't so funny anymore. Even in the tossing seas, Kreshenko heard the pounding of feet up the outside stairs. The wing door opened, and a very wet second captain, *Peter the Great*'s first officer, stepped into the dry space. He removed his hat and then used his right hand to shed some of the seawater from his short-cropped blond hair.

"Captain, you wished to see me?"

Kreshenko held out the message flimsy. The younger man, destined for great things in the surface navy, read the orders. He too reread them two more times. The captain knew this kid to be bright and good at his job, and he was pleased to see that these new orders scared the hell out of Second Captain Dishlakov as much as they did himself.

"Has someone in Moscow gone completely mad?" Dishlakov said as he gave the message back and then removed his rain slicker. He angrily tossed the wet plastic coat into the far corner of the bridge wing.

The captain held a finger to his lips as a mess steward brought in tea. They remained silent while their hot tea was poured. The second captain took a seat next to his commander. The steward left.

"Not wise to show your emotions in front of the crew, my young friend. It doesn't pay to let on that the new Russian attitude in Moscow has completely gone off the deep end. We'll keep that little fact to ourselves. Lord only knows the crew will catch on soon enough."

"Yes, Captain."

"Now, what in the hell do you suppose they mean by *loiter in the area, await passengers and large contingent of special operations personnel*?"

"All I see is that Moscow thinks holding station on the edge of a powerful hurricane is child's play, Captain. Do they understand the risks?"

The captain laughed and then sipped his glass of tea. "God, this tea is getting worse and worse." He made a face and then set the glass in its pewter holder down. He watched the level inside the glass roll to one side and then the other. "As to your question, my friend, no, they do not know, nor do they care. We have been, and always will be, expendable." Kreshenko looked over at the innocent face of his first officer. He knew that the brother lost weighed heavily on his mind and colored his judgment on higher authority. "And it seems even more so the past few years with our fearless leadership. It seems our people in Moscow have never learned the more valuable lessons on aggression. We seem to be backsliding, and there is nothing a mere sailor can do about it."

The first officer got up from his heavily cushioned seat and then dogged the hatchway. They would not be disturbed.

"Captain, perhaps it's not well that you speak so openly about the current leadership in this manner. You know I have the same opinions, but my family is in a far better position to protect me than your family is you. I believe the official position is that the *Pyotr Velikiy* was lost due to your half-brother's careless actions upon taking command of his ship. Regardless of the official lie, you seem to be a target lately."

"Yes, my family was also in on the Gorbachev debacle. We helped bring down the Soviet regime; I know the stories. But this message with no explanation? It's just typical of the way things are being run now."

"Orders, Captain?"

"Inform the *Ustinov* and the *Levchenko* of our orders. We will hold station at the edge of the hurricane and await our passengers."

"Aye, aye, Captain."

"Crazy sons of bitches. Has the world gone completely insane?"

The mighty Russian battle cruiser heeled sharply to starboard as she and her two escorts started steaming in a circle, awaiting their destiny and a voyage into seas they could never have imagined.

ALEXANDRIA, EGYPT

The man with blond hair knew this was not a regular police procedure; as a matter of fact, he was well aware through his informative friends that these men were not regular police at all. These imposters failed to even abscond with the right uniforms. The five had the clothing of the local Alexandria Police Department. The uniforms were all ill-fitting, and one of the embroidered patches on the shoulder of one looked as if it had been stitched on in a hurry with the wrong-colored thread. The man suspected he had hit the mark and was now in the custody of their antiquities police, the highly secretive Pharaoh's Guards Regiment formed after the riots of 2015 in order to protect Egypt's heritage from vandals. He knew them to be a new, supposedly counterterrorist unit of the Egyptian government brought to fruition to protect Egypt's history from being destroyed or stolen. But he knew their work was geared more toward the theft of their *own* national heritage for secretive sales to the highest of world bidders. Interpol knew them to be the men behind the terrorists' attacks on their own unsuspecting people who dealt with ancient Egyptian works. Right now, the man handcuffed to a steel chair would have taken the terrorists or even Interpol. This was one situation he was not going to make it out of if certain men were even a few minutes off on their slim timetable.

"Who do you work for?" the man sitting in a chair in a darkened corner asked for the fifth time.

"I work for myself. My business card is still in your hand. Just because I came into possession of the object in question before you gentlemen could steal it does not mean I'm not who I say I am."

"Yes, Mr. Klaus Udell, of"—the man held the business card up to the light—"Dresden, Germany."

"Yes, I run a fashionable antique shop on the outskirts of—"

Whack. The open-fist blow to the side of his head made his vision find that ever-elusive tunnel that usually preceded being knocked the hell out. The man shook his head and stared at the black-bearded man who had delivered the sneak attack. This thug he would remember.

"If you insist, I admit it's not that fashionable a shop." His blue eyes never left those of the bearded man, who now moved to the side of the chair. That irritating smile was still etched on his dark features.

"Humor. I'm so glad that you have some. You are going to need it, my friend. The days of Europeans pilfering our heritage are over. An example must be made." The man finally stood, and the official identification was made. This was the gentlemen you see on the Discovery Channel and National Geographic. He was famous inside and outside of Egypt. Dr. Hasan Mobbari, national director of the antiquities bureau for the government of Egypt.

"Well, I see you have made enough fame and fortune to fool your bosses into thinking you're looking out for their best interests. Smuggling antiquities from your own people and department must be pretty lucrative."

The small man laughed. "Very lucrative." Mobbari walked over and faced the handcuffed man. "Why do I get the sense that my presence here and my nefarious outside interests have not come as a surprise to you?"

The man in the chair only smiled with blood staining his lower lip. Then he looked toward the man who had hit him. The smile eased off.

"In case you have not noticed, I am a thief. Thieves know certain details about life in our game. You are one of those details. I am what is called an opportunist, a veritable black sheep in the antiquities world."

"Black sheep?" Mobbari asked, confused.

"It's an American turn of phrase. I sometimes hang out with some, well, let us just say, shady and despicable individuals."

Mobbari actually flinched back a step when the man had raised his voice when he said the word *despicable*.

The smaller man quickly regained his composure.

"It makes little difference just who your thieving friends are; they cannot help you at this time. We are very secure here in the museum. It is Sunday, we are closed, and the security department, well"—he laughed again, more heartily this time—"they're mine also." He lifted the blond-haired man's chin up. "Now, let us speak on the subject of the crown of Ramses II."

"Is that something you have misplaced? For a fee, I could possibly put out some feelers and assist in finding this, well, whatever it is you're looking for."

This time the blow was straight into the side of his jaw. His head burst with stars, but that didn't stop the handcuffed man from turning and facing the bearded attacker. His eyes were intense and filled with malice as he took the brutish man in.

"This facetious attitude will not help you avoid the pain that is coming your way, my German friend. All this talking is meaningless anyway. I am afraid your filthy ilk, your partners in crime as it may, have betrayed you."

The knock came loudly on the steel door. The sound echoed off the walls as if they were in a huge cave system. One of the uniformed men went to the door and slid a small door back and looked. He closed the viewing port and then turned to face the head of Egypt's antiquities department.

"Two museum staff with a small crate."

"Ah," Mobbari said, smiling as he leaned down and into the face of his guest, "opportune timing, I must say. My German friend, it has arrived."

The blond man looked up as the smile on the face of not just this arrogant fool but his minions also became larger. It was if they all had a secret that he wasn't privy to.

"Let them in. I'm sure Mr. Udell would be interested to see what we have recovered."

The two men in white coveralls were allowed in. They had a small wooden crate between them. They set it on a table and then began to open it with small crowbars. Mobbari and his men were involved and excited as they watched the object being uncrated, enough so they paid no attention to the deliverymen. The top of the crate came off and then the sides. The two large men stepped back as all eyes went to the straw-filled case.

Hasan Mobbari reached into the crate after donning white cotton gloves and pulled out a magnificent headpiece designed and built over 3,400 years before by the brilliant artisans in the court of Ramses II. The crown was white and had an inner crown of red; there was the golden cobra in its most menacing posture on the front—ready to strike. All this detail culminated in the most famous crown in history. The two differently colored parts indicated the kingdoms of Upper and Lower Egypt. Mobbari held it up to the light and then toward the blond man sitting in the steel chair.

"Magnificent piece!" Mobbari exclaimed.

"So, you were just torturing me for the pure enjoyment of doing so?" the man asked as he spit another mouthful of blood onto the cement floor. His eyes once more went to the bearded face of his assailant, who only nodded with pleasure and smiled even wider.

"Not at all. It is and will be far more fun," Mobbari said as he finally lowered the crown. "You see, I have contacts inside your world also. The men who turned you in, Herr Udell, informed on you when my rather extensive net was closing in around them. Not only did we recover the crown in your fifth hotel room—very resourceful, by the way—they also gave us your real name and profession—Mr. Henri Farbeaux. Or should I address you as *Colonel*?" Again, the irritating laugh. "Without even knowing it, we have captured a man wanted in nearly every country in the known world."

The five other men laughed also. The two larger men in the coveralls did not. They had removed the silenced dart guns so fast that the men were still laughing when the .22-caliber Phisolene anesthetic–filled glass darts slammed into their necks, chests, and even one man's forehead.

"Oh, shit. That had to hurt," a blond man said as he removed his baseball cap and his museum overalls. "The instructions from Pfizer said don't hit anyone above the neck."

The other man, this one with black hair, eased over to Mobbari and removed the crown from his shaking hands. "Well, I told you for years I was a better shot than you, Swabby," the dark-haired man said.

"Who are you men?" the antiquities director asked in as a defiant voice as he could muster after seeing his men fall to the cold flooring.

"Who they are makes no difference, you traitorous thief."

All eyes turned to the door as ten men, followed by one in a black suit, entered the room. The ten civilian-attired personnel started kicking at the downed men and began removing them from the room, not too gently either, the handcuffed man noticed with pleasure. He also noticed they left his bearded attacker behind because of his sheer size.

The dark-haired man who was still wearing the white coveralls placed the crown of Ramses II back into the crate and then placed the wooden sides and top back on. He faced the man in the black suit as he in turn placed a set of handcuffs on Dr. Hasan Mobbari.

"General, thank you for the cooperation."

The tall, thin Egyptian pushed Mobbari to the floor until the portly man was on his knees, and then the newcomer held out his hand.

"Knock it off, Jack. We've come too far for that kind of formality." The man looked around at the unconscious men being removed and then over at the air gun Carl was still holding. "Although I must learn where it is you get such fantastic equipment."

Colonel Jack Collins shook the general's hand with a smile. "We have an extensive toy box."

General Hasne Shamakhan, Egyptian Homeland Security, smiled again and then lifted Mobbari to his feet. "Thanks for this, Jack. We've been after this scum for quite some time, but we never could gather enough proof." He looked down at the visibly shaken television star. "This bag of refuse has pulled the wool over our eyes for far too many years. Now, he will pay for his thievery and murder. Is that how you say it—*wool over the eyes*?"

"Yes. But most times wool is easily stripped away."

The other man walked over to the chair and the angry prisoner sitting there glaring at the three men looking at him.

"Hey, Henri. What's up, man?"

"I find it difficult to see how my battering at the hands of these men is worth a few industrial diamonds," Henri Farbeaux said as he wiggled his hands that were still cuffed behind his back, indicating it would be nice to have them removed. "And the next time there is a change in plan, I would appreciate being informed of such."

"Oh, you knew all along the deal wasn't going to turn out like you wanted." The man leaned close to Farbeaux and whispered so the Egyptians couldn't hear. "We let you keep the blue diamonds from the displacement machine. Your service to the United States was well rewarded. All that money just for a few whacks to the old jaw, sounds like a hell of a deal to me." Captain Carl Everett, US Navy, smiled again as he produced a small silver key. "Want out of there?"

Jack smiled at the Egyptian general as Carl and Henri once more began their back-and-forth of mutual hate and respect.

"Thank the president on my behalf, Jack. Now that this is done, I must ask the inevitable question: Why is the US Army taking an interest in foreign antiquities?"

"Let's just say we were in the region and were asked to help out a friend. Don't get used to it, though; this was a onetime favor. As for the president, he's always willing to loan out people like us; it's his way of keeping us out of trouble at home." Jack stopped smiling and then looked at an angry Henri Farbeaux. "But I must state it was Henri here who took the biggest chance. By the way, he made your security look rather foolish inside the museum."

"Yes," the thin man said as he pushed the antiquities thief toward the open door. "We'll have to thank Colonel Farbeaux another time for pointing that little flaw out." The Homeland Security director turned and smiled at the Frenchman as his cuffs were removed. "After today, Colonel, your days of stealing within the borders of my nation are finished. At any rate, thank you for your assistance." He became as serious as he could in warning. "The next time we will not be so welcoming, grateful, and friendly."

The three men watched as the general left with his prized prisoner, stepping over the still prone form of the bearded man who had assaulted Henri and who was in the process of being cuffed by one of the Egyptian Homeland Security men.

"Gentlemen," Farbeaux said, still rubbing his wrists from the chafe the handcuffs had given him, "you have fallen to the lowest order of men. You have taken advantage of my good nature and deep sense of gratitude for my earlier freedom from the American authorities in Brooklyn."

"Knock it off, Henri. You owed us for those blue diamonds you stole from the Wellsian Doorway. I think a payment worth $17 million is quite sufficient for your services in regard to assisting us in bringing Mr. Everett back from history, and for your expertise in your field of endeavor in recovering the crown of Ramses, and for helping us recover this." Jack reached into his coveralls and pulled out a small object. It was a large piece of Americana stolen years before from the Smithsonian. Jack held the original surrender note from the pen of Lord General Cornwallis, asking General George Washington for terms of surrender of his British forces at Yorktown during the American Revolution. The old paper was in a plastic case and had been inside the offices of one Hasan Mobbari. Niles Compton and the president of the United States saw no need to explain their real intent to the Egyptian authorities. The president—nor, for that matter, Niles Compton—didn't care for red tape all that much. This theft of American property was not something to take public.

"I am so pleased to have assisted you in getting that little piece of history back into your hands. The diamonds were still not worth the humiliation of being slapped around by brutes with the IQs of a jackal. You could have also made your appearance somewhat earlier into my torture session."

Jack laughed and patted Henri on the shoulder as the Frenchman finished rubbing his wrists. "Come on, Henri. We'll give you a ride out of here. You never know about the Egyptians; they could have a change of heart about allowing you to leave."

Farbeaux turned away from Jack and faced Carl. "I really don't like you, Captain." For emphasis on his words just as the last Egyptian was standing the bearded man up to escort him out, Farbeaux kicked the beast in the groin, doubling the man over. He fell, and then Henri kicked him in the side of his jaw. He then straightened and calmed himself.

"Ah, but I thought we were becoming close friends, Froggy?" Carl said, but his attention was also drawn to the inherent temperament of the Frenchman when it came to vengeance. "Now, we have a plane to catch."

Colonel Henri Farbeaux turned to face Collins, and then with a wary eye on Carl, he said, "I'm sitting next to you, Colonel."

3

KIROV-CLASS BATTLE CRUISER *PETER THE GREAT*
FOUR HUNDRED NAUTICAL MILES NORTH OF HURRICANE TILDY

First Captain Kreshenko stood on the expansive bridge of *Peter the Great* and faced the window that looked out over the stern. The helipad on the swaying deck looked to be a mile away. Kreshenko frowned just as the giant warship dipped her prow into the heavy seas. He couldn't imagine what it was like even a hundred miles closer to Tildy. His ship was taking a pounding, and he was nowhere near the killing swirl of the hurricane. He watched through his binoculars as the heavy-lift helicopter, the Mil Mi-26, NATO designation Halo, hovered shakily over the stern. His crewmen were battling the seas, trying to guide the giant helicopter down to the pitching and rolling deck. Thus far, in three attempts, they had come close to crashing the hovering behemoth into the superstructure all three times.

"Are they insane?" Second Captain Dishlakov said as he slammed his fist down upon the reinforced window frame. Both officers watched as the Halo came in for its fourth attempt. "Fools!"

Kreshenko hissed as the huge helicopter's tail rotor came close to striking the radar boom at the uppermost top of the mast. The tail boom spun crazily, and the captain thought to himself that he was possibly about to lose his ship to a fool's stunt. He cursed as the Halo finally straightened and then rose once more into the rain-filled black skies.

"That's it. Tell whoever that is to get the hell away from my ship. RTB immediately. This is not only going to cost those idiots their lives, but we could lose this ship. I'm not having it. They can throw me in the deepest Gulag in Siberia. I'm not losing my ship because some brass-hat son of a bitch has a wild hair up his ass. Call them off, Dishlakov!"

Peter the Great rolled to port, and the dark seas crashed over onto the helo deck. As the radio call went out, Kreshenko was satisfied when the giant helicopter started to rise and turn away.

"Thank God the pilot has some common sense."

"Should we clear the landing party from action stations, Captain?" Dishlakov asked.

"Yes, I'm sure those boys are wet enough. Let's—"

"They're coming back!" called one of the bridge lookouts.

Kreshenko was stunned as he turned back to the window, and through the wash of rainwater, he saw the Halo Mi-26 returning to the battle cruiser. This time, the captain took up the microphone. "Communications, order that bird away from my ship! If they attempt to land, I will shoot them out of the sky."

"Sir, the Halo is flashing command override on your order. They say they are coming in."

The captain cursed, and then, to his shock, the Halo came low once more over the fantail. He then saw ropes shoot out from the open doors of the air force bird. His eyes widened when he saw men rappelling down these ropes to the helo deck below. Several of these brave fools landed hard on the steel deck, but they kept coming. They streamed from both sliding doors of the Halo. He turned to his first officer as he watched this insanity through his binoculars. Dishlakov had noticed the same thing as the captain, and as he lowered his glasses, they exchanged worried looks. Each of the first fifty men to the deck was heavily armed. Finally, as they turned their attention back to the badly swerving helicopter, four men in different clothing rappelled down the rubber-treated ropes to land softly onto the pitching deck.

"Second Captain, go below and bring the commander of this band of fools to my cabin, take the others to the ship's mess, and station a marine guard on them until I get some confirmation on just who these idiots are."

The captain watched as the Halo, with her belly empty of men and equipment and after the last large bags of gear were lowered down, rose back into the black sky and then made a sharp turn to the north. Kreshenko slammed his fist onto the windowsill once more and then stormed off to his cabin.

Two hurricanes were about to explode into the North Atlantic that day, and one was about to happen on board his ship.

It took the captain thirty minutes to finally get to his quarters after securing flight operations. His men were battered and seasick, and after he made sure they got something hot into them, he stormed into his cabin.

The big man was dark haired and was using one of the captain's towels to dry his head. He didn't even notice when Kreshenko burst through the cabin's door. He stared angrily at the man wearing black Nomex battle BDUs, the uniform commandos the world over were now wearing. In place of the Russian Federation flag was a Velcro patch depicting a black camouflaged star. The captain looked on his bunk and saw the belt with the holstered weapon. His eyes went from the bed to the newcomer, who seemed to be making himself at home.

"Ah, First Captain Kreshenko. Is it too much to ask if you have a drink anywhere close by?"

The captain watched the man as he smiled and then simply tossed the towel onto the tiled deck. Kreshenko closed the door and retrieved the towel as *Peter the Great* rolled to starboard. As the captain tossed the wet towel into his private head, he turned to face the stranger. He saw the man wore no rank on his collar and that he was one of those film actor types that always seemed to walk out with the women after the drinking establishments closed. The captain had seen his ilk his entire life and despised the breed.

"I don't have alcohol in my cabin. I try to shy away from it at sea."

"Ah, I had heard that you were a prudent man, Captain. Thank goodness I always come prepared," he said as he retrieved his bag and produced a bottle of very expensive vodka. "Thank goodness it survived the flight." He held the bottle up so the captain could view the label. "This was a gift from old Putin himself, the moron," he said as a way of telling Kreshenko to be careful in his approach about his visitor endangering his precious ship.

Instead of commenting, the captain walked to his desk and came back with two glasses.

"You see, I knew you were a man of action, Captain," the stranger said as he tore the protective plastic from the cork and then poured two glasses. "Just as your brave brother and his crew." He held a glass up and then toasted, "To the new Russia."

Kreshenko remained still, not moving for the glass. Finally, in deference to the toast, he nodded. The man acted as though he hadn't noticed Kreshenko's small displeasure at the term *new Russia* or the mention of his dead brother, but Kreshenko knew that the man had. It was in this man's cold eyes, and the captain knew immediately this visitor was no military person, or at least hadn't been one for many years.

"What are you doing on my ship?" Kreshenko asked as he pushed aside the glass of vodka, which was still untouched.

The other man smiled, his eyes moving from the captain of *Peter the Great* to the still-half-full glass. He reached out and took the glass and drank the fiery liquid down. He closed his black eyes momentarily and then let out a satisfied breath. He then tossed the empty glass to the captain, who fumbled with it and then secured it before it crashed to the floor. The stranger unzipped his BDU top and then pulled a large envelope from its dry place.

"You endangered my ship and crew with that little stunt."

"Yes."

The captain looked at the envelope and then grudgingly accepted.

"May I assume my men are being dried and fed?"

"Your men are being taken care of," Kreshenko said as he sat at his desk and broke the wax seal on the package.

"Perhaps to speed things along, go to the last page and examine the signature on the bottom."

Kreshenko, with his eyes firmly affixed to the man he had instantly taken a dislike to, flipped through the sixteen pages, and then his eyes settled on the last name and signature, the commander in chief of the Russian Navy.

"Okay, you have impressive credentials. That still gives you no right to endanger my ship."

The man laughed once more and then retrieved the bottle of vodka and poured again. He drank and then sat upon the captain's bunk without asking.

"Captain Kreshenko, from this moment on, your ship will be in constant danger. So will the other two vessels of your rather small battle group."

"Just who in the hell are you?" he asked, not bothering with the set of orders. He had seen that this man's name had been blacked out on the official copies.

Once more, the glass was filled, and the stranger drank deeply. He started untying his boots. "Why, I'm the man who's ordering you to turn *Peter the Great*, the *Ustinov*, and the *Admiral Levchenko* around one hundred and eighty degrees."

This time, Kreshenko recovered far more quickly than the newcomer thought possible. He sprang to his feet, slamming the orders down on the desk.

"Back into the hurricane?"

"Yes, back into the hurricane."

"Once more, sir, who are you?"

The man pulled off a wet boot and sock and then fixed the captain with a cold look. "I am Colonel Leonid Salkukoff; I am the assistant director of internal historical studies from Odessa. And I am here to repair a mistake from many, many years ago. A mistake we have well benefited from, but it has now run its course and its usefulness." The tall man stood and faced the captain. "And you, my good captain, your crew, the other two warships, well, they are expendable in that endeavor. Now, shall we get *Peter the Great* turned around to meet our destiny?"

Kreshenko was feeling ill as he reached for the phone on his desk. "I want a flash message sent to both Red Banner Fleet North and to Presidential Command Authority in Moscow." The captain held his hand over the phone as the radio room scrambled to make the connection. "We'll see if President Putin is as accepting of the consequences in sending his prized flagship of the Red Banner Northern Fleet into danger as cavalierly as yourself."

Kreshenko was stunned when the man completely undressed and was preparing for a shower when he stopped and smiled.

"President Putin has no say in this, Captain. The sooner you learn this harsh fact, the better off you will be."

"You're telling me that the president has no authority to order this ship back to home waters?"

Again, the irritating smile. "Captain, let me explain something to you," he said as he wrapped a dry towel around his muscled hips and stopped in the doorway leading to the captain's private head and shower. "Beyond certain offices in our government, the office of the president of Russia has never existed. Since the so-called fall of the Soviet State, the presidency, nor even the politburo, has been in charge of our country and never will be."

"What are you saying?" Kreshenko was starting to become furious, but at the same time, a sick feeling of knowing struck his guts. He and his dead brother had spoken about it in private times, but they always thought it nothing but a conspiracy theory to scare the progressives in their country.

"You'll learn more in the orders, but suffice it to say, Captain, playtime in the world is over. I'm afraid the average person won't be able to recognize Mother Russia in the next few years. The arrogant fools in the West will learn that the cold war was not lost by us. We won it the day we *convinced* them we lost it. Now, get this ship turned around or I'll have you shot and turn it around myself." The man calling himself Colonel Leonid Salkukoff lost his humorous smile as he ducked into the private head and the warm shower that awaited him.

Captain Kreshenko placed the phone down and then grimaced as he hit the intercom to the bridge.

"Second Captain Dishlakov, let's get *Peter the Great* and our two escorts turned around. We're going back into the hurricane. Let's get all three ships buttoned up tight and prepare for rough seas. Set storm warning conditions throughout all three ships."

As he sat and read the extraordinary orders he had ever been given, the captain felt the bulk of Russian advanced weaponry heel hard to starboard as she turned away from home and back into danger.

LOS ANGELES—CLASS ATTACK SUBMARINE USS *HOUSTON* FOUR HUNDRED NAUTICAL MILES SOUTHWEST

It had been four hours since the message containing the *Houston*'s mysterious bogey had gone up the chain of command from *Nimitz* to Norfolk and then finally to Washington. In that time, Captain Thorne became convinced that CINCLANT and NATO command had totally lost their minds.

"Boat's at a hundred feet and holding," said officer of the deck Jacobs as he called out the depth. There actually had been no need to do so because the closer the submarine got to the surface, the fiercer the rolling of her bulk became. "I take that back. We're rolling. Thrusters starboard!"

Thorne looked at the young lieutenant JG and slightly shook his head, wanting the young officer to calm down for the benefit of the crew. The man acknowledged that he received the captain's silent advice and visibly settled.

Captain Thorne examined the orders he had received via ELF, the low-frequency method of communicating that was coded and protected from snooping ears. He shook his head as the *Houston*'s first officer joined him. He was tucking in his shirt as he approached Thorne and the message flimsy he held. The captain handed Lieutenant Commander Gary Devers the flimsy.

"You have got to be—" The first officer was cut off by a sharp roll as *Houston* actually breached the surface with her sail tower, exposing her numbered designation to the early morning sky. Number *713* stood out in all its white-painted glory before dipping back into the dark green tumult. They had gone from one hundred feet to almost nothing in one swell of the rough seas. "Jesus, that was embarrassing. Thank God we don't have to hide from a warship at these shallow depths. Exposing ourselves like that would be a good way to get a Russian missile sent our way," the first officer said as *Houston* finally settled.

"Up scope," Thorne said as he held tightly to the periscope stanchion. As Thorne looked around him, he saw the anxious faces of the mere kids watching his every move. When the scope was up, he peered into the eyepiece. "Gary, let's give the old girl a goose. Give her a shot of air, will you? Bring her as shallow as you can without exposing that damn sail to the elements again."

"Aye, Skipper. Make your depth seventy-five feet."

"Aye. Blowing negative to the mark. We're coming shallow to seventy-five feet," the chief of the boat repeated.

Throughout the length of *Houston*, loud pops were heard as the hull relaxed as she came to a shallower depth.

"There she is," Thorne said as the scope cleared the high seas for the briefest of moments. The captain started using his Morse lamp high upon the radar antenna. *Houston* rolled hard to port as the men were heard cursing as they fought for handholds.

Through the beeping of the Morse signal, Devers could read: *Disabled vessel, this is USS* Houston, *a United States submarine off your starboard beam. Are you under power or do you need assistance? I repeat, this is a United States warship. Do you need assistance?* Finally, he pushed a button on the periscope, and although he knew he couldn't hear it inside the thick-hulled sub, he had just sent out a blast of air through his warning horn affixed to the sail.

"Captain, we're drifting right toward that hunk of junk," Devers called out from the plotting station.

Thorne slammed the handles up and then lowered the scope. He reached for the intercom. "Communications, keep trying on all frequencies until she responds."

"*Conn, radio, aye.*"

Thorne leaned against the navigation console and then looked at the plot. "How soon until the *De Zeven*, *Shiloh*, and *Bunker Hill* arrive on station?"

"An hour, give or take five minutes. They're having a far rougher time with Tildy than we are."

"I imagine," Thorne said as he examined the plot on the navigation board for what seemed like the thousandth time. "Plot the hurricane against the last weather report and prediction, will you, Gary?"

The first officer designated the edge of Tildy and then plotted the estimated position of the hurricane's eye as close as he could with the information the boat's computer had. The virtual reality app made the hurricane swirl as if it were a motion picture animation. The captain placed a finger in the estimated position of the eye, the calmest part of the storm, and tapped the spot.

"There it is. If CINCLANT and the president want that ship boarded, there's the only place it will be possible. I estimate five hours until the hurricane's eye if the phantom's drift remains the same. If not, we'll have to have one of the heavy cruisers attempt to take her in tow."

Devers leaned over and silently concurred with the estimate. "Captain, maybe those in power have thought this through, but what if the Russians find out we're attempting to board that derelict?"

Thorne laughed but immediately regretted it when he saw the anxious young faces of his control room crew.

"I guess at that time we'll find out just how important this hunk of junk is to someone, won't we?"

"Yes, Captain."

"Okay, let's take one more look. Up scope," he said as the chrome-and-plastic scope rose from the deck. "Damn, that thing is riding pretty low in the water. Either she's taking on water and foundering or she's far heavier than her listed displacement tonnage. If that's the case, we need to—"

The flash in the eyepiece of the periscope sent the captain back hard enough that he almost lost his footing. It was as if the sun had exploded in the advanced optics of the scope.

"Captain, what—"

A pressure wave slammed into *Houston*, swinging her bow around fifteen degrees before her thrusters corrected her programmed position. She rolled hard to starboard and then to port as she finally started to settle. The captain gained his composure, and then, rubbing his eyes, which felt like they had been burned from his skull, he grasped the handles of the scope again and looked. He closed his eyes once more and rubbed them. He peered through the eye-piece again, expecting to see nothing but flaming wreckage on the surface of the rolling seas. Again, a bright flash and the Russian ship vanished. Before he could say or do anything, another bright flash that lit up the dark skies again wreaked havoc with his vision and the optics. The lens cleared, and then the vessel was back, rolling and pitching and sinking into a deep depression.

Houston suddenly went dark. Not even her emergency lighting came on. All her boards went out along with the overheads. Then, just as quickly, electrical power sprang back to life.

"Electromagnetic pulse?" the first officer asked, concerned when the captain started moving the periscope to the left, right, and then settling once more.

"I don't have a clue, but that damn ship is still there. Chief of the Boat, I want a damage assessment and diagnostics run on everything."

"Aye."

The captain again slammed the handles of the scope to the up position and then lowered it. He looked around the control room at the anxious faces staring at him. He took a deep breath and then nodded at his first officer.

"Okay, take her to five hundred feet and hold station. Use thrusters to keep us even with the *Simbirsk*. Sonar, conn, I want shifts rotated every thirty minutes. I want fresh ears listening for any untoward intruders to our little drama."

"Conn, sonar, aye. No contacts at this time other than our three sisters a hundred miles off. We did have a spike in the infrared band ten seconds before power shut down and another spike in radiation output at the same time."

"From *Houston*?"

"Negative, conn. It came from our phantom."

Throughout the boat, the rumors were really starting to fly. It seemed the USS *Houston* and her surface cronies were about to attempt the boarding of Russian state property, and they knew those same Russians wouldn't be too fond of that little development. Now, they realized that whatever that ship was, it could possibly have the potential to send *Houston* and her crew to the bottom of the Atlantic.

The USS *Houston* went deep with her crew's knowledge that there was something out there that rattled one of the most experienced submarine skippers in the world.

4

THE WHITE HOUSE
WASHINGTON, D.C.

Rear Admiral Harley Dickerson—Scooter to the men and women who knew him best—was waiting outside the national security advisor's office with none of his staff present. General Maxwell Caulfield, former head of the Joint Chiefs of Staff, had been talked into taking the advisor's job after the Overlord incident the previous year. He saw his old friend as he strolled into his outer office. After greeting his assistants and getting his missed calls, he turned with a curious look toward the man waiting patiently. He read the messages as he smiled toward his visitor.

"Scooter, what in the hell brings you out of that dungeon at the Pentagon? You spooks haven't had enough after our little alien encounter?"

Harley Dickerson stood and shook his friend's hand. They had worked together closely during the past three years of dealing with the Overlord incident. Dickerson was a liaison between DARPA, the US Navy, and several other darker entities inside defense circles.

"Max, we need to talk," was all Dickerson said as he leaned in with Caulfield's hand still clutched in his own.

The general raised his brow and then glanced at his two assistants. "I've got a briefing with the president in"—he looked at his watch—"fifteen minutes, Scooter. Can it wait? We have a developing situation at sea regarding the Operation Reforger IV exercise. We had to cancel the damn thing last night, a little coup for our friends the Russians, but if—"

"Max, make the time—now."

Caulfield saw the anxiety in the younger man's face and then simply gestured to his open door. "Liz, no calls for the next few minutes."

Once inside the small office, Caulfield offered Dickerson coffee, and he refused, opting to open his briefcase instead. Caulfield sat behind his desk. He looked at the pictures of his family and the uniform he once wore. The old marine corps blues were a part of his past life now. Today and forever afterward, Maxwell Caulfield would be wearing what it was he was wearing today, civilian suits from varying Men's Discount Warehouse stores. And as his assistants both quipped, he had absolutely zero taste in civilian clothing. Yes, he missed the far simpler life of a marine.

Dickerson tossed a small stack of photos and typed pages onto Caulfield's desk and then sat back down. Max saw the man he knew as unflappable bite on a thumbnail as he picked up a photograph and scanned it. The black-and-white image depicted a very grainy view of a large ship. It was low in a depression inside a deep trough of water, something Caulfield had experienced many times in his career aboard ships. The vessel was in heavy seas.

"One of ours?" he asked, looking up at Dickerson.

"No. This was taken through the periscope of a tailing submerged asset in the North Atlantic last night. This was transmitted this morning to our offices and those of the chief of naval operations."

"Why isn't Jim Hardy bringing this to me, then?" Max asked as his eyes bored in at Dickerson. This was a breach of military etiquette. His boss at the Pentagon should have been briefing him personally on anything having to do with Operation Reforger IV.

"The admiral isn't in this loop, only my department at intel. Besides, by the time I started explaining things to him, this thing could blow up in our faces."

"What could blow up?" Caulfield asked.

"Max, we have a seventy-five-year-old ship of war out there that was reported sunk before the end of World War II. The name of the vessel is the *Simbirsk*, a Russian battle cruiser verified as being sunk by the German navy in 1944."

Before Caulfield could register this shock, Dickerson tossed a file onto his desk after unlocking it from a compartment in his briefcase. Max Caulfield looked up with the photo of the *Simbirsk* still in his hand.

"And this?"

"A file on a warship of our own."

"Don't keep me guessing here, Scooter. I don't have the time for it," Caulfield countered.

"A destroyer escort, same vintage as our Russian war casualty. This file is on the USS *Eldridge*. This is all we have on her. It seems the Department of the Navy, or at least at the time, the Department of War, lost the entire file just after the incident. Many people in my group think it was intentionally lost by the navy department on orders from none other than President Roosevelt. The rumor is the navy boys tried to do something rather extraordinary that had not been cleared with the war department. That was right around the time that Admiral Stark, the chief of naval operations, lost a lot of influence at the White House."

Max looked at the file and then looked up at his visitor after viewing the second photo. "This another war casualty?"

"No, Max, she wasn't. She went on to serve the navy well throughout her deployments the rest of the war. We even sold her later to a foreign government. No, she had a very distinguished career."

"Scooter, this is boring me to death. You bring me a partial file and then claim the rest has been lost. What in the hell is going on here?"

"General, that's the ship that was the centerpiece of a little-known theoretic application undertaken by scientists from Chicago University and Harvard, jointly with the Department of the Navy. All this took place in 1943, and that experimental application turned disastrous for the navy."

"What application, Scooter?" Caulfield said with resignation lacing his voice.

"That theoretic application was thought to produce what we would come to know as stealth technology. That theory and later action would be tagged by every conspiracy nut in the free world as the Philadelphia Experiment."

Twenty minutes later, after his assistants had told him that the president was waiting on his morning security briefing, General Maxwell Caulfield asked for and received a private meeting with the leader of the free world that lasted just thirty-five minutes. In the three minutes after, the United States Armed Forces quietly went to a higher alert status.

The partial file on the Philadelphia Experiment had been read by a sitting president of the United States for only the second time in history.

EVENT GROUP COMPLEX
NELLIS AIR FORCE BASE, NEVADA

The conference room was full. All sixteen departmental heads were present. Alice Hamilton was even there, popping in for meetings on a regular basis. Alice had been a part of the Group since 1947. She read the report filed by Jack and his excursion into Egypt. He reported the sting operation in cooperation with Egyptian Homeland Security had gone off without a hitch. Alice looked up and smiled as she saw the visible relief in the faces of Jack and Carl's two replacements, Jason Ryan and Will Mendenhall. They were both still put out that the colonel had not included them on the mission, anything to get them out of the complex and into the field where they thought they belonged. Alice then flipped pages of her notes and then faced Sarah McIntire, who was sitting next to Master Chief Jenks.

"We have a report from Captain McIntire and Ms. Korvesky on their investigation into the expansion of the level forty-seven vaults."

Sarah wanted to roll her eyes as she stood and reported on the granite strata she knew would not support further expansion in that area of cave system. Before she could finish, the double doors of the conference room opened, and an air force security officer allowed the new head of Computer Sciences into the room. Dr. Xavier Morales used his powerful arms to propel his old-fashioned wheelchair inside. He rolled directly to the head of the long table and Director Niles Compton. Sarah gratefully gave the twenty-four-year-old computer genius the floor. She was happy not to be spouting geological formations that no one but herself fully understood. Anya, for her part, winked at Sarah, being grateful herself for the respite.

Just as Morales stopped, another man was allowed into the room—Professor Charles Hindershot Ellenshaw III came in and held up a file so Xavier could see. Charlie nodded and then took his place at the table, excusing the young lady who had been substituting for crazy Charlie and the Cryptozoology Department. Morales waited until the doors were once more secure. He handed his own file to the director.

"Doctor, you have something more important to share with us than Captain McIntire and Ms. Korvesky's report on the unstable rock strata of our complex?" Niles smiled and then opened the file folder. Morales had it marked as *Director's Eyes Only*. Compton read. The straight line on his mouth told Alice Hamilton and the others in the meeting that he didn't like what it was that the Computer Sciences director had brought him. Ryan and Mendenhall exchanged looks, as they had yet to see the young Mexican American excited about anything other than his new love affair with the world's most powerful computing system, Europa.

"How did you come across this information, Doctor?" Niles asked as he handed the folder over to Alice, who perused it very quickly. The other department heads were left wondering.

Morales looked around, somewhat apprehensive about his answer.

Niles took a deep breath and then patted the closed file with his fingertips.

"Okay, I'm going to have to place this meeting on hold until the same time tomorrow. Sarah will enter her strata report into Europa and copy all departments on its content. Thank you. Drs. Morales, Ellenshaw, and Pollock and Alice, I need a moment, please."

The room slowly emptied, and Niles stood and made his way over to his desk and then sat. Alice took her customary place to his left with her electronic notepad ready. The others took seats in front of the large desk once used by Garrison Lee, and General George C. Marshall before that.

"First, Dr. Morales, when you insert Europa's influence into another Blue Ice system inside government circles, it has to be cleared with either myself or Virginia first."

"I understand that, sir. The computer break-in was not initiated by me or anyone in the complex. Europa herself initiated it after receiving several key-words from flagged communications that she routinely monitors with your endorsement, sir."

"I'm not following," Virginia said.

"It seems someone with A-1 security clearance programmed Europa to seek out certain keywords from government communications. The keywords in this case were *Eldridge, Simbirsk, phase shift*, and a few others. In this particular case, she hit on all the words coming from the White House and the Pentagon."

"Two are the names of ships. The other is an advanced theory on the implementation of redacted covert cover—stealth technology, or in this case, phase shift. It's the ability to hide the radar signature from prying eyes. The other keywords mentioned in the order to Europa were *Operation Necromancer* and *Schoenfeld*. I know because I was there when then director Garrison Lee, myself, and Pete Golding placed them there in 1997."

Xavier looked shocked, as did Charlie Ellenshaw. As for Alice and Virginia, they were both confused. Then it was Alice who closed her eyes and remembered something from the past about Garrison Lee and the one event he could not get out of his thoughts, an event rarely spoken of by the former director of Department 5656. Whatever it was buried in that memory, Alice knew it had scared the hell out of Garrison, a man who feared almost nothing in life.

"Does this have to do with what happened in Philadelphia in '43?" she asked Niles.

"Yes," Niles said. "It seems our friend and mentor was an eyewitness to the event."

"May I ask what in the hell you are referring to?" Virginia asked.

"The Philadelphia Experiment. And yes, it really did happen, much to the regret of many a young sailor."

"Why would Senator Lee be interested in the so-called Philadelphia Experiment after the fact?" Virginia asked, trying to grasp what was being implied.

"He was a witness to the results of that failed experiment. It scared him enough that he and Pete Golding made sure Europa kept an eye out for any hint of the government starting up that program again." Niles pursed his lips as he thought about his earlier call from Lord Durnsford.

Without another word, the director hit a small switch on his desktop, and a monitor rose from the wood. The screen was a solid blue in color until a flash and the seal of the president came on. Niles waited.

"Can you excuse me for a moment, please?"

The four people got up and left the conference room.

Niles sat and listened to the president, his friend of many years, explain his side of what was developing in the North Atlantic. Then Niles explained his earlier conversation with his asset inside Great Britain, whom the president never asked about but could have guessed as to the asset's identity. Niles went into detail about their concerns over an operative inside the Russian authority who was even now making his way to the area in the North Atlantic in question. A decision was made, and the presidential meeting was over. Niles closed the screen and then moved back to the conference table and waited as the others came in. They quickly settled. Charlie still held his file folder and was awaiting his turn to put in his two cents.

"I just finished with the president, and he has confirmed that we have something brewing in the North Atlantic. I will explain later. For now, let's start with Virginia. Place your nuclear sciences division on the highest alert."

"The entire department?" she asked.

"Xavier, get with communications and liaise with the air force. We need Colonel Collins and Captain Everett rerouted. Stop them in London and get them to report to RAF Station Ramsfield for possible transport and sea drop. As I said, we don't know much, but I want us ahead on whatever the president decides to do. I also have a friend of our government who needs a word with not only Jack but Colonel Farbeaux also."

"What are we speaking of here, Niles?" Alice asked.

"The president was informed that the navy has come in contact with a derelict vessel inside the hurricane zone where a resupply war game was scheduled. It seems one of those keywords Dr. Morales spoke of and Garrison Lee warned us to look for has shown its face. The president has ordered that this ship be taken in tow and claimed as salvage. The US Navy brass wants that ship, and now, so does the president. Unfortunately, the Russians have an eye toward their property and want it back. CIA and MI6 in London have reported a very unsavory character is heading out there now. This department is currently liaising with our friends in Great Britain on this Russian character who is someone of high interest. That's all I have on that. But our friend Henri Farbeaux is a key to a point the British have made, and our French asset will be needed on this little excursion."

"I hope there is a sea lawyer available to the president, because the Russians will take exception to us boarding their ship," Virginia said, knowing something about sea law.

"And it seems they are heading full steam back into the area. I imagine they may want that ship badly enough that they are willing to risk the lives of close to a thousand sailors to get it. Our naval assets in the area have three warships bearing down on them at high speed while battling a hurricane. They are taking this seriously. And"—everyone looked up at the *and*—"when the president spoke to our friend Vladimir Putin, he says he knows nothing about this. NSA and CIA concur that he isn't lying. It looks like we have something going on here that doesn't include the official Russian government. We and the Brits are very anxious to learn more about this specialist the Russians are sending out there."

"Do you think we are dealing with a rogue element inside that government?" Alice asked with concern.

Niles smiled, as he knew Alice would be the first one to see the link. "We just don't know enough yet. Now, Professor Ellenshaw, I have something for your department also."

The crazed white hair of Charles Hindershot Ellenshaw III perked up.

"Get with Dr. Morales and file everything we have on the phase shift experiments of the '30s and '40s, also all we have on the ships involved. I want this information coded and placed into the new laptop system Xavier here just developed. Virginia, give them a hand on the physics aspect of converting light to energy; it may come in handy."

A confused Virginia nodded.

"Okay, Charlie. What have you got there in that file?"

Ellenshaw slowly handed the file over, and Niles opened it. He pulled a wrinkled, weatherworn page that looked as if it were torn from a book. It depicted a pirate with a long, curly and flowing beard with sword held high as he and his band of pirates attacked some unsuspecting ship. The second item he pulled out was a black-and-white photo. Niles pursed his lips and let out his breath as he handed the photo and the picture over to Virginia and the others.

"Those were the only items filed under the Philadelphia Event in '43. I suspect they were placed there by Director Lee sometime after he took command in 1947."

Virginia and Alice were both stunned by the photo and even more perplexed by the colorful picture of pirates.

"The photo is what came back with the *Eldridge* after the phase shift accident. According to Garrison, there were more than fifty of these creatures on board, protected from the effects that killed all the exposed crewmen by being inside when the ship returned from wherever it had been. That picture of pirates was found in the pouch of one of the attackers."

"Attackers?" Charlie asked, pushing his glasses back onto his nose.

"Yes, it seems while the *Eldridge* was away, she had been boarded by whatever those creatures are. The color picture is from a licensed Russian reprint of *Treasure Island*, published in Moscow in 1934. How and why this creature had this on its person is not known."

"Amazing," Charlie said.

"I'm glad you find it fascinating, Doctor, because you're on the makeshift field team." Niles turned away from the stunned Ellenshaw and faced Virginia. "Inform Master Chief Jenks that his engineering skills will also be needed." He held up a hand to Virginia before she could voice her complaint. "No, you can't go. The master chief is far more versed in naval applications than you, and his engineering is off the scale. Get him all the information you have on the theory of phase shift so he has it available. Also get Commander Ryan. He's going also. And tell Will Mendenhall no also. He has duties here."

"Do you want to inform Sarah and Anya their homecomings with Jack and Carl will be delayed?" Alice asked as she closed her electronic notepad.

"No, this is now a closed event. Only the people mentioned as team members and those in this room are to have operational knowledge of this. Thank you." Niles closed the meeting, as he needed the time to think about just what he was sending Jack and Carl into. He looked up as Xavier was close to being through the door.

"Doctor, make sure that Europa terminal is functioning correctly. They'll need her out there."

"It's working, sir. I'll double-check it."

"Thank you."

The director was left alone. He stood and made his way to the large credenza in the corner and poured himself coffee and then returned to his chair and sat heavily into it. He picked up his phone and then hit one number. Through a series of screeches and bleeps, his call was finally connected. The face was the familiar one with the exception of his dress and his missing bow tie. Lord James Durnsford looked sleepy as he came fully awake.

"Niles, old man. Unlike you, us old sots like our sleep."

"It's officially on, James. The president has approved your request and my mission. I'll leave it to you to deliver the bad news to Colonel Collins and our French friend."

"Oh, delightful."

HER MAJESTY'S NAVAL BASE (HMNB)
PORTSMOUTH, ENGLAND

Henri was looking at both Collins and Everett as if they had set him up for another fall as the trio was directed from the airstrip toward the command center of Her Majesty's Naval Base in Portsmouth. They had been led into a very comfortable room and told to wait. When asked for what and for how long they had to do so, the Royal Navy marine guard just raised his brows in a *your guess is as good as mine* look.

"Maybe a little reward money for old, bad man Farbeaux?" Henri said sarcastically, not looking at either American.

"Relax, Henri. We already tried to ransom you off to any of them—MI6, Scotland Yard, the Rolling Stones—but alas, none were interested, so take it easy," Carl said with his ever-present smile.

"If it's any consolation, Henri, this was for you," Jack said as he slapped a folded ticket onto Farbeaux's arm.

The Frenchman looked at the ticket and then took it and opened it. It was a first-class British Airways ticket to his home in Tuscany. He looked from Jack to a grinning Everett.

"So, at least for that part of your little Egyptian sting, you were telling the truth," Henri said, shaking his head. "May I use this now?" he asked with hope of excusing himself from the company of two men he admired but disliked very much.

Jack looked at his watch. "I don't think that's up to us any longer. It seems we have been diverted."

Farbeaux let out an exasperated breath, and Jack decided to explain something the man needed to know.

"Henri, imagine that if Dr. Morales and Europa can find out just what it was you were up to in Egypt, how long would it be before the police in Alexandria, or even"—here, Jack looked around the room with its British Union Jack staring them down—"if MI6 caught on? You were there to steal something that wasn't yours, and we just happened to need the cover of your enterprise in our recovery of American property."

"The Egyptians hadn't caught on because they don't have the computing power that little maniac does at your little prairie dog burrow in Nevada."

"Objection! Argumentative," Carl said as he stretched his long legs out before him. "We like to think of it as our underground insane asylum."

"For once, I agree," Henri mumbled. "So, may I assume your little operation has hit somewhat of a snag, since we find ourselves virtually under arrest?"

Before Jack could tell Henri to relax once more, the door opened, and a familiar face poked in. Henri's brows rose in worry as he saw it was Lord James Durnsford, the head of MI6. He stood and greeted the man they had met during the Overlord operation.

"Lord Durnsford, what brings you to Royal Navy jail?"

After taking Jack's hand, the career intelligence man looked around the room, not understanding. Then he smiled and then chortled at Collins's American humor.

"Royal Navy jail. Very good, Colonel, very good. But as you can see, just a boring little office filled with boring little men." The portly nobleman nodded at a curious Everett and a suspicious Farbeaux. "I see our help in the recapture of this scallywag has paid off handsomely?" he said, smiling toward Farbeaux.

"Yeah, but in all actuality, Colonel Farbeaux holds a special place in our president's heart, and ours also."

"Yes, it seems we all owe a debt to many men and women—you and the captain here being two more of them. Gentlemen," he said as he walked over and sat down in a chair and folded his fingers into themselves as he smiled uncomfortably. He reached into his coat pocket and produced a message flimsy and handed it to Jack. "That message explains to you the little mess science has recently, or not so recently, gotten us into."

Collins exchanged looks with Carl and Henri. They both appeared to be listening, but both were also suspicious of one of the more brilliant spies in world history. One just never knew where it was Her Majesty's intelligence services were coming from.

"Mess?" Jack asked.

"Yes, a rather big mess we haven't quite figured out yet. Now, we here at MI6 know you are on detached service, Colonel, and you will never divulge your real duties to your country, but let's just say we have suspected for quite some time who and what government entity you really work for."

"I'm in the army, he's in the navy, and he . . ." He paused when Henri smiled at him, waiting. "He, is, well, he just is."

"Yes, of course you are." His smile faded as he became serious. He leaned forward to emphasize what it was he was about to say. "What would you say, Colonel, that if we were to go digging into files from the old Soviet regime, and even in today's rather aggressive Russian administration, we here in British intelligence may possibly have discovered an outfit that, not unlike the one you claim not to work for, and one that even rivals my own entity in this country, is quite active within the Russian government and has been for over eighty years? An entity run completely autonomously and without fear of Russian leadership?"

"I would say MI6 knows a little too much about friendly governments and not enough about the aggressive ones." Jack didn't care for British intelligence's rather extensive guesswork on the Event Group.

"Good show, old boy. Good point." He lost the smile. "Now, what would you say if one of the leadership of this mysterious group was now on his way to the very spot where the NATO resupply exercise Operation Reforger IV was just canceled, and they were heading there at high speed with one of the more lethal commando teams the world has ever seen in their company?"

"I would say let them fly off. What are they going to find, dumped garbage from the warships that had been in the area?" Carl chimed in, but he did sit up in his chair a little more erect.

"Normally, we would just observe, but this is not a normal situation as described by your president and your think tank under his leadership that is buried in some godforsaken desert somewhere, and the United States Navy, and all of NATO Northern Command." Lord Durnsford stood up from his chair and placed his hands behind his back as he faced the Frenchman. "The president of the United States is calling in that favor, Colonel Farbeaux."

"You mean calling in that favor for the fifth time in three years?" Henri said with a dirty look at Jack. "Owing him or any of these people is like owing money to the American mob: you never pay off that debt."

"Yes, very good, Colonel. Now, it seems the security leadership of this mysterious Russian group, based somewhere we believe in the deepest, darkest, very much frozen wastelands of Siberia, has encountered you on more than one occasion. It seems you were even in this group's custody at one point. Perhaps you know of whom I speak? Please, share what you know with Colonel Collins and Captain Everett. It may just come in handy."

Henri allowed his breath to escape with a hiss as he angrily looked at the British intelligence man in his tweed suit and bow tie. He knew exactly who this man was referring to, and he didn't like the memory of the man at all. He faced both Jack and Carl.

"There are rumors around which the United States, Great Britain, and Russia, possibly Germany also, have a deep closet of historical secrets. Maybe you have heard these rumors?" He looked at Collins with a crooked grin. "I can clearly state that the Russian element is in fact a reality, among other groups, that is." He looked from Jack to Lord Durnsford. "This group, unlike the rumors toward others, is a ruthless entity and is a smaller part of a whole. The intelligence services of the United States, Great Britain, France, and Germany have long suspected that the whole is in charge of the parts. In other words, gentlemen, this group of men, from their varying departments within the government, actually runs the Russian state and have for the past eighty years, more so as perestroika moved forward. The freedoms the Russian people thought they were getting were all a sham."

"You mean Putin and the politburo aren't in charge?" Carl asked as if Farbeaux were joking. He could tell by Lord Durnsford that Henri's words had the spark of truth behind them, which made Everett's normally strong body feel ill. "I mean, in general conversation, why didn't you ever say anything?"

Farbeaux looked at Carl with a questioning glare. "Just what would have been the benefit to myself for doing so, Captain?" He said the word *Captain* as if it left a bad taste in his mouth.

"The head of this Russian group's intelligence, their security arm, is a man whom you may have met, Colonel Farbeaux. A ruthless individual who was trained by the true leadership cast of this underground organization to this group, and one man in particular whom we have yet to identify. We here at MI6 believe he is responsible for this mirror group and acts as the internal security for all of them combined."

"I don't know his employers or this mysterious group's governing body you speak of. But a Russian I once heard of murdered an entire town in the Ukraine for hiding state artifacts after the fall of the Soviet Union. If it's the man I am thinking of, yes, I did meet him once. In deference to my two American friends here, the man is the most capable killer and guardian of Russian history and state secrets I have ever heard of. He will kill children to keep the world from knowing what it is they know. Yes, he is a man who makes the world a ruthless and hateful place. And also a man I care never to meet again."

"The very gentleman of whom it is I speak. Colonel Farbeaux, I'm afraid I have some bad news for you, sir. The president, in conjunction with the British prime minister and NATO command, has activated your temporary military status to active duty, and said status has been affirmed by Paris. You are now, once more, attached to the United States and British armed forces. You are to accompany Colonel Collins and Captain Everett on a joint NATO mission to recover something this mysterious Russian group may have lost. You will have no trouble finding this lost item, since your navy has just now begun to take her in tow in the North Atlantic. Your specific orders, Colonel, are to identify this man for Captain Everett and Colonel Collins during their mission to observe naval assets in the area and the mysterious circumstances surrounding what is now happening."

The three men remained quiet as Lord Durnsford smiled down at the seated officers. Another message flimsy was produced by the British master spy. This one he again handed to Jack. He read.

"Are you joking?"

"We here at MI6 never have developed that sense of humor you Americans so readily ascribe to. No, no joke, Colonel."

Jack handed the message to Carl.

"Proceed by military transport to confidential location and recover war matériel currently in NATO possession. Said war matériel is a derelict, and NATO has declared provenance and has initiated salvage rights over its discovery. You and your selected group will proceed to said undisclosed location, investigate, and determine if this war material should be considered a threat to the national security of NATO treaty nations." Carl looked up from the flimsy. "Signed, Compton, advisory board chairman to the president on military and international affairs."

None of the three men made comment about the disguised cover for their own director.

"Okay, what's up, Lord Durnsford?" Collins asked as Henri stood and paced, not liking where this thing was going. "And why Henri? We could just get a description and go from there."

"Colonel Farbeaux's one job is to identify this man for our governments, and if at all possible, one of you three will kill him. Circumstances as to why this assassination is necessary will be readily apparent upon meeting this psychopath. I stress, Colonel Farbeaux, only if you can identify this man as the Butcher of Kharkov."

"And us?" Everett asked.

"You, Captain and Colonel, will be in charge of a boarding party that will secure said war matériel. The final part of your instructions is to make sure Colonel Farbeaux follows his orders and, if need be, fulfill the directive as described in your orders."

"You said this matériel was just taken in tow. Are we speaking about a ship?" Jack asked.

"Yes, we are, Colonel. A very large and even stranger ship than you could ever believe. A ship that was sunk during World War II and is now making a reappearance in the North Atlantic at a most inopportune time."

"And why would this Russian murderer be there?" Everett beat Jack to the burning question.

"Because"—Lord Durnsford grinned broadly—"this particular ship belongs to the Russian Navy, and they have sent their number-one killer and his mysterious group to recover it. All our little puzzle pieces have now fit together somewhat nicely thanks to some highly questionable purloining of information from a very inquisitive source and his equally criminal computer somewhere within your national borders."

"Oh, that's just great," Carl mumbled as he sat down. He didn't go on to say they were now headed into danger thanks to a twentysomething kid and his maniacal new girlfriend named Europa.

"Yes, yes, it is great, Captain, as that may be the most important ship ever to set sail in the history of the world." He smiled broadly. "You see, we believe, as do your own higher management, that this ship is only the second vessel in history to have gone to, and returned from, another dimension."

The three men exchanged looks. After what they had just gone through to return Carl to this world, they had no doubt that this older scientific achievement had really taken place, and that was the reason why they all felt ill at that very moment.

"Gentlemen, the rest of your team will join you here shortly. They are taking a very fast aircraft and will arrive on time. Once you've breached Tildy, you can join the fun there with a squad of Her Majesty's Royal Marines traveling with you." Lord Durnsford walked to the door and opened it to leave.

"Who is Tildy?" the Frenchman asked.

"Why, it's only the bloodiest, most hair-raising hurricane in the past five years. Good luck, gentlemen."

Henri sat hard into a chair.

"My distaste for you has grown exponentially with every experience I have ever shared with you two . . . gentlemen."

5

ANDREWS AIR FORCE BASE
WASHINGTON, D.C.

After the mission briefing explaining what it was Compton expected from the security man, the cryptozoologist, and the engineer on what their duties were to be once they joined with Jack and the others, none of them were feeling very perky after the supersonic flight from the western United States to Washington. Master Chief Jenks was beside the hangar, throwing up his early morning breakfast. Charlie Ellenshaw would wince every time the engineer heaved. He shook his head as he turned to face Jason Ryan, who was saying farewell to the second pilot to have flown them from Nellis Air Force Base in Nevada to the East Coast. Those two aircraft and the speed at which they got to Washington were the reasons for Jenks's upset stomach. Ryan looked from the second pilot, after shaking his hand, to the F-15E Strike Eagle he had used to fly the master chief supersonic over the continental United States. The double-seat fighter had made life rough for Jenks. As for Ellenshaw, Ryan had learned that nothing of a mechanical fear ever entered into the cryptozoologist's mind.

Ryan slowly pulled his flight suit off, and Ellenshaw did the same. He looked at Jenks and smiled.

"Ready for round two, Master Chief?"

Jenks wiped his mouth and then unzipped his flight suit. "What do you mean?"

At that moment, a large hangar door started to slide open. The bright sunshine of the dying evening illuminated an amazing sight as the giant aircraft was rolled out of his hidden lair.

"Oh, shit," Jenks mumbled. "You flyboys and your damnable toys."

"Wow," was all Charlie could manage.

Ryan, disappointed that he wouldn't be flying on this leg of their journey, was just as stunned as his companions when he saw the supersonic bomber as it rolled free of the hangar. The B-1b Lancer bomber was an evil-looking aircraft if Ryan had ever seen one. Its sleek design made her identifiable to any aggressive nation that this bird meant serious business.

"Gentlemen, our ride awaits. We should be in England in under two hours."

Over the sound of the Lancer's engines spooling up, they once more heard Master Chief Jenks as he again dry heaved in anticipation of another record-setting flight—this time over the Atlantic.

LOS ANGELES—CLASS ATTACK SUBMARINE USS *HOUSTON* NORTH ATLANTIC

The closer *Houston* got to the hurricane's eye, the calmer the seas became. That was the break they had been waiting for as Captain Thorne looked at the video screen whose picture was being provided by their own periscope. Technically, he was in command of this maneuver, and he was watching with fear etched on his face as the Aegis battle cruiser USS *Shiloh* fought the diminishing swells as they battled with the somewhat calmer eye of Hurricane Tildy. He watched nervously as the eight-man rigging team had scrambled aboard the derelict Russian vessel *Simbirsk*. The team had successfully managed to get the tow cable attached with only one moment of sheer terror involved when one of the *Shiloh*'s crewmen almost went overboard when one of the larger swells of green sea had swept over the deck of *Simbirsk*. Thorne exhaled as did most crewmen on the bridge as the two ships were finally mated.

"XO, send out the order again to Captain Johnson on board *Shiloh*. The riggers are not to enter the interior of the ship. They are to await our team arriving from England."

"Yes, sir."

Thorne turned back to the video monitor and spied the activity aboard the Russian ship. It looked as if the cable had been strung and the *Shiloh* began the slow move from the perimeter of Tildy to its exact center. The eye of the hurricane would protect them well enough *if* the course of the bad weather didn't suddenly change. He saw on the monitor the powerful turbines of the *Shiloh* spring to life. His eyes went to the other two escorts as they took up station in front of and behind *Shiloh*.

"Okay, let's button her up and observe. Chief of the Boat, take her down to two hundred and get us on a pace with our surface assets."

"Aye. Give me ten degrees down bubble and bring her up to four knots."

The command was passed, and *Houston* once more went deep. Thorne took the 1 MC mic from the stanchion.

"To all crew, this is the captain. For the duration, we will be running silent. We fully expect company on this little foray, and we don't need to let them know that we are here. Sonar, conn."

"*Conn, sonar*," came the reply.

"I fully expect any visitor to come from the northeast. They may have a submerged asset accompanying them. Keep your ears sharp, no surprises."

"*Conn, sonar, aye.*"

"Chief of the Boat, as soon as we settle in, I want *Houston* to belly up to the *Simbirsk* and get real cozy with her underside. I figure it's a good place to hide. To the rest of the crew, we will be deep for the next hour, so let's get some hot food in our bellies and some rest."

As the deck angled sharply downward, the crew of USS *Houston* knew they wouldn't have the appetite for the hot food nor the rest the captain had just ordered.

Apprehension of Russian warships bearing down on them through the raging temper of Hurricane Tildy had dulled their sensations of hunger and weariness.

EVENT GROUP COMPLEX
NELLIS AIR FORCE BASE, NEVADA

Dr. Niles Compton waited outside the classroom. He looked at the digital clock in the hallway and then felt Will Mendenhall beside him. Niles nodded at Will and then gestured by his nod toward the classroom directly across from the one he was standing next to. Will went, and he too waited.

A soft chime sounded, and the classrooms along the long and winding corridor opened, and associates of the Group exited. The military and civilian personnel smiled and conversed in soft tones until their eyes fell upon the director. It was as if high school students suddenly came upon the principal. Most hurried past with a worried glance back. Will Mendenhall smiled at the effect the director had on the newer people. He was rather intimidating with his eye patch and glasses that covered only his good eye. He was scary before with just the knowledge of his brilliance; now, it was both his appearance and his brain.

Niles waited until the classroom was empty and then strode inside. Sarah McIntire was there putting her teaching materials into a briefcase when she saw the director walk in.

"What brings you down to level eighteen, Doctor? A little brushup on geologic formations?"

Niles placed his hands into his pants pockets and smiled. "Unless it has something to do with the cave system around us caving in, I'll leave the expert stuff to you."

Sarah smiled and then snapped the clasps to her case closed.

"You have a minute?"

Sarah tilted her head, and then a curious look crossed her face. "Don't tell me Jack's already in trouble," she said as she left the classroom and stepped into the elevator.

Compton smiled just as both Will and Anya Korvesky stepped inside. Anya was also carrying her teaching aids in a case on her Introduction to Surveillance 101. She looked at Sarah with the question written on her face.

"Level seven, please," Niles said to the Europa-controlled elevator.

All three waited while Niles watched the digital display of the floors passing by when he suddenly stopped the elevator's progress. The air-cushioned ride stopped.

"Look, Virginia had to know because of her position as AD, so she was brought in on a loop the president wanted kept to a minimum. I wanted to tell all three of you the truth of what's happening, both in the North Atlantic and of our suspicions in Russia. Jack and his team have been diverted to the situation I referred to in the Atlantic; reasons will be explained later. I wanted to explain this to you because for the next day or so, I will be working with Dr. Morales on a research assignment ordered directly by the president involving suspicions with our Russian friends. I will not have the time to take with you three asking questions. Yes, the assignment Colonel Collins is on is dangerous. They will be in harm's way. You'll just have to trust me when I say it will be explained when this is all confirmed. For now, leave Dr. Morales alone to his work. Bite the bullet. Personal relationships aside, this is business of the most serious time."

Sarah started to say something, but Niles cut her off by ordering the elevator to continue. Sarah got the hint and shut up. The doors opened, and Niles stepped out without a word, and the doors closed again. The three occupants stood there not knowing what had just happened. The elevator started to move downward on its silent, air-cushioned ride.

"Well, I guess our boys are in trouble again," Will said.

"And we were left out of the loop."

Sarah looked at Anya. "Is there some light you can share on what the director was referring to when he brought up the Russians?"

Anya shook her head. "Wasn't my area of expertise, and getting anything out of Mossad, as you know, is difficult at the best of times. No, I have nothing."

"All I know is Jason and Charlie are now moving to the East Coast by supersonic transport," Will replied.

"And?" Sarah said, looking at Mendenhall.

Anya smiled. "He's mad because he doesn't get to play with the other kids."

Will frowned and hit the floor button instead of using the voice command.

"You're damn right I am. Bastards."

HER MAJESTY'S NAVAL BASE (HMNB) PORTSMOUTH, ENGLAND

The sun was an hour away from broaching the skies to the east when Jack, Carl, and Henri were driven to the farthest reaches of the British naval base at Portsmouth. The United States Marine guards were silent as they pulled up to a large dock area. Jack glanced back at Carl when they saw the inordinate amount of navy shore patrol. It was also noticed that none of these patrolmen had their standard sidearms and nightsticks. They were fully armed with British-made L85A2 IW standard assault rifles. Collins counted no fewer than thirty-five of the naval security men. The marines remained quiet and offered nothing other than a "Good morning" to the three men as they stepped from the American-made Humvee.

The three found themselves looking around at the mass of personnel but, with the heavy roll of fog in the area, couldn't see anything much beyond the pier they stood upon.

"Colonel Collins?"

Jack turned at the sound of the voice. A tall man in a green flight suit stood with a clipboard in his hands. He saw the Union Jack in a lighter shade of green on the man's shoulder. Next to him were two other men dressed similarly. These two carried four large duffel bags.

"I'm Collins," Jack said as he stepped forward.

"Sir, I am Flight Lieutenant Daniel Killeen. These are for you and your men, Colonel."

The two men standing next to the Royal Navy officer stepped forward and handed three duffel bags to Henri and Carl. One other they sat next to Jack.

"I believe we were able to accommodate everything that was requested by your State Department."

Jack exchanged another look with Carl. The mention of the State Department was a surprise. They quickly deduced that Niles was running a game on somebody. It was the never-ending song and dance in regard to covering up anything and everything about the Event Group. Jack knew it was wise not to comment on the observation. He leaned over and unzipped the bag at his feet. His brows rose as he spied the contents.

"The M4s and ammunition are from the stores of USS *Breckenridge*. She's a destroyer escort visiting Portsmouth. My boss says your boss felt you would be more comfortable with American arms rather than British."

"No offense meant," Everett said as he lifted one of the small M4s from the bag and examined it.

"None taken, Captain." The Royal Navy man then reached back, and one of his men slipped a parcel into his hand. "Also, this was forwarded through your embassy for delivery to you. I have instructions that say to tell you it's a gift from a Dr. Morales." A confused look crossed the officer's face. "He states you may need Marilyn Monroe's advice at some point. He said in his instructions to you that it is a closed-looped system and is not attached to the rest of her body. I hope you understand what that means, because we, sir, do not, which was obviously intended."

Collins smiled as he took the larger-than-normal laptop computer from the British officer.

"Thank you. It does make sense."

"I'm beginning to believe that kid knows his stuff," Carl said as he and Jack again exchanged amused looks.

Lieutenant Killeen looked at the wristwatch under his rolled-up sleeve. "The other members of your party will be arriving shortly. They are currently en route from London. It seems at least one of the new arrivals was extremely unhappy about their flight accommodations thus far."

"Jenks," both Carl and Jack said simultaneously.

"Yes, I believe that was the name your air force crewmen claim. They seem not to like that man very much."

Henri opened a duffel and pulled out a black Nomex BDU. He held it up to Collins with raised brows.

"Relax, Colonel, you've always looked good in black," Everett said as he placed the M4 back inside the first bag.

The thump of heavy rotors broke the still of the morning. The fog parted as the British officer again looked at his watch. "Right on time."

Jack, Carl, and Henri watched as a United States Navy Seahawk helicopter, the naval version of the army's Blackhawk, slowly pushed the fog away and settled down to the ancient wooden pier. They heard the loud cracking and popping as the large helicopter and her extreme weight taxed the ancient dock. Collins was beginning to wonder just how far out in the boondocks they were if the pier was that old. Someone didn't want others to even know they were there, or didn't want prying eyes to see something the British wanted kept hush-hush.

With the four-bladed rotors still turning, the sliding door on the port side opened, and an angry Master Chief Jenks hopped out, pushing the crew chief's helping hands away. He removed a cold cigar and was about to chew the young man's head off when Jason Ryan jumped out and got in between them. He was followed by a purely thrilled Charlie Ellenshaw, looking ridiculous in a blue flight suit that had been supplied to him by the US Air Force. Ryan waved at the waiting trio and then gently nudged the angry master chief forward.

Ryan saluted Collins and then shook hands with both Henri and Everett.

"So, how was your little flight?" Jack asked as Charlie joined them.

"I'll tell you how it was." Jenks lit a fresh cigar and then angrily looked at Collins. "At times that air force jockey flew so low I thought we hit several seagulls."

"From my understanding, we've lost more B-1s to bird strikes than enemy fire," Everett said with a smile.

"The flight was good, Colonel," Ryan answered quickly while looking at Jenks in a successful attempt at shutting his complaining down. "The master chief, like myself, I fully admit, doesn't like anything he's not in control of."

"What in the hell does the air force know about control? That jock was all over the sky!"

"Jenksy, my understanding is that the B-1B Lancer not only had to hide from Russian eyes, but it also had to avoid a little thing called Hurricane Tildy," Jack said as he started to distribute equipment.

"While almost doing double the speed of sound. It was quite a ride," Jason said as he accepted a Nomex commando BDU from Everett.

"Yes, positively thrilling," Charlie agreed as he looked at his new commando BDU. Again, his eyes widened with pure delight.

"Gentlemen, please, we are now officially behind schedule. You may prepare and dress aboard our transport."

The six men looked around at the rising fog, confused as to their mentioned transportation. And again the British flight officer looked at his watch.

"Ah, listen. Here she comes."

A whine pierced their ears. The old pier they stood upon shook and rattled, and even more ancient nails popped free of the grip they had at holding the old wood together. Suddenly, an earsplitting sound erupted from the sky, and they all felt the heavy downdraft as a large craft penetrated the remaining fog. The four jet engines easily evaporated the veil of fog closest to the wooden pier as the strange-looking aircraft started to settle.

"My God, I thought she was just a rumor," Ryan said as he allowed the black Nomex suit to fall back into the open duffel.

"We hope the Russians have a similar way of thinking," the Royal Navy officer said as he watched the fifty-five-foot airframe settle onto her extensive undercarriage. It looked like a larger version of the American-built Boeing V-22 Osprey VTOL, the vertical takeoff and landing system designed for the US Marine Corps. Instead of propellers, this version held four turbofan jet engines for each engine stanchion at the far edges of the tilt-wing craft. These started to wind down as the newest version of the amazing machine landed.

Jack looked at Ryan, who stood amazed. The aircraft was black and had a Royal Navy bull's-eye emblazoned in even blacker paint along her fuselage. As she settled, a rear ramp slowly started to open.

"Gentlemen, this is your ride into the Atlantic," Killeen said as he also examined the aircraft. "This is a joint venture between your Marine Corps and our Royal Marines. There are only four like it in the world—two here and two at Camp Pendleton in California. They are all still going through testing. This one is assigned to us. I give you the V-25 Night Owl. She's capable of carrying seventy-five fully equipped commandos and introducing them into hostile theaters of war with stealth and speed. She is capable of supersonic flight with her swept-wing delta design. She is one amazing piece of equipment, I can assure you."

The six men exchanged uneasy looks, and it was of course Jenks who had to voice the concern they were all feeling.

"Okay, that's a good speech. Now, tell us how many copies have you lost in her testing phase." Jenks stared at the officer and puffed on his cigar.

"Six."

Jenks just nodded. "If my engineers had a success rate like that, we would have been out on our asses faster than—"

"Okay, Master Chief, we get it," Jack said, eyeing Jason as if Jenks's outburst was somehow his fault.

"Gentlemen, I assure you we will get you to your destination . . . alive."

Lieutenant Killeen smiled as he slapped the master chief on the shoulder, which elicited a scowl, and then gestured for them to board the amazing-looking aircraft. "Your magic carpet awaits."

"I remember when the navy actually used ships. Wasn't that a freakin' novel time."

They all smiled as Jenks turned and left for the boarding ramp.

"As much as I hate to agree with that foul little man, I myself have serious reservations about flying into a hurricane with that thing," Henri said as he too followed Jenks.

Jack swallowed as the V-25 Night Owl started to spool her four wing-mounted engines up. Carl leaned into Collins.

"You okay?" he asked. "Did you bring your music?"

Collins shook his head.

"Well, I'm sure we can dig something up."

Jack swallowed again as he watched Charlie, Ryan, and Jenks board the Night Owl. Everett took both duffel bags in hand and then gestured for Jack to go ahead.

The assault upon a ship that had become even more famous than the specter of the famous ghost ship the *Flying Dutchman* was under way.

Tildy's circling winds were now over 155 miles per hour.

6

KIROV-CLASS BATTLE CRUISER *PETER THE GREAT*
NORTH ATLANTIC

The mighty warship rolled heavily to port, knocking most of the crew on the battle bridge from their feet. A one-inch-thick window smashed inward as the green sea poured into the bridge. The large space of bridge was filled with the stench of vomit as men could no longer bear the attack on their inner ears and the motion sickness caused by the merciless rolling seas.

Captain Kreshenko regained his feet with the assistance of Second Captain Dishlakov.

"Seal that breach!" the XO shouted above the roar of the hurricane.

"Hang on!" someone shouted as another forty-foot wave cascaded over the immense deck of the battle cruiser.

Kreshenko cringed as he heard steel being sheared away from their uppermost mast. Electrical circuits shorted out all across the electronic suite of the battle bridge. Fires erupted as Kreshenko calmly replaced his hat.

"Captain, we are receiving a distress call from the *Ustinov*. They say they have lost their forward missile mounts and are taking on water in their engineering spaces."

Kreshenko and Dishlakov ran to the aft windows and raised their binoculars to the north. At first they couldn't see the missile cruiser, and their hearts simultaneously skipped a beat. Then they saw the smaller cruiser's radio and electronic warfare mast rise above the crashing sea. Their momentary relief was stolen away as they watched an explosion erupt on the forward spaces of her deck. The fireball rose until the raging sea and high winds consumed it.

"She's going to buckle, Captain!" Dishlakov shouted as more seawater rushed in through the damaged bridge window on their own battered warship.

"Helm, give me twenty degrees to port. We'll circle slowly and assist as best we can. Have a rescue team ready to take on survivors if needed."

"Aye."

"Belay that order, please."

Both officers turned as a man came through the port hatch, shaking water from his rain gear.

"Helm, bring her around," Kreshenko again ordered.

"I said disregard that order," Colonel Salkukoff said as he stripped the rubber parka from his body.

"We have a ship in trouble. Those are Russian sailors out there. We *will* assist."

Salkukoff smiled and then nodded toward the Russian marines stationed on the battle bridge. With his nod, both guards pulled out their sidearms. One was leveled at the nineteen-year-old helmsman.

"Captain, it will be you who causes the death of your helmsman if he obeys that order. We are near to breaking through into the eye of the hurricane, so we shall remain on course. Do you understand?"

Before the glaring Kreshenko could respond, *Peter the Great* heeled hard over to the starboard side. This time it felt as though the giant battle cruiser could never recover. She was close to capsizing.

"Helm, turn her into the roll!" Kreshenko yelled over the din.

Another heavy wave crashed into the ship as the order was given. This time they all felt the pressure as *Peter the Great* was totally submerged for the briefest of moments before she rose back from the killing seas and took a large imaginary breath of life.

"Captain, we have a distress call from the *Ustinov*. She has buckled along her centerline mass. She has hull plate separation. They are requesting assistance."

Dishlakov looked from the two marines holding their weapons on the captain and the helmsman toward the barbarian who was ordering their ship to turn their backs on a sister vessel in distress.

"Captain, we have lost the forward missile-loading hatch. We're taking on water in the forward spaces."

Kreshenko cursed as the calls kept getting more desperate and frequent.

"Send out a call to the *Admiral Levchenko*: assist the *Ustinov* and take on her crew."

"No, I want the *Admiral Levchenko* to form up with us. We will break into the eye together. The *Ustinov* is on her own. Send a message to her captain and crew; they will never be forgotten for their bravery," Salkukoff said as blandly as he could.

As *Peter the Great* went down into another trough, Kreshenko pushed his way past his men to face the Russian colonel. When one of the marines faced him with a loaded weapon, Kreshenko merely batted the handgun away angrily. "Stand down, marine," he said menacingly. The rest of the bridge crew became aware of the confrontation and watched. Most were ready to assist their captain after the recent order to abandon their fellows had been said aloud, which would have angered any sailor the world over.

"Captain, if you do not follow my orders, I will command your weapons officer to target that cruiser and finish sinking her. Do you understand?"

Kreshenko was silent as he took a firm hold on the helm console when the battle cruiser once more fought her way back to the surface of the roiling seas.

The bridge-wing hatch opened, and ten of the colonel's commandos entered the bridge. These men didn't look seasick at all. They all had automatic weapons held at port arms. The colonel never removed his dark eyes from the captain. He was sure his bluff was about to be called when the announcement was made.

"*Ustinov* just broke her back!" one of the bridge lookouts called.

Kreshenko screamed a curse as he snatched the binoculars from his first officer and focused to the north. Tears of rage and frustration filled his eyes as he fought to see through the ravages of the hurricane. He felt his heart sink as the raked bow of the *Ustinov* rose high into the air at the same moment her stern section with her proudly proclaimed name in Cyrillic rose and then, astonishingly, the two halves of the ship crashed together, shredding steel and men in one massive action. She had snapped in the middle. A giant wave struck the forward section and slammed it into another advancing wave. Then her stern slipped beneath the waves, and as it did, a tremendous explosion illuminated the dark world in which they had entered. Kreshenko lowered the glasses and angrily tossed them to Dishlakov. He stormed toward Colonel Salkukoff, who stood bracing himself against the rolling waves.

"Captain, *Admiral Levchenko* is turning to assist," the radar officer reported with his eyes firmly on the drama taking place only feet away.

The standoff between the Russian colonel and the captain of *Peter the Great* was a force of wills.

"The *Ustinov* is gone, Captain," Second Captain Dishlakov announced as he turned and allowed the binoculars to fall from his hand.

Kreshenko's eyes never left the colonel's.

"Helm, resume original course and speed. Radio, send a message to the destroyer—form up on *Peter the Great* until we breach the eye."

"Aye, Captain."

"Most wise, Captain," Salkukoff said as he gestured for the marines and commandos to lower their weapons.

"Two hundred and fifty-six officers and crew were on board that cruiser."

"True Russians all, Captain."

The giant cruiser once more bashed her way into a deep depression and then fought her way back up.

"So, we are back to praising the dead again for their heroic sacrifices? Eighty years of meaningless deaths ordered by men like you was not enough? You wish to return to the days of not being accountable for Russian deaths?"

The colonel gestured for the hatchway to be opened by his men.

"Inform me when we are close to breaching the eye, Captain. That's when real sacrifices may have to be made."

All eyes on the bridge watched the man and his men leave. Then their eyes went to the two marines who had sided against their captain. They holstered their weapons and then lowered their eyes. Kreshenko went to the forward windows and stared out into the killer hurricane. He was joined by Second Captain Dishlakov.

"I knew her second in command. He just had a new baby daughter a week ago," Dishlakov said as he took up station next to his bearded captain.

Kreshenko didn't respond. As far as he was concerned, his entire crew had just become pariahs in the eyes of the Russian Navy and, for that matter, most other navies around the globe. They had just turned their backs on sailors in peril and allowed them to drown.

"Keep a close eye on *Admiral Levchenko*. She's tough, but she's not as tough as the cruiser we just lost. Tell her to form up and stay close." His eyes shot to the closed hatchway. "We may need her more than ever if we make it through this hurricane."

Dishlakov caught the meaning, and then he started giving orders.

Peter the Great, along with her tough little destroyer escort *Admiral Levchenko*, was only thirty minutes away from entering the eye of Hurricane Tildy.

LOS ANGELES—CLASS ATTACK SUBMARINE USS *HOUSTON* HURRICANE TILDY—THE EYE

With the calmer seas, the small task force made a slow circle inside the hurricane's eye. The *Houston* was still submerged beneath the four-foot seas while *De Zeven*, the Dutch frigate, kept station a thousand yards behind the American Aegis cruiser *Shiloh* and the disabled Russian cruiser *Simbirsk*.

"Radar, conn," Captain Thorne said aloud as he peered once more through the periscope, "any surface contacts outside our own?"

"*Conn, radar, nothing, Captain.*"

"Sonar, conn, any submerged contacts?" Thorne swung the periscope around 180 degrees.

"*Conn, sonar, just three whales heading out of here. We're clear at this time.*"

Thorne was about to do something no submarine commander ever ordered lightly.

"Chief of the Boat, surface."

"Aye, Captain. Blow negative to the mark, fifteen degrees up bubble. Give me full rise on the planes." The chief hit the alarm warning, and the beluga call was made. "Surface, surface."

For the five hundred crewmen of both the Dutch frigate *De Zeven* and the missile cruiser *Shiloh*, an amazing sight greeted them as the massive, spherical bow of USS *Houston* broke the surface of the sea. She rose high into the air and then slowly settled back as the calmer waters inside the eye washed away from her sleek black hull. The white numbers on her sail tower shone brightly in the falsehood of sunshine that was the eye of Tildy.

Captain Thorne was the fourth man through the conning tower hatch. His lookouts were posted high on the electronics array as *Houston* came free of her natural element. Thorne scanned the area and was satisfied that his boat was as safe as it could possibly be for the moment. He turned and scanned every and all areas before he felt he could relax. He reached over and hit his intercom switch.

"Gary, inform *De Zeven* and *Shiloh* this is only a courtesy visit. They are to maintain current course and speed with a straight cut across the eye at thirty-minute intervals. If anyone's watching, that should keep them on their toes."

"Aye," came the answer. *"Captain, we have a secure communiqué from Fleet, your eyes only."*

"Send it up," Thorne said, wondering what sort of maniacal order he was now being given.

A boatswain mate popped his head up through the hatch and handed Thorne the message flimsy on a clipboard. He signed for it and then read. He read it again. He let out a pent-up breath and then hit the intercom once more.

"Gary, somebody's got a real seashell up their ass. Inform *Shiloh* that she'll be taking on representatives of National Command Authority in about half an hour. If whoever they are make it through the hurricane, that is. Inform them to make ready helo recovery. Also, inform *De Zeven* that she'll have to be close aboard for any sea rescue operations that may have to be conducted."

"Aye, aye."

Thorne adjusted his view of the 130-mile wide eye and spied the heavy, roiling clouds that made up the outer fringes of the killer hurricane. It was like they were inside a glass jar with a menacing swirl of twisting black clouds marking the circular boundaries of life or death. His binoculars went to the ancient battle cruiser *Simbirsk*. He could see the *Shiloh*'s riggers were still securing her towline and maintaining the strain. The men were having a much easier time of it than they had before entering the eye. Thorne relaxed.

Thus far, they had not had another blast of electromagnetic pulsing as they had before. The *Simbirsk* sat lazily behind the Aegis cruiser as if she were nothing more than a normal disabled ship being assisted. The darkened silhouette of the Russian warship gave the captain a severe reaction. It was one of fear, and that was something Captain Thorne was not comfortable with. Once more he hit the switch on the intercom as the cool spray of seawater washed over him.

"Weapons, keep a running track on our Russian mystery. If she does something I don't like, I want to be able to put two fish into her fast. Warm up two ASROCs."

"Already done, Captain," Gary Devers called up.

Now, he had not only torpedoes targeted on the battle cruiser, he had the sophisticated antiship missile system targeting the phantom. Still, Thorne didn't feel safe. His eyes moved to the swirling hurricane. The cylindrical pattern reminded Thorne of a cage. A very violent cage. His eyes settled on a spot to the north. He wondered if there were any surprises waiting to emerge from the dark skies circling around the small grouping of ships.

"Okay, let's button her up. Dive, dive!"

Within fifteen seconds, the bow of *Houston* slowly sank beneath the waves.

ROYAL NAVY TRANSPORT V-25 NIGHT OWL
TEN NAUTICAL MILES NORTH OF TILDY

At twenty-two thousand feet, the ride was rougher than any of the men aboard
had ever faced. The Royal Marines were in no better shape, and it made the
Americans wonder if they would be any good at their jobs if and when they
would be needed. Jack was wondering the same thing about him and his own
people. The only ones who seemed to be handling the rough weather well
were Henri Farbeaux, Jason Ryan, and Carl.

The V-25 hit a bump in the road, and every man aboard went high in their
seats until their safety harnesses stopped their flight to the Night Owl's roof.
They all heard the whine of the turbofan engines as they spooled up to regain the altitude they had just lost. Jack closed his eyes and held his belly
pack tighter to his chest. It was Everett who noticed the colonel's discomfort.
Henri did also but kept his eyes neutral.

Everett leaned over and nudged Collins on the arm. "Having a rough go of it?"

Jack looked briefly at Carl and then shook his head. The Kevlar helmet kept
Carl from seeing Jack's eyes, but he knew the colonel had just lied to him. As far
as Everett knew, he and Sarah McIntire were the only two people on the planet
who knew that Jack had become terrified about flying. The man had over two
hundred parachute jumps in his career, with eleven of those combat jumps, and
now after all these years, it had finally started to overwhelm the career officer.

"Give me the music and I'll have the pilot pipe it in back here," Carl said as
he watched the colonel. Collins shook his head once again. "What, you don't
have any music?"

"Left them all in England," was all he could say.

Carl looked at Jason Ryan, who was sitting straight across from them next
to the master chief and Charlie Ellenshaw. Charlie looked even paler than
he usually was, and the mess of vomit at his feet and many others' attested to
the fact that none of them were used to this. Then Carl's eyes roamed over to
the Royal Marines, who were off in their own worlds of misery. He spied them
and then made a choice. He unsnapped his harness, and it was Collins who
looked at him as if he had lost his mind. The V-25 shook and rose. It then fell
and rose again as Everett crashed across the small aisle and leaned into the
man he had chosen.

"Any of you men bring any music with you?" he shouted, catching the attention of several others next to the marine.

"Excuse me, sir?" the young white-faced sergeant asked above the whine of
engines and the rage of the hurricane.

"Music. Did you men bring any music?"

The sergeant shook his head while his look asked Carl if he had gone nuts.

"I think Blavey has some," a large man said as he leaned over and faced Everett.

"Who is that?" Carl asked.

"That's him, sir. He's a Karaoke nut. Brings his CDs everywhere. Against regs, but he tends to forget about protocol when it comes to his music. He's a bleedin' Elvis impersonator." The large corporal nudged the slight man next to him. Carl saw the kid looked as if he weighed no more than one hundred pounds. What kind of Elvis impersonator was he? "Hey, Blavey. Wake up. The captain wants one of your CDs."

The boy's eyes opened wide as if someone had just informed him they were crashing into the sea. He jerked awake fully and focused on the men around him. Everett could see that the kid hadn't been dozing; he had been praying. With a zombie look on his young face, the kid reached into his pants pocket aligned along the side of his calf and produced several silvery CDs. He held them out to Carl as if he didn't care one way or the other if he accepted them or not. Carl took one and then handed the rest back to the kid. He took it to Jack.

"Looks like Elvis is all we have," he said, holding out the one CD he had taken. Jack just stared straight ahead.

Charlie Ellenshaw nudged Jason Ryan, who was busy smiling at all the sick humanity around him. He knew them all well—every one a landlubber. He smirked. Charlie nudged him again, and Jason's eyes rose to see what had attracted Ellenshaw's attention. He saw a white-faced colonel and was shocked to realize that the colonel had become terrified of flying. He had suspected it for quite some time, but he and Will Mendenhall had yet to see it for themselves. He was so shocked he wanted to turn away at this very strange sign of weakness that had developed in the man he respected most above all in the world, the bravest officer he had ever even heard of. He silently told Charlie not to look. Now, the reason for the colonel playing music during stressful times became evident. It was his way of taking his mind off his situation.

Jack didn't seem to hear Carl. He knew the problem was getting worse, and he had been able to hide it for the past few years as it slowly developed, first in his subconscious and then displaying itself in the most inopportune moments. He knew now that flying was quickly becoming a real phobia for him. The Overlord experience he knew had finally cemented his fear in unrepentant terms. It was a fear he would have to deal with upon the completion of this mission. The colonel didn't notice Carl leave his side and advance toward the cockpit.

Ellenshaw looked at Ryan, and Jason shook his head that he should just stay out of it and watch.

Everett returned and then took his spot next to Jack just as the V-25 took another nosedive toward the raging surface of the sea far below.

"Copilot to crew," came the call over their helmet headsets. "Five minutes to IP. We will circle and then very quickly make our descent into the eye of the hurricane. Until that time, we have a particularly peculiar request from our American brethren."

The blast of music exploded into everyone's ears as the CD that was given to the flight crew came blaringly to life.

"The warden threw a party in the county jail. The prison band was there and they began to wail. . . ."

Every head of the thirty-five men perked up at the sound of Elvis Presley as he screamed out his hit from a million years before, "Jailhouse Rock."

Carl smiled over at Jason and Charlie. But it was Henri who guessed as to the reasoning behind the music. He had always wondered why Colonel Collins insisted on rock music before a jump or anything harrowing that had to do with flying. The music actually was therapy for him. He smirked as he realized he had just learned a large secret he could use to irritate the arrogant American colonel as much as possible. His smile grew when Collins perked up, and he nodded as if to himself as his eyes closed and his body relaxed. The music from his father's and grandfather's time calmed him, and he had never in his life known the reasons why. He knew psychiatrists would have a field day with him on their couches.

"Now, that's the way you sing it, Blavey!" the Cockney-accented sergeant said as he nudged the kid next to him in his never-ending tease about his Karaoke. The young corporal took a cue from Jack across the way and visibly relaxed. Most of the men felt the relief the music provided.

That would have to be noted in the past tense, since the V-25 Night Owl took a nosedive for the deck. The signal had been given. It was time to enter the eye of the hurricane.

Tildy awaited the assault team with her open arms.

HURRICANE TILDY
FIVE HUNDRED NAUTICAL MILES SOUTH OF GREENLAND

The Night Owl came into full contact with the edge of the eye, and she nearly buckled. One of her four GE turbofan engines was actually drowned by the inrush of water as she tried desperately to escape the high winds that threatened to rip her from the sky. Inside, every man held on for dear life as the death plunge through the swirling and raging clouds convinced them they were into their final minutes of life. A brief but brutal gust of wind that measured 130 miles per hour slammed into the V-25 and turned her upside down. The pilot fought the controls, fearing he was about to shear off both wings as he brought the hydraulic systems online to invert the stabilizers for vertical flight.

TICONDEROGA—CLASS AEGIS MISSILE CRUISER USS *SHILOH*

Captain Ezra Johnson, a graduate of Mississippi State University, had fought his way up the naval ranks. His skin color had not been the detractor he had always thought it would be. Instead, the black captain had found out that the only real prejudice in the US Navy was the fact that he and many others were not graduates of the US Naval Academy at Annapolis. Any officer was looked down upon for that little failure in education; despite this fact he had steadily climbed the ladder until he landed his command aboard the advanced missile cruiser USS *Shiloh*. He had accomplished this through knowing naval operations better than he knew the alphabet.

At the moment, he was cursing the higher command authority that had authorized this crazy maneuver. The British, NATO command, or even his own president had lost their collective minds to try to pull off this kind of stunt in the middle of a hurricane. The weather was still wet and the seas rolling inside the eye of Tildy, but even this was too much to try to land a VTOL aircraft aboard his ship. With the towline connected to the Russian cruiser, it was a maneuver that could spell certain destruction for his ship and crew.

As he stared through his binoculars on the starboard bridge wing, he again cursed his luck at having drawn this command from NATO organizers. While Captain Thorne on *Houston* was the outright ranking commander of this rear guard group, he was well aware it would be his call on whether or not the landing aboard his expensive missile cruiser would go forward. As of right now, he was willing to call off the whole thing. He swung his glasses to the starboard as the Dutch frigate *De Zeven* took rescue stations on her starboard beam. He moved the glasses to the towline and then to the forward decking of the Russian derelict in his charge. The line was holding as the ship lightly entered a small swell of sea and then settled.

"Minimal radar contact, Captain, bearing three-four-five degrees north."

Johnson swung his binoculars around and spied the blackened skies swirling menacingly to the north. He knew whoever was flying this mission had lost their minds. He turned and nodded at his XO. The executive officer then reached out and hit his intercom.

"Stand by to take on aircraft. All stations, the smoking lamp is out. Rescue stations, rescue stations."

The radar officer aboard *Shiloh* was a patient man and always allowed his radar men a full range of training. This time, however, his eyes never left the scope of the operator he leaned over. He was watching not just the incoming aircraft but a spot on the screen that had held his attention for the past thirty minutes. It was a solid blip on the scope that was there one minute, gone the next. Then when he thought it was a trick upon his eyes, the officer thought he saw two red blips appear and then vanish. He knew the heavy seas of the hurricane were causing havoc with everyone, including himself.

"Captain, we're getting an intermittent contact just eighteen miles north of us. The heavy swells may be masking someone out there."

Captain Johnson nodded. Captain Thorne aboard *Houston* had passed along CINCLANT's concern about Russian interference. But he also knew the Russians were very prudent about keeping their capital ships protected at all costs. Unless this signaled a change in Russian naval philosophy, Johnson wasn't that concerned.

"Keep a close eye out, but concentrate on the job at hand."

"Aye, Captain. We have our inbound, thirty-two miles out and closing fast."

Johnson shifted his focus and then quickly spied the edges of the eye. Tildy wasn't easily giving up her secrets, as he couldn't see anything other than hell raging across the world. Then he saw the V-25 burst through the clouds at breakneck speed.

"What are those fools doing?' he asked as his eyes widened when the Night Owl broke into the clear. It looked as though she had one of her four engines smoking and nonresponsive. She hopped, skipped, and jumped as she fought to level out. He mentally pushed the bird down and across the calmer seas of the eye.

It took the V-25 fifteen minutes to cover the calmer air of the now dormant eye of Tildy. They came on fast, as the pilot of the VTOL was anxious to get his damaged bird into its nest before Mother Nature explained to him in no uncertain terms who exactly was in charge.

"XO, take the conn."

Johnson tossed the XO his binoculars and then went to the bridge wing to oversee the landing operation.

"XO has the deck."

Ezra Johnson didn't envy the British pilot in his attempt to get his three-engine VTOL down to the deck. He shot over the three ships three times as he tried to get his bearings on the fantail of the large missile cruiser. The towline in particular was causing the Royal Navy pilot much concern.

"Goddamn, these pilots are nuts!" he shouted above the din of engine and sea noise.

The V-25 Night Owl came in low and fast.

LOS ANGELES—CLASS ATTACK SUBMARINE USS *HOUSTON*

Captain Thorne was drinking a cup of coffee and sitting close to the navigation console. His crew was getting anxious as the radio called out altitude and distance of their new arrival to the area. Every time he heard the words *abort landing*, he cringed, as he knew how dangerous landing a VTOL could be, especially with a towline close to the helo deck.

"*Conn, sonar, we have a close-in surface contact, bearing two-three-seven degrees north, sixty-seven miles out. No, check that. Possible double contact, same bearing.*"

Thorne closed his eyes for the briefest of moments when his own hidden fear was announced to his control room crew. He calmly placed the coffee cup down and stood. He took the 1 MC mic and raised it, but before he spoke, he saw the anxious faces of his young crew. He smiled. It felt false to him, and he stopped.

"Sonar, conn, how strong is the contact?"

"*Intermittent at times, but course and speed are holding steady. Whoever they are, they're in a hurry. Engine plant noises indicate cruiser and possible destroyer.*"

"Get me as much information as you can. We'll get you closer; I need detail."

"*Aye,*" came the brief answer.

"Okay, let's play. Gary, all ahead flank, course two-three-seven degrees north. Let's give this one a wide angle. Okay, let's put the spurs to her."

"Aye, Skipper. All ahead flank, give me five degrees down angle on the planes, take her to six hundred. Let's go get 'em, Chief," XO Devers called out. He was satisfied when his people went straight into their work, more confident, more relaxed. It was just the fact that they were now doing something other than just babysitting.

"Weapons, with one and two loaded for war shot, we'll need tubes three and four also. Gentlemen, let's warm up the Harpoons."

The Harpoon missile was the deadliest weapon aboard. The crew realized the NATO Reforger operation was no longer a game.

USS *Houston* sped toward the oncoming threat.

ROYAL NAVY TRANSPORT V-25 NIGHT OWL

Jack turned his head as he snapped closed the strap to his Kevlar helmet. He saw the brighter skies outside and immediately went into his military role as leader. He nodded his unspoken thanks to Carl, who only winked in return as he adjusted his own equipment. He made eye contact with Henri, who only smirked at him. This made Jack just as uneasy as he had been before the music of Elvis had calmed him. Henri Farbeaux now knew one of his weaknesses.

"One minute, one minute," the copilot called out as the Night Owl slowly dropped down to three hundred feet. The V-25's crew chief managed a walk-through and checked everyone's safety equipment.

The pilot was fighting the debilitating lack of lift on his right side where one of the two wing-mounted engines had died. The Night Owl kept wanting to dip in that direction, forcing him to think about aborting the landing altogether.

Suddenly, a red alarm sounded. Then a piercing scream came into everyone's ears through the bird's intercom system. Only Everett and Ryan knew what the warning was about.

"Jesus, we're being painted!" the copilot shouted out in shock and surprise. "Oh, crap. We have missile lock!"

Above the scream of engines and the rocking of the V-25, every man aboard knew now that there was an enemy out there and they had just made their intentions known.

The NATO salvage mission was now under attack.

TICONDEROGA—CLASS AEGIS MISSILE CRUISER USS *SHILOH*

"Captain, someone just illuminated the Night Owl. Whoever it is, they have missile lock!"

Johnson turned back into the bridge. "Who has missile lock?"

"Unknown, sir. We have that intermittent target inside the hurricane but nothing concrete." Johnson saw the operator jerk his head up in shock and surprise. "We have two missiles in the air!"

"Track origin and match bearings. Target ASROC. Get the close-in weaps ready."

Above deck, the swirl and hum of the close-in weapons system, two Phalanx Gatling guns, one fore and one aft, turned and started tracking the incoming bogeys with the most powerful defensive radar system afloat—the Aegis

Electronic Warfare System. The many-barreled gun started rotating, warming up. She was now ready for a gunfight.

Ezra Johnson knew that he was only trying to keep the target ship guessing, as the *Shiloh* had no lock on the source. All he could hope to do is make the aggressor blink.

As the crewmen of *Shiloh*, *De Zeven*, and the unseen *Houston* watched, the V-25 set off their countermeasures. Chaff—small bursts of aluminum foil that were ejected in packets—and hot magnesium flares exploded from the tail section of the Night Owl. Then another, then another as she laid down a false signal for the enemy missiles to track in a virtual waterfall display of fire and aluminum. The Night Owl veered sharply away from the missile cruiser in the hope they could at least draw fire away from their main asset in the area.

Johnson turned away from the departing V-25 and turned his attention on the area where the incoming hostile threat would emerge. He saw the first of the two missiles free itself of the high winds inside the hurricane. His jaw muscles clenched as one of the large missiles struggled to regain control after breaking into calmer air. He let out a sigh of relief when the missile suddenly took a nosedive and crashed into the sea. Johnson knew they would not have the same luck with the second enemy missile as they had with the first. It came directly at the maneuvering Night Owl.

"Rolling action missiles, lock on and fire!"

In the combat control center, a signal was sent out, and the small, multifaceted missile system came to life. Sixteen extremely small missiles left their tubes and streaked outward toward the incoming threat.

"Get the R2-D2s ready. They're going to need help!" the captain hissed as he just ordered his only two close-in defensive systems to life.

Johnson grimaced, as he knew the odds were favoring the enemy and that the V-25 Night Owl was going to die.

The Russian SA-N-6 antiair missile dropped low to the sea in its rush toward the V-25. It came close to catching the topmost part of a large swell of sea but hopped easily over it. The American rolling action missiles detonated thirty-five feet in front of it, but the Russian-made system kept coming. The missile then climbed to altitude. It was on a straight line toward the Night Owl. Too late—the Phalanx, a system made by the Raytheon Corporation, acted like a garden hose. One thousand rounds of twenty-millimeter cannon fire greeted the missile. Only one of these struck the weapon as it kept climbing toward the weakened Night Owl. The Phalanx had also failed.

The missile struck the V-25 just below the left stabilizer. The wing immediately buckled as the twenty-five-pound warhead detonated. The VTOL was thirty-five feet above the sea when the wing collapsed, and the Night Owl slid over onto her side and fell into the sea. It hit with a sickening crunch as the fuselage snapped into two pieces. Men scrambled to free themselves from their harnesses as the entire V-25 started to slip very quickly beneath the calmer waters of the eye.

Men and equipment started to float to the surface as the Dutch frigate *De Zeven* made her way to the crash area. She slowed as men became visible, and the rescue mission started in earnest.

LOS ANGELES—CLASS ATTACK SUBMARINE USS *HOUSTON*

Captain Thorne cursed himself for allowing his surface assets to be fired upon. His weapons officer was reporting that *Houston* could not get weapons solutions for either vessel entering the eye of the storm.

"Weapons, as soon as those ships clear the hurricane, target two Mark-48s for each. ASROC, prepare to launch."

Battle stations was the call, and *Houston* came alive as never before.

TICONDEROGA—CLASS AEGIS MISSILE CRUISER USS *SHILOH*

Captain Johnson cursed. He slammed his fist into the steel railing of the bridge wing as *De Zeven* made her run to save lives.

His first officer came out to the bridge wing and handed him a communication. The XO's face had lost all its color.

"What is it, Sam?" he asked as he reached for the message flimsy.

```
TO ALL NATO SHIPS IN THE AREA, STAND DOWN OR
AGAIN BE FIRED UPON. THE VESSEL YOU HAVE IN TOW
IS THE PROPERTY OF THE RUSSIAN PEOPLE, AND YOU
WILL SURRENDER IT IMMEDIATELY.
SIGNED, KRESHENKO.
```

"What do we do, Captain?" the XO asked.

"Target same area. Get the ASROCs warmed up. Send this to Kreshenko, whoever he is: 'NATO invites you to come and get it.'"

Johnson knew his anger had overwhelmed his better judgment. Instead of calming things down, he just exacerbated the situation. He watched his XO vanish into the bridge area, and then he turned and examined the spot he thought their enemy would emerge from the outer edges of Tildy. His guess was only off by a mile.

"Oh, my God."

The largest battle cruiser in the world with another, smaller escort ship broke through the outer edges of the hurricane and into the calmer eye. She made for a spectacular scene as her raked bow cut the seas apart in her race to face the NATO force. Johnson immediately recognized the form of *Peter the Great*, one of the nastier fears of all Western navies.

The Russians had arrived.

PART TWO

CRACKED MIRRORS

Unlikely people,
From unlikely worlds,
Are never meant to be together.

—Carlos Gutierrez,
"Alternate Reality"

7

Jack pulled up a sputtering Charlie Ellenshaw. He had yanked him up by his floating white hair to the surface, where both men spit out salt water and tried their best to stay afloat. Collins looked around as heads began to bob to the surface of the softly rolling sea.

The last thing of the Night Owl he saw was the tail boom as it slid beneath the water. He spied Jason Ryan soon afterward surface with a gagging and spitting copilot of the V-25. Then he saw Henri and Carl as they assisted the Royal Marines. Collins and Charlie swam toward Ryan.

"Any other crew get out?" he shouted.

Ryan made sure the copilot was all right and then turned to face Jack. "No, I couldn't find the master chief, either."

Suddenly, the water erupted next to them as Jenks surfaced. He pulled heavily on something, and then the frightened face of the Royal Navy pilot came into view. He threw up seawater as Jenks pulled off his flight helmet.

"Come on, breathe, you limey bastard!"

Finally, the pilot took a deep breath and then vomited again.

"That's it. You'll live."

"You always act surprised when your plans go straight to hell. Flying through a hurricane usually means bad things to the rest of the world, but you Americans always think you can pull off the impossible."

Jack looked over at a drenched and bleeding Henri Farbeaux. "Glad to see you made it, Henri."

Collins started counting the heads that were visible. He stopped at thirty-six. That meant they had lost seventeen men. He slapped the water angrily, as he knew that whoever had fired that missile was now in deep debt with the Royal Navy.

"We lost one hell of a lot of people, Jack."

Collins looked over and saw Everett. He had gathered some of the equipment bags that had almost gone down with the V-25.

"I know. Let's get aboard that damnable ship and get this over with before some asshole tries that again."

A line hit the water next to Ryan's head as he joined them. They turned and saw that it was the *Shiloh*'s rigging crew aboard the *Simbirsk* who had thrown the ropes.

Jack watched as the *De Zeven*, initially tagged for the rescue, turned and made her way back to *Shiloh*. Evidently, Captain Johnson wanted his escort back to multiply defensive weaponry in case they were attacked again. Prudent thinking as far as Jack was concerned.

"I hope they have coffee going on that tub," Jenks said as he tied the thick rope around the pilot and signaled *Simbirsk* to haul him aboard.

Jack looked at the World War II Russian cruiser and saw that she looked as if she had come out of her commissioning birth just last week. She was in pristine condition and looked like any warship from that era. There was one notable exception—the coiled wiring that covered her hull from stem to stern. They looked like old-fashioned coil springs from an army cot. They were gray in color to match the ship's paint scheme. He saw the American riggers on board as they managed to throw five more lines into the water. Collins felt a strange electrical sensation gently coursing through his body. It wasn't painful, but he knew it was there. It was like the feeling you get just before a close encounter with a lightning strike.

"Shall we see what all the hubbub is about, Colonel? At least to take cover in case someone starts shooting missiles at us again."

Jack nodded at Carl, who also turned to see the ghost ship in front of them.

The Russian battle cruiser *Simbirsk* waited like an old haunted house from stories told to make you frightened of your own shadow when you were a child. It was Ellenshaw who put the right words to it.

"That ship has gone bad," he said as he was pulled toward the derelict by the lifeline.

At that moment, a Russian-made Ka-27 antisubmarine helicopter swooped low over the floating men and the towed *Simbirsk*. The counter-rotating blades made a heavy *whump* as they passed. Jack's eyes narrowed when the Russian was joined by an American Seahawk. They dueled in the sky over their heads, each helicopter coming closer and closer together in ever-more dangerous maneuvering.

"I guess Hurricane Tildy is the place to be. All the best people are here."

As soon as Jack and his remaining men were aboard, he was handed a radio. Now that his team had arrived, the mission had become his operational command. Everett stood next to him, trying to shake some of the cold water from his nylon BDU. Before Jack raised the radio to his mouth, he quickly made sure everyone was safely aboard. After the excitement of their arrival, it took him a moment to remember the code name for the operation.

"This is Dynamo actual, over," he said as he caught his breath from the strenuous climb to the high decking of the old warship.

"Dynamo actual, this is Captain Ezra Johnson. I think we can drop the pretense here. I think the damn Russians know about our presence, over."

Before Jack could respond, the Russian helicopter broke with the Seahawk and turned and swooped low over the bow of the ship—low enough that all aboard dove for cover. Collins raised his head with an angry look but forcibly calmed himself as the twin counter-rotating blades buffeted the exposed men. The Royal Navy lieutenant was organizing his remaining men to prepare to resist an onboard assault. He dispersed them throughout the upper deck into hidden positions. Jack nodded at the young officer's move.

"I see your point, Captain." Jack gave Carl a knowing look. Everett, for his part, was assisting Jenks and Charlie Ellenshaw with their equipment check. They had lost some gear and were worried they wouldn't be able to make their analysis of the Russian ship with what they had left. Carl shook his head slightly at Jack, indicating the trouble. "What is the current situation? Over."

"Well, if that rust bucket over there had radar, you would be able to see a most disturbing sight. We have a Kirov-class missile cruiser and her escort bearing down on us. They are currently sixty miles out and closing at flank speed. No more ordnances have been popped off, but I don't expect the situation to hold. I have my orders also, over."

Jack and the others knew what those orders were. If for any reason they could not secure the vessel, it would be sunk as a hazard to navigation. That was a polite euphemism for "If we can't have it, you can't either."

"With the loss of some of our equipment, it looks like we can start leaning in that direction. Do we have time for a general inspection of her power plant? Over."

"Unless the Red Baron up there starts shooting, I would say you have about three hours, over."

Collins was about to respond when a voice broke into their secure channel. The uninvited intruder was even clearer than the straight line-of-sight signal from *Shiloh*.

"To the illegal boarding party currently aboard the Simbirsk, *this is Colonel Leonid Salkukoff. You are committing an act of international piracy, and the Russian government asks you to stand down and return to us Russian state property."*

Collins heard the voice of the Russian and responded, "I am sure I don't have to stand here and explain to you the finer points of international law governing the open seas of the world. This ship is a derelict and unmanned. It is also a hazard to free navigation. By right of salvage, NATO has claimed this vessel."

"Who am I speaking to please? Over," came the accented voice. Jack knew that whoever it was, it was coming from the circling helicopter over their heads due to the heavy sound of rotors heard in the background.

A quick look at Carl and a smirk. He clicked the transmit button. "This is *Dynamo*, over."

"Ah, we can play this game all day, Colonel Collins. We will play until the whistle sounds, and still, the inevitable outcome will not have changed one iota. Over."

Most of the men on the deck of *Simbirsk* heard Jack's real name being uttered by the Russian. They all stopped and listened as the situation had suddenly just changed direction.

"Okay, Colonel, you know who I am. Your dramatic and revealing moment has passed, and here we are with the same dilemma we had just a second ago."

"Colonel, we can have this discussion all day, but at the moment, our missile cruiser Peter the Great *has been tracking a submerged target in her area. May I suggest you tell your submarine to back down until we can come to some form of understanding? Over."*

Collins acknowledged the dreaded news by the look on his companions' faces. Everett, the navy man, along with Ryan, saddled up closer to hear the exchange. They knew an attack on a submarine would be devastating. It was in the calmer waters underneath the waves while *Peter the Great* was on the surface with a clear sonar signal to pick up on, where, because of the high seas, *Houston* would have trouble getting a fire solution. The Russian had the advantage. Jack grimaced when he saw the choices in front of him.

"A temporary stay only, Colonel, nothing more. Let us communicate without the specter of a massacre threatening your sailors. Over."

"Captain Johnson."

"Shiloh, here."

"Captain, on my authority, order *Houston* to stand down. Further orders later. Over."

Just two clicks sounded on the radio informing Collins that the captain understood.

"*Now you see, Colonel, cooperation between nations can be a simple achievement. We have—*"

"You fired on a United States ship of war, Colonel. That is what—"

"*We fired upon common pirates. Can we skip your game of American dodgeball, Colonel? I suggest a cease-fire until we can have a discussion in person. My forces will stand down in a joint effort at the cooperation I mentioned a moment ago. Over.*"

Jack looked around him. The ancient Russian ship. The towline leading to another vessel full of young men. And then he looked across at the Dutch ship, whose sailors even now lined her outer railing watching with anticipation. Then his eyes rose to the swirling cage of the hurricane they found themselves in. The black wall swirled around them like a tube of evil darkness. His eyes fell to Carl, who only nodded at Jack that they had no other choice at the moment.

"Agreed."

"*How many men do you currently have aboard, Colonel? Over.*"

"We have thirty-six officers and men aboard. All fully armed, Colonel."

"*Coincidentally, we have almost the same number. And we are armed also. So, we have an agreement; all forces will stand down until we can have a civilized discussion on our differences of opinion. Over.*"

Jack lowered his eyes and his radio as he quickly thought. He looked up and caught Ryan's attention.

"Mr. Ryan, take a few of these marines and stash some weapons in a few of the companionways. I don't care much for liars, and that is just what we have here."

"*Colonel, my patience wears thin. I do not care for flying all that much. I understand you have the same affliction. Over.*"

"Okay, this is getting downright creepy, Jack. How in the hell does he know that? No one in our own department has a clue but us," Carl said as he knelt beside Collins.

"We're not going to find out by not letting the bastard board." Jack angrily clicked his radio to life and stood as the helicopter swung low once more over the deck. "Permission granted to land aboard *Shiloh* for transfer to *Simbirsk*. Over."

"*Oh, I think we can manage something a little more time friendly, Colonel.*"

Collins heard the scream of the Russian-made navy helicopter as it came low toward them. It rose and then settled beyond the high radio mast of the cruiser, toward the stern. It vanished.

"Damn it!" Jack cursed as he was tossed an M4 automatic weapon. "Mr. Ryan, get Jenks and Charlie into the wheelhouse after you get some weapons in other locations and wait. Carl, get a squad of marines, and let's greet our guest."

It took Jack, Carl, and sixteen of the Royal Marines three minutes to cover the seven hundred feet of deck to the stern of the old cruiser. When they arrived, the last man rappelling from the helicopter was seen as his booted feet struck the deck just aft of the number-three gun turret. The man allowed the rubberized rope to fly free as he quickly unzipped his body armor to allow cooler air to enter. He looked around the stern of the *Simbirsk*, and then he spied the two Americans and their greeting party of sixteen Royal Marines. He smiled and gave the men a jaunty salute.

Jack stood waiting with his exposed weapon at his side. He felt someone next to him and saw that it was Henri Farbeaux. Jack's eyes saw the dirt and grease on his BDU and knew that the Frenchman had already been inside the cruiser.

"Exploring, Henri?" he asked out of the side of his mouth.

Farbeaux's eyes never left the man who was smiling and walking toward them with thirty-two men dressed just as they were. The Frenchman's eyes narrowed.

"I thought I would do the job I was kidnapped to do, Colonel. Then maybe my part in this foolishness can come to an end sooner rather than later."

"Well, is that him?"

Henri watched the Russian's approach. His mouth went into a straight line.

"Yes, it is him." He faced Jack. "Do not trust this man, Colonel. His mission here is to destroy your assets and kill every one of you."

"Why don't you tell us what it is you really think, Froggy?"

Henri looked at Everett, who smirked. "This may be one situation you won't find so amusing, Captain. I do not see an acceptable outcome here."

Carl saw the seriousness in Farbeaux's face and decided to stop chiding him. He didn't particularly care for that look on the former French Army colonel's face.

A man who stood the same height as Jack came up and stopped. He eyed the two men beside him and then the Royal Marines to his right and left. He looked behind him at his own black-clad warriors.

"At ease. Inform your men to sling weapons, Captain."

Jack watched as the men with their black helmets and Russian-made Nomex BDUs on did as ordered. He also noticed that these soldiers were far more heavily armed than his own contingent.

"There. Now, we can all be friends," Salkukoff said as he faced Jack. He stood rigid for the briefest of moments and then gave Collins a very fast and ill-mannered salute. Collins just as quickly returned it. "I hope I did that right."

He smiled over at the larger Everett and Farbeaux. "It's been quite some time since I played soldier."

"Colonel, your mission here is illegal. I request that you and your men fly back to your cruiser and let the courts decide what happens next."

The smile remained as Salkukoff tilted his head as if he were attempting to understand a language he did not know.

"So you can rape this vessel for her technology? Colonel, you of all people know better than that."

"Rape the technology of a ship over seventy years old? Colonel, in poker, you never show an opponent just how weak your hand really is."

Salkukoff turned his head, and instead of answering Jack, he faced Henri Farbeaux.

"Colonel Collins has a very diverse sense of humor. He accuses the Russian government of wrongdoing but at the same time has in his employ one of the greater antiquity thieves in modern history." He stuck his hand out to Henri. "Colonel Farbeaux, I find you in the strangest locales."

The Frenchman looked at the outstretched hand, and then his eyes moved to the colder, darker eyes of the Russian.

"I am a thief, yes. All here can attest to that fact." He didn't notice nor did he care that Salkukoff dropped the offered handshake. "But you are a murderous pig of the first order. I was witness to your bravery on the battlefield."

A knowing look crossed the Russian's features. "Ah, the Ukraine. They were thieves, Colonel, just like yourself. They paid the price. You, sir, have yet to meet our justice."

"And that time is not here and not now," Collins said as he stepped in front of Henri. "This man is under my protection."

Salkukoff smiled even wider. "As you are mine, Colonel Collins. While aboard the *Simbirsk*, you will be offered our hospitality. At the end of this, we will see if you wish to pursue matters in another direction."

He stepped past Collins and then eyed the vessel around him. He shook his head and then ran a hand along the bottom of the number three-gun turret.

"They don't construct them like this anymore"—he turned to face Jack— "do they, Colonel?" He saw that the American was going to remain silent. "Today's surface ships of aluminum and composites, they would never have withstood phase shift dynamics."

Collins and Everett exchanged quick, nervous looks.

"I believe you may have an engineer aboard?"

Jack stood silent as he eyed the man before him. The Russian brushed the rust off his hands and looked at the group of NATO representatives. "No, you did not bring along your brilliant Master Chief Jenks, the man responsible for getting your response to the alien incursion into the air. I must say a thrilling sight to see something as large as that battleship rise into the blue skies of Antarctica. It gave me goose bumps."

Collins was having a hard time not only hiding his anger but also his shock that even the master chief was known to this man.

"Uri, it looks like you will not get to have the intellectual exchange you had hoped."

A smaller man emerged from the group of Russian commandos. He was wearing glasses and had a distinct look of discomfort about him. He removed the helmet from his head and then held it at his side.

"A shame. I am a great admirer of the master chief. I have read all his work on hydrodynamics and naval engineering. Marvelous mind."

"May I present—" Salkukoff started to say.

"Dr. Uri Gervais, chief engineer of the Orion project."

Jack turned and saw the master chief with Ryan and Charlie standing next to him. Jenks lit his cigar and then eyed the smaller man before him.

"He's the man behind Russia's effort to get to the moon."

Jack looked from Jenks to the small scientist before him. The man looked as if he wanted to be anywhere but here. Collins could also see that the older scientist was terrified of Salkukoff.

"Professor, it was my understanding from our intelligence briefings that you wouldn't be caught dead in the company of assholes like this."

All eyes went from the cigar-puffing Jenks to the Russian professor and then to the colonel, who merely laughed at the insult from the career navy man. Dr. Gervais, for his part, said nothing. The man looked downright uncomfortable.

"And our briefings on you are as accurate as yours are on the good doctor. Now, shall we see about our mystery ship and where she could have been hiding since World War II?" He stepped past Jack and the others and made for the hatchway that led into the darkened interior of the ship. Collins and Everett both noticed the satchel charges being carried by every one of the Russian commandos. It was clear what their intent was if they could not recover the *Simbirsk*.

The Americans and British followed the Russian strike team into the phantom of the Atlantic.

8

NORTH ATLANTIC OCEAN
HURRICANE TILDY—THE EYE

The smell of oil, grease, and sweat permeated the air inside the blackness of the *Simbirsk*. The lingering aroma of baked goods and meat, beets, and other smells greeted them. The Americans allowed Salkukoff and his men, with the exception of the twelve who followed them, to lead the way. The Russian colonel held up a diagram as they slowly eased their way down a deserted and dark companionway.

"Ah, here we are," he said as he indicated a hatchway that led downward. "Engineering spaces right this way."

"Do you guys feel it?" Charlie asked as he caught up to Jack and the others.

"What, Charlie?" Jack asked, wanting everyone's impressions about the situation.

"Ghosts. I don't know, but this ship is all wrong. I felt it while in the water, and I feel it now."

"Just your nerves, Doc," Ryan said with not much conviction. Even the clattering of their footsteps on the metal stairs made a hollow, echoing sound that felt like a harbinger of something waiting for them below.

"As soon as we get the generators working, we can—"

Before the colonel could finish his statement, the lights inside the stairwell flared to brilliant brightness. Every man stopped and looked around. They all heard the far-off mechanical sounds and the generators running. Bilge pumps cranked to life, and the flow of bilgewater started spewing from the side of the *Simbirsk*. Jack managed to look behind him at Jenks, who just shrugged in ignorance as to how the lights could have come on without anyone turning them on.

"Perhaps your claim on international salvage rights has just been denied, Colonel Collins. It seems she may have not been abandoned after all," Salkukoff said as he continued downward. Both the Russian and Collins himself were aware that maybe they should have brought along the bulk of their men instead of leaving them to glare at each other above deck.

As they traveled down the eight decks to the engineering spaces, they all felt the power around them. Every once in a while, the hair on their arms and necks would gently rise as if an electrical current were swirling around them.

In the back of the line of men, Jenks turned to the smaller Russian professor. He tossed the cigar away and fixed the gray-haired man with a fierce look.

"From my understanding, Doc, you were thought to hang out with better people than this current staff you have. What in the hell happened to you?"

Gervais looked sheepish at first, but when he saw that the Russian colonel and his men—with the exception of the Russian rear guard behind him and Jenks—were far enough away, he leaned toward Jenks and spoke in low tones.

"Things are changing in my world, Mr. Jenks. Some would say not entirely for the better."

Jenks let the *Mister* pass without comment since he knew the good professor didn't know navy protocols. He did, however, pop a fresh cigar into his mouth as his eyes went from Gervais to the Russian commandos who were following. He lit the cigar and said nothing as the professor pushed by him as if the conversation might have already gone too far.

"Things are a little squirrely around here," he said as the trailing Russian commandos gestured for him to continue forward.

The line of men stopped at a double set of heavy steel doors. None of the professional navy men had ever seen hatchways such as these on a warship. It was as if they were made to keep something out—or in. Salkukoff spun the heavy locking wheel until it stopped. They all noticed that it had turned as if it had been greased just yesterday.

"Jenks," Jack said quickly as he held his hand out and stayed the doors from opening. The Russian turned with raised brows.

The master chief, with Ellenshaw in tow, stepped forward, and Charlie dipped into a large duffel and produced a small device. Jenks held out a Geiger counter. He listened, as did the others, with great interest. Without a word, Jenks held his hand out behind him, and Charlie placed a small ball-like device into his hand as he accepted the radiation counter back from Jenks.

"You wanna step back, comrade?" he said as he eyed Salkukoff at the supposed insult by the master chief.

Jenks eased the right side of the double steel doors open and tossed in the small ball. They all heard it clatter to the steel deck as Jenks quickly slammed the door closed. The master chief leaned against the cold steel and then silently counted as Charlie brought up a small computer and then started taking readings. The ball was the invention of the Nuclear Sciences Division and was designed to sniff out radiation and deadly chemicals such as anthrax and other dangerous substances. The sniffer began working.

"The counter shows nothing. No radiation." He looked at his wristwatch. Then he looked at Charlie Ellenshaw. "Well, Doc?"

"The sniffer is clear. Zero."

Jenks turned and then opened the door and then gestured for the Russian to enter.

"She's clean. No rads and no chemical contaminant to speak of."

"That would be impressive, Master Chief, if our science back in the '40s was as advanced as you seem to think. Why would this ship have radiation permeating the air?"

Jack walked easily past Salkukoff and stepped inside the engineering spaces. "Then I take it you understand just where this ship has been for all these years, Colonel? Maybe the place it has been is a radiation-filled area. Have you thought of that one?"

A smirking Jenks and Charlie pushed by the silent Russian. The good professor Gervais was next.

"Apologies, Colonel. I never thought of that," the small, portly professor said in passing.

Salkukoff watched as the line of men entered the spaces. His eyes settled on the back of Jack Collins. He held his temper and stepped inside. He walked past Gervais with a small nudge.

"Don't embarrass me again, Doctor."

Jack and the others stopped as they came to the center of the room. Far beyond was the hatchway leading to the engine spaces. He nodded at Jason Ryan and two of the marines. "Go see what shape the power plant is in."

"Go with them," Salkukoff said to four of his own men. He gave Jack the briefest of smiles.

"What in the hell is that?" Jenks asked loudly enough for all conversation to stop.

Collins and the Russian colonel turned and saw what Jenks was seeing. Along both sides of the space was a thick glass partition. Behind that glass, only inches from the outer hull, was what looked like large lightbulbs. At least a million of them crowded the space. They looked to be situated on a conductive pad of ceramic. Wiring of every thickness ran from the ceramic platform to large consoles of dead indicator lights. They saw the workstations for at least fifty engineers. On the front of the twin aisles of electronics was what looked like a power generator. What was most disturbing to all was the fact that the stations looked recently occupied. Coffee cups with black coffee still inside, and tea glasses with the liquid still in them were everywhere.

"No dust, rust, or rot of any kind," Charlie said as he picked up one of the glass teacups. The pewter stand that held it looked brand new. He quickly replaced it on the console he took it from. He saw a piece of bread on a small saucer and poked at it with his index finger. While not exactly fresh, it was still edible. He pulled his hand away and looked at the other faces of interest around him.

"The damn thing looks as if it were launched yesterday," Everett said as he and Jenks looked closer at the workstations around them. Ryan picked up a clipboard and examined the Cyrillic writing.

One of the Russian commandos stepped forward and took the clipboard from Ryan's hand. Jason looked angry but held his temper when Salkukoff stepped forward.

"Until we can get things worked out, we would rather not share much information. You understand, Colonel?"

"Shiloh *to Colonel Collins*. Shiloh *to Collins, over*," came the voice of Ezra Johnson over Jack's radio. At the same time, Salkukoff also got a call on his own walkie-talkie.

"Collins, go."

"*Colonel, CIC is picking up a spike on our infrared monitors. Sea temps have risen six degrees in the past ten minutes. Over.*"

"*Peter the Great* has the same information. That combined with your Aegis defense system makes the information almost an absolute."

Jack looked up at Salkukoff. "The timing of these spikes coincides with the lights coming on."

"I think we can chuck coincidence out of the freakin' window," Jenks added.

"Chuck?" Professor Gervais asked.

"American slang for throw or toss," Ellenshaw explained.

"*Instructions, Colonel? Over.*"

Collins again raised his radio to his mouth, but before he could say a word, the humming started. It was so intense that men had to quickly cover their ears. Then the lighting dimmed as the large lightbulbs sitting on their ceramic base started to glow softly.

One of the Russian commandos reached out and placed a hand onto the thick glass that separated them from the machine inside. The man was trying to steady himself from the onslaught of sound.

"No!" Jack yelled when he saw the movement.

Before anyone could react, a small bolt of electricity shot from the ceramic base of the machine, penetrated the glass, and slammed into the man's hand. His body jerked, and a spasm coursed through him, and then he collapsed to the steel deck. All eyes widened when they saw the sparkle of light that coursed over the commando's extremities. Then a loud pop was heard, and then the

Russian soldier just vanished before their eyes. As suddenly as everything had started, it wound down. Lighting returned to normal, and then the bulbs inside the glassed-in chamber dimmed to almost nothing.

"*Shiloh, Shiloh*, this is Collins. Update on those readings, over."

"*Shiloh to Collins, we lost power momentarily but are back up. Readings are down to almost nothing. Sea temps still remain high.*"

"Copy and stand by; out for now."

Ryan and the Russian professor leaned over to the spot where the electrocuted man had been. There was a vague outline where he had fallen prone to the deck, but nothing else. Professor Gervais moved his hand over the cold steel of the deck and immediately pulled it back when the steel gave way by at least two inches. It was like poking a bowl of Jell-O. Then the deck solidified once more. Jason and Gervais looked up and then over at Collins.

Salkukoff smirked as if the joke were on Collins. "Before we start tossing accusations around, Colonel, perhaps we should—"

The sound of the generator starting to spin wildly filled the space. Each man knew this assault was different. Electricity filled the air. The smell of ozone wafted freely, and men started to gag. The bulbs inside the chamber flared to life once more, only this time they were so bright that they burned the eyes of those who turned that way. Each man, through natural instinct, hit the deck.

"*Shiloh, Shiloh*, seal the ship! Get every man belowdecks!" Jack screamed into the radio just as Salkukoff was doing the same with *Peter the Great*.

Suddenly, everyone felt the electricity shoot through their bodies. The noise was ear shattering, and the deck beneath them actually warped and became sickeningly pliable. The sound of the powerful generator nearly burst the eardrums of those closest to it. Charlie Ellenshaw screamed in pain and was soon joined by all.

The very air around the writhing men turned into a wave of nausea-filled movement and liquidity.

The last sensation Collins had was the feeling of falling.

Outside, the world was on fire. The burst of power from the *Simbirsk* flowed over and around the men on her upper deck. Those closest to the hatchway leading below vanished in a puff of blackened dust as those farther away just burst into flames. The towline to *Shiloh* melted and then snapped with a twang, sending the far end into the *Shiloh* and her riggers, slicing them in two. Then the heat wave struck *Shiloh* and sent her fantail high into the air until it came crashing down into the sea. Every one of the riggers burst into flame or was thrown into the boiling waters surrounding the large cruiser. Everything that was flammable on the outer decks melted or flamed so brightly it looked like a magnesium explosion.

Inside the bridge, Captain Johnson hit the deck hard, as did his control crew. Windows smashed inward, and then to the captain's horror, he felt the deck beneath him start to tremble and then actually wave up like an early morning surf. It was like he was lying in a soft pool of water. Seeing this, one would think the deck and other steel members of the ship didn't dance under them, but to the sensations the body felt, they were moving and felt almost as if the very atomic structure of the deck and hull was breaking down. Johnson tried to stand and, with much effort, finally managed. As he did, it felt as though the deck had become a piece of melting rubber. He looked out of the broken bridge window just as the *Simbirsk* vanished in a bright explosion of light and sound.

Before he could react, the USS *Shiloh* and her burning and battered Dutch escort ship, *De Zeven*, blinked out of existence 1.2 seconds after the Russian ship.

The pressure wave expanded outward. It was now a wall of water and heat that resembled a nuclear detonation. It traveled at the speed of sound outward from a spot that was now nothing but vapor and the largest whirlpool ever created on the surface of the world's oceans. It was gaining power exponentially as it moved out and *down*.

LOS ANGELES—CLASS ATTACK SUBMARINE USS *HOUSTON*

The pressure wave was almost as intense below the sea as it was above. It caught Thorne and his crew unawares as the thump of seawater from above slammed into them. Lights went out, and the power plant screamed to keep her station between the Russian cruiser and his own surface assets. It wasn't enough. Water lines broke, and the heavily welded seams of the boat started to be stretched beyond her engineering. Not one but two forward torpedo tube outer doors were twisted at such an angle that not only did her outer doors collapse, it warped the heavy pressure door inside. The interior forward spaces of *Houston* were now open to the sea.

"Emergency lighting!" Thorne said over the din of yelling men at their stations.

"*Conn, sonar, we have a massive surface detonation. Unable to pinpoint at this time.*"

Before Thorne could answer, the bow of *Houston* dipped down. Then they all felt the acceleration of the boat as it started a plunge for the seafloor two and a half miles below.

"Blow ballast. Give me full rise on the planes. All back full! Shut off those damn alarms!"

As the command was relayed, Thorne felt the bow fall to an even steeper angle of dive. He heard the two powerful GE nuclear reactors scream in protest as the engineering department took *Houston* to 115 percent power. She would either redline or explode in the next four minutes.

Then the real pressure strike hit. The stern of the *Houston* was thrown up and then actually overtook her forward momentum, and the giant attack sub somersaulted downward. Finally, her bow planes dug their teeth in, and *Houston* righted herself as the wave flowed past them.

"Helm's not answering, Skipper," XO Devers called out. He was bleeding from his head and was soaked after getting one of the many leaks shut down. "Engineering says we're close to redlining." All the men were injured in some way from their circular ride to the roof and then being slammed to the deck. Most quickly recovered and resumed their watch. They were now hanging on to their stations as the world tilted downward. What was even more disturbing was the fact that several of the crew felt their hands travel completely through their consoles. Their feet were also being sucked into the steel of her deck. As men nearly panicked, they looked down and around but could not actually see the deck and other solid objects bend or soften. It was if they were sensing it but not able to see it. Most thought they were hallucinating these factors.

Thorne grimaced, as he knew he was moments away from losing his ship. He quickly turned to the navigation console and studied the map. He then ran for the sonar shack. The run was downhill and totally out of control as the down angle increased. Thorne finally arrested his run and entered the tight space of the sonar room. He immediately saw the sonar supervisor was busy putting out an electrical short with a fire extinguisher.

"*Captain, we're at nine hundred feet, approaching crush depth.*"

Thorne ignored the frantic call from the control room and instead leaned over the nearest sonar operator. His eyes moved rapidly until he found what he had been looking for. It was the same thing he had just spied on his navigation chart.

"*Eleven hundred!*"

"Jesus, we implode at twelve hundred," one of the youngest operators said in a shaky voice.

"Stow that shit, mister," Thorne said as he quickly calculated what it was he was looking at. He hit the intercom. "XO, fifteen degrees starboard. When I give the command, flood the aft torpedo room and give me full rise on all the planes!"

"Aye, Skipper. What do you have in mind?"

"I think we have to crash-land *Houston*."

Without explanation, he called out to his sonar operators, "That mountain range, find me a shelf . . . now!"

"A what?" one of the operators asked in confusion.

"A place to land this damn thing!"

All four operators went facedown into their scopes until the one who had commented on their crush depth pointed. "Large shelf, bearing five degrees starboard."

The order went out to basically call for *Houston*'s destruction. The venting inside the sealed and isolated aft torpedo room was open to the sea, weighing the stern of the giant submarine down and bringing her bow up. The powerful electric motor of the boat still screamed in reverse as *Houston* plummeted.

"Thirteen hundred and fifty feet!"

"Come on, come on. Rise, damn you, rise!" Thorne prayed aloud. Then into the intercom: "All hands, brace for impact!"

The USS *Houston* slammed into a shelf on the side of the Challenger Rise mountain peak. The long, ledge-like protuberance circled the mountain in a twisting road-like run downward. *Houston* hit at a little over thirty knots. Her bow plowed into the rock and sand with a noise like that of tearing paper and ripping steel. She bounced once, twice, and then finally came down on the small valley shelf, sliding to a stop only seven hundred feet from a drop of two and a half miles.

Captain Thorne never realized they had made it as the lights and *Houston*'s power plant shut down, along with the conscious minds of her entire crew. She settled onto the bottom with no power, and the sensation of a liquefied deck and hull plating once more became solid to those sailors who had become aware of it.

USS *Houston* was sitting alone on the bottom of a world that had changed around them in a momentary flash of brilliant light and sound.

KIROV-CLASS BATTLE CRUISER *PETER THE GREAT*

Captain Kreshenko, along with his entire bridge crew, saw the devastation coming right at them. He saw through his binoculars the massive wall of water as it built in ferocity. He knew without thinking that the *Simbirsk* and the two NATO vessels had been destroyed as he had lost them soon after the bright burst of light from the area thirty miles out. The initial detonation looked momentarily as if a giant bubble of light had formed over the old Russian ship, and the American and Dutch surface vessels were caught in that bubble.

"Order the *Admiral Levchenko* to take the wave head-on!"

"Too late!" Dishlakov said as he watched in horror through the bridge windows. Kreshenko saw the heated wave of water and light as it struck the smaller destroyer and flipped her completely over from stern to bow, not once but twice. The tough old ship snapped into three sections and then settled into the calming waters. Then a tremendous explosion erupted underwater, and then that wave of destruction also reached out for *Peter the Great*. Just as both walls of water, electric-filled light, and fire reached them, every man ducked as the ship was caught in the massive bubble the Americans had experienced.

The captain's last thoughts were wasted trying to grasp the might of the American weapon that had been used on them. They had fired on NATO ships, and this was their just reward for doing so.

Fire erupted over the deck of *Peter the Great*. Every man who was exposed burned to death or melted into her superstructure as the intensity of light and flames from the exploding destroyer consumed all flammable material just as it had on board *Shiloh*. Men scrambling to get belowdecks found their feet sinking into the solid steel plating of the decking. One man tripped and fell. His head and shoulders smashed into a bulkhead, and the upper portion of his body vanished. His legs kicked momentarily until he died. Others fell completely through to other decks far below. The sensation of pliability was no longer just that; it was real, and the Russian battle cruiser was experiencing it.

Kreshenko felt his ship roll to starboard and not right itself. He knew *Peter the Great* was going to capsize. The last sensation he felt was the rolling of the enormous cruiser and the strangeness of his own steel deck as it warbled and waved underneath him. He attempted to raise his head to give the order to abandon ship when the decking came up with his movement. It was like his face had been stuck in tar. He collapsed with his mind flowing in horrid understanding.

Then *Peter the Great* vanished in a flash of light that would have been mistaken for a nuclear detonation—if anyone would have been left alive to have witnessed it. The bubble of light that had emanated from *Simbirsk* engulfed them and then contracted to a smaller ball, and then the air and sky popped like a rubber band being stretched beyond endurance.

The sea inside the eye of Hurricane Tildy was calm and also void of all life— sea or land—for one hundred miles in all directions. Even aquatic life caught in the phase shift vanished beneath the waves.

As the North Atlantic began to settle, the outer edges of the eye of Tildy collapsed, just like a falling curtain. Its dark clouds flowed downward into the sea and upward into the sky as if some giant god had waved a magic wand and disbursed the hurricane. The darkness of the swirling clouds fell into the roiling waters, and then the storm and the clouds that made up her bulk dissipated and then vanished.

Hurricane Tildy was gone as if never there.

9

KIROV-CLASS BATTLE CRUISER *SIMBIRSK*

Jack awoke to men screaming in agony. As he tried to raise his head, he felt the skin on his cheek being tugged at. He pulled harder and then felt the searing pain as some of that skin was torn free. He shook his head and felt the area where skin had been. His fingers came away bloodied. He looked next to him as Carl was slowly rising from the same eerily pliable deck. Jack saw that Everett had lost some skin also but knew he was all right as he stumbled over to assist Ellenshaw, who was lying still over one of the engineering consoles. The calls for help came in English and Russian.

As for Colonel Salkukoff, he had been saved when he fell on one of his men. That man was now dead. Half in, half out of the floor decking. Others were in the same pose of death. But it became quickly evident that this effect did not apply to all areas of the mighty ship. Collins quickly deduced that the laws of physics did not apply to every scene of death. Some men were fried beyond recognition, while others had succumbed to the strange atomic makeup of the ship itself. Jack quickly looked for his team and was glad to see the master chief and Ryan had survived and were even now administering first aid to those who needed it.

Everett faced Jack, and at first, Collins failed to hear his words. He shook his head, and then Carl's mouth movement started to make sense.

"Jack, come on. We have to get the hell out of here!"

Again, he shook his head and then nodded. "Grab everybody. Charlie, Ryan, help those men. Come on, Swabby, let's go see if anyone else is alive."

Around them, the sound of the powerful generators was winding down like some giant turbine. The ship felt as if the power had been drained and she was now starting to sleep after a major tantrum.

As the Royal Marines and Russians worked together, Jack and Carl, followed quickly by Salkukoff, started for the double hatchway. All three barreled past dead men who had either been melted into the deck or electrocuted. A quick estimate counted twenty-two men dead just belowdecks. They all knew there was no rhyme or reason to the extent of the deaths or what had caused them. Some parts of the ship were affected, while others had remained as they always were—solid and unflinching.

As they took the stairs two at a time, they heard the giant generator finally slam to a stop. Then the lights once more went out. This didn't slow them, as Carl flicked on a powerful flashlight. After five minutes of fighting to get above deck, they were stunned at what greeted them. Dead men were everywhere. Even Salkukoff was taken aback at the power of what just happened. His briefings failed to explain just what the parameters of the old experiment had been. Now he knew. Whoever operated this phase shift system from the '40s had given themselves a death sentence.

"Good God, Jack. What in the hell happened?"

When Collins didn't answer, Everett turned and saw what it was that held his attention. The skies to the north, south, east, and west were clear of any cloud cover whatsoever. Hurricane Tildy had vanished as suddenly as it had arrived. The seas were calm and floating debris was the only leftover from the mighty hurricane. But all of this was not the disturbing factor. The ocean was a purplish color. Gone was the sea green of the North Atlantic. In its place, a light violet water world met their amazed gazes as its swells met the hull of the *Simbirsk* with a mild lapping sound.

Carl nudged Collins and nodded at what was floating to the surface and at their new surroundings. Jack then saw the bodies floating in the waters surrounding *Simbirsk*. The trail of dead sailors led straight to the USS *Shiloh*. She was listing heavily to her port side by at least fifteen degrees. There was no crew upon her outer decks. They saw the crashed and burned Seahawk helicopter just outside her hangar. It was a smoking heap of wreckage. Fires were raging across her deck. Even as they watched, several of her crew finally managed to break into the upper deck with fire hoses and suppression gear. They were fighting to save their ship.

Carl grabbed Jack's arm and pointed to the starboard side of the *Shiloh*. There they saw the last visage of the Dutch frigate *De Zeven* as she slowly rolled over, the massive flames engulfing her superstructure, hissing as they hit the violet-colored waters. Her proud fantail raised high into the air and then silently slid into the sea. They saw a few of her crew surface and cry for assistance. Several of the *Shiloh*'s damage control teams threw lines into the water as they tried desperately to save their fellow sailors. At close to a half a mile away, Jack still had to hold Everett's arm as he tried to make it to the railing to jump from the relative safety of the *Simbirsk* in an effort at saving the Dutch seamen. He angrily realized Jack was right and pulled his arm free.

Jack looked around him at their own situation. The *Simbirsk*, minus her casualties above on her main deck, had come through the battering intact. There were no fires and no damage other than to exposed personnel. Collins reached for the radio on his side and raised it to his lips.

"Collins to *Shiloh*, Collins to *Shiloh*, do you read?"

"It's no use, Colonel. You'll get no response."

They turned and saw that Salkukoff was just replacing his own radio. He watched the effort across the wide expanse of the *Shiloh*'s crew battling their fires. He shook his head.

"Our radios, even your digital watches, aren't working. It's as if we were involved in an EMP burst. Electronics everywhere, with the exception of the sealed area down below, have been fried. *Peter the Great* is not answering. If not an EMP, I can only assume she's gone also."

Jack looked at the radio and confirmed that he wasn't even showing a power light. He quickly gestured for Carl to throw him his radio, which had been switched off during the electronic ambush by the *Simbirsk*. He tried to call again with the undamaged radio but received no response from Captain Johnson.

"Carl, see if we can get a signal lamp up and running, I don't care if you have to use smoke signals—I have to speak with Captain Johnson. We need a navy corpsman as soon as they can spare one."

"You got it, Jack," Carl said and then vanished into the bottom of the wheelhouse.

"How in the hell could we have suffered an electromagnetic pulse?" Collins asked aloud.

"Baffling, to be sure, Colonel," Salkukoff said as he joined Jack next to the railing. "I estimate we lost well over half of both complements of our men."

Jack nodded as he turned with the wish to see the conning tower of the USS *Houston* break the surface of the sea. But he knew there would be no way such a fragile boat could have withstood the powerful event they had just survived.

"However, I think the discussion of how and why can wait. In case you haven't noticed, Colonel, the ocean is the wrong color."

Of course Jack had noticed, but he wasn't willing to think about the whys and why-nots of their current situation. The first priority was to save lives and then establish contact with *Shiloh*.

"Also, it seems our lady Tildy has given up her fight." There was debris from their vessels, bodies, and other flotsam, but strangely, Jack saw what looked like palm fronds and other organic plantlike material you would usually see after a powerful storm had swept through.

"Yes, I did notice, Colonel." Jack turned and faced the Russian. "Perhaps it's about time we come clean here. This event is a variation on what conspiracy nuts in my country called the Philadelphia Experiment. What was yours called?"

"Operation Czar. I guess someone back in the day thought it witty to make something disappear like the czar and his family. Although it needed to be done, it was still all rather tasteless."

"Rather tasteless? The murder of innocent children is just rather tasteless? We'll have to get into detail about taste some other time," Jack said angrily. "Until then, Colonel, maybe you didn't notice, but look over there."

Salkukoff turned in the direction Collins had indicated. His eyes widened when he saw what had made the American far paler than a moment before.

"Either we've been blown off course by about ten thousand miles and ended up off the coast of Hawaii, or we're not in Kansas anymore."

The island was green and beautiful. It sat in front of them like a postcard of some fabulous vacation spot only found in the South Pacific. Collins reached for his binoculars in their case and then raised them to his eyes. He could see birds and trees from their distance of five miles away. At this range, none of the species of bird could be discerned. The birds were just birds, but their feathered plumage was spectacular and stood out even from that distance, colors he had never seen before. The trees were an entirely different matter. They were tall and had thick branches halfway up and then at their crown. Some were the familiar palm trees, others unrecognizable. The rolling waves crashing against the island's deep brown sands were violet and gleamed in the early morning sun. The most glaring sight was the rise of a small mountain at the exact center of the island.

"Where in the world are we?"

"I think the question is, what world are we in?" Jack turned away just as Ryan walked up to report.

"Thirty-seven dead. I haven't had the time to count uniforms. But rest assured it's most everyone."

Jack patted Jason on the shoulder and then pointed to the island off their port beam.

"What the f—"

"You're a navy man. Ever seen an island like that before?"

"No. The mountain alone is far too big for any island I've ever seen outside of Hawaii. It looks like a dormant volcano. What in the hell happened, and where are we?"

Before any answers could be thought about, it was Charlie Ellenshaw who stepped free of the wheelhouse with his mouth agape. He stuttered, and when he found no voice, he just pointed.

Jack, Salkukoff, and Ryan both turned and saw the most stunning sight any of them had seen since their nightmare had begun. The setting early morning moon was still visible on the horizon. Only it wasn't exactly the moon they all remembered. The moon, which they had all stared at, kissed girls under, and marveled at her power and beauty, was still there, only it was now just a battered and smashed rock in space. Its white surface was broken into millions of smaller pieces, with the largest of these at its center. The rubble revolved around the ancient disk and spread out across the sky in a long tail of utter destruction. The moon had been smashed into gravel for the most part and looked as if the gravitational forces were turning it into a Saturn-like ring system around the largest section of the old moon.

"Colonel, may I suggest we get your Master Chief Jenks and my learned Professor Gervais down below and shut down that damn power plant before we go somewhere else we don't really want to be?"

Jack didn't answer, as he spied something that eased his mind somewhat. He pointed with a small smile on his face.

The USS *Shiloh* was breathing once again. Her engines sprang to life, and the roiling of white water churning at her stern told Jack they were once again under power.

"They're signaling, Colonel," Ryan said as he eased the binoculars from Jack's hand.

Across the distance of a mile, Collins, Charlie Ellenshaw, and Salkukoff saw the flashing signal lamp from the starboard bridge wing of *Shiloh*.

"Will come about for assistance. Pulse shielding of most electronics worked as designed. Weapons system down. Communications down. Casualties heavy." Ryan turned and faced the colonel. "They're asking if we need medical assistance." Jack only nodded, and Jason said he would get Carl to pass it along. Collins was as content as Charlie to stare at the comforting sight of the Aegis cruiser making her wide turn in the deep purple of this strange sea.

"She's also reporting that all contact with the *Houston* has been lost." Ryan lowered the field glasses and faced the colonel. He sadly handed the glasses back and then slowly walked away to help Jenks and Henri.

Jack watched the naval aviator and knew he was feeling the loss of the Dutch and American sailors on both vessels. Navy men took losses of ships very seriously.

As he turned back, Collins knew that *De Zeven* and *Houston* might not be the last to be lost. With one last look up at the shattered moon, Jack put his arm around crazy Charlie Ellenshaw, and then they went belowdecks.

"Let's see if this Russian bucket has any of that American coffee we gave to Comrade Stalin back in the day."

Ellenshaw smiled, agreeing that it would be nice to do a normal thing like drinking coffee.

As for Salkukoff, his eyes and field glasses were raised in an entirely different direction. They were trained toward the north and the line of smoke that rose from the violet-colored sea beyond the visible horizon. He only hoped it was his one remaining surface asset that he could count on.

He could only hope that *Peter the Great* was out there somewhere so he wouldn't have to use his ace in the hole.

Three hours later, *Shiloh* was tied up alongside *Simbirsk*. No fewer than ten lines held the two ships mated together as the grisly task of collecting the bodies continued. Several corpsmen from *Shiloh* made the horrid task of removing the bodies from the deck where they had melted into the pliant steel. Three of these medical corpsmen were women, and Jack was proud that they were the only three who did not continuously vomit at their tasteless task.

Jack was watching the crew of *Shiloh* as they slid the remains of the Seahawk helicopter from the fantail of *Shiloh*, where it hit the water and then vanished. Collins felt his eyes slowly closing as the sounds of men and women working coupled with the soft lapping of the strange seas against the hulls of the two ships worked to relax him for the briefest of moments. The days without sleep were getting their revenge. He felt the tap on his shoulder. He turned.

"Thought you could use some of this," Master Chief Jenks said as he handed Jack a clear glass cup of hot coffee. "Damn Russians don't have real mugs on this tub, just tea glasses."

Jack smiled as he accepted the coffee. "When we get back, we'll file an official protest with the Russian government."

Jenks nodded. He then faced the island five miles away and sipped coffee.

"Any theories or opinions?" Jack asked.

"Not a one, Colonel. But I do wish Ginny could see this ocean and that island. Be a good honeymoon spot if it weren't for the circumstances."

Collins lowered the coffee and fixed Jenks with a funny look. "I think you've got it bad, Master Chief. Imagine that the Big Bad Wolf has fallen hard for Little Red Riding Hood."

"Ah, it's nothing like that." Jenks tossed out the black coffee with a grimace on his face. Then he faced Jack. "Yeah, I guess it is like that."

Collins smiled and then nodded, finally realizing that the old crew-cut navy man actually *was* a human being.

"As for opinions and theories, I think you have to ask the nerd king about those. He has a far better grasp on that than I do."

"Charlie?" Jack asked, frowning at the taste of the burned coffee.

"He says we are not on Earth anymore—at least our Earth."

"Is that right?" Jack asked. The theory seemed to fit what they had witnessed thus far. He frowned again and then thought the better part of valor was to not drink any more of the seventy-year-old coffee, or at least coffee that was brewed inside a death ship. He handed Jenks the glass when he spied Captain Johnson on deck below them supervising the aviation fuel cleanup. He picked up the bullhorn.

"How is the chow over there?" he called out.

Johnson turned and saw the colonel for the first time. He waved and then accepted his own bullhorn. He raised it to his lips.

"The mess was the first thing we got up and running. You know the navy can't function without coffee and a sandwich to shove down their necks."

"That's why the phone call, Captain. I don't know if we can trust seventy-five-year-old canned beets and Spam."

"I get your point. I'll have the galley send over a hot meal and fresh coffee."

"How are your electronics?" he asked through the high-pitched whine of the bullhorn.

"We should have communications and radar back up within the hour. We had the necessary circuit boards in ship's stores. The weapons systems are something else. They are fried. So, for right now, we have only our .50-caliber and five-inch Bofors systems available."

Jack lowered the bullhorn in exasperation. In the strange world they found themselves in, he was not happy about the weapons situation. "Captain, we need to get together and talk. Let's get everyone on *Simbirsk* and figure out where we go from here. We should have some answers soon on just where in the hell we're at."

"Is that little toy of yours turned off?" Johnson said, not joking one bit.

"We think. But then it was turned off before this little adventure started, so we'll see."

"Then I reluctantly accept." Johnson lowered his head and then spoke again. "Also, we have over one hundred men we have to get buried. May I suggest at sunset?"

"I'll confer with our Russian guests and confirm."

Johnson waved once more and then tossed the bullhorn to a passing sailor.

Collins turned to the master chief. "I'm getting real tired of burying kids." Jack tossed the bullhorn to the deck, where Jenks retrieved it and then watched the colonel's back as he sadly moved off.

"Amen to that."

KIROV-CLASS BATTLE CRUISER *PETER THE GREAT*

Captain Kreshenko prayed that the pumping and counterflooding would work. His warship was still listing at fifteen degrees to her port side after nearly capsizing after the initial wall of water, light, and heat had struck. He had had little time in feeling sorrow for the lives lost on the escort destroyer *Admiral Levchenko*. His ship had lost almost as many crew as their doomed escort. He was down 175 men from the assault of the American weapon.

"The pumps are catching up, and the counterflooding is working, Captain," said a tired and worn Second Captain Dishlakov as he came into the shattered bridge of the giant cruiser.

Kreshenko saw the disheveled state of his first officer. The man was burned on the right side of his face, and his arm may have been broken, as he was holding his left with his right as he reported. The captain frowned as he took the man in.

"Now, your orders are to go below and get some hot soup and tea, Vasily. I'll need you in the next few hours. Have the doctor check that arm, and get something for that burn."

"I'm all right, Captain. We need to get our electronics suite up and running."

"Communications is a priority at the moment."

"What about our weapons systems?"

Kreshenko chuckled. "In case you have not noticed, my old friend, we lost. Our priority now is to communicate with Moscow and get our men home. First we have to make contact with the only naval force in the area and hope that tempers have calmed to the point where we're not shooting at each other anymore. Besides, I'm still not sure if my ship can make it home, and I am not losing any more of my men to this craziness. We'll go and find the Americans and hope we don't have to fight this thing all over again."

He saw the questioning look on Dishlakov's face and tilted his head, waiting for his response. It took him only a moment.

"Captain, what about the color of the sea, the shattered moon?"

"I have no answers for that, Vasily. I am not that sure I want to know. We have to go on the assumption that it is all explainable and that our only duty is to these men aboard our ship."

"Yes, Captain." Dishlakov turned to leave.

"Vasily?"

The first officer stopped and turned, still holding his broken arm. "Sir?"

"If we get communications up, our priority is to contact Moscow, not our dear operational commander Salkukoff. Understood?"

"I never had any intention of contacting that arrogant son of a bitch . . . sir," Dishlakov said and then saluted with his good right hand.

Kreshenko smiled at his friend and then turned his attention back to his damaged ship.

"Engine room reports engines are now operational."

The captain turned to his chief engineer and nodded. "Okay, as soon as we have propulsion, get the air defense systems up and running."

"Sir, we have no missile capability, and we won't have. We don't carry the necessary electronic stores aboard the ship. Moscow, in her infinite wisdom, never figured we would actually ever sustain damage from what we may assume was an EMP burst."

"Imagine that—Moscow miscalculated. Wonders never cease, do they? But alas, the twenty-millimeter weaponry will have to do for offense and defense, now won't it?"

"Yes, sir." The man saluted and then quickly moved away.

Kreshenko felt the powerful engines spring to life beneath his feet. He took a deep breath as the mighty ship started to breathe once more. Her powerful generators started supplying far more than emergency power, and the ship sprang to electrified life.

"Helm, all ahead slow one-third."

"Aye, all ahead slow one-third."

"Steer south-southwest, fifteen degrees. Stay on course. Let's get what weaponry we do have warmed up and ready. Let's go find the Americans."

Peter the Great started forward, her four massive bronze propellers churning the violet-colored waters at her stern.

She was going straight at the unsuspecting Americans.

10

Jack and Carl met Ezra Johnson at the gangway that had been placed between the *Simbirsk* and the *Shiloh*. It was Carl who broke the ice with the captain the navy way.

"The last time we met, Captain, I was a shavetail ensign and you were a JG, if my memory serves."

The black captain smiled politely, but Everett knew the man didn't remember some lowly SEAL from years back. Carl gestured the captain to join the team and their Russian counterparts near the fantail of the *Simbirsk*.

There had already been a flare-up between Captain Johnson and Colonel Salkukoff. Johnson refused to transfer his dead sailors over to the *Simbirsk* for burial. The exchange had become heated over the undamaged walkie-talkies when Johnson even insisted that the NATO contingent lost in the phase shift be transferred over to *Shiloh* for burial. It was Jack who had stepped in and told both parties to conduct separate services for each group. When the two men finally met face-to-face, the hatred was palpable. Johnson could not go lightly with someone who had fired on his ship and killed his men.

Johnson took his place at the table that had been set up at the fantail. Coffee and tea were served by the mess staff that Johnson had reassigned to Collins while they were aboard the *Simbirsk*.

Standing at the head of this table was an unlikely candidate to be chairing the meeting. Charlie Ellenshaw had come a long way since the Brazil mission, his very first field excursion. Crazy Charlie, a moniker that was being used less and less these days, adjusted his wire-frame glasses on his nose and then looked at Jason Ryan, who had just placed the portable Europa laptop on the table in front of Charlie. Jack caught the warning look from Jason to Charlie about the security surrounding Europa that Ellenshaw was using. The Russians could never learn about the supercomputer's abilities. Charlie nodded as much to Jack's satisfaction. The cryptozoologist looked down at Master Chief Jenks, and the cigar-chomping navy man nodded and gestured that he had the floor.

Jack watched the faces around the table. Salkukoff and Gervais were the only two Russians sitting in the meeting. Collins also noted that Henri Farbeaux was nowhere to be found. The Frenchman had been preternaturally silent during the last few hours. Jack had not questioned him about his orders from MI6 about what was expected of him. The less he knew about how and where Farbeaux would kill the Russian, the better.

"In the past few hours, we have made considerable progress in defining the technology of the phase shift equipment. I'll leave that to Master Chief Jenks and Professor Gervais, who understand the science far better than I. My task was to discover just where it is that we find ourselves." With a cautious look at Ryan, Charlie opened the laptop up and then turned it so most could see the screen.

"How fortunate you brought a laptop computer along that just happened to be shielded against an electromagnetic pulse."

The portable Europa laptop was a closed-looped system that only used the standard hard drive for computing. Although the small device was not directly linked to the enormous system in Nevada, its computing power and memory rivaled most corporation databases; therefore, this laptop did not have to breach the differing planes in order for Europa to help them. Jack started to say something in explanation to Salkukoff, but surprisingly, it was Ellenshaw who held his hand up to stop Jack's words.

"This is a military-grade system. So yes, it is shielded."

Salkukoff didn't say anything else. He just nodded in Collins's direction as if to say, *Touché.*

"As I was saying, by directing our camera to the sky, our system was able to determine without a doubt that we are indeed on Earth. Not only that, the phase shift has done nothing other than alter the plane of existence. The time and distance is a constant. Nothing has changed."

"Time and distance?" Salkukoff asked.

"Yes. What Professor Ellenshaw is saying is that we have not lost one minute of one day in the shift. It is the same date, the same time. Just our surroundings have changed."

Salkukoff looked at the Russian professor and nodded.

On the computer's screen was a picture of Earth with the representation Charlie and Europa Jr. had figured out for what their current Earth looked like. All heads leaned forward.

"As you can see, based on temperature and because of the shattering of the moon, the world is possibly covered in water with only the highest peaks on our maps showing. For instance, the island we see to the east is part of the Challenger Rise series of mountains in the North Atlantic. These mountains in our world are close to a mile below the surface of the sea. This tells us that somewhere in this world there are differing high water marks, perhaps brought on by massive earth movements and displacement. We just don't have any of the answers yet."

The screen was dotted with sparse islands of land speckled throughout.

"Where are the landmasses of our world?" Johnson asked. "I've climbed Mount Rainier, so where is it? Where are the Adirondacks? Where are the Blue Ridge Mountains?"

"From Professor Gervais's and my own calculations, with the assistance of Master Chief Jenks, we have come to the conclusion that whatever happened to the moon destroyed most of the landmasses we know from our own Earth. Entire mountain ranges were swallowed whole. The Earth shifted on its axis, and we have what we see here today. We don't have definitive answers here, gentlemen. It's best-guess only, no real science to back us up. If we just had one or two weather satellites, we could get more concrete answers, but in the alternate world we find ourselves in, those satellites were never launched. We are truly on our own."

"What about the ocean? Why violet?" Everett asked.

"We have analyzed the seawater. The color is produced through a series of different factors." Charlie brought out a graph prepared by the portable

Europa. He unfurled a long roll of paper. "As you can see, we have a varying number of different contaminants, from volcanic, sea life, and other organic minerals. Why violet? Your guess is as good as ours.

"That's all we have on our environment for now," Charlie said as he sat down and looked at Jenks, who made no move to stand up. He puffed on his cigar and then fixed Salkukoff with a withering glare. That look was followed by Henri pulling out a chair and sitting next to Ryan. Everett looked at Jack, and for some reason that look made the colonel wonder just what the Frenchman had come up with during his absence.

"The phase shift generator and application nodules have been disabled."

"Application nodules?" Jason asked.

Jenks puffed on his cigar and then fixed Ryan with his intense stare. "Those lightbulb-looking thingamajigs, young captain. It seems our Russian allies were a little more advanced in 1944 than we were ever led to believe," he said while fixing that stare onto Salkukoff. "It seems they had access to weapons-grade uranium long before we thought it possible."

"I cannot answer for that; it was a little before my time," Salkukoff said with a smirk.

Collins watched Henri as the Russian spoke. He was convinced that at least the Frenchman knew the Russian colonel was lying.

"Well, I took some scrapings from the conductor," Jenks continued with a warning look toward Jack, "and what I saw was a bit surprising. The core material came from our own Hanford nuclear facility, the same batch as supplied to the University of Chicago and signed for by Professor Fermi himself. I would say someone of ill intentions grabbed some for comrade Salkukoff's distant relatives."

"How did you come to that conclusion, Master Chief?" Salkukoff asked.

"As I'm sure you know, comrade, every breeder reactor leaves fingerprints. That's how we verified your atomic program in the '50s was a legitimate concern. Your original stockpiles came in from the Ukraine. During our phase shift experiments, they didn't have the correct power settings on board the USS *Eldridge* to get them anywhere but the shortest way to kill close to two hundred sailors. The Russians came along with a vast improvement, as they were able to get by the power restraints with the addition of stolen American enhanced uranium."

"Yes, yes, the evil Russians once again thwart the forces of good in a time of war," Salkukoff said as he tossed a pencil on the table. "I find your tone accusing and unacceptable. This should not concern us here, Master Chief Jenks. Can we get the cursed thing back on, and can we get home?"

"We have yet to determine that."

Jenks waved to Charlie that he was done. He angrily threw his cigar over the railing.

"I want to know what this gentleman's intentions are toward my NATO assignment," Captain Johnson said. He had gotten a full measure of Salkukoff, and the captain found the Russian to be most disagreeable. The captain stood up and faced the Russian. "You fired upon my ship, sir."

Salkukoff shot Jack a look as if Collins had betrayed him. Jack decided he wasn't playing his game.

"I think the captain deserves an answer."

Salkukoff kept his eyes on Collins. Then he too stood and faced Johnson.

"You and your NATO allies were in the process of stealing Russian state property. We stopped you from doing so—and will do so again at the conclusion of our mutual predicament."

"That is an unacceptable—" Johnson began, but the emergency siren from *Shiloh* started blaring.

A runner came up and handed Johnson a message flimsy. His look from message to Russian was clear. He wadded the paper up and threw it at Salkukoff. Collins watched all of this as he stood.

"What is it?" he asked.

"*Peter the Great* has been spotted on the horizon; she's coming on full speed."

Collins looked at Salkukoff. "I think you'd better establish communications, Colonel, before your people start something none of us will survive."

"You'll excuse me if I don't wait for this bastard to do the right thing. I have a ship and crew to protect." Johnson left the table and ran for the gangway.

As the others gathered at the railing to watch the crew frantically throwing off lines, it was Salkukoff who came up to Jack and held out a handheld radio.

"Tell your Captain Johnson that *Peter the Great* has their orders; there will be no confrontation."

Jack eyed the radio and then fixed Salkukoff with that blue-eyed glare that made the Russian very uncomfortable.

"You'll excuse me if I side with Captain Johnson. Your trust points have slipped in the past hour. I think he's going to err on the side of caution."

Salkukoff smiled and then lowered his radio.

"*Peter the Great* is flashing a signal," Everett said as he looked toward the horizon and the small pinpoint that was the giant cruiser as it steamed their way.

"She's asking for a cessation of hostilities," Carl said as he lowered his binoculars.

"Yes, Captain Kreshenko will follow orders. You can tell your nervous Captain Johnson we mean no harm."

Jack remained looking at Salkukoff and then lifted his radio. "Captain, stand down."

He saw the form of Johnson stop and then look back to the *Simbirsk*. Collins saw the captain staring up at him. Then the alarms stopped. Jack saw men lining the railing with small arms, and the .50-caliber and twenty-millimeter weapons started tracking *Peter the Great* as she came on.

"If that bucket has a working missile system, it doesn't matter what we end up believing," Everett said as he came up and stood by Jack.

"Forget it, Toad; they're as useless on board that ship as they are on board *Shiloh*. If they were working, our little Russian ass over there would be a little more forceful in his welcoming of his boys."

"I hope you're right, Jenks," Jack said. "If not, I just ordered those men to stand down and die."

"He's not wrong. Salkukoff would never give away an advantage like that. He'll wait to attack us when we get ready to attempt leaving. He will hope to leave us here."

They all turned and looked at Farbeaux as he approached.

"He'll do nothing as long as we have most of the brainpower working to get us home."

"What makes you—" Ryan started to say.

"I'll leave that to you, Colonel."

Ryan looked at Jack and wondered what it was he knew that his security department didn't. Then he looked at the cold way Henri was looking at the back of Salkukoff. Collins broke away from the Americans.

"Colonel, flash message *Peter the Great*. Lay up alongside *Shiloh* and have this Captain Kreshenko join us aboard *Simbirsk*."

"Wise decision, Colonel."

Jack didn't say anything as Salkukoff passed along the message. He walked away where he was joined by Farbeaux and Everett.

"Jack, it's damn obvious this Salkukoff is out to get their little science project back."

Collins looked from Carl to Henri.

"That is exactly what our friend here is going to stop, preferably in the nick of time."

Henri said nothing as he watched the specter of *Peter the Great* grow ever bigger as she approached.

"What is it, Colonel?" Carl asked when Farbeaux said nothing.

"I believe it will be a matter of who kills who first." Henri smiled that unsettling smile he had. "Number one, he knows exactly why I am here. Number two, he has the same death order as we do. Only his is far more encompassing in scope. Whoever is pulling this man's strings has given him orders to kill us all."

Henri Farbeaux let that sink into the Americans' psyche as he walked away and joined Charlie Ellenshaw. Jack, Carl, and Jason Ryan watched the Frenchman leave.

"What do you think, Jack?" Carl asked.

Collins laughed aloud as he watched Captain Johnson unhappily order his crewmen to tie *Shiloh* back up to *Simbirsk*.

"What do I think? I think we'd better listen to that man's opinion when he says Salkukoff is out to secure this ship." He turned and faced his two friends. "And when it comes to lying and killing, Henri has the upper hand on us all. I think I'll go with the colonel's hunch."

Everett exchanged looks with Ryan.

"Oh, that makes me all jittery inside."

"We're in trouble, aren't we?"

"No, of course not," Carl answered as Jack walked away. "We have our intrepid hero Farbeaux calling the shots. What could possibly go wrong?"

Jason looked down at the violet waters of this strange sea. He said nothing about the pessimistic view shared by the captain. He looked again at the water and the far-off island.

"Okay, Mendenhall, this is one time I would be happy to trade places with you."

In the far-off distance, *Peter the Great* started blasting her collision horn, announcing her imminent arrival.

Suddenly, the strange violet sea of this new world was getting ever more crowded.

LOS ANGELES–CLASS ATTACK SUBMARINE USS *HOUSTON*

Captain Thorne accepted the clean shirt from his XO. He started to put it on and then saw that Gary Devers was waiting.

"Oh, sorry. The two bodies have been removed, and we managed to get the outer doors closed to the forward torpedo compartment. The torpedo room is useless to us. The aft torpedo room has been pumped free of water and will be operational within the next four hours."

"I'll trade the torpedo room for ballast control in a heartbeat."

Thorne finished buttoning his shirt and then faced his XO. "Still no luck?"

"We're trying to cross match the circuit boards from fire suppression to ballast control. No luck thus far. We do have good news on communications. We were able to get the radio up, and the ELF is breathing again. Nothing but static."

"After we get the remaining forward spaces clear of water, try the boards from the pumps. Strip them if you have to. We'll have just one shot at getting off this shelf, and I want all options covered as best as we can get." Thorne left the aft torpedo room before the corpsman and his men cleared the two bodies, which was something Thorne wanted not to see at the moment.

"Skipper?"

Thorne stopped and waited for Devers.

"The crew thinks we were nuked. Or at the very least our surface fleet was nuked. I think they need a word."

"A word about what? That we don't know anything yet?"

"I was thinking—"

"Stop thinking, Commander. Let the crew think what they want at this time. We don't know what happened, and I'm not about to lie to them and say it was the hurricane—which, by the way, according to water conditions, has vanished. Why do I want to scare these kids any more than they already are?"

"I see your point, Skipper."

Thorne was starting to turn away when he stopped and lowered his head. He turned with a half smile on his lips.

"Gary, right now I'm afraid my voice will betray the fact that I'm as scared as hell. That won't help anyone. I want them, hell, I *need* them to believe we can get this boat up and out of here, not what it is they will face when we do surface."

"Yes, Skipper, I understand."

Thorne smiled and then turned away. He picked up a phone outside the aft torpedo room after he heard his engineering officer ask for him.

"Thorne."

"*Reactors are breathing again, Captain,*" reported the reactor officer.

Before Thorne could answer, he heard the main ventilators kick in. He felt the cool air and closed his eyes. He then heard the washing machines in a far-off compartment start up and a loud cheer erupted throughout the boat. He opened his eyes at the sound of cheering, and then he winked at XO Devers. One of his biggest worries was the horrible thought that after both his reactors had scrammed, they wouldn't be able to get them back up. He felt the relief flood through him just as the main lighting came blaring to full life.

Devers watched as Thorne lowered the phone without saying anything further to the reactor officer. He eased the phone from Thorne's hand.

"Well done, Lieutenant. Now let's see if we can get ballast control back up. One step at a time, boys. One step at a time." He reached out and hung up the phone. He saw Thorne was still holding his head down, and the first officer knew his captain was relieving himself of some of the doubts that had crept into his thinking. He saw his shoulders slump and knew he was trying to control his emotions. He patted the captain on the back and moved forward without him.

"To all crew members. The movie tonight will be *Poseidon* starring Kurt Russell. All personnel off duty may attend."

Devers heard the crew give out a cheer. He knew it was just an announcement, but it was a normal announcement. And that was good.

USS *Houston* was not only breathing once again—it was starting to come back to life.

11

KIROV-CLASS BATTLE CRUISER *PETER THE GREAT*

The motor launch ferrying Captain Kreshenko and his first officer over to the *Simbirsk* rode lightly over the small swells of ocean. Sailors from *Shiloh* lined her rails after transferring freshwater to the old Russian cruiser to see the great warship up close. Her missile launchers gleamed in the late afternoon sunlight. She was prickled with defensive armaments that looked far more operational than their own. They watched as the Russian sailor tossed one of the Americans a line until Kreshenko and Dishlakov could hop from the whaleboat to the gangway. They were met at the top by Colonel Salkukoff. The three men saluted, and then the colonel gestured for them to follow. Introductions were made, and then the inevitable confrontation between warring sea captains reared its ugly head. Johnson refused to salute the Russian captain.

"What gave you the right to fire upon my ships and aircraft?" Johnson asked angrily.

"The right of any captain to defend his territory, and this ship is Russian territory." Kreshenko gave Captain Johnson a wide berth.

"That subject will remain closed for the moment, gentlemen. We're here to find out if we can get these sailors home without killing everyone."

All eyes went to Jack Collins. Of the eleven men standing at the fantail, it was Kreshenko who looked perplexed.

"What do you mean?" he asked Salkukoff in Russian. The quick exchange registered with everyone when the color drained from Kreshenko's features.

He leaned against the steel cable that wound around the *Simbirsk*. He looked to be in shock.

Jack took this time to face Captain Johnson. "Look, I know you are angry, Captain. But I need cooperation from these men. Until I get it, you will cease trying to pick a fight that we cannot win at the moment. Besides, you're accusing the wrong man of firing on your assets. The man you want, the one who gave orders, is that man right there."

Johnson saw that Collins was pointing at Salkukoff. Johnson grimaced, but he quickly relented and just nodded.

As the group settled in once again around the table, it was Jack who tried to calm things down and bring the men leading this insanity to some form of compromise. He specifically looked at Henri Farbeaux. He had not said much since meeting Salkukoff in person, and Jack knew that not knowing what was on in the Frenchman's mind usually led to major trouble.

"Captain, welcome aboard. While we can argue rights of salvage forever, I believe the problem at hand should take precedence."

There were nods around the table, but mostly from the American contingent. The Russians placed poker faces on their countenances.

"Captain, I am proud to say that Master Chief Jenks, Captain Everett, Mr. Ryan, and I served with your half brother during the Overlord operation."

Captain Kreshenko stood and nodded toward Jack and then simply sat down.

"Before we get into our mutual problem, we have to discuss the defensive posture while we are in this situation. Captain, may I assume you are having the same difficulties as ourselves in regard to the EMP invasion of our integrated systems?"

Kreshenko looked at Salkukoff, who gestured that he should answer the question.

"Yes, all defensive and offensive missile weapons systems are down. We don't have the necessary replacement boards in ship's stores. Like your *Shiloh*, we have only close-in weapons. Basically, small arms."

"Thank you, Captain, for being honest. As you may have heard, we are in the same boat, no pun intended."

Kreshenko looked at Salkukoff, and he said that the small pun was nothing to even think about. It seemed the American sense of humor evaded the Russian captain.

"We currently have both weapons officers from *Peter the Great* and *Shiloh* evaluating the sixteen-inch gun system aboard *Simbirsk*. They seem to think those big guns might do us more harm than good if we attempt to fire them. They'll keep going on their evaluations until they are told otherwise."

"Captain Johnson, with your command boards for the Aegis system down, do you still have drone capability?" Jack asked, trying to get Johnson back on track as far as cooperation went.

"We had to change out transmitter boards on the Raytheon drone. We cannibalized three personal cell phones and a navy satellite phone, but she'll be up and running within the hour."

"Good. We'll need it. I want that island scouted." Jack turned to Salkukoff. "Colonel, now that we know that weapons-grade uranium was used in the process for the phase shift experiment, how safe is it for my people and yours to be working around it?"

"I would think at this point safety is the least of our concerns. Are not all hands expendable in this endeavor?"

Most faces registered shock around the makeshift conference table. Jack remained standing while facing down this cold-blooded man he knew was not hesitant to kill or maim those in his way. Jack leaned forward with his hands planted firmly upon the tabletop.

"Let me make this clear to you, Colonel: where we come from, no one is expendable. You may blame politicians or think-tank generals, but never assume a field commander will ever give up the life of his people willingly. I repeat, there are no expendables on this or any ship here."

Salkukoff just smiled. He nodded at Jack, and the colonel felt the Russian was merely mocking him. If truth be told, he felt like shooting the bastard right in front of everyone.

"Radar. Both *Peter the Great* and *Shiloh*. Gentlemen, not knowing what's out here can kill us all. Besides the drone, we need an early warning system up and running. Captains, make that a priority." He faced Captain Kreshenko and his first officer, Dishlakov. "Captain, right now, we have to throw off any animosity we may have toward each other. If we cease our cooperation, none of our men, mine or yours, will ever see home again. For most of us around this table, that may not affect too many lives. But we all have kids out there who do have families, who do love their children, and they want to get home. They don't want to get into a pissing contest. That stuff is for the real world, not this one."

Kreshenko looked at Dishlakov. Barely understanding the language, he raised his brows in question.

"He means we don't need to see who has the biggest muscles," Charlie said, clarifying the "pissing contest" comment.

Jack was just getting ready to get people back to work when again alarm bells started to sound, and men started running to prepositioned action stations aboard *Simbirsk*.

"Watercraft coming in from the south!" an American lookout from *Shiloh* shouted.

Jack and the others went to the railing. Carl handed Collins a pair of field glasses.

"Where away?" Carl called out as he raised his own glasses to his eyes.

"Ten points off the stern," a Russian sailor called out.

Jack had trouble finding them. Then Everett nudged Jack. "To the right, coming right at us."

Collins adjusted his view, and there they were.

"Holy shit," Ellenshaw said as he became excited and wrested the binoculars from Master Chief Jenks, who scowled.

"Look at them all," Captain Kreshenko said aloud. "Amazing. It's as though we are in the South Pacific."

Seven hundred yards away, riding low in the water, the reason for them to get so close without the lookouts seeing them, were at least a hundred small boats. Some were larger than others, but most were no more than thirty-five feet long. They had sails and outriggers, the sort used by fishermen all around the world. The sails were brightly colored in flashes of orange, blue, and yellow. The larger of these boats rode in the center of the teeming mass. The smaller boats surrounded the larger in a protective cocoon.

"Count?" Jack asked as he scanned the insides of the boats for the first time.

"I have one hundred and twelve small boats and six large. No armaments visible," Everett called out.

"I have the same count," said Dishlakov.

Charlie was aghast. "Armaments?" He quickly moved away from the railing and faced Jack. "Colonel, it's obvious that these people are fishermen. These people are like the Jundiai fishermen in the Galapagos Islands. They use the larger boats for hauling the smaller boats' catches. That's all. Colonel, do these people no harm."

"Calm down, Charlie," Collins said as he centered his glasses on the largest, middle boat.

"My God. Look at their skin color," Dishlakov said.

Collins focused and saw that the skin color was perfectly white. The people were small, maybe five foot or a little more, and their hair was blond. As the boats came closer, the men on the *Simbirsk* could see the newcomers' curiosity was as great as their own. Heads moved, popped up, and they jabbered, but they soon calmed as they came alongside *Simbirsk*.

The fishermen came close, but their sails remained unfurled, and they slowly started to slide past the giant warship.

"Mud—they use it to protect their skin from the sun and sea. That's why they're white skinned." Charlie turned to Jack and Carl with a large smile on his face. "They're almost prehistoric. This is amazing!"

Several of the officers lining the railing stepped back when they heard Ellenshaw's words of excitement. They all had the same smiles and inquisitive looks on their faces as they watched the strange, thin, white-haired man dance a jig. Jack couldn't help it; he smiled at Everett. Charlie was in his element. He lost his smile when Charlie started waving his hands in greeting.

Jack watched the first of the boats slide past. The small fishermen of the largest boat just looked up at them, less excited to see the strangers than they were to see *them*. As Collins watched on, the small man standing at the front of his boat—Collins could see that this was their leader—simply watched the strangers in their high perch on board *Simbirsk*. The thin, bearded man looked up, and their eyes met. Still the boats silently slid by. All eyes of this indigenous people looked up with what could only be described as mild curiosity. They saw the large men looking down on them as they sailed past with their massive haul of fish, but the strangers held no more interest to them than a large log in the water would in regard to their safely navigating their way.

Charlie became quiet as the last of the boats slid by and toward the island five miles away.

"What is it, Charlie?" Jack asked.

"The fish inside the larger of the boats. I didn't recognize any species. Of course, I was not as close as I would have liked to have been. Still, I failed to recognize any of those fish."

"Captain, what do you say we get that drone in the air and see what our fishermen are up to on that island?"

Johnson nodded and left.

Jack's eyes then went to Colonel Salkukoff. The man was just watching the fishing fleet as they became smaller as they went home. His eyes finally looked up, and he saw the American looking at him. The Russian held the look momentarily, and then Jack watched him walk away with Captain Kreshenko in tow.

Carl and Farbeaux came up to Jack, and they all watched the Russians walk away.

"Gentlemen, what are your impressions of Captain Kreshenko and his man Dishlakov?"

"Typical Russian Navy," Carl said as he watched the retreating backs of the Russians.

"There is hatred, or at the very least a stern dislike there, I think," Farbeaux offered.

"I agree. Kreshenko didn't fire on *Shiloh* and her escorts, and he didn't order us shot down. That order came from Salkukoff, and the Russian captain resents it."

"Precisely my thoughts," Farbeaux said.

"Henri, I wasn't too thrilled with that order MI6 passed on to you. No man should be placed in that situation." Jack turned and faced the Frenchman. "But that man cannot return with us. I think the world would be a better place without him."

No more words were said as the announcement was heard coming from *Shiloh*.

"Prepare to launch drone."

TICONDEROGA-CLASS AEGIS MISSILE CRUISER USS *SHILOH*

An hour later, Captain Johnson was throwing a fit. A US Marine guard stood in front of the hatch leading to the combat information center and refused to allow the two Russians inside the extensive and far-reaching advanced electronic center. Pictures and visitors were not ever allowed inside because they could compromise the security of the Aegis combat system. No Russian had ever even seen a drawing of the advanced radar and control apparatus.

"Captain, I will take full responsibility. Make sure none of your Aegis systems are in operation for the duration of their visit. Nothing but dark screens. But they must be allowed inside so they can independently verify what it is the drone will see. We need their trust and cooperation. Master Chief Jenks and their Professor Gervais are pretty close to discovering why that damn phase shift engine keeps coming on by itself. We will eventually need it to turn on when we want it to. For that, we need Gervais. He knows more about the mechanics involved than the master chief."

"Stand down," Johnson told the two marines. "I will enter the visit in the ship's logbook."

Jack watched the captain open the hatch, and then he and the others went into the most highly secretive compartment in any US Navy vessel—the Aegis Control Room.

Everett nodded when he saw that not only were the monitors and main screen of Aegis shut down, they were also covered with tarps to keep the Russians from viewing the Aegis brain. Carl's eyes went from Salkukoff to the Russian seamen. The captain and Dishlakov were wide-eyed at the CIC. This was nothing compared to what they had to work with. Kreshenko could not believe they lived in the same advanced world as the Americans.

"The time is coming where we will have such toys, Captain."

Kreshenko looked down and saw that it was Salkukoff who had spoken.

"The question then is, how many people will he kill to get this technology?" Dishlakov said as he joined his captain. Kreshenko said nothing but watched as the colonel walked away and stood next to Collins.

"What have you got, Mr. Franks?" Johnson said as he approached a console with a lone officer manning a joystick. The large main display screen was on, and all eyes went there.

"Approaching the island right now, Captain. Professor Ellenshaw, you requested contaminant readings—we have them here." The remote control pilot, a lieutenant, pointed to data scrolling across the screen in bright green letters. "Our sensors are within 5 percent plus or minus accuracy. They were just recalibrated before we left for Operation Reforger IV."

Charlie adjusted his glasses, and Jack watched the green lettering scroll across his wire-rimmed glasses.

"No radiation and no contaminant particulate," Charlie mumbled as Jack tried to hear. "No pollution of any kind." Again, Ellenshaw pushed his glasses back up. "I wish the master chief were here. I think he would find this ash count interesting."

"Why?" Salkukoff asked before Jack could.

"Sulfides, fluorides, and pumice—a lot of volcanic discharge. If I didn't know better"—he turned and smiled at Jack—"I would say that we were looking at what the air quality would have looked like during the early Bronze Age. Heavy volcanic activity is the indicator."

"In the North Atlantic?" Carl asked.

Ellenshaw smiled. "You mean our North Atlantic, or this one?" Charlie sniffed and then saw that Carl wasn't smiling.

"Look at that beach," one of the US Navy crewmen said as he pointed at a scene that looked as if it had been taken recently at one of the more fabulous Hawaiian resorts. The beach was wide, and the sands were the color of soft mocha chocolate. The drone rose higher. The beach was littered with palm fronds and other detritus that scattered on dry land after a major storm. They all noticed that the hurricane had touched this world as it had in their own. Most wondered if it was the same hurricane that had affected their world and started by the *Simbirsk*.

The palm trees were the predominant species of plant in and around the beach area. The more the drone flew into the island's interior, the more varied the species. Plants of every size and shape engulfed the green island.

"Look at that," Everett said as the drone passed over a large village.

From an altitude of eight hundred feet, the Raytheon propeller-driven drone displayed an amazing sight. The village was huge. Grass huts, some large, some small. Community buildings and boats. A large, violet stream-fed lagoon at its center. But most amazing of all were the hundreds upon hundreds of men, women, and children going about their late-afternoon chores. Fish cleaning, boat repair, children playing, and wives cooking. The camera zoomed in, and they saw these people closely for the first time. They were heavily tanned, and there were indeed several varying races of humans. All small, but some were tanned heavily, or Caucasian as far as they could see, while others were black.

"Mixed raced. That in and of itself means we are in a very special place."

Jack looked at Charlie, who studied the scene far below the drone with a rapturous eye.

"How do you mean, Doc?"

"I mean, in our own shared history, differing races rarely mixed before the advent of trade and travel. This . . . this is amazing."

"There could be another explanation, Doc," Everett said aloud.

Charlie again pushed his glasses up on his nose and then turned and faced the captain.

"What is that?"

"Mutual defense against a common enemy," Salkukoff said.

The men around the remote control console became quiet as the drone moved over the large village. Only Salkukoff looked annoyed at the direction of the summarization by Ellenshaw.

Ryan entered the CIC and joined the group.

"Colonel, according to Charlie's data," he leaned in and whispered, "we have four hours until sunset. Maybe we should take a Zodiac over and introduce ourselves. As the security liaison on this mission, I find it vital to see if this asshole is right about a common enemy. Because if these peaceful-looking fishermen have bad guys they're afraid of, I have a feeling we won't like them very much ourselves."

Before Jack could comment on Ryan's suggestion, the remote operator brought the drone to a higher altitude, and then all conversation stopped.

On the large monitor, a long line of natives was returning from the large mountain that rose high at the center of the island. The trail they traveled was wide and worn. The travelers upon this road had large baskets strapped to their foreheads, and those baskets were large enough that they ended only at the smalls of their backs.

"Well, it looks like they have more than just fishermen. Is that villagers gathering food from the mountainside?" Jack asked aloud.

"No, I don't think so," Charlie said as he squinted toward the screen. "Lieutenant, could you get a better shot at a lower altitude?"

The naval officer complied, and the picture from the drone's camera system shifted as the operator sent the sixteen-foot-long aircraft into a shallow dive and then brought the zoom lens in tight on the long line of women, children, and men.

"Not gatherers." Charlie looked away from the picture and then faced Jack. "Mining, perhaps." He pushed his glasses back upon the upper portion of his nose.

"Well, we suspect fishing, and now they may be mining something. Ryan is right; maybe we'd better get in a boat and make a courtesy call on our hosts. They didn't seem hostile up close, at least the fishermen didn't," Jack said as he faced his team as the remote drone rose back up into the sky and then circled the large village.

"Uh-oh," the remote control officer said as they all looked at the screen. "I think our little spy mission has been found out."

On the screen, all the faces of the villagers were turned skyward as the miners made their way into the camp. All eyes were turned upward as the noise of the propellers cutting the air gave them away.

"Sorry, Captain. Flew a little too low."

Women scrambled to get their children inside. Men and others pointed toward the drone and gestured animatedly.

"Bring her back to the barn. We're scaring these people," Johnson said, slapping the young lieutenant JG on the back.

"I think we should not concern ourselves with these island people nor fear scaring them. They have nothing to do with our predicament."

Jack looked from the retreating drone on the screen to Salkukoff. He thought about not saying anything but decided that he really despised this man.

"Colonel, we like to learn things. Aren't you Russians always saying knowledge is power?"

"Yes, we are, Colonel Collins. But we also have a limit to cooperating with people who don't make it a priority to return to our own world. I suggest we concentrate on getting the phase shift equipment operational and leave this place."

The colonel got up and abruptly left the CIC. After a moment, Kreshenko and Dishlakov stood to follow. The captain paused and faced Jack.

"Colonel, I would very much like to accompany your landing party if you'll have me."

Jack only nodded his assent. The Russian captain returned the gesture and then made for the hatch.

"Captain?"

Kreshenko faced Collins once more.

"Make sure your boss comes along also."

The Russian raised a brow and then placed his saucer cap on his head and left with Dishlakov right behind him.

Once outside, the Russian XO turned to his captain.

"Why does he want Salkukoff with you?"

The captain smiled. "Because Colonel Collins feels the same as ourselves. He knows Salkukoff cannot be trusted. And that the man is possibly insane."

Dishlakov watched the captain leave to prepare to accompany Collins and his shore party.

"Stand by to launch Zodiac. Marine force X-ray report to departure ramp."

The USS *Shiloh* prepared for their first friendly invasion of a country not of their own world.

The large Zodiac held twenty-five men: Jack, Ryan, Everett, Henri, Jenks, Farbeaux, Charlie Ellenshaw, Second Captain Dishlakov, Captain Kreshenko, and Colonel Salkukoff, accompanied by seven US Marines, four British Royal Marines, one navy motorman, and three Russian commandos. They sped toward the island. Jack had ordered the officers to only carry small arms. The US Marines carried their sidearms and M4 assault rifles, the British their ever-present Heckler & Koch automatic assault rifles. The Russians had the standard-issue stockless AK-47. Jack had specifically ordered the M60 machine gun removed from the mount at the head of the rubber boat.

The Zodiac made little noise as the 150-horsepower motor allowed the Zodiac to slide along the top of the violet seas efficiently. Jack watched the shoreline as it grew ever larger. There was no one on the beach throwing spears at them. *At least not yet*, he thought. Still this new world seemed so preternaturally silent. Collins turned and faced the security element of their landing party.

"The NATO marine and Russian security detail will stand by the boat and keep radio contact. The officers will approach the village alone. We don't need the natives getting jumpy. Remember, we still do not know if this is the first time they will have encountered people from our world." He shot Salkukoff a look, and the Russian just smirked knowingly as always. "So, your element will secure the boat and listen for signs of trouble."

The Zodiac actually picked up speed the closer to the brown sands they got. The bow struck the softness of the beach, and then the rubber craft slid easily and noiselessly onto the shore. Jenks was the first one out. He quickly tied the boat off on a tree trunk that had floated onto the silent shores and then looked at the screening palm trees that guarded the interior like a wall of browns and greens.

"What a sight," Jenks said as Charlie joined him. "Ginny would have loved this."

Ellenshaw smiled when the master chief mentioned Virginia. Charlie had yet to express to the assistant director how pleased he was for her and the gruff lifelong navy man.

"Of course, she would be complaining that these folks have it bad because they don't have lights and a running toilet, but other than that, I think she would love this joint. Hell, Doc"—he slapped Charlie on the back, nearly dislodging his glasses—"this is better than old Subic Bay on a Saturday night!"

Ellenshaw really didn't understand the reference about the wild naval base in the Philippines of yesteryear. He just smiled for the master chief and his impending happiness.

"Great place for a Marriott," Jason Ryan said as he took in the beauty of the scene before him.

"Oh, come on. Only a navy man like you would put a damn tourist trap in a place like this," Jack said as he placed his hands on his hips and studied the terrain. "Gunny, place two men just inside the tree line and wait for our return." He turned and faced all the security element. "There are to be no outward hostile acts. We're visitors here and come uninvited, so act accordingly." Jack noticed only the British Royal Marines and their American counterparts nodded. The Russian commandos looked to Salkukoff for confirmation.

Kreshenko interpreted Jack's orders for the benefit of the Russian commandos.

"Rules of engagement, Colonel?" the gunnery sergeant asked.

Collins looked around at the tranquillity of the island. "Yes, your ROE is this: run if fired upon or confronted in any way. We'll hook up by radio if things go south. These people are not to be harmed for any reason."

"No shooting," the large marine said, loud enough that everyone heard, even the black-clad Russian element.

Jack waved the officers forward, and the visiting team stepped into a world that had not existed on their own planet in over one hundred thousand years.

12

Collins, Everett, Ryan, and the other professional military personnel felt the eyes on them from the moment they stepped into the trees lining the brown shores. They moved steadily through the exotic landscape, with Charlie Ellenshaw the only member of the landing team to actually stop and appreciate the vast array of botany and fauna that no longer existed on their own plane of existence.

"Colonel, some of this vegetation and many species of flower have not existed in our world for many thousands of years," he said as he gently held a flower up that none of them had ever seen before. "This is a far more familiar landscape of Antarctica two hundred thousand years ago than is indicative of today's fauna."

Jack turned and faced Ellenshaw and placed a finger to his lips in a shushing gesture. He glanced at the Russians. The three men acted as though they failed to hear the professor's observation, but he wasn't so sure. For all he knew, Salkukoff knew all about their little time travel journey into the past. Nonetheless, Charlie got the hint.

"Tell me, Doc, why do you think this fauna survived here and not on our world?" Ryan asked. Jack knew he did it to get the conversation off Antarctica.

"My main suspect would be, of course, pollution and oxygen content. They haven't had to deal with greenhouse gases and contaminants the way our world has."

As Jack moved through the bush, he suspected that Charlie's observations were right on.

There was movement ahead, and Everett held up a fist, bringing the small safari to a stop. Carl went down to one knee and waited. It wasn't long before the crashing of bush and leaf became louder, and then they all heard the sound of laughing. They all knew the sound of children.

Jack looked back at the three Russians. Salkukoff was the only one who had drawn his gun. Collins caught his attention and shook his head and held his gaze until the colonel replaced the weapon into his shoulder holster. The look lasted a moment longer as Salkukoff continued to stare at Jack.

Before Everett could react, a child burst through a stand of small trees and right into his thick arms. The young boy was followed by two giggling girls of about the same age. After Carl caught the boy, he fell backward until the child was on top of him. The girls crashed into the scene, and that was when the startled screaming started.

"Damn!" Collins hissed. For the first time in years, he was caught off guard and was slow to react. How do you stop little girls from screaming without scaring them even further? As he watched, frozen to his spot, he saw that Carl was doing the only thing he knew to do. He held his hands up in the air, allowing the boy child to stand up and scramble backward. The two girls took their partner by the hand and then quickly disappeared into the underbrush of jungle-like trees and undergrowth. Carl fought to his feet with his eyes wide.

"I think you scared her, Captain," Salkukoff said as he stood from where he had been kneeling.

"Well, I—"

Everett caught Jack's look, and it wasn't because he was staring at him. It was the fifteen long, pointed spears that poked through the small palms and bushes. Collins pointed, and Everett turned right into the sharpest spear tip he had ever seen. Again, and for the second time in as many seconds, he raised his hands into the air and took a step back.

The Russians backed away, as did Charlie and Ryan. Jenks, Carl, and Jack held their ground but stood stock-still and didn't flinch, and they all had their open hands in the air. After only a few steps, Captain Kreshenko felt the jab of a sharp object in his back, and he slowly turned, raising his own hands into the air.

Jack turned in time to see a small man with blond hair and brown skin step from the bush. He held no spear. He wore breeches made of some sort of fish-type skin and nothing from the waist up. He had a very lethal knife in a scabbard on his hip, and his necklace was made from small seashells. The brightly colored bird feathers were placed at varying intervals into his blond hair. Charlie started to lower his hands when he saw the inhabitants up close without their protective coating of mud. He thought they were a magnificent mixed race of people. He started to smile as his hands came down until five more of the native men stepped from the line of trees. Their ten-foot-long harpoon-like spears were held at the ready. Charlie placed his hands back into the air.

"Gentlemen, don't move an inch. I think they're more concerned about their children than they are us." Collins smiled as best he could under the circumstances and nodded.

The blond-haired leader, whose hair was done in braids, looked from the Russians to Jack and then moved forward, unafraid of the strangers. As he did, fifteen more of the fishermen stepped onto the trail.

"Oh, crap," Charlie said, watching history come alive for him once more. His field assignments had been of the most startling kind of late.

"Hang in there, Doc," Jenks said as he eyed the weaponry aimed at them. He saw a bow and arrow aimed their way and spears longer than most American Indian lances he had ever seen in museums. "These aren't weapons the way we think of them. They're tools to these people."

"Well, I don't see them as a hammer or nails," Ryan said as he took a step back from an advancing fishing spear. "That spear tip looks sharp."

The leader of this advanced scout team stepped forward. His tilted head and his curious expression fixed on Collins. The man, who stood about five feet eight inches tall and was muscled beyond reason, advanced on Jack rather quickly, and the colonel thought he was going to feel the business end of the man's short, strong knife. The man motioned for his hunters to lower their weapons. Then he reached out and quickly pulled Jack's nine millimeter free of his shoulder holster. He looked it over with curiosity and then looked back at his men, and the newcomers were taken by surprise when the small man laughed. He jabbered something in strange, halting words, and then the other hunters started laughing along with him.

Jack met Carl's eyes, and the confusion was evident on both of their uncomfortable faces. The laughing continued and then stopped when the leader of the group simply tossed Jack's semiautomatic into the air toward him, where the colonel was forced to catch it. The man walked up to Charlie, who still had his hands in the air. The scientist had lost the welcoming smile and was nervous when the brown-skinned man reached up and pulled Ellenshaw's glasses from his face. He placed them on his own small nose and then looked around. He quickly reached up and pulled the glasses off and threw them onto the ground.

"I guess they didn't match his prescription," Jenks said with a chuckle and the cold cigar in his mouth.

The leader rubbed his eyes, thinking that the glasses must have robbed him of his clear vision. Quickly his attention turned on the chuckling Jenks, and the headman's eyes went from being rubbed to them looking at the master chief with interest. His eyes narrowed as he looked at Jenks, and he crouched low as he took the man in.

Jenks quickly stopped chuckling at Ellenshaw's discomfort. The man cautiously approached him, and then his hand slowly rose to his face. The small man's movement was so quick that Jack and the others thought the man had sliced the master chief's throat. The leader of the small band of fishermen and miners had Jenks's cigar in his hand, and he examined it. He then smelled it, and then his tongue reached out and tasted it. His face was a mask of horror as he quickly crushed the smelly cigar and then threw it away.

"Hey, those are a little hard to come by out here," Jenks said in protest.

"I guess it wasn't his brand, huh?" Charlie quipped, eliciting a dirty look from the master chief.

The man looked at the other visitors, and with a couple of clicks of his tongue, the others lowered their spears. Then they just simply walked away back to the underbrush. Jack and the others slowly lowered their hands and watched the fishermen and the far filthier miners leave. Collins smiled and then looked at his group. Without answering their unasked questions, the colonel just turned and started to follow the residents of this bizarre world down the trail.

LOS ANGELES—CLASS ATTACK SUBMARINE USS *HOUSTON*

Captain Thorne was on his back inside the sonar shack, cursing and trying his best to get the new cable attached to the equipment. They had stolen from Peter to pay Paul. The cable was from the PC that crewmen used from time to time to send loved ones e-mails. It had been sacrificed to repair the sonar and radar suites. Finally, he made the cable connection, and then he pushed himself from under the console.

"Well, give a shot, Lieutenant."

As Thorne watched from the deck, the lieutenant silently prayed and then hit the switch. There was a loud electronic beep, and then the display screens came up. The four sonar men couldn't hold in their unbridled enthusiasm, and they let out a cheer. Thorne was helped up by the lieutenant and patted on the back.

"You did it, Skipper."

"One down, eighty more items to go. How is the XO coming along with our air supply?"

"He says we still have plenty of air, just no way to get it into the compartments. He has most of the crew busy cleaning up seawater, and that should keep their minds busy for a while." The young lieutenant JG looked around, and then the captain caught his drift and moved away from the young sonar men.

"What is it?" he asked as he wiped his sweaty brow.

"Captain, the XO says the ballast control panels are totally scorched. We have cannibalized everything from personal equipment to the damn washers and dryers for the right boards, and nothing even comes close."

"Okay, what we have to do is build new boards for ballast control." Thorne stopped and thought a moment, and as he did, there was another cheer that erupted throughout the boat as fresh air once more started to flow through the ventilators. He took a deep breath and got as close to the vent as he could to catch the cold air.

"New boards?" the lieutenant asked.

Thorne felt the cold air wash over him, and after a moment, he fixed the officer with a determined look.

"I want circuit boards from everything not being utilized and others that we won't need. Boom boxes, personal iPads, anything. Gather everything up and get it to engineering, and then we can piece something together. Just a blow switch will do." He slapped the boy on the back. "Go. We'll worry about diving some other time. Right now, we have to get up to the sunshine."

The lieutenant turned and left, not catching the worried look from Thorne about their chances.

As he gave orders to his sonar men, Thorne lost his balance as the *Houston* was starting to lose its hold on gravity. The submarine started to slide down the shelf they had landed upon. He held on for dear life as the sliding increased. The sound of smashing rock and sand reverberated throughout the ship, and every man knew what was happening. Most closed their eyes and waited for the inevitable slide to the proverbial deep end.

Thornes cursed inwardly. As suddenly as it started, he felt the *Houston* catch on something, and the slide downward was arrested.

Captain Thorne again closed his eyes in a silent prayer, and when he opened them, he saw the frightened faces of his sonar men. He was starting to run out of encouraging words for the crew. His gaze went from young face to young face.

"What do you say we find a solution to our ballast problem and get the hell out of here?"

The faces relaxed as Thorne delivered what he thought would be his last encouraging words.

If the *Houston* had windows, the crew would not be as happy at Thorne's words as he thought. The USS *Houston* was only sixteen feet away from the precipitous drop of two and a half miles to the seafloor far below.

COMPTON'S REEF—THE ISLAND

Charlie had named the new island Compton's Reef. The name was funny to most, but Collins had cringed when Ellenshaw had mentioned the director's name. That would be something Jack would take up with crazy Charlie later.

As they moved, the sounds of life were all around them. They smelled food cooking. They smelled the grasses that lined the trail they traveled upon. They also heard the sounds of laughter, playing, a community living life the only way they knew how—day to day.

After only ten minutes, Jack broke into a clearing, and the sight that met his astonished gaze almost made him weak in the knees. For the first time, he wished Sarah could see what it was he was seeing at this very moment.

"Wow!" Ryan said as he stepped out of the bush and stood beside the colonel.

Inside the clearing, there were well over three hundred huts of varying size and shape. The largest one in the center of the large village looked as if it were some form of community center. Women sat around its exterior and did their chores, chopping leafy vegetables and other cooking activities. Men were off to the side, repairing nets and fishing spears, while other men placed the baskets they had observed being brought down from the mountain in even rows at the edge of the large community. Even the children, who were still playing, laughing, and running, were involved in the village's activities by carrying water from the large stream-fed lagoon.

Jack quickly estimated that the inhabitants must have been at the very least three to four hundred strong. The most amazing thing was the fact that outside of mere curiosity, the folk of this community gave them only cursory looks and glances. Even several of the blond-haired women looked over at the men and giggled as they noticed them. Their worlds were not that much different, Jack figured.

"This is amazing," Charlie said as he adjusted his recovered glasses and took in the scene. "It's like something out of a Jack London or some South Seas romance novel."

Ryan was looking at a group of young women who were sewing items that looked as if they came from a bolt of sharkskin material. They looked his way, and he smiled back at them.

Jenks popped a cigar into his mouth, thought better of it with their present company, and then pocketed the stogie.

The Russians eyed the scene, and Collins didn't know what their thoughts were. They stood and watched the activity with mild interest. It was Salkukoff who joined Jack, Ryan, and Everett.

"As you can see, Colonel, these people are not a threat to our ships. So, may I suggest we cut this visit short and get back to saving ourselves?"

Collins was curious as to why the Russian was so adamant about not spending time in this village of innocents.

"Forget it. We have to learn all we can about these people." Charlie angrily looked at the Russian colonel. "We can draw conclusions on our own environment by study," he said as he looked sideways at Salkukoff as if he were a barbarian.

Ellenshaw immediately went to a group of men who had large nets strung up in the branches of two trees as they used large wooden needles to repair the links of line that made up the net. He immediately smiled and watched silently. The men nodded at Ellenshaw and then continued jabbering and sewing.

Jack was mystified at the easy way Charlie took things. His naïveté amazed him. How simply the cryptozoologist looked at life. Jack smiled as did Everett and Ryan.

"Never stand in the way of science, Colonel. I thought you would have known that doing the things you do with history."

The shocked look on Salkukoff's face told Jack he had hit pay dirt on the Russian. The small brief supplied by Compton's new orders had come in handy on just who this man was suspected of being.

"And suddenly, you know far more about me than previously thought, Colonel Collins."

Jack just dipped his head and then moved off toward the center of the village.

"Ryan, did you bring that package from *Shiloh* you got from their mess?"

Ryan looked at Jack and then remembered. He quickly reached into his small pack and brought out a clear neoprene bag. It was full of individually wrapped saltwater taffy in varying colors. He tossed the bag to Collins.

"Didn't anyone ever tell you not to feed the animals, Colonel?" Salkukoff said with a dirty little smirk.

Jack noticed the Russian's eyes constantly meandered over to the assembled baskets lined nearby and then just as quickly looked away. The American, after noticing this, pretended to ignore him, and then he opened the bag. He caught the attention of a small girl as she moseyed across to the stream running in the center of the village by holding up a piece of the tantalizingly colorful taffy wrapped in paper. The girl, not knowing what the item was, just went about her business.

The small child had several large halved coconut shells and used them to dip into the stream. After filling the coconut shells with freshwater, the girl placed the other half of the shells over them and sealed the small containers. She was about to get up and return to her chores when the dark shadow of Jack fell upon her. She stood quickly, spilling some of the water. Her eyes were big, round, and the bluest Collins had ever seen. He was joined by Everett and Ryan as the girl's eyes went from man to man. Jack smiled down at her. He unwrapped an orange-colored piece of taffy and offered it to the small blonde. She looked from the gift to Jack.

"She won't take it, Colonel."

Everett looked at Ryan and smirked. "Five bucks says she does, flyboy."

"You're on. You'd better—" Jason stopped when Carl started laughing.

The small child had placed her containers of water on the ground and accepted Jack's offer without much trepidation. She examined the orange-colored candy and then sniffed it. She squeezed her fingers closed and squished it somewhat, and then she smiled up at Jack.

Ryan and Everett examined the child. She was wearing what looked like sharkskin shorts and a halter top of grass. As the girl popped the taffy into her mouth, it remained open as the sensation and taste of sugar hit her taste buds. Her eyes widened, and all the visitors to the village that day smiled and laughed at her reaction—everyone with the exception of Salkukoff, who watched without mirth or humor. He shot Kreshenko and Dishlakov an angry look, but this time they ignored him and then joined the rest of the landing party as more children came over to where they stood.

When Jack saw the curious children start to advance on them, he quickly handed out handfuls of taffy to the men around him. Soon there were over seventy-five children ranging in age from a couple of years to fifteen or so. The amazing part was that the parents of these children watched and smiled at not only the scene before them but the strangers themselves.

"They are totally trusting," Charlie said, rejoining the group. "No inhibitions, no fear."

"I'm afraid we equate this gentle world to our own and are very sad to realize our world comes up lacking, Doc," Everett said as he handed a piece to a mother who had come to see what the children were laughing over. All the children had their mouths and cheeks stuffed full of candy.

"I suppose," Ellenshaw said as the children started to move away.

"All right, what is it, Doc?" Jack asked. "I know that look. You're worried about something."

"I'm concerned about that," he said as he pointed to a hut in the far corner of the village. "They must have an enemy. It's not us, but there's something in this world these kind and gentle people fear."

Jack and the others followed Charlie's gaze, and then they saw what it was he saw. The large hut was surrounded by war shields and axes. Spears and bows. Slingshots hung from small poles, ready to be snatched up at a moment's notice.

"I see what you mean," Jack said.

Before they could move to the hut and examine the villagers' weaponry, they were approached by the same small man who had confronted them on the trail. He went to Jenks and then took his hand and started pulling him away. Other men joined in and started escorting the visitors toward the far end of the village.

"Now, did you geniuses ever consider that fish may not be the only meat product these folks eat?" Jenks said as he looked behind him as the man pulled on his hand and arm.

"As much as I hate to admit this, I think that antisocial bastard may have a point," Ryan whispered to Jack as they were led away. "I mean, we could be on the menu tonight."

Before Jack could tell Ryan to stay cool, they all smelled it. Jenks heard his stomach rumble, and even the two Russian Navy men perked up at the smell of roasting meat. They were led to a small clearing near the far side of the large village, and that was when they saw several of the blond natives of this new world bring out a large roasted boar on a long pole. The visitors were escorted to small blocks of tree trunk, and the women gestured that they should sit. They were all amazed to see that these simple people had a social gathering place for their main meal of the day.

As the men sat down and exchanged looks of wonder, a deep bass sound echoed throughout the island. Salkukoff was the only one of them to tickle his gun with his fingers. As he stopped and looked up, he saw Jack and Farbeaux looking at him.

Henri had been the only man outside of Salkukoff who hadn't been more appreciative of their new surroundings. Jack leaned over and spoke in low tones to the Frenchman.

"What is it?" Jack asked over the sounds of the horn being blasted.

"Our Russian colonel was the only man here not to be surprised by that hut over there and the weapons it contains. He wasn't even curious. Dishlakov and Kreshenko were, but not him." Henri faced Jack. "We also have to get a look-see inside those baskets, because if you have been watching Salkukoff as I have, you would have noticed a disconcerting way that our Russian friend has of eyeing them. Why is that, Colonel?"

Jack looked over, and the Russian was staring right at the two men. Collins said nothing but knew Henri was right, having noticed the same thing.

As the seashell horn was blasted by one of the larger fishermen, other horns started their refrain. Soon adults were arriving from all parts of the island to join the group meal. Men, women, and children greeted the others who had joined them.

"Now *this* is a barbecue," Jenks enthusiastically said as his mouth started to water. "This has got to beat shit on a shingle, huh, Doc?" he said, nudging Charlie on the arm and almost knocking him from his small tree stump, joking and mentioning the military's main meal of the past 150 years of chipped beef on toast.

"I am quite famished myself," Ellenshaw said as he rubbed his arm from the master chief's gentle pop.

Women started singing a song in their native language, when the village's men joined in. It was rough but harmonious. They sang as everyone sat down for their evening meal. Their bodies swayed to the sounds of the song that even the young children had joined in for.

"We are truly barbarians in a gentle land," Henri said, sparking strange looks, as the Frenchman had never once shown sentimentality about life back home. Jack and Everett figured the man was just waiting for the villagers to bring out something that the antiquities thief could steal. But as Jack looked on, he could see a change in Farbeaux. He was genuinely impressed by what he was seeing.

The horns calmed, and the singing slowed as food was passed around. Jack was handed a large wooden bowl with fish and pork. There were greens that looked close to seaweed. He sniffed the food and found the fragrance of the seaweed was something he would never have expected. The fish was done to perfection, and the roasted boar was succulent.

"I may never want to leave this place," Ryan said as he popped a long strand of seaweed into his mouth, slurping it up like a strand of spaghetti. The young women around the great campfire giggled and exchanged words about the handsome young naval aviator. Again, Ryan made them practically swoon when he popped a large piece of pork into his mouth and then rubbed his belly in overexaggerated pleasure over the taste of the meal. All around them, the villagers ate and laughed as if the visitors were a normal part of life. Jack chewed on the delicious roasted boar and then leaned over to talk to Ellenshaw, who was busy studying the wooden bowl and its craftsmanship.

"Doc, what does our traveling link with Europa make out about their language?"

An astonished look came to Ellenshaw's face as he snapped his fingers. "Damn, I almost forgot!" He reached into the pack at his feet and brought up the closed-looped system that was their very limited remote brain of Europa. He flipped open the aluminum top. He whispered, "Europa, can you identify the language being spoken by these indigenous people?" Charlie held the computer outward without drawing attention to what it was he was doing.

It only took a moment, and it was straight up. *"No, Doctor."*

"No syntax, no morphology, is there nothing close to one of the languages you are familiar with?" Again, Charlie held the laptop up so Europa could hear. He also used the camera system to scan the people as they spoke. He just hoped that the portable laptop housing Europa Jr.'s limited memory would allow him to gain the information he needed. Not being in direct contact with the supercomputer was limiting, to say the least.

"Doctor, from their hand gestures and spoken language, it is calculated that the indigenous peoples involved are utilizing both spoken and sign languages. There is a total of two million six hundred thousand combinations on record. Limited memory on the portable system has curtailed a more detailed study."

Ellenshaw closed the top and then placed the laptop back into his pack. He shrugged at Collins. "I wish Pete or Dr. Morales could expand this new memory system for the portable Europa more."

"I'm sure they didn't expect us to run into language problems," Everett said as he placed his bowl aside.

"Look at that," Kreshenko said as he was looking at the sky overhead.

The sun was setting, and what came up next was still a frightening and amazing sight: the moon with her trail of debris spread out across the sky like an incomplete ring of Saturn. The sparkling white material that used to be the same moon they used to stare up at was almost fluorescent in color and made every man at the campfire that night feel small and unknowing.

"How long do you figure the tail of that moon is, Colonel?" Kreshenko asked.

"My guess would be close to about three hundred and fifty thousand miles." Wonder seized all their minds.

The evening was full of laughter and of families spending the end of their long day together. Fathers helped sons, and mothers laughed with daughters. Neighbors shared jokes and laughter, and the visitors were included in some of these exchanges just as if they could understand everything that was being said or discussed. Jack and the others were reduced to their lowest forms of response; they nodded and smiled enough times to look like bobblehead idiots.

"Shiloh *to Collins*," came the radio call.

Jack stood, and as a small blond-haired villager smiled and jabbered about something that Jack was sure the man thought he understood, he happily nodded and acted as though he had indeed understood the joke, or was it just a story? He didn't know but smiled and bobbed his head and then moved away to take his radio call. Everett joined him.

"Collins," he said into the radio when he was a few feet away from the boisterous villagers.

"*Colonel, I have Professor Gervais here, and he wishes to speak with Master Chief Jenks*," Captain Johnson said from the deck of *Shiloh*. "*He seems really agitated about something.*"

Everett got the attention of Jenks, who had a small child on his lap and was teasing her by making her think he had just pulled her nose from her face. The girl giggled and squealed with laughter when she discovered that the nose he had pulled off was actually his thumb that he wiggled in front of her. Jenks made eye contact with Carl and then easily sat the girl down and then joined the two officers. Jack explained who was calling and then handed the radio to Jenks.

"Jenks here," he said and then popped a cigar into his mouth. He waited a moment and grew frustrated. "Who is this?" he asked, looking at Jack.

"Supposed to be Professor Gervais."

A look of knowing came onto the master chief's rough countenance.

"Press the damn button on the side, Professor. Jesus."

"*Oh, oh, I see. Thank you.*"

"Okay. What's up, Doc?" Jenks said and then smiled at his small Bugs Bunny joke. He saw that Jack and Carl only stared at him, and then he removed his cigar and then spit. "Goddamn humorless pukes." He turned back and then looked at the radio. "Come on, push the button on the side every time you want to speak. Don't they teach you anything over there in Putin land?"

"*Oh, again? I see,*" came the voice over the radio as Jenks was sure Captain Johnson was explaining the transmit switch on the radio to the old professor. "*Master Chief, we have activity on the phase shift equipment that is quite fascinating.*"

"And that is?" he asked into the radio as he removed the cigar once again as he looked at Jack and spoke in low tones. "And we were afraid of Russian science all these years, and they can't even operate a radio."

"But yet they still came up with phase shift technology," Everett said, raising his eyebrows at Jenks.

"Smart-ass."

"*The equipment seems to be powering up once again. Low output, but we are detecting a ramp-up by 0.1 percent.*"

"Come on, Professor, that could be anything. It could just be residual energy being disbursed by the equipment to static electricity buildup. You are in a ship constructed of steel, you know." Jenks rolled his eyes at the Russian professor's naïveté.

"*Yes, I have figured that into the equation and have found no evidence of that. Therefore, I will monitor the phase shift system until you return, but there is now another concern about a changing situation that I will let Captain Johnson explain.*"

There was silence once more as Jenks handed the radio to Jack. "Here. Navy officers give me the galloping trots."

"Hey!" Everett said with a mocking tone.

"Present company included, of course."

Everett's eyes narrowed, but the master chief just shrugged.

"*Colonel, Johnson here. It seems that when the professor first detected the buildup of energy from that machine on the Simbirsk, we started getting interference on the Shiloh's and Peter the Great's radio band frequencies we have just repaired. Were you or any of your landing party using a radio at that time?*"

"Negative. We were invited to dinner by our hosts. Thus far, this is the first call."

Carl nudged Jack's arm, and the colonel looked up at where Everett was nodding. Salkukoff was nowhere to be seen. Neither was Henri, for that matter.

"Noted, Captain. Inform the good professor that Master Chief Jenks will return to the ship momentarily. Out for now." Jack lowered the radio and then gestured for Carl and Ryan to find Salkukoff. "Jenks, stay with me."

Before anyone could move, a shrill scream echoed through the bright moonlit night. The scream could be heard from some distance away. Around them, women gathered up their children, and the men, much to Jack and his team's surprise, started running for the large hut where they had seen the village's weapons stored.

"Oh, this don't look good," Jason said as he watched the frantic activity. As he studied the scene, he nudged Jack on the arm and then pointed.

Jack turned and saw what was being indicated. In the clearing where the baskets of whatever the villagers had been mining had been lined up, a place that had been unguarded since they all had moved into the next communal clearing for their evening meal, the baskets had mysteriously vanished.

Before Collins could comment, they saw one of the women, a larger, more rotund one with streaming long and braided blond hair, gesturing wildly in the center of the village. It looked as though she were frantically looking for someone. Jack saw that it was the same mother who had gathered up the child that Jack had given the saltwater taffy to just three hours before. Several of the armed village men confronted her, and she was crying and waving her hands wildly. Then the men, along with thirty others, broke from the group and started to run for the jungle surrounding the village.

"Jason, you and Jenks find Henri and that damn Russian. If the Frenchman already fulfilled his mission, we could be looking at a whole lot of trouble with the rest of the Russians. Get them back here."

"Right," Jason said as he and Jenks left the center of the village.

Jack pulled his nine millimeter as did Everett. They both started to follow the menfolk of the village. They ran past a startled Kreshenko and Dishlakov, and Collins waved for the Russian Navy men to follow. They were unarmed, but Jack wanted to keep an eye on them also. With Salkukoff missing, he wasn't taking any chances.

The group of close to thirty-five villagers and guests sprinted into the low underbrush surrounding the large village.

They had gone about eight hundred yards from the village. Jack and the others were having a hard time catching up with the fast and agile natives. They jumped over tree stumps and bushes just as if it were bright daylight and they could see perfectly. Jack heard the villagers stop up ahead, and then he saw why. They had circled around something on the grassy floor of the trail. Several of the small men turned away, and they could hear the moans of despair coming from them. Collins approached slowly, easing his way past the circle of villagers, who, for the most part, stood there with spears dangling from limp arms, their heads bowed. Jack felt Carl and the Russians next to him. A man was on his knees crying and reaching for something in front of him. The small man was pulled away from whatever it was by the elder of the clan. It was the same man who had greeted them upon their arrival. As he led the man away, the elder caught Jack's eyes, and the look was not only one of sadness but, strangely enough, also one of resignation. Collins holstered his handgun and leaned down to see.

"Oh no," Second Captain Dishlakov said as he saw what was there.

Crumpled in a heap was the small blond girl with the golden smile Jack had shared candy with earlier. Collins went down to one knee, and he felt the sadness invade his soul like a virus striking his system. He checked the broken girl for a pulse but found none. A familiar anger filled his mind as he lowered his head.

"Why would someone do this?" Kreshenko said as he looked around the darkness.

Jack reached into his small pack and brought out a flashlight and clicked it on. The remaining villagers jumped back at the magical object Jack had used to bring a false sunlight to the gruesome scene before them. With an ease of motion, Jack moved one of the villagers out of the way, and with his free hand, he grasped the long spear, and with delicate care, he removed it from the chest of the little girl. Collins stood as Kreshenko stepped forward and pushed by the silent men of the village and removed his black class-A navy jacket and then reverently placed it over the girl's still form. He took a step back and looked at the men, who had lost all enthusiasm or anger at what had just happened to a child of their clan. Kreshenko didn't understand these people.

"It looks like she was taken right from the gathering. Look." Jack shined the light on the girl's exposed wrist. It was red and discolored as if she had been pulled. All eyes also locked on the same thing Jack had seen. Clutched in the girl's right hand was the melted, softened piece of saltwater taffy. The child had never eaten her candy. She must have admired the color and its softness too much to waste by eating it. Collins swallowed the lump in his throat. "She must have at least been free enough to scream, and then whoever did this plunged this into her," Jack said as he retrieved the spear from the ground at his feet and easily tossed the long shaft over to Carl. "Look at it, Swabby."

Carl did as he was asked and examined the long spear. The differences were noticed right away. The bloody tip was not flint or any other kind of natural material. It was iron.

Immediately, the newcomers started looking around them. They now knew there was danger here facing these native villagers in this tranquil place.

Collins moved the flashlight around the clearing, and he saw that a long line of perpetrators had used the trail recently. The underbrush was trampled, as whoever it was had headed toward the opposite beach from the side of the island that they themselves had landed on.

The Americans and Russians were eased aside by the villagers as they gathered around the still form of the covered body. They easily picked up the small
bundle, and they moved off with it. Kreshenko and Dishlakov started to follow
the slow and sad procession out of the jungle.

"No," Jack said as he clicked off the flashlight.

The Russians stopped and turned to face the American with a questioning
look.

"Let's get the others and get back to the ships and leave these people to
grieve in their own way. I don't think they'll think us rude or anything like
that. As a matter of fact, it worries me that they almost seemed emotionless or
maybe even expectant of what happened. We'll leave them alone for now and
get answers tomorrow."

"Colonel, you are thinking deep thoughts, and as a captain of a capital warship, I have come to learn the signs of a man who has something on his mind."

Collins looked from the retreating forms of the villagers and faced Kreshenko.

"Yeah, Captain, I do have something on my mind."

"What is it, Jack?" Everett asked with the spear still in his hand. He noticed the weapon and then easily snapped it into two pieces over his knee and
then angrily tossed it to the ground.

"These people just had a child murdered by something or someone. But
their reaction was one of resignation. It's like they experience this all the time.
I think they originally thought the child may have been taken by an animal,
maybe a big cat or something, and that was their intent, to kill or stop whatever
it was. Then they saw what had killed her, and they all became not angrier but
frightened or even resigned to the situation."

The night became stiller than it had been earlier, or was it that the newcomers had just felt the night close in around them far more than it was before
they found the murdered child?

"We'll learn more tomorrow. We'll expand the search of the surrounding
seas and see what else is out there. Right now, we need daylight," Jack said as
he started to move away.

"Yes, in the daylight," Dishlakov said as he eyed the dangerous world
around him.

In the bush only a few feet away, the bright green eyes with black pupils watched
as the men moved away. The long-fingered hand reached out from the brush
and grasped the broken spear that Everett had just discarded. The eyes blinked,
and the creature stood erect. The eyes watched, and its recessed ears, buried

deep into the sides of its head, listened. It hissed, opening its mouth, exposing the clear, small, and very sharp teeth of the predator.

The creature moved back into the darkness and was engulfed by the night.

Jenks and Ryan found Charlie Ellenshaw, who was lurking behind a tree. They thought the crazed cryptozoologist was still back in camp, but here he was in the middle of what was fast becoming a dangerous jungle. Jason eased up behind Ellenshaw and tapped him on the back, which made Charlie yelp in fear as he fell forward, thinking that whatever was out here had come upon him. He looked up and then exhaled a pent-up breath.

"Jesus, Captain, are you trying to give me a heart attack?"

"Come on, don't be a wimp, Nerdly," Jenks said with a chuckle.

"What in the hell are you doing out here, Doc?" Ryan asked.

"Following Colonel Farbeaux. He looked very determined to get somewhere."

"Damn," Jason said as he looked at Jenks. "I hope he hasn't done anything yet."

"Done what, Commander Ryan?"

They turned and saw Henri standing only feet away from them. Jenks grabbed his chest and yelped just as Ellenshaw had just done a brief moment before and cursed the Frenchman.

"Where's Salkukoff?" Ryan asked pointedly, almost afraid of the answer.

"Right over there," Farbeaux said with a gesture of his head.

"Why did he vanish?" Jenks asked.

"I don't know, but he was speaking with someone on the radio."

"I thought he didn't have one," Charlie said, confused by the inquiries being made.

"He wasn't issued one by us or the Russian captain. Their equipment wasn't working when we left. Our radios were shielded, at least the handheld radios were." Ryan looked around and tried to catch sight of the Russian. "Who was he speaking to?"

Farbeaux kept his gaze on Ryan. "All I can say is that the language returned was Russian."

Before Jason or Jenks could ask another question, they heard the underbrush being parted and footsteps as they approached. Colonel Salkukoff stepped out in his expensive bush clothing. The only thing that was missing, the Americans had joked earlier, was the pith helmet seen in old Tarzan movies.

"Out for an evening stroll, gentlemen?" the arrogant man asked as he pushed by the group. He stopped and faced the Frenchman and the others, including

Ellenshaw, who was just now standing up. The Russian's eyes took it all in. "Or were you on a spy mission sent by your clever Colonel Collins?"

"Yes, they were."

Everyone turned and saw Jack, Carl, and the two Russian Navy men. They were standing there silently, listening and watching.

"I see, so all pretense of trust is now gone?" Salkukoff asked with a large smile.

"No, not at all, Colonel. There never was a pretense. We never trusted you."

The smile grew even larger.

"Colonel Salkukoff, after you vanished from the meal our hosts were generous enough to lay out for us, you came up missing. Now we have a small child murdered. Coincidence?" Jack asked as he stared at the dark-haired man.

"I will not stand here and be interrogated by you, Colonel Collins. I won't answer to your ridiculous and dangerous insinuations. I don't kill children."

"But yet you do. I saw your gentle nature in the Ukraine, Colonel. So, I know that you do, most assuredly, kill small children," Henri said as his blue eyes never left those of the Russian.

"We'll discuss this later. Right now, we have to get Master Chief Jenks back to the *Simbirsk*."

Salkukoff started forward and then stopped in front of Farbeaux.

"Very soon, Colonel Farbeaux, we are going to have a serious disagreement."

"I look forward to it," Henri answered as Salkukoff stepped by him.

"But for now, Colonel Collins has suggested that we return to the ships. Captain Kreshenko, Second Captain Dishlakov, join me, please."

With a bow of his head toward Jack and the others, the Russian captain and his XO reluctantly fell in beside Salkukoff.

"What do you think, Jack?" Carl asked.

"Again, I think our Russian colonel knows far more about this place than he's telling."

"Does anyone want to know what I think?" Jenks asked as he slowly and deliberately lit a fresh cigar.

No one asked, and Jenks accepted that.

"Well, if you *are* interested, I think our French thief here should have placed a bullet in the head of that murderous son of a bitch while you were out here in the dark."

Most heads turned and looked at the master chief. He smiled back at them.

"But no one asked me, so let's get the hell back to that ghost ship and try to get out of here before this Salkukoff asshole turns the tables on us. Because in case you didn't notice, gentlemen, that bastard has had a plan and an agenda long before we arrived here." Jenks snorted, puffed on his cigar, and then moved by the others toward the beach and the boat ride back.

Collins lay back as the others joined Jenks. He stepped up to Henri, who had been rather silent the past few minutes.

"I was afraid you had killed him already," Jack said when he was sure no one was in earshot.

The Frenchman shook his head and placed the small .30-caliber handgun away. He had been hiding it behind his back the entire time he was facing off with Salkukoff.

"I would have, but when I came upon him and his secret radio, I found this. He must have stepped right over it. It was on the beaten track made by the attacker or attackers. I assume more than one by the way the brush was trampled." He reached into his pants pocket and then held out a small object. "Remember, Colonel, the power source enhancers we used for the Wellsian Doorway?"

Jack knew the power enhancers well from their adventure through time with the help of the Traveler's Wellsian Doorway, the very power enhancers stolen by the Frenchman after those events. He nodded to inform Henri he remembered. Henri then dropped what looked like a small rock into his hand. Jack examined it in the shattered moonlight. He looked from it to Farbeaux.

"That's right, Colonel. Uncut, directly from the ground. I suspect this one fell from one of those mysterious baskets the miners brought in—you know, the ones conveniently lined up in the village?"

"Blue diamonds." Jack turned the unprocessed mineral over in his hand. It was still crusted with dirt as if it had just been taken from the ground.

"I noticed elements of the diamonds earlier when you were engaged in making nice with the natives."

"Inside the village?" Jack asked, amazed he hadn't seen them.

"Yes, their spear tips and their arrowheads are made of blue and red diamonds."

"Industrial blues," Jack said.

"Yes, the blood diamonds are good for nothing but money, but those, we have seen what they can do as energy enhancers."

Henri was right. If someone were here to mine this stuff, they could easily corner the energy markets on a massive scale back home.

"Colonel, I think you just discovered Salkukoff's hidden agenda that the master chief just mentioned."

What the two men and former enemies had discovered was not even feasible in their minds. How could the Russian manipulate blue diamonds from another plane of existence? They were thinking that he couldn't do it. Then again they were both experienced enough in facing the impossible and adjusted their thinking. After the Antarctica Event, they were on a course to believe almost every outrageous theory possible.

Farbeaux stood his ground, not moving as he pulled another item out of his pants pocket. He unfurled it, and Jack again turned on his flashlight to see it clearly. Henri stretched it out.

"I found this also while you were being fed. It was inside the villagers' armament hut."

"Is that what I think it is?" Jack asked just as Jason returned to both men, curious as to what they were talking about.

The flag was black material of a sort that was woven and thicker than most, but they could see that it closely resembled a flag. On that flag was a symbol every one of them recognized from their childhood. It was a pirate flag. The old skull and crossbones.

"This is getting strange," Jason added. "Remember the page from *Treasure Island* Garrison Lee found on the *Eldridge*?"

"There seems to be a connection here, and I'll be damned if I can figure it out," Jack said as he gave the flag back to the Frenchman. "Henri?" Jack said as he stopped on the game trail heading back to the landing boat.

"Yes, Colonel?"

"Neither Salkukoff or the *Simbirsk* can survive this."

Farbeaux nodded.

"As a matter of fact, as far as that goes, if it comes to that, we stay here with both the *Simbirsk* and Salkukoff. All other concerns at this point are secondary. That man cannot return to our world with that ship."

Around them, the jungle came alive with night sounds once more.

13

As the American-built Zodiac disembarked the Russian contingent accordingly between the *Simbirsk* and *Peter the Great*, Master Chief Jenks immediately removed the Europa system laptop from Charlie's bag and opened it. As the rubber boat rode smoothly over the soft movement of the strangely colored seas, Jack moved in next to him.

"Europa, was your task completed?" Jenks asked.

"Assigned task completed at 1735 hours, Master Chief."

"I can't get used to Marilyn Monroe talking to me."

Jack smiled as he heard the same argument he had been making since his arrival at the Group eleven years before. "I know how you feel."

"Europa, run program Chameleon."

On the small screen, Jack and Jenks watched the system start to scroll. The master chief smiled at Jack, and then he whistled.

"Ooh, good little spy we have here. Be sure to keep her out of my private server."

Jack watched the specs pop up on the entirety of the phase shift experiment as conducted by the Russians in the mid-'40s, complete diagrams and reports on the completion of the stolen American design.

"There you are. They used unrefined uranium for their power source. Actually, in some areas, the nuclear question was years ahead of the American enrichment program of that time," Jenks said as the reflection of the findings continued to scroll across the screen and onto his face.

"Yeah, but our boys in New Mexico were going another way with it," Jack retorted.

"Yeah, and didn't that make the world a happier, kinder place?"

"Europa wasn't compromised when she took over the Russian professor's computer?" Jack asked, always concerned about the security of the most advanced computing system in the world, even if the laptop was only using 0.0001 percent of her capacity.

"Nah, that kid Morales, the new king nerd in the Group, said Europa has never been caught in the act."

"Good. Now, how does this damn thing work?"

"Jesus, Colonel, do you have an extra three years for me to explain it to you?"

"That bad, huh?"

"Yeah, that bad. This stuff would give Virginia a raging migraine."

At that moment, the Zodiac lightly bumped the boarding ladder, and the men were assisted to the deck of *Shiloh*. They were met by Captain Johnson, who looked worried. When Jack made the last step up, Johnson steered him away from the others.

"What's up?" Collins asked.

"Number one, we tried several times to contact you by radio. We couldn't raise you. My electronic warfare boys tell me we were being jammed."

Jack pursed his lips, knowing that the Russians were up to their old parlor tricks again. But why now and why when other Russians were with them in their exploration of the village?

"Can you burn through it?"

"Yeah, now that we know someone is screwing with us, no problem. We'll set the radios to random and roving frequencies."

"What else? You don't seem the type that gets worried over jamming."

"Two other developments. One—we're picking up a few sonar readings that we cannot figure out. The computers say they are transient in nature. But it sounds like hammering, voices on occasion, and escaping air. Computers are saying they are nothing more than biological sea life."

"What do you think?" Jack asked, knowing that if the sounds from the sea bothered Johnson, he had better not ignore them either.

"No clue yet; we'll keep evaluating. Now, number-two concern. Radar is working on and off. But at 1645 hours, we detected small craft moving toward the island. That was when the attempt was made to contact you. Don't know the size or the disposition of these craft, but they did go to the island on the opposing side as your landing. Did you have any company at that time?"

Jack turned away just as Everett, Charlie, and Jenks walked up. He faced the captain once more. "Yes, there were visitors. One of the island's children was murdered."

"Children?" Johnson asked.

"We'll brief you in the wardroom."

Johnson nodded and moved off with the returning marines.

"What is it, Jack?" Carl asked when he saw his face.

Instead of answering Everett's concern, he faced Jenks. "Look, Master Chief, we need to learn and learn fast how we can get that phase shift equipment operational with some modicum of control."

Jenks frowned. "That will take some time. In a few hours, I should learn enough with the help of Captain Johnson's electronics team on how to at least turn it on without blowing ourselves up."

"Jack, why the white face?" Carl persisted.

Collins reached into his pocket and retrieved the dirt-encrusted blue diamond and rolled it over in his hand. He also explained the flag Henri had discovered.

"Swabby, I'm beginning to think our Russian friends know a hell of a lot more than they are letting on about this mysterious world we have here. We're running so far behind in this game, we may never catch up." Jack looked up and saw Carl was still in the dark. "Look, Salkukoff may not be a regular visitor here, but they knew somehow what it was they were going to find. These." He held out his hand and showed the blue diamond.

"That's assuming an awful lot," Everett said. "I don't suppose you have proof."

"No, no proof. My only evidence is the fact that whoever is running things in Moscow these days would have never risked the life of their most experienced man unless it was for a reason that could not be ignored. He's here for one of two reasons. Either he knew these were here and the Russians are somehow taking advantage of it, or he was sent to stop the phase shift project forever."

"Seems like if that were the case, Salkukoff would just have blown the ship out of the water as soon they entered the eye of Tildy," Charlie Ellenshaw offered.

"Maybe our friend had just those orders," Farbeaux said as he joined the group.

"Running his own game against the wishes of his bosses?" Carl asked, raising a brow.

Jack tossed the blue diamond into the air, and Charlie fumbled and then caught it, and then it dropped to the deck and slid over the side and into the sea. Ellenshaw looked horrified.

"Don't worry about it, Charlie," Jack said. "I suspect they have a whole mountain streaked with them. There's plenty more where they came from."

They all watched Jack move into *Shiloh*. The Frenchman soon followed.

"You know what makes me the most nervous?" Everett said to Charlie, Jenks, and Ryan.

"What makes you nervous, Toad?" Jenks asked.

"When both of those men are confused and without answers concerning the motives of a man like Salkukoff, we may have a major problem on our hands."

"I'm not following," Jenks said.

"He means, is Salkukoff following orders or is he in this for himself?" Ryan answered for Carl.

"You guys are some worrisome sons of bit—"

Jenks found himself standing alone as the others followed Jack in the hopes of figuring this out before the Russian knew they were on to him.

Inside the wardroom of the *Shiloh*, Johnson, Carl, Jack, and Farbeaux sat with the captain and his officers and ate a light meal. In the far-off corner, coffee was being consumed at an extraordinary rate by Jenks, Charlie, Ryan, and the electronic warfare department of *Shiloh* as they tried to figure out the complicated design of the phase shift engine on *Simbirsk*.

"What makes you think that the sneaky little bastard won't just up and vanish on us without us in tow?" Ezra Johnson asked, voicing the fear of his officers sitting around the table.

"Master Chief," Jack called out until Jenks looked up from the newly printed schematics stolen from the Russians' own computer. "What guarantee do we have *Simbirsk* won't up and disappear on us in the middle of the night?"

Without looking up from the plans, Jenks reached into his front pocket and tossed something all the way across the wardroom, where Jack caught it and then held it up.

It was a small crystal-looking ball with several leads connected to it.

"What is that?" Johnson asked.

"It's the power converter from the phase shift generator. One of a kind. They can't start her up again without it. Unless they take some of those unrefined blue diamonds and construct a new, vastly improved converter."

"And the master chief is just tossing the damn thing around?" Johnson's first officer asked in shock.

"Jenks said the crystal is damn near indestructible. That's why it was the only essential part he chose to steal."

"I may be off point here, but just who in the hell are you people, Colonel?" the first officer of *Shiloh* asked.

Collins chose to ignore the same question he had been asked by everyone, from the leaders of the free world to his own mother.

"Captain, what is the EMP damage?"

"Some good news, some horrible. We have nothing but close-in weapons support. Four .50-calibers and handheld weaponry from the armory. Good news is that we do have the Phalanx system, but no radar for her targeting. No offensive or defensive missiles. Fire control on those systems was totally disabled. Radios are now working along with radar. Sonar, as we discussed, is still spotty at best."

"Are the Russians in the same predicament?" Jack asked with hope.

"Their pulse shielding is damn near the same design as our own," Johnson answered.

"What are you talking about, sir? It is the same design. Just like their missile control, all stolen from us before their prototypes were even built."

Johnson smiled at his XO as everyone on board ship knew how the Russians obtained most of their sophisticated systems.

The men inside the wardroom continued their duties on through the midnight hour, and they would work until they were comfortable with their strange situation.

Within an hour, they would never be comfortable again.

KIROV-CLASS BATTLE CRUISER *PETER THE GREAT*

Four Russian sailors stood at the fantail of the giant warship, smoking and drinking tea during their off shift. They had been slaving below, trying in vain to get their missile systems operational. They had found themselves in the same shape as the Americans as far as replacement parts for those systems—they just had too much electrical damage to fix. Captain Kreshenko had ordered all crew not on duty to be armed from the arms locker. The night watch was tripled, and the radar shack was to be triple manned. The few British and American marines assigned to *Peter the Great* were mostly hanging out forward, as they didn't mix well with their new Russian friends.

The sailors joked, but again, like the Americans, their laughter and joking was limited to their work and not their situation. All you had to do was look out at the strangely colored sea in the shattered moonlight to figure that one out.

The four men were just getting ready to head below and go to sleep when one of them heard a sound he didn't recognize. He went to the railing and looked down. At first, all he saw was the lapping of sea against the hull of *Peter the Great*. Then his eyes widened when the broken moonlight showed something just beneath the violet-colored waters. The face looking up at the sailor burst through the froth and covered the seventeen feet to the fantail before the sailor could pull his head back. The other three men watched in stupefied wonder as their companion went over the side without uttering a word. They heard the splash and ran to where he vanished. Then before they could even look over the side, more figures burst from the sea and gained the main deck of the Russian warship.

The intruders were dressed in sharkskin pantaloons. Many had a form of vest, and all twelve of them had very sharp harpoon-like spears. They started to stab and decimate those at the fantail with what resembled ancient swords of a curved nature and the long spikelike spears. One man managed to pull his Makarov pistol and get a shot off as an ax came down on his hand. The man screamed and looked into the face of his attacker. His eyes widened beyond what he ever thought they were capable of.

The face was light green in color, the skin nearly transparent, as the sailor could see the muscle and veins just beneath. The tentacle-like appendages curled and uncurled at the corners of its mouth, and each was adorned with a brightly colored ribbon of material. For all the world, the creature looked as if it had stepped directly from a pirate novel. The eight tentacles swung with every motion from where they were attached just below the neck. The scales on the attacker's chest were thick and darker green than its face. The thing hissed as it brought the ax down again. This time, the sailor's scream was quickly silenced.

More shots rang out as the deck watch saw what was happening at the fantail. As spotlights started illuminating the chaotic scene below, alarms started sounding throughout the ship.

Peter the Great was being boarded.

TICONDEROGA-CLASS AEGIS MISSILE CRUISER USS *SHILOH*

Jack came near to spitting out the cold coffee he had just sipped when the alarms started sounding throughout the cruiser.

"Action stations, action stations surface. All hands, action stations surface."

"Is that bastard moving on us already?" Everett asked as he followed *Shiloh*'s command team up and out of the wardroom.

As men scrambled out of their bunks or into their varying departments, Jack and Everett let Captain Johnson and his men go to the bridge while they went to the main deck just below. They were the only men above deck.

"Maybe this isn't the best place to be," Jack said.

"You heard the captain. We don't have any missile control. They can't let loose with anything, so the deck is as safe as anywhere at the moment. Look!" Carl said, pointing six hundred yards away.

Peter the Great was lit up like the Fourth of July to the Americans. Tracer fire and the loud *thump, thump, thump* of her heavy twenty-millimeter gun were going crazy. Spotlights crisscrossed the water, and that was when Jack saw the enemy. Hundreds of small boatlike vessels were streaming toward the giant Russian battle cruiser. Her deck guns were laying down a withering fire. Tracers reached out like a laser beam and cut several of the small boats to pieces. Through binoculars, they all saw the largest of the ships at the center of the attacking smaller boats. The flag waving at the topmost of the mast was the exact duplicate of the flag Henri had found: the skull and crossbones of a pirate vessel.

"What in the hell is going on?" Jenks said as he, Charlie, and Jason joined them at the railing.

"Look out!" Collins cried as a spear thrown from somewhere in the dark streaked by and struck the hatch that Henri Farbeaux had just stepped from. The spear struck the steel of the hatch, and the tip bent, and the shaft nearly took the Frenchman's head off. Jack then reacted far faster than anyone realized as he quickly unholstered his nine millimeter and shot three times at the greenish figure reaching out for the railing. As he fired, several more hands were seen reaching over the cable. Some had long, curved iron swords. More gunfire erupted from the *Shiloh*'s .50-caliber machine guns on the bridge wings.

Just as Collins lowered his nine millimeter, a shattering scream filled the air as several of the strange attackers burst from the side of the ship. They were all armed with the same weaponry that had killed the little girl on the island that had been newly christened Compton's Reef. *Shiloh* then added her own powerful searchlights to the already surreal scene before them. Ropes made of organic sea material were thrown over the railings, and grappling hooks made of fish bone entwined between rails and cables. Farbeaux reacted fast and went to the sides and started cutting the ropes before the creatures climbing them could get a full foothold on the main deck. As Henri cut through the seaweed-like material, Jason joined him and started firing over the side. His first round caught one of the horrid-smelling attackers in the face, and the beast screamed. It was high pitched, and if it weren't for the heavy gunfire from *Shiloh*'s crewmen, the noise of the injured boarder would have been earsplitting. Just as the head recoiled, the rope was cut, and the creature fell backward into three more.

Captain Johnson couldn't believe what was happening. His ship was actually being boarded. Not since the heady days of the civil war between communists and nationalists in 1928 China had an American ship of war been attacked in this manner. Johnson grabbed the 1 MC microphone and then said the words no American warship captain had uttered in close to a hundred years: "All hands, repel boarders, repel boarders!"

Several of the strange weapons crashed through the bridge windows, and then one of the .50-caliber Brownings and one of the heavy searchlights illuminated the attackers in their boats to the port side of *Shiloh*. The brutal size of the American rounds caught the boats and their crewmen and chopped them to pieces.

"XO, get the anchor up. Engine room, get me some power up here. Helm, steer straight ahead. Get us moving!"

On deck, Jack heard the anchor start to raise, and *Shiloh* surged to life. He turned quickly and saw Master Chief Jenks and Charlie Ellenshaw as they were firing M4 assault rifles over the side. Thus far, they had kept their attackers at bay, and only a few had managed the treacherous climb to *Shiloh*'s deck. There were bodies floating all around the large missile cruiser. As Jack raised his head, one of the attackers who had made the climb screamed as it launched itself at him. He moved too slowly and was knocked down, and the creature seized that opportunity and pounced. Jack tried in vain to get his pistol up in time, but the attacker wedged his hand between it and the deck.

Jack looked into the animated face of his adversary, and he didn't care for what he was seeing at all. The clear, small, sharp teeth were in full display, and the drool from its mouth spiraled down as the beast saw the opportunity. It raised the mother-of-pearl knife high into the air, and Jack prepared himself for the sharp blade to crash into his chest. The gleaming earrings and other pearl-like adornments rattled and shook as the beast, who dressed like the pirates of old, prepared to kill him.

Suddenly, the head of the attacker swung sharply to the left as a rifle butt crashed into its skull. The beast went limp, and before Jack knew what had happened, Carl was helping him to his feet. The M4 was at his side as he faced the colonel.

"Sorry. Ran out of ammo. Had me scared there for a minute, Jack. You're slowing down a little, enough so that you let Flipper's ugly cousin almost gut you."

"I could say the same for you, Swabby. A little later and I would have been sushi."

As the scream of heavy-caliber bullets streaked over into the waters, *Shiloh* started her run. The foam and burst of power at the stern caught several of the attackers as they climbed their ropes and made it to the stern railing, just as *Shiloh* took a powerful leap forward in the water. Violet spray and foam flew high into the air, and her thrust forward slung the boarders from the railing.

As Jack regained his breath after the brief struggle with death, he felt the deck beneath him heave as *Shiloh* used her two powerful turbojet engines to spring forward. Almost all personnel on her exposed deck lost their footing due to the acceleration of one of the world's fastest warships.

The night sky was crisscrossed with blue, red, and green tracers. Star shells started to explode from the five-inch main mount on the foremost section of *Shiloh*, and their magnesium flares lit up the night sky. Luckily, they didn't need computer guidance to fire the five-inch gun straight into the air. It was better than nothing.

"Look!" Charlie said, pointing toward the two anchored Russian ships.

Peter the Great was also slowly starting to move. Her anchor had been cut loose as her powerful engines were throttled to their stops. Only the *Simbirsk* was idle. And to all their horror, she was also burning from her forecastle to her bridge. Flames licked at her forward sixteen-inch gun mount, and an explosion could be seen rising high into the sky.

Collins suddenly sprang and moved quickly to the stairs leading to the bridge. He entered and saw Johnson directing the intense fire from his station at the bridge windows.

"Captain, get us over to the *Simbirsk*. She's starting to burn!" Jack yelled.

Johnson had to be given credit for not even questioning the direction. He immediately ordered *Shiloh*'s helm hard over.

"Damage control, stand by to board *Simbirsk* and assist in firefighting."

Jack nodded at Johnson and made his way down to help in the endeavor to save their only ticket home. *Shiloh* sped through the floating carnage of the attackers. It rammed smaller boats with their screaming crewmen and crushed them beneath her massive weight. The twin propellers slashed and mutilated those creatures that had escaped the ramming. The battle was one of the more ruthless scenes any of the experienced Event Group personnel had ever witnessed.

Of the three ships anchored that night, one was burning heavily, and the other two had been boarded by an unknown threat. All of this from sixteen small boats and the tenacious creatures that crewed them. The last thing they saw was one of the searchlights picking up the largest of the ships as it moved off into the dwindling moonlight, the pirate flag flying magnificently on the topmost sail.

The attack lasted no more than seven minutes.

14

Three hours later, the fires on board *Simbirsk* had been put out. The crews of *Shiloh* and *Peter the Great* examined the damage as both cruiser captains had straddled the damaged World War II warship in a protective layer that any enemy would find hard to get past. A total of over six hundred men lined the decks of both with automatic weapons as they all scanned the sea for further threats.

The two captains, Jack Collins, Carl Everett, Henri Farbeaux, and Salkukoff met at the burned fantail of the *Simbirsk*.

"The phase shift power plant, was it damaged at all?" Captain Kreshenko asked, looking at Jack.

"Professor Gervais and the master chief are evaluating that as we speak. Thus far, it looks as though the quick thinking of Gervais saved us from the enemy getting to the equipment. He and his assistants locked themselves inside the engine room and dogged the hatches. They couldn't get in and were butchered by the Russian, American, and Royal Marine contingent sent by you. Obviously, we need more security aboard *Simbirsk*. We can't risk losing that ship at this point."

"Are you suggesting that these . . . these creatures were after the power plant?" Salkukoff asked with skepticism written on his stern face.

Collins now turned his attention to Salkukoff. "Well, let's see here, Colonel. Their boarding parties never made an attempt to get belowdecks of either

Peter the Great or *Shiloh*. But they did the *Simbirsk*. I've never been a big be-
liever in coincidence, and if your files on me are as accurate as I think they are,
you should know that."

"As you say, they are accurate files, Colonel Collins. So why do we not cut
to the chase, as you Americans say? Ask me your questions, and maybe I can
allay your suspicions about my mission."

"I'll bite. What are your orders?"

At this, even Captain Kreshenko raised a brow, as he wanted the full details about Salkukoff's mission as well. He could see that the American colonel
was as suspicious about this man as himself.

"To put it bluntly, Colonel, I am here to assure my superiors are not em-
barrassed by this ship and the ways and means we received the technology."

"Destroy her," Jack said with a smirk. "But now you find yourself at cross
purposes, don't you?"

"Yes, I would indeed like to survive this, but it is not my highest priority."

"This has nothing to do with the phase shift experiment, does it?"

All eyes went to Jack, curious at the question he had just asked. Carl even
stepped closer to the Russian.

"You're out to protect the way in which that material was stolen originally.
Not only that, you're here to stop us from finding out those sources are still
active within our government, possibly even our military. That's why you didn't
sink *Simbirsk* during your egress into the hurricane. You needed to know just
what it was that *we* knew."

"You Americans love your conspiracy theories, don't you? This is not one
of your films where the hero always figures out the dastardly scheme of the evil
man. This is real life, Colonel Collins."

"Yes, it is." Jack turned to Kreshenko. "Captain, did you confirm with
Moscow the colonel's orders?"

The Russian captain just nodded.

"And where did that confirmation originate? Moscow?"

"No." Kreshenko looked at Collins and shook his head. "Colonel, you
are placing me in a difficult situation."

"Yes, Captain, I am. You have close to five hundred men you're responsible
for, just as Captain Johnson does. We need to know if the only enemy we
have is out there." Jack pointed to the open sea. "Now, this man knows why
the *Simbirsk* was targeted and why they tried to get belowdecks. We need to
know why."

All eyes again went to the Russian colonel.

"You weren't sent to destroy *Simbirsk*; you were sent to salvage her and bring
her home to the motherland, right?" Jack smiled as he knew he was getting

warm to the truth—the same truth that Niles Compton and British MI6 wanted to get at.

"What is that?" Kreshenko asked. "What could possibly be here that Russia needs?"

"Industrial blue diamonds," Henri answered for Jack.

"And he should know. He's stolen enough of them from us to make the identification," Carl said as he too eyed the Russian.

"The misguided captain is most assuredly correct, Colonel. I do know my diamonds." Henri turned and looked at Kreshenko. "In ten years, the most advanced nations of the world will be fighting over this very limited resource for energy purposes. These fine fellows have come to utilize them in the most industrious of ways. I see them as money, but you men see them as power. Why they abound in this world and not our own will have to be explained by a geologist"—he looked at Jack and their shared memories of Sarah McIntire—"but I suspect that is the reason we have the company of your presence."

Jack smiled and nodded at the Frenchman, who dipped his head at the colonel's favored look.

"Speculate all you want, Colonel. My superiors want their ship and their experiment back," Salkukoff said. "And as for your question, yes, we have recovered *Simbirsk* before. In 1989, she reappeared in the Black Sea with several of those disgusting creatures on board. Before we had a chance to recover her, she vanished once more. Three hundred of our men went with her. We did recover some of these from her superstructure before she did her disappearing act. Failing to recover our property will lead us to destroying her. Even with you on her, Colonel."

"Who do you work for? Whoever they are must think you are expendable, because without your *Simbirsk*, you're as stuck as we are," Jack persisted.

"I work for my government, of course." Salkukoff never allowed his eyes to leave Jack's.

"The orders, as confirmed, never originated in Moscow, Colonel. I must insist you answer Colonel Collins's question," Kreshenko said.

Salkukoff stepped back and then looked at all of them. "I work for my government."

"President Putin is not the head of that government, is he?" Henri asked.

"Does it really matter, Colonel Farbeaux?"

"Colonel, you have to see this," Charlie said as he came forward with Jenks in tow. The master chief was also holding a small fire extinguisher. Ellenshaw saw the serious faces of the men standing in an angry circle, and he and Jenks stopped. "Uh, we're all still friends here, right?" crazy Charlie asked, lowering the rag he had been trying to show Jack.

"I have a feeling we're not, Professor," Kreshenko said, but he was not looking at the Americans. He was staring straight at Salkukoff.

Carl turned to Charlie. "What have you got, Doc?"

Ellenshaw was silent at first as he caught the heavy vibes streaming off the angry men.

"Doc?" Everett asked again.

"Oh, this." He held out an old red rag. It had a clear substance dripping from it. "It was recovered from the stern decking, and we suspect it was how the fire was started. Chief?"

Jenks nodded. Ellenshaw allowed the rag to drip onto the old wood decking of *Simbirsk*. Then Charlie eased over to Jenks and accepted a small square of steel.

"As you see, this substance doesn't burn the wood deck, correct? Now watch this," Ellenshaw gingerly laid the small piece of steel onto the substance. Suddenly, the liquid activated, and a magnesium-type of flare-up happened. The steel melted right before their eyes, and then when it touched the wooden deck, it slowly fizzled to nothing.

"Damn," Carl said as he kneeled to examine the spot. "Chemical?"

"Organic," Jenks said. "In the late '70s, I heard rumors that the navy was experimenting with the glands of certain fish and other sea life, and they were amazed to find some of these same properties. This stuff more than likely originated with some kind of fish—clam, who knows? But it was a substance that was harvested, to be sure." Jenks looked over at the assembled men. "Evidently, our aggressive friends from the sea are a little more knowledgeable than we gave them credit for."

Without warning, Jack quickly reached out and deftly removed Salkukoff of his holstered weapon and then tossed it to Everett. Kreshenko looked momentarily shocked, but Salkukoff did not.

"Easy, Captain," Henri said as he stepped up beside Kreshenko.

Everett looked from the Russian captain to Jack. Then he went to Kreshenko and handed him the Russian pistol.

"Captain, I suggest you place this man under arrest until such a time as we can get the hell out of this screwed-up world," Collins said.

Kreshenko shocked them all by handing the pistol back to Salkukoff. "Consider yourself under arrest, Colonel. You still have the privilege of defending yourself, but you are hereby prohibited from venturing belowdecks of *Simbirsk*."

"A wise decision, Captain," he said as he holstered the pistol.

Jack looked at the two Russians and shook his head and then turned away, followed by Carl and Henri.

Ellenshaw looked at Jenks.

"We have got to start being in on these meetings."

"Yeah, we end up missing the good stuff."

Master Chief Jenks easily tossed Kreshenko the fire extinguisher and left with Charlie.

Just after 6:00 A.M., alarms were sounded again on all three ships. Men crowded around the railings and watched as the alarms died down to nothing as the fleet of villagers started to sail by on their small wooden ships. With their brightly colored sails pushing them through the strangely colored sea, sailors from both nations watched them go by. There were catcalls and whistles when the men of both navies saw the women inside the boats as they prepared their fishing nets for the day.

"Look at that," Carl said as he stood next to Jack. "It's like the world moves on for them. Death by those fish-looking pirate bastards must be close to an everyday occurrence."

"I'm afraid you're probably right, Swabby."

As the hundred boats moved silently past the warships, one of the men with mud covering his face raised a hand. Unlike the day before when there was not even an indication that these small people even realized they were there, this time there was a greeting. Jack watched the headman as he lowered his arm. Jack's mind was filled with the glee of that little girl as he gave her the salt-water taffy. Then the memory broke apart as he saw her face in death not three hours later. He turned away from the railing.

"You're having the same thoughts on Director Compton's edict on getting involved with indigenous people?"

Jack watched the small fishing boats vanish into the rising sun of the east and then turned and nodded. "I tend to lean more toward the Garrison Lee way of doing things."

"Yeah, kill the bad guys, and then we'll figure out the rest."

"Yeah, this noninterference stuff, sometimes it's hard to see and grasp, even coming from one of the smartest men in the world."

A Russian commando approached Collins, and with a sour look on his face, he reported, "Colonel, I have been sent to inform you that Colonel Salkukoff has requested you join him aboard *Peter the Great*." The Russian saluted, but Jack held firm. The hand remained raised just below the man's helmet. The commando finally caught on. "We have a prisoner."

Jack finally returned the salute, and the Russian left with an arrogant gait. He brushed by two American sailors, and one of the men made a turn to go after the commando, but Captain Johnson walked by at just the right time and shooed the men back to work. The captain, his eyes momentarily on his men, finally turned and went to Jack and Carl.

"This is getting a little tense around here," Johnson said as he joined the two.

"I don't think it's going to get any better," Jack said. "Fighting a common foe hasn't resulted in forgetting old animosities, has it?" Collins said, and then he faced Johnson. "It seems we've been invited over to *Peter the Great*. Want a look-see at this marvel of the seas?"

"Wouldn't miss it for the world," Johnson answered as he gestured toward the gangway and the waiting Zodiac. "But you know, I think I'll take a marine strike team with us. I like to share my experiences."

"And Henri," Jack said, smiling. "I like the way the Frenchman gives Salkukoff the creeps."

"I like that aspect also," Johnson agreed.

"We're starting to think more alike every hour, Captain," Carl said as he and Jack followed the captain of *Shiloh* to the waiting Zodiac.

Deep in the bowels of *Shiloh* and her darkened CIC, several radar men were busy making adjustments to their repaired systems and failed to see that the horizon had momentarily filled with a blip that, if they had seen it, would have been comparable in size to an entire battle group, just sitting there on the horizon.

Their own three ships were about to face the entire home fleet of their aquatic enemy.

LOS ANGELES—CLASS ATTACK SUBMARINE USS *HOUSTON*

Tempers and fears remained high as sailors accustomed to having everything they ever needed supplied to them by the navy had been exhausted. They fought tooth and nail with repairing so many systems that none of them suspected they would ever see home again. Several times, *Houston* started sliding down the mountain shelf as her weight turned against them. The ballast tanks remained filled with seawater as they battled the pumps that would eject that water from their tanks.

"Okay," the chief of the boat said from a crawl space. "Try her now."

With relief exploding from his pent-up breath, Captain Thorne heard the outer and inner vents open and then just as quickly close. He squeezed his eyes shut in offered prayer, as did the tired and frightened men around him.

"That did it, Chief," Thorne said as he winked at the young ballast control technician next to him. The chief crawled out of the small enclosed space. He was covered with sweat.

"Remind me to write one hell of a nasty letter to the Electric Boat Division about making more room behind these damn consoles!"

Thorne assisted the small career navy man to his feet and slapped him on the back. "I'll deliver it myself, Chief." Thorne turned and nodded back into the control room. "Okay, Gary, give her a shot of air, and we'll see if the chief's magic works."

Inside the control room, Gary Devers nodded at the ballast control officer. The man closed his eyes and then turned the small switch that activated the powerful pumps. They heard it throughout the boat as the ballast pumps kicked in. Every man heard the pumps start doing their job as water was beginning to be forced from the ballast tanks.

A loud cheer went up throughout the entire length of *Houston*. Captain Thorne stepped through the hatchway and watched the faces of his XO and of his ballast control officer. He waited for the word.

"Pumping ballast from the boat to the sea!" the officer called out loud enough that another cheer shot through the boat.

"Gary, have the engines ready for all back."

"Aye. Make ready for full astern, and then—"

The explosion sounded distant, but every man knew exactly what it was. Ballast control had blown another one of her precious circuit boards as the makeshift system was unable to withstand the load of the powerful pumps.

Houston settled and calmed as the pumps wound down. The lights flickered and then steadied as USS *Houston* started to slide down the large shelf they had come to rest upon. The boat scraped and shuddered as every man felt the boat start to speed up. And then, as suddenly as the slide of death had started, it skidded to a stop and then silently went back to her death slumber precariously close to the end of the shelf.

Thorne placed his head into the crook of his arm and then cursed their luck. They had gone through every circuit board that they found, washing machine parts to privately owned stereo equipment. Even the old movie projector had been used. It all seemed hopeless.

"Close the outside vents. It doesn't seem *Houston* is ready to leave just yet," Thorne said with a wink to those control room crew who were watching him. This time, he saw the hopelessness in their eyes as the realization struck them that odds were fast climbing they would never see the open sky again. Thorne once more brought up the 1 MC mic. He started to talk but faltered, and then he momentarily hung his head. Instead of talking to his crew like he should have, he replaced the mic and then started forward, away from the despondent eyes of his young crewmen.

As he made his way forward, he passed his sailors, and they avoided his eyes.

"Captain, have a minute?"

Thorne stopped as he wanted to turn and tell whoever it was that he had all the damn time in the world, just as they all did, but stopped when he saw the weapons officer. He just nodded once.

"Skipper, I have to report something, and I just don't know how."

Thorne focused fully on the young man before him. He raised his brows as he refused to allow his voice to betray his distress over *Houston*'s situation to show.

The officer offered the captain a small jar. Thorne took it from his hand and looked at it. He rolled the bottle over and then held it up to the light. He lowered it, and the confusion on his face was evident. The water inside had a purplish hue to it.

"What is this, some kind of contamination?"

"No, sir. The water we took on during the initial attack, or whatever it was, was normal. Seawater, nothing more. This here is still seawater, but as you can see, it's not the right makeup of color and other nutrients from the oceans of the world."

"Just what in the hell are you saying, Lieutenant?"

"Skipper, when we were hit, we were in a normal surrounding of ocean water. After the flooding was controlled, we sprung a few leaks here and there, but it was controllable. But what we didn't expect was what came through those leaks. This," he said as he tapped the water in the small jar. "I tested the ballast tanks also, Skipper. They're full of this stuff. The seas we're in are violet in color and lacking commercial contaminants. Nothing—no oil or other pollution we find in oceans all over the world. No matter where we are or how deep, we always have dirty seas. But this, it's like the ocean has never seen an oil- or diesel-powered ship. Ever."

Thorne was even more perplexed and lost. He looked at the water and then at the young face of the lieutenant.

"How many crew know about this?" he asked as he handed the sample back.

"Just me and my weapons people. But word's spreading fast, Captain."

"Well, there's not a lot we can do to investigate that right now, Lieutenant." Thorne paused and bit his lip and then came to a decision. He took the lieutenant by the shoulder and then leaned in conspiratorially. "Lock your men up. Tell the cooks in the galley to send you all your meals. You're now too busy to stop your leaks to venture forth." He winked. "We can't let this spread. These boys have too much on their plate already. Hold them until we find out one way or the other about ballast control."

"Yes, Captain."

Thorne nodded, and the lieutenant turned and left. Alone, Thorne faced the cold bulkhead separating some of the men's sleeping quarters from the forward torpedo room.

"Help us out here, old girl." He patted the steel beneath his touch. It was cold.

"Skipper?"

Thorne turned to see XO Devers standing there with a young man off shift from the torpedo room. Thorne nodded as he felt betrayed by his voice once more.

"Machinist Mate Ramirez says he might have an answer to our problem. He says it's dangerous, but he believes it may work in getting the pumps back online."

Thorne looked at the young man who stood nervously waiting. The captain recognized the boy but could have sworn he had never exchanged so much as a hello before this day.

"Machinist Mate?"

"The Mark 48, Captain."

"A torpedo?" Thorne asked.

"Yes, sir. I know the Mark 48 from its tail fins to her warhead. I believe inside her guidance system there is a board we can use to rig the ballast pumps."

"I have a feeling you have a *but* to offer here, Ramirez."

"Yes, sir. It's a big but for sure. Almost the size of my wife's." He smiled but found no one was smiling with him.

"Go ahead, Machinist Mate Ramirez. It's the day for bad news."

"We have to take the Mark 48 completely apart to get to that guidance chip."

"I suspected that much, Ramirez," Thorne said.

"Yes, sir. I know you did, but we have to disassemble the actual warhead. It's the chip on the circuit board that tells the Mark 48 when and where to detonate. It's real sensitive. Even a small charge of static electricity will set off the warhead."

Thorne closed his eyes and then suddenly opened them.

"Can you do it without blowing us from here back home? Although that's far more acceptable than where we are now."

"Yes, sir, but it's like brain surgery. The boat can have no movement at all."

"Well, great. With the gravity slides we're experiencing, I don't know how we'll be able to pull that off."

The XO and the machinist mate waited.

"Okay, Dr. Ramirez, let's get surgery ready."

USS *Houston* might not be as dead as earlier believed. But then again, with Machinist Mate Ramirez taking apart one of the world's most powerful torpedo warheads on a boat that only wanted to slide into a deep oblivion, suffocating might have been preferable.

Thorne closed his eyes again and this time prayed for his entire crew. He touched the cold steel of *Houston*'s hull once more.

"One break is all we ask for, Gray Lady."

In answer to his prayer, *Houston* began another slide toward the jagged edge of the mountain.

Their break might have to come in some other form.

PART THREE

PIRATES OF THE PURPLE SEA

Exult, O shores, and ring, O bells! But I, with mournful tread,
walk the deck my Captain lies, fallen cold and dead.

—Walt Whitman,
"O Captain! My Captain!"

15

Niles looked up from his hushed conversation with Xavier Morales as the others sat down. The missing heads of all the departments suggested Niles had some news concerning their mutual friends in the North Atlantic. They were wrong.

"I want to say something about what is really happening. It's not just about the colonel and his mission team in the Atlantic. The entire battle group is missing. This rumor you may have already heard, as I failed to stop the scuttlebutt before it started. It's true. They are not lost, just missing. That is not why I asked you here. I figure you deserve a more detailed mission objective. Virginia may need some input from someone other than me or Xavier. She may need your input also. I put Xavier and Virginia in the clean room of Europa and sequestered them to do some very deep research through Europa. She did her job and may have a bread-crumb lead as to what the Russians are playing at where our field team is concerned. We suspect that things inside the Russian government are not as they appear. These facts are being forwarded to our friends in Britain, as they have suspected the same thing for the past thirty years. Virginia?"

Virginia stood at her normal seat at the conference table and cleared her throat and then nodded.

"The information we gathered through Europa and her cyber activities is not only disturbing, it's terrifying. It seems we have been duped since the great military purges of Stalin's in the '30s. We have learned that not only is the Russian government not in control of that nation, they haven't been since the spring of 1941. With the start of Hitler's Operation Barbarossa, the German invasion of the Soviet Union, Joseph Stalin became nothing more than a fig-urehead of that nation."

"Tell them your suspicions, Doctor," Niles said with encouragement.

"The people behind this charade since 1941 are now preparing for all-out war with the West."

"We worked closely with them during the Overlord operation; we had no indication at that time of any deception," Alice said.

"That is because we were dealing with people who had no knowledge of this hidden government outside the office of the president. Putin may not even know he is not in charge. He is nothing more than a mouthpiece but thinks it's him calling the shots. Just like every leader that country has had since Stalin. They are all figureheads. They fall from grace, no problem, next man up as ap-pointed by this hidden group," Virginia said as she shook her head at the dis-belief of her own voice.

"Okay, now you know as much as we do. Virginia, prepare a presentation, and I'll speak with the president as soon as you have it."

Virginia just nodded as a brief thought of Jenks and the others flashed through her mind. She was prepared to do as ordered, when she stopped and then pulled out her electronic notepad. "We do have one more item that is as confusing as the rest. It seems the Russians are out to acquire as many indus-trial blue diamonds as they can get their hands on."

"And why are blue diamonds so important to the Russians?" Niles asked Virginia.

"That we don't know. But one thing is for sure: the Russian government as we know it does not exist, and what their plans are for them we haven't a clue."

Niles remained sitting and thinking as Virginia sat back down. He looked at Alice in the hopes she had some advice as far as why the Russians would want blue diamonds, but her face said that she was just as stunned as he was. She just shook her head.

"We have to stand down for now until we have more information. I'll get word to our friends in MI6 somehow and see what they can come up with.

"Captain, you haven't commented since you came in. Is it that you're wor-ried about Jack and the others? Or is the thought of the Russian agenda for war against the West?"

Will Mendenhall gathered his briefing materials and then faced his director.

"I think war has already been declared here, Doctor, and we're just learn-ing who is declaring it. It might already be too late."

Niles watched as they filed out of his office and conference room. He picked up the phone and made the connection to the Oval Office.

"How in the hell do I start this conversation?"

KIROV-CLASS BATTLE CRUISER *SIMBIRSK*

Master Chief Jenks watched as Professor Gervais covered the ground that he and Charlie Ellenshaw had already covered without the Russian scientist's knowledge. Jenks wanted to see how up front the good professor was in telling the Americans the truth of the science of phase shifting.

"As you see, gentlemen, the phase shift occurs when the correct frequencies are struck between the field generator on board *Simbirsk* and the surrounding air. For a reason no one's science can explain adequately is why the vessel vanishes at all. The electrical field generated around the ship disperses and then takes the ship with it into an adjoining dimension that fits the electrical field frequency. This world just happens to be on the same frequency as the phase shift field. Eventually, by adjusting varying frequencies, we can discover new worlds, new peoples, new assets for our own."

"Professor, trust me when I say we have had some experience in this area." Jenks paced around the glass separating the field coils for the phase shift engine and placed a hand on one of the large lightbulb-like electromagnetic pulse projectors. He removed it quickly when he remembered Charlie's hypothesis that it was these innocent things that burned sailors to death when their electrical field was released. "The *Simbirsk* cannot hit the same frequency twice, much less continuously send it to the same dimension. It would be random at best. So why does the *Simbirsk* travel to the same one every time?" Jenks turned and faced the small Russian, and Charlie saw that the man was apprehensive at best. "You would have to have a targeted transponder to guide the shift to that same location, thus here we are in Candyland with the purple sea. So, you see my concern here, Professor? The electromagnetic field and the frequency of this world cannot be random, as you suggest. You don't know the frequency. You would need a transponder, a signal to lock on for that correct freq."

"How do you know it would take a corresponding beacon or transponder? Maybe this is the only other dimension there is," Gervais said, thinking his argument was sound enough for the Americans to become believers.

"I don't want to get into the whole Einstein thing about there being a varied world of differing dimensions. That stuff gives me a massive headache. But rest assured, Professor, we know for a fact that dimensions are vast and varied. Time, space, all that $E = MC^2$ crap, while not proven"—Charlie smiled as he glanced at Jenks—"is a fact of life."

Jenks saw the worry on the face of Gervais. "Believe me, we've been down a lot of roads, and we suspect Mr. Alien Brain Einstein was pretty accurate." Jenks moved back to the small worktable with the diagrams Professor Gervais didn't know the Americans already had. "Now, why don't you tell us what it is you people are really up to here?" Jenks lit a cigar, knowing that was forbidden to do inside the phase shift engine area.

"I don't understand," the Russian said as he glanced toward the main hatch, where a Russian commando watched them.

Jenks reached into his pocket and produced a second blue diamond that Jack had given him for this little confrontation. "You have a field element here already, don't you, Doc?"

Gervais looked from the filthy diamond to Jenks and Charlie. Ellenshaw was smiling, as he loved confronting people about the truth or lie of their predicament.

"Field element?" he asked, looking again at the Russian watching them. He seemed more attentive than he had been just a moment before.

"What ship is out there, Professor?" Jenks persisted.

"I don't know what it is you mean."

Charlie stood and did his best prosecutor pose as he faced Gervais. Jenks allowed the cryptozoologist to have his moment.

"I think it's time you come to the side of the Lord, Professor. That man you have calling the shots is a maniac sent to cover up the fact that your government, or whoever he works for, has known about this place for a very long time and has sent people here to gather up industrial blue diamonds. For what purpose?"

Gervais clammed up.

Charlie leaned on the table, his hands only inches from the Russian scientist. "You know, I have learned a lot about people by accompanying the very best while they were doing what they do best, discovering who the real bad guys are." He looked at Jenks, who nodded. "You, my good man, are in the company of very bad people, who in turn are being ordered around by more, even worse people. Why are you here?"

"You know that Salkukoff is here for one reason. He cannot allow anyone to learn the real truth of what's happening here. He is going to try to kill us all," Jenks added.

"He will succeed. He always does."

"Now, was that so hard? Being human is hard sometimes, and I know that for a fact," Jenks said.

"So, you have been in this dimension before?" Charlie asked, surprised Gervais had given up so readily.

"Yes, twice." Again, they saw him look at the Russian commando, who was overtly watching them. "Certain elements inside Russia have discovered a new and improved way to destroy mankind. During the rush to find new weaponry for the common good during this outer space incursion, we discovered a way to destroy organic material and leave the surrounding area—buildings, cities, and geological formations—untouched."

"Neutron physics?" Jenks asked.

"That's been outlawed by international agreement," Charlie said, and for some strange reason, that elicited a small laugh from Gervais.

"With industrial diamonds, we can now generate power from a laser platform in space. We can target entire cities or countries. But the power it takes will require abundant industrial blue diamonds to operate. Salkukoff has information on your strange group under the desert and knew that you had recovered every available blue diamond on the planet for Operation Overlord and some other mysterious project in Brooklyn conducted a few weeks back."

A knowing look between Charlie and Jenks belied the fact that the Russians had an inkling of the Wellsian Doorway. How much they knew, that would be for Colonel Collins and Niles to figure out later.

"Salkukoff and others believe the Americans are on the same trail for the same technology. You are correct in one regard—he knew your group would be coming to the North Atlantic when the *Simbirsk* mysteriously arrived out of nowhere."

"And his plan is to . . . ?" Jenks persisted.

"His plan is to discover what you know and then to make assurances you never get back home."

"What assets from your nation are here?" Charlie asked.

"I don't know. They don't take me into their confidence. The two times I came, I was blindfolded and kept in isolation. It seems we were transported by ship, but every time I was allowed to depart, again I was blindfolded. I do know it was a ship, as I am prone to seasickness. That fact they couldn't hide from me. I am also aware that with the original transport to this world by *Simbirsk*, she had a well-equipped library. One of the books in that library was one Dr. Ellenshaw mentioned in passing yesterday. It was *Treasure Island*. Somehow, Salkukoff uses that book, which was found by our aquatic friends, and used it to his advantage. He interfered most assuredly in the development of this species toward an aggressive nature. He uses that pirate nature to secure the diamonds."

"Come on, Dr. Zhivago, we figured that out when we saw the damn pirate flags on those boats. Now tell us something useful before that maniac kills more innocent people," Jenks said angrily.

"All I do know is that Salkukoff and his higher management use one species against the other. That they use the indigenous life-forms here to gather the diamonds for transport back to our dimension. One group gathers; the other group secures and then transfers the diamonds to their new masters."

"So, you people have enslaved one group and given power over them to another. Do you ever stop and think before you do something as shameful as slavery, no matter what the cause is?" Charlie looked at Gervais, and Jenks could see that the kind and gentle cryptozoologist was furious. "All of this for gathering the science to kill your fellow man?" Charlie said with indignant outrage.

"Professor, why do you suppose the villagers greeted us with caution but not outright fear?"

"Because they are your slaves, and they were used to seeing men from our world in theirs," Charlie said as things started to fit. "They dig the diamonds, and the aquatic species keeps them in line. Amazing inhumanity."

Gervais hung his head. His shame was apparent. "I believe the mission here is coming to an end. Salkukoff and his people have grown paranoid that their mission has been compromised. They are still far short of acquiring enough of the diamonds for any extensive weaponization purposes, but they have decided the risk of exposure is now too great to continue. Now, that's all I know, gentlemen."

Jenks looked at Charlie. "That's all we're going to get from Mr. Wizard here." Jenks slapped the small man on the back hard. "Thanks, you sniveling little coward."

Gervais now knew he had been ambushed by the Americans. Once more he looked up, and he saw that the Russian commando had vanished.

"Looks like the cat will be out of the bag soon enough, Doc." Jenks also saw that their guard had vanished. It was obvious the Russian commando had more important things to report to Salkukoff. "I hope you have a good reason ready as to why you spilled your guts."

Charlie paused and looked down at Gervais.

"You make me ashamed of being a scientist. Our jobs are to explain and teach the rest of the world to everyone. Here you have enslaved a gorgeous people and raped their land so you can possibly kill other innocents." He slammed his hands down on the table. "You deserve what's coming to you."

Jenks puffed on his cigar and then paused at the spot the commando had occupied moments earlier.

"You have an offer of sanctuary aboard the *Shiloh*. I suggest you make use of it."

Jenks and Ellenshaw left the professor alone to contemplate his future.

Jenks and Charlie reported to Jack and Carl. His suspicions were confirmed, and as he looked out over the violet seas, he knew the Russians had an unknown phase shift asset out there somewhere. He turned and faced his two intrepid interrogators.

"So, these sea creatures are attacking us and the villagers in support of the Russian game here? And you are convinced the Russians already have what amounts to an occupation force? And he now has a suspicion that Salkukoff is finished with this little experiment and is packing it in?"

"According to Gervais," Jenks offered.

"Radar from neither *Shiloh* nor *Peter the Great* has shown anything that could be considered an asset here, Jack—no ships, no aircraft," Carl reminded him.

"A nearby island?" he asked.

"Not that shows up on radar. Compton's Reef is the only substantial island for seven hundred miles that our limited resources can tell," Carl explained. "There is an above-water reef thirty miles to the southwest. Coral mostly. We'll get the drone to overfly it as soon as we can. That may well be a place for our Russians to hide. Now we know why Salkukoff wants the *Simbirsk* back so badly. They need it for this occupation force to get home with their plunder."

"Could they be hidden on the island we just visited?"

"Possible, but improbable," Charlie said. "Those people were not concerned about us because they were used to seeing men of our dimension because of the Russian incursion. They would have guided us to that element if they had them there, thinking at the very least we were together. They are too innocent to be any sort of ally in this."

"I agree," Jack said, lightly hitting Ellenshaw on the arm as he moved past him. "Okay, we have some time to track this Russian element down. Until then, we have two problems. One, how can we defend these ships against the force of aquatic attackers we faced last night? Two, can we discover if Kreshenko and his crew are a part of this? If not, do they have an inkling of what is really happening not only here but in their own country?"

"My suspicion is that no one in the Russian military is aware of this secret society that runs things over there. Kreshenko believes his orders still originate in Moscow. We know that they don't, but do he and his crew?"

They turned and saw Henri Farbeaux as he stepped in from the shadows.

"Can Kreshenko and his men be convinced that he is on the wrong side of this?" Jack asked the only man in the world who knew this form of criminality.

"My honest evaluation?" Henri asked as he looked at the strange sea surrounding *Simbirsk*.

"If that's possible," Carl said as he jabbed Farbeaux one more time.

"Sometimes it is, Captain, but rarely," the Frenchman said as he turned back to face the group of Americans. "I must stay true to form, at least in Captain

Everett's opinion, and say we cannot take that chance. *Peter the Great* and her crew are now the enemy no matter which way you play this. Kreshenko will follow his orders. The same orders I have for Colonel Salkukoff must apply to all Russian military personnel from this point on."

"What are you saying?" Charlie asked, almost afraid of the answer.

"What he's saying, Doc, is that *Peter the Great* and her entire crew have to meet the same fate as the man they answer to, and that is to eliminate them all if possible," Jack answered for Henri. "See what you can do, Henri. I don't relish the thought of a sea battle here and now. We have to find a way to convince the Russian Navy of our intent to save their lives."

"And the hidden asset they have in this dimension. Even if we convince Kreshenko, they all have to be destroyed and all access to these blue diamonds removed. Whatever that asset is, they may have extensive firepower. The one advantage we have is the fact we know they need the *Simbirsk*."

"One little flaw in these theories, gentlemen, is the fact that these so-called allies from the sea attempted to burn *Simbirsk*. Why would they do that unless our friend Salkukoff had another way home?"

Henri had just thrown the proverbial wrench in the works by saying what everyone else had overlooked.

"My God," Ellenshaw said aloud.

"In my experience, Professor Ellenshaw, God has very little to do with what we do for a living. He abandoned men like us long ago."

Henri Farbeaux walked away after giving them all the hard truth of the day.

Jack faced Jenks, Carl, and Charlie. He saw Ryan approach. He looked hot and sweaty. He stepped up to Collins.

"What did you find out, Jason?"

"Well, you won't believe it. It's like visiting a wartime museum down there. Colonel, this ship is packed full of ordnance. The damn Russians never removed a thing."

"Are you going to let us in on it or what?" Jenks asked.

"I sent Mr. Ryan on a small tour of the facilities on *Simbirsk*. Tell them, Jason."

"The turrets are fully functional. They have over a thousand rounds of sixteen-inch projectiles in her magazines. High and dry, and fully functional, and as deadly as the day the old Soviet Union made them."

"What does that mean?" Ellenshaw asked.

"It means, Doc, we now have something a little more substantial in case we need it, either against our fish-faced pirate friends or . . ." Everett just nodded toward the anchored *Peter the Great*.

Charlie Ellenshaw walked away, shaking his head. Collins knew the old hippie well enough to see what was coming.

"Where does this madness end?"

Not one of the career military men had answers to Charlie's question, especially Jack Collins.

He was also not the only one to know that the United States and Russia were already in a state of war.

16

LOS ANGELES—CLASS ATTACK SUBMARINE USS *HOUSTON*

Captain Thorne pushed the cushioned headphones harder onto his ears as he tried in vain to hear what it was his experienced sonar men were hearing. He cocked his head and then shook it.

"I don't hear anything that doesn't sound like static."

"It was there, Skipper. We heard it on three different occasions."

Thorne removed the headphones and looked at his sonar officer. "Are you sure it wasn't whales or something else biologic?"

"Computers say no. Our program eliminated biologics almost immediately. It says mechanical."

"Surface?"

"We don't know, Skipper. But it seems it has a pattern. Possibly search and then silence. We just don't know."

"Keep on it. It may be a moot point if we don't get those ballast pumps operational."

"Yes, sir."

Thorne left the sonar suite and found XO Devers. He guided him into the mess where he sat down at a table. The cooks were busy, and they were alone.

"What do you think?" Devers asked after he himself had reported the spotty contact earlier.

"It makes my decision not to release the emergency tracking buoy and transponder look brilliant. It's a good thing we didn't if we have a hostile close aboard."

"Agreed. It was a stroke of luck you waited until our situation was dire enough to tell the world we were sunk—of which that aforementioned situation is fast becoming, by the way."

Thorne smiled at Devers.

"Well, let's take our minds off our mysterious visitors until we can do something about it."

Suddenly, there was movement as *Houston* began to once more slide down along the diminishing shelf. Thorne grimaced as the noise of scraping steel against sand and rock sent shivers down the spine of all who heard it. Both officers grabbed the tabletop and held on. Their bodies swayed in a sudden stop as *Houston*'s bow caught on something and her slide was arrested. Both officers let out a pent-up breath.

"Now that, Skipper, is hard to take your mind off of."

Thorne just nodded.

The time USS *Houston* needed to save herself was sliding away faster than their slow ride down the mountainside.

KIROV-CLASS BATTLE CRUISER *SIMBIRSK*

Jack was belowdecks with Carl and Jason and their ever-present company of Russian commandos who watched their every move. They had not seen Colonel Salkukoff in three hours. Kreshenko reported that "His Majesty" had retired for the afternoon. Jack suspected he was missing for other reasons, but since the crew of *Shiloh* was prohibited from access to the old Russian cruiser, there wasn't much he could do about it. The personnel he had aboard was all he could expect. With the Russian captain Kreshenko still a mystery, they knew they couldn't take him into any confidence or suspicion they had.

"There they are," Ryan said as he raised the heavy steel gate to show them the *Simbirsk*'s firepower.

Everett whistled. "Now that's old-school stuff there, Jack."

The sixteen-inch projectiles were lined and stacked on pallets. They were secured by heavy bands of steel bracing and looked as deadly as ever. A thousand shells filled the reinforced magazine.

"The powder bags are stored over there and seem to be high and dry," Ryan said as he pointed to another powder magazine. "They also have .50-caliber and twenty-millimeter ammunition, enough to invade a small country. That's not even mentioning the five-inch shells for the six mounts on deck."

"Evidently, the old girl never got a chance to fire on that Nazi sub she encountered," Jack said as he closed and secured the magazine.

"Are you thinking what I'm thinking here, Jack?" Carl said as he opened the powder magazine storage locker. He stepped back and whistled again as over four thousand silk powder bags were covered in a heavy tarp.

"I think I am. This could be our only fallback in making sure *Simbirsk* never sees her home again."

"Hopefully after we hitch a ride home on her, so let's not get ahead of ourselves here," Jason said with not a smile near his mouth.

The old-fashioned alarm bell sounded throughout the empty bowels of the old cruiser. The three Americans quickly gained the stairs and climbed to the upper decks. The four Russian commandos were right behind them.

The sun was bright and beat down upon the one hundred men who had been transferred over from *Peter the Great* and now lined the rails, manning AK-47s and the *Simbirsk*'s old twenty-millimeter guns. Jack went to the railing and looked out over the seas at where the excitement seemed to stem.

"Look at that," Jenks said as he joined them, wiping his hands on another old rag. Ellenshaw was with him and had to remove his glasses and clean them in order to see the magnificent sight before them.

Coming in from the north was the fishing fleet at full sail. The colors were amazing. Jack turned as more excitement erupted behind them. They ran around turret number two and went to the starboard side. There had to be at least another fifty boats with full loads of women and children heading toward the anchored *Simbirsk*, *Shiloh*, and *Peter the Great*.

Jack was in awe of the native spectacle. They could hear music—flutes, small drums, and gaiety. Collins smiled, and then he heard one of the Russian sailors charge his AK-47, and as Jack watched the young man, he raised the assault rifle to his shoulder. The colonel easily reached out and gently lowered the raised barrel. Other sailors saw this, and they too relaxed.

"Easy. I don't think they're sending their wives and children out to attack."

The Russian sailor smiled, then faltered, and then the large American slapped him on the shoulder with a wink.

"Can't blame the Ruskies for being a little shaky. After all, they've all seen those other ones up close," Jenks said as he turned to Charlie. "They make our pirates from the storybooks look like pussies."

"By the 'other ones,' I suppose you mean what seems to be the dominant species here?"

"Yeah, those jokers. Those fish boys. Bunch of nancies, if you ask me."

As the fishing fleet and the boats from the village came closer, everyone relaxed. Jack looked over and saw the crewmen of both *Peter the Great* and *Shiloh* were also lining the rails, weapons relaxed as they stared in awe at the approaching wave of humanity.

"Ooh," the young sailor said beside Jack. The boy rubbed his belly as he spied the roasted pigs and birds that filled the boats from the island. The music seemed South Pacific in its natural sounds of whistles, drums, and flutes. Russian sailors started cheering their guests as they came on. Even the Americans on *Shiloh* cheered.

Ropes were thrown from both landside and seaward as the boats came in. Russian sailors tied off the ropes and then threw over old rope ladders and lowered the gangway as close to the violet sea as they could get. Sailors started assisting women, men, and children aboard the Russian battle cruiser. Food by the boatload was handed up to the happy men of the *Simbirsk*.

"It seems our hosts have invited themselves to dinner, Colonel."

Collins and his company turned and saw that Captain Kreshenko had joined them. He was wearing a white shirt with his rank on the collar. His first officer, Dishlakov, was at his side.

"It does seem, Captain," Jack said as he turned back and watched the joyous, very much smaller men and women step aboard the largest object they had ever seen before. They touched the rough steel of her turrets and the wood of her deck. They were amazed by the portholes and bridge windows. Several of the more agile men climbed up cables, jabbered something in their native tongue, which would elicit laughs from their visitors, and then the brave man suddenly jumped from the cable and dove forty feet into the violet waters accompanied by many a cheer from the Russians, the British, and the Americans.

The fishing fleet tied up, and load upon load of fish was handed up to waiting arms. Fruits, vegetables, and other exotic growth were brought on board.

"Perhaps we can set aside suspicions and our natural animosity for one evening, Colonel. I will inform your Captain Johnson that he and his off-duty crewmen may join us. Unarmed, of course."

"Of course. And I'm sure Captain Johnson would be happy to accept."

"Of course, we will see to it that the on-duty personnel on board *Shiloh* receive their share of this marvelous bounty."

With that, Captain Kreshenko and Second Captain Dishlakov turned and left.

Jack turned to Carl, and the SEAL and just shrugged. "A breakthrough?"

Collins only raised a brow to the observation.

"Huh. He probably just wants to separate the crew of *Shiloh* and then murder us all during the freakin' dessert course," Jenks mumbled and then went to assist an older woman on board as she struggled with her grip on one of the old rope ladders.

Ryan watched the master chief and then turned to face Jack and Carl.

"He might just have a point about being whacked at dessert. I think I saw that movie."

The foredeck of *Simbirsk* was covered in old World War II green blankets that had once been donated by the United States to her Russian allies at the opening of the war against Nazi Germany. Food of varying varieties extended fifty yards and covered an immense section of deck. Kreshenko had allowed another hundred sailors from *Peter the Great* to join them, and they and *Shiloh*'s crew eyed each other from opposite sides of the blankets. The villagers and the men from their mining operations and their fishing fleet were interspersed with both crews and seemed not to notice the distrust among them. It was obvious distrust was not something these gentle people understood. The gathering had made Jack wary because he didn't know what the natives' play was. It was almost as if they sensed these men were different from those previous thugs that had introduced a form of slavery to their island. Collins knew he felt an obligation to their cause but could not find an avenue that could help them, other than all-out war with their Russian companions. That would ensure that none of them ever saw home again.

Jack's eyes continually roamed the faces on deck, but thus far, there was no sign that Colonel Salkukoff intended to join them. Also missing was Professor Gervais and most of the Russian commandos. Jack pointed this fact out to Everett, who agreed that he too had noticed.

One point of decent news was the fact that for the past half hour, Captains Kreshenko and Johnson were in deep conversation as they walked the deck, speaking only where they were assured they were alone.

Both crews seemed to be accepting of their guests. Americans and Russians alike were kind and very amused by the antics of the villagers. Food by the pound was being consumed by all. Baked fish and other delicacies were placed on steel plates supplied by the engineers, and acetylene torches were used to the amazement of the fishermen and others to heat the fresh bounty of the strangest fish species any of them had ever seen. They were strange enough that Charlie Ellenshaw cringed every time one of these was thrown hissing onto the hot steel. He was running from man to man, trying to see what it was they had caught before the fish vanished forever before his inspection. Crazy Charlie was so excited that he had men from both nations laughing at the way in which he tried inspecting everything before it was consumed. He even went as far as taking a plate from a Russian sailor and looking it over, much to the shock of the man eating it. Still, the crews seemed at ease enough for the moment to excuse the excesses of the past two days.

Jack was also smiling as he watched the excitement of his friend. That was when he saw Henri standing aloof next to the number-one turret. He was in the dark far beyond the powerful deck lighting. Collins silently stood and placed his hand on Carl's shoulder to keep him from following.

"It looks like our Frenchman has something on his mind. I'll be right back."

Jack walked over and stood next to Farbeaux as the Frenchman watched the festivities.

"A beautiful people," was all he said.

"Yes, they are. It's a shame our kind has interfered here," Jack said as he watched a group of young girls no older than ten dance for the sailors to raucous cheers. The female members of *Shiloh* wowed the young girls with parcels full of makeup and small mirrors. It seemed the vagaries of female social standards translated well to species rather than the situation.

"Coming from our world, it seems we should be used to the loss of innocence. We have learned acceptance of a certain amount and go on justifying it in that manner," Henri said as he exhaled deeply. He finally turned and faced Jack. "Professor Gervais is dead."

Collins forced himself to relax as he stepped closer to the Frenchman. "Not by your hand, I hope," he said as he felt the anger already start to well up inside.

"I do not kill harmless old fools, Colonel. You should know that about me by now. No, the good professor hung himself right next to the phase shift engine."

Jack exhaled and then leaned against the bridge bulkhead. "Suicide," he said as he inwardly damned himself by not making Jenks stay close to Gervais at all times. Now, so many answers and a possible ally in their escaping this mess were gone.

"Yes, but it seems strange that four fingers on his right and two on the left were snapped in half. Do you suppose he had difficulty in tying the noose around his neck?"

"You saying it was forced?"

"In the circles I have been privy to, Colonel, men such as Gervais never commit suicide. They blame, they become sorrowful for what they have done, some turn to Jesus, others to the bottle, but most never go out that way—too much of a coward. No, he was murdered."

"My investigation says suicide, Colonel Farbeaux. Otherwise, you would have been the first person questioned if there were the least bit of suspicion as to the cause of death."

Jack frowned as he realized the Russian had come upon them unheard. He could see Henri tense up at the sudden appearance of Salkukoff and his six commandos. Two of them were removing the covered body of Gervais from down below.

"Unfortunate, to say the least," Jack said as he turned and faced Salkukoff.

"He has served his purpose on this mission, Colonel Collins. He has confirmed the phase shift system is still functional. His recommendation to me an hour before he decided to exit this world was that we could make the attempt at getting back to our own dimension at any time."

"That has yet to be agreed upon by my engineer, Master Chief Jenks."

Salkukoff smiled and placed his hands behind his back and then rocked on his heels.

"I'm afraid your calculations are far beyond your understanding of the situation, Colonel Collins. You assume that you still have jurisdiction in this matter. *Your* right of salvage, I think you quoted upon our initial meeting."

Jack remained quiet, as he knew this wasn't his play. It was Salkukoff's.

"For tonight, we will allow these men to enjoy themselves." He started to turn. "It would be a shame for us to have hostilities while our innocent guests are aboard." He started walking and then stopped and faced Collins and Farbeaux once more. "After all, they have a hard enough life as it is facing the Wasakoo."

"The very same Wasakoo you turned into pirates?"

"That was a fortunate coincidence. The Wasakoo had already stumbled up the book on board *Simbirsk* during the original experiment. We just happened to take advantage of it. The idiots actually think *Treasure Island* is like a bible of sorts. Pretty adventurous of them, agreed? Good evening, gentlemen."

They watched the Russian and his escort of killers move away and smile and taste the offered food. Two more went the long way around while carrying the covered body of Gervais.

"May I assume the good colonel knows a little more than he did just last night?" Henri inquired. "I think we just met the architect of this whole situation. The Wasakoo—do you think he even knew he spilled the beans?"

"All he did was confirm the facts we already know, Colonel. I mean, who could make something like the Wasakoo up? I mean, if I made up a name, I would have chosen Klingon, or Romulan, or the Sith, or something." Jack smiled.

"I am always amazed at the way in which you come to your conclusions, Colonel. Totally amazed."

Jack merely walked away without further comment. Henri watched and then slowly followed, shaking his head at the irreverent way he joked during the most stressful times.

The radar operators on both *Peter the Great* and *Shiloh* were relieved early for their chance to join the visitors and eat their food. In the confusion of operators changing shifts, they all missed the large red blip that appeared and then vanished just as quickly.

Death was over the far horizon and was watching them closely.

Salkukoff and his commandos had transferred the body of Professor Gervais to a waiting whaleboat. Twenty-six commandos sat waiting for Salkukoff to join them as the colonel conferred with Captain Kreshenko.

"I have concerns, Colonel Salkukoff. Even though my men are jovial at the moment, I don't expect them to take the news of this apparent suicide well. They all knew of the professor's importance in getting them back home. Morale will plummet."

"That is why we are removing the body to *Peter the Great* for storage. Allow your sailors this time to forget about their situation and enjoy the company of these"—he paused as he gestured to the hundred small boats tied to the anchored ships—"people."

Kreshenko watched as Salkukoff waited for more questions, but the captain merely stepped back to allow the colonel his way. He watched the dark-haired man step easily into the whaleboat and then turned away. He paused when he saw the Frenchman looking at him in the light of the strangely shattered moon overhead—even stranger now that the smashed orb was rising higher into the sky with its trailing tail of moon debris.

"Interesting man," Henri said as he stepped forward and faced the Russian sea captain.

"Interesting term, maybe? But the man is one who I've known for a very long time. Maybe not him, but others like him. They have been hiding in the shadows since the fall of the old regime." Kreshenko looked directly into the Frenchman's blue eyes. "These are men who rejoice in the troubles and sorrows of our world." He started forward to rejoin the men at the bow and their revelry with the villagers but stopped as he came astride Henri. "I suspect he would have little or no compunction to bring that chaotic philosophy to this world also."

"Captain?"

Kreshenko stopped but did not turn.

"We all may have to make some hard choices in the next few hours."

Kreshenko allowed his shoulders to slump as the Frenchman made it clear that their survival might just depend on him and only him. But still the captain moved off in silence.

Farbeaux turned and went to the stern railing of the old warship and watched as the whaleboat started off toward *Peter the Great*. He saw the boat pause momentarily, and then it slowly moved off again. His eyes went to the anchored

Shiloh and saw that her above-deck crew were relaxed, as most of them had just returned from the fabulous feast brought to them by the villagers. Again, his eyes turned away and watched the violet-whitish foam from the Russian boat as it vanished around the port side of *Peter the Great.*

"Is it bothering you as much as it is me?"

Henri heard Jack's voice but remained fixed on *Peter the Great* five hundred yards away. "If you knew my thoughts at the moment, Colonel, you wouldn't like them."

Collins stepped up and stood next to the Frenchman. Although Jack would never fully trust Henri, he knew his instincts were infallible when it came to pegging the intentions of bad people. He knew Farbeaux was one of those bad men who used common sense in the way he did business.

"Where will he strike first?" Jack asked as his eyes also remained on the giant missile cruiser anchored across the way.

"It will not be where we suspect it will come, Colonel," Henri said as he finally turned away from the sea and faced Jack. "That man cannot allow even his own people to return to our world. They have seen and heard far too much. Whoever is pulling Salkukoff's strings wants their venture here and their treasonous activities toward Moscow kept quiet. And I suspect that for many years they have excelled in doing just that—silencing those who know of them."

"Kreshenko?"

"I don't know what is running through that man's mind. He's disciplined, he's loyal to a fault, and he is a career navy man. I suspect Captain Everett or that little naval aviator, Ryan, would have a better chance at getting into his head."

"I've recommended that already. One thing is for sure: until we have an accurate guess as to what that murderous bastard has planned for us, we need Captain Kreshenko to make the right choice."

Henri chuckled as he gestured for Jack to precede him back to the bow and the festivities there.

"So, we are hoping for a career Russian military officer to make the right choice between helping us Westerners or committing wholesale treason?"

"That about sums it up, Colonel."

"Luckily, there is a precedent that shows the average Russian is capable of a little revolt against authority on occasion."

"That, Colonel, sir, is what we are banking on."

Sailors from both nations helped the villagers load their belongings into their small boats. The native people of this strange world were not going home

empty-handed. Americans and Russians both gave freely of their own possessions. Children were leaving with so much candy, cakes baked by both mess
crews, and other items such as mirrors and clothing. The villagers were now
wearing everything from New York Yankees caps to Russian national hockey
team jerseys. The natives were leaving with assorted pots, pans, and utensils
that amazed and wowed each and every one of them. The sailors waved their
good-byes from the railings of both *Simbirsk* and *Shiloh*.

Captain Kreshenko, who had not said a word to anyone during the final
stages of this diplomatic endeavor, allowed the men of *Peter the Great* and *Shiloh* to continue to mix. There were now well over three hundred men compris-
ing both crews on the old battle cruiser. They mingled and spoke in broken
English among themselves, and as sailors, they all had similar stories of their
duties and of home. Even Captain Johnson and his officers were enjoying learn-
ing more about Russian procedures. Even more surprising was the fact that
the strict Captain Kreshenko allowed it.

Charlie Ellenshaw was abnormally silent as he stood alone watching the sails
of the fishing boats grow smaller in the moonlight. He leaned heavily against
the railing and didn't notice the master chief step up next to him. The old navy
man was eating something that resembled a banana but was totally dark green
in color, but looked ripe after peeling.

"I didn't see you eat anything tonight, Nerdly."

Charlie turned and saw the master chief and shook his head. "Sometimes
I don't know how you and Colonel Collins can do it."

"What's that?" Jenks asked as he tossed the green banana peel into the sea.

"Professor Gervais. I believe he was a kind and gentle man who was murdered because of someone's political or military aims. I feel terrible I spoke to
him in the manner in which I did. Just terrible."

"I'll excuse you for that one, Doc, since you are an endangered species of
hippie and all of that. We do it because if we don't, others will meet the same
fate as the good professor. This is a screwed-up world we live in, even here in
this whacked-out place. And I know you probably think Gervais was a good
man forced to do bad things, but that's the choice most people in the scientific
field must decide on for themselves. Now, as for what I would do?" Jenks paused
and lit his after-dinner cigar. "Simple—I would have blown the whole project
to hell and back before doing what he did. All he had to do was say something."
Jenks slapped Charlie on the back. "I think you're one of those opposite-
thinking kind, Nerdly. I think you would have screamed to high heaven if you
knew about this experiment. And that, Chucky, would have gotten you a note
on a toe tag in the morgue."

"Thank you . . . I think," Ellenshaw said.

"Ah, what the hell does an old sea dog know about it?" Jenks said and then guided Ellenshaw away from the railing. "All I want to do is get home and then live the rest of my life with a woman who will do all the thinking. Now, let's get you some of those leftovers and get something into that skinny-ass body of yours."

Charlie smiled, knowing that even a heavy brain like Jenks could think about the good of things.

"I envy you, Master Chief," Charlie said as Jenks slapped a large piece of pork into his hand.

"Ah, crap. I envy you, Nerdly, having three names like you do. Charles Hindershot Ellenshaw III," he said, looking up at the moon and its trailing comet-like tail. "Now that is really a name you can sink your teeth into."

Charlie smiled, as this was the first time Master Chief Jenks ever called him by his real name.

As the two men turned away from the sea, they failed to see the underwater bubbles pass by the bow of the *Simbirsk*. They were heading straight for Compton's Reef.

17

TICONDEROGA-CLASS AEGIS MISSILE CRUISER USS *SHILOH*

Jack, Carl, Ryan, Henri Farbeaux, and a weary Captain Ezra Johnson watched from the darkened CIC far beneath the main deck of the heavy cruiser. They spied the activity on the wide-screen monitor on the bulkhead. Other members of the CIC teams were monitoring radar and sonar, but they watched the activity on the monitor, as did the officers.

The drone was flying high over *Peter the Great*. Most of the sailors were still settling in from their evening with the islanders. The night watch had been posted, and the crew, for the most part, went belowdecks for some well-earned sleep. Jack smiled when he saw that a lot of the Russian boys were wearing traditional United States Navy headgear. The reason for the covert flight was an attempt to spy on Salkukoff and his commandos. As the propeller-driven drone circled *Peter the Great*, they saw nothing of the colonel.

Captain Johnson patted the shoulder of the drone's remote control specialist. "Bring her back home, Jenkins. We're not going to see anything that that bastard doesn't want us to see."

"Aye, sir," the young man said as he input the correct orders into the remote system. The drone would fly back and land softly in the water next to *Shiloh*, where she would be recovered and recharged.

"Well, that was a bust," Ryan said as he rubbed his eyes.

"Captain, we're picking up something strange on the horizon," young Seaman Jenkins said as he pointed to the large monitor. "We have a bright glow to the south."

"Adjust angle of turn and bring the camera up."

The drone turned, and instead of overflying *Shiloh*, she pointed her nose camera toward Compton's Reef.

"What the hell?" Johnson said as he took a tentative step closer to the large monitor, as if getting closer to it he could actually see more detail. What the high-definition camera system told him and the others was that Compton's Reef was burning.

Jack and the others were out of CIC in a flash. All sleepiness and weariness were now gone. As they hit the steps leading up, the general quarters alarm sounded throughout *Shiloh*.

"All hands, man rescue stations. All sea rescue elements to their stations; this is no drill. I repeat, no drill. Man rescue craft!"

Jack and his men gained the main deck, and all they could see was the *Shiloh*'s powerful searchlights probing the seas between herself and the island. Even *Peter the Great* was in the process of launching rescue crews in whaleboats.

"Marine strike team report to boat ramp six."

"Let's go," Jack said as he started making for the stern, where the marine unit would be launched. "Carl, radio the Royal Marines stationed on *Simbirsk*. They are to hold station at any cost. Tell them to keep their heads on a swivel, as this could be a ruse of some kind."

"Got it, Jack," Everett said as he raised the radio and made the call.

Altogether, there were three Zodiacs filled with the marine strike team assembled on *Shiloh*. They were closely followed by the Russian complement of shipboard marines in their larger whaleboats. There were no less than a hundred fighting men moving toward the burning island, along with the other Zodiacs filled with corpsmen and damage control specialists from *Shiloh*.

As their boats struck the brown-colored sand, they heard the screaming coming from the village at the center of the island. The two varying marine elements broke into two groups with the Russians going to the left and the American marines to the right. They moved quickly as the screams of the islanders became louder. The flames reached far above the coconut trees and palms. The flaming tendrils reached out for the setting moon.

As Jack broke into the open, he couldn't believe what it was he was seeing. The creatures, the Wasakoo, as Salkukoff had informed them, were running from hut to hut, setting them aflame. Their long spears were dispatching those women and children who were too slow to move. Curved swords were slicing into women and children alike. Warriors from the village were putting up a brave fight, but Jack could see they were losing badly. Collins aimed his nine millimeter and shot the closest of the green-skinned creatures. The tentacled giant turned with a loud, screaming hiss and started toward Jack just as fifteen M4 automatic weapons opened fire beside him.

Farbeaux and Carl broke into the clearing and came face-to-face with one of the Wasakoo. The beast had a spear in hand, poised to throw, and in one of the eight tentacles it had circling its neck, it held a pearl-handled bone knife. Farbeaux and Carl both fired their handguns at the same instant.

The Russian marines opened fire from the opposite end of the village as they caught those Wasakoo who were now in flight in the open. The shots slowly dwindled down as the attackers were quickly dispatched. Jack swallowed hard and then reached for the radio.

"Captain, Collins here, over."

"*Johnson, go.*"

"Captain, we need the rest of the medics and more medical supplies ASAP, over."

"*We were watching from the drone. I've already dispatched additional medical and rescue teams. I informed Captain Kreshenko. He's also sending what he can. Oh, shit. Those green fish bastards are escaping on the western side of the island. No, never mind. The Russian marines just saw to it they aren't going anywhere.*"

"Thank you, Captain," Jack said as he replaced his radio.

Charlie and Jenks were late arriving, as no one waited for them to enter one of the landing craft. As they advanced slowly into the clearing, they saw the devastation. The bodies of the very people they had just shared a feast with were spread throughout the clearing. Their homes were in flames, and Russian and American sailors were doing all they could to not only secure the area but to assist the wounded and dying. The anger among the young sailors and marines of both nations was palpable as one dead child or woman after the other was turned over and examined. The gifts that had been given to the islanders were strewn throughout the shattered village.

"Did we cause this?" Charlie asked as he leaned over and felt for a pulse of a young boy who had the entry wound of one of the large spear points in his back. He lowered his head when he found the child lifeless.

"No, Doc, we didn't," Jenks said as he sadly faced the destroyed village and its people. His eyes fell on the men of the community. They had died bravely, as they all had weapons in their hands. He shook his head and wondered if Charlie was right after all. These people had lived here for how many thousands of years and hadn't been wiped out by this aggressor species before this, so why now? He spit and tossed his dead cigar away, no longer wanting that small simple pleasure.

Collins found Farbeaux, Everett, and Ryan standing by one of the bodies of the fishermen who had brought them the bounty they had just consumed. It was the elder of the village lying there with his throat slashed and a spear in his side. He was dead, and Jack Collins cursed himself for not thinking about posting some form of security detail for these innocent people.

"Jack, you'd better take a look at this," Carl said as he stood from his kneeling position.

Collins slowly walked over, and he was joined by a stunned Master Chief Jenks and a tearful Charlie Ellenshaw. Carl tossed something, and Jack caught it in the dwindling moonlight. He held the object up and examined it in the flames. His eyes narrowed as he looked at it.

"This one was wearing it," Carl said as he kicked out at the still form at his feet. The tentacles around the creature's head moved, but it was only a nerve reaction. The long, thick muscled appendages moved and then settled.

The object that was removed from the lifeless body was nothing more than a canvas pouch with a long strap attached. Jack held it up closer to the fires and saw the Russian writing on it. He tossed it to Henri, who was fluent in Cyrillic writing.

Henri looked up after a quick examination and raised his eyebrows in confusion.

"What is it?" Ryan asked as Henri handed the canvas bag to him.

"What did it say?" Charlie asked as he pried his eyes away from the slaughter around him.

"Rostov-on-Don."

"What is that?" Ryan asked as he gave the bag back to Henri.

"It's a city in southern Russia." Jack turned and saw Kreshenko coming onto the scene accompanied by six Russian marines. Of Salkukoff and his black-clad killers, there was no sign. Kreshenko's face held the visage of a man shocked beyond measure at the carnage around him. Collins took the carrying bag from an angry Henri Farbeaux and approached the captain and tossed him the bag.

"Can you explain this? It was found on one of the aquatic creatures. He was wearing it."

"Rostov-on-Don," he read aloud, loud enough that his accompanying marines all looked pale in the firelight.

"I cannot," Kreshenko said. "This does not make sense to me."

"Do you think someone in your company might know?" Jack asked, not allowing Kreshenko to know his anger was close to being out of control.

The captain slapped the bag into a marine's hands and then nodded and turned and quickly left the village that had turned into a massacre site.

Jack turned and nodded for everyone to help and assist the medical teams as best as they could. He pulled Henri aside.

"Why would a bag with the name of an obscure Russian city be on one of those creatures?"

"I don't know, Colonel. Perhaps it was taken from *Simbirsk* on one of her magical appearances into this world, just like the book *Treasure Island*."

Jack nodded and started to turn away.

"What are you thinking, Colonel?"

Collins stopped and turned.

"I would conclude that you were probably right, Henri, with one exception: the Russians, nor anyone else during the '40s, had a little-known invention called Velcro."

Farbeaux watched Jack walk away to assist the dead and the dying and shook his head.

"Yes, I could see how that places a big hole right in the middle of that theory."

18

Jack sat against a small charred log and counted the bodies. Three hundred and twelve of the kind and gentle villagers were lying dead in the early morning light. The sun rose against the backdrop of smoldering grass huts and the meager possessions of this simple people. He knew that at least some of the villagers had escaped the carnage, but he suspected they would never see them again. How could trust ever be regained once lost? Their lives had been affected by strangers more than once, and in all instances, the newcomers had fallen far short of a just treatment of these natives.

"It's not your fault, Jack."

Collins looked up and shaded his eyes from the sun rising behind Carl. The career navy man sat at the end of the burned log and lowered his head.

Jack and Carl looked from the scene of devastation around them as Charlie and Jenks walked up. Jack stood, as did Everett. They were all covered in soot and were filthy from searching for survivors inside their shattered homes. Ellenshaw was worse than anyone. He was burned in several places, and his hair was even more of a mess than ever. Beyond Charlie's condition, they could all see the morale of the combined sailors and marines had taken a serious hit. Russian marines sat with American marines, and all were in shock at what had happened. One such Russian was holding the broken hockey stick he had given one of the male children. He angrily threw it away and then stood and left.

"My search parties have not turned up any more of the surviving islanders, Colonel. I am afraid we have made our friendship with the native people a moot and very much lost point after this."

They turned and saw Kreshenko and his XO, Dishlakov, as they examined the village for the first time. In the rising sun, they closed their eyes against the devastation.

"Captain, it's time you chose a side."

Kreshenko looked at Jack, as his words seemed to have fallen on deaf ears. Captain Kreshenko held the look a moment and then turned away. Dishlakov looked as though he wanted to say something but stopped short. He turned and followed his captain.

"Second Captain Dishlakov," Collins called out to the man's retreating form. He slowed and then stopped without turning. "We are all responsible for this slaughter."

Dishlakov hung his shoulders and then left the clearing.

"We're going to have to do this without them, Jack," Carl said as he watched the second captain vanish into the scorched undergrowth.

Collins looked around him at the burned homes of their new friends. His mouth went into a straight line.

"I agree. But first, our friend Henri has a job to do," Jack said as he removed the radio from its case. "And I'm going to help him."

Carl watched the colonel turn away to speak privately with Farbeaux, and he didn't like the look on Jack's face one bit.

TICONDEROGA-CLASS AEGIS MISSILE CRUISER USS *SHILOH*

Jack had his eyes closed inside the darkened and air-conditioned interior of the *Shiloh*'s CIC. Everett, Henri, and Ryan, along with Captain Johnson, sat beside him as their eyes watched the screen above them. The view was aerial, and it showed the vastness of this violet sea. The drone had been launched five hours before, and even on its power-conservation settings, it was now low on power without seeing anything to the southwest. Their theory on a reef or another small island was now getting weaker and weaker.

"That's it, Captain. We have hit the PNR. We have to bring her back to the barn," announced the young lieutenant JG from his seat.

"The point of no return had been reached, Colonel. We have to bring back the drone or lose her."

Collins opened his eyes and sat up. "Bring her back. This is like searching for a needle in a stack of other needles." Jack stood and stretched. He slapped the operator on the back. "How long until you can get the remote recharged and in the air again?" He glanced at the digital watch on the bulkhead. "We have to find out where these creatures come from and if the Russians have any surprises for us out there."

"Thirty minutes' return trip and another twenty to change her batteries and another five to download her old programming and install new."

Captain Johnson silently nodded in agreement.

The remote control operator sat up straight in his chair and then gestured toward the monitor.

"We have something, thirty-six miles out."

On the monitor, the men inside the CIC saw an amazing sight. The complex makeup of natural coral material spiraled into the afternoon sky. In brightly colored towers made up of the organisms that constituted the living reefs of coral, they saw the home of the aquatic species that had been allied with Salkukoff. The computer display, as generated from the visual information supplied to *Shiloh* by their drone, scrolled across the screen. The system immediately identified no fewer than seventy of the giant coral towers as they rose from a naturally supported bed of reef that stretched for fifty miles or more. Jack saw thousands of boats tied up in and around this exotic community.

"Look. As clear as the water is, you can see the structures are more under the water than they are above," Ryan said as he leaned closer to the monitor.

Battlements and other defensive positions lined the uppermost reaches of the coral towers. They could see thousands of the aquatic species as they went about their chores for the day. It was almost medieval in its makeup.

"Charlie should see this," Carl said as he watched the amazing scene below the drone's cameras.

"Captain, sonar."

Johnson moved quickly to his four sonar operators. He leaned in and saw their waterfall displays and immediately saw the anomaly. Then as he watched, the contact went dark again, and the waterfall display of color went back to its pristine shape of straight lines.

"Have you checked your equipment?"

"Yes, Skipper. Diagnostics says we are back to 100 percent reliability. There is something out there."

"What is it?" Jack asked as he, Carl, and Jason crowded around.

"A soft sonar contact bearing the same course as that reef. Not sure if it's real or not. Hell, it could be below or above the water. Being just over the horizon, radar is no good."

Collins moved away, deep in thought.

"I can tell you're thinking the same thing I am. Why would Salkukoff leave his only way back home?" Carl said as Ryan also nodded in agreement that it was indeed strange for the Russian to take that chance.

"He has to have an alternate source of the phase shift equipment. My guess is another ship."

They all turned back to the monitor that was being overflown one last time by the drone. They had garnered the attention of the Wasakoo, as many of them were pointing to the sky. By their frantic gestures, the sight of the strange bird-like drone awed and confused the aggressive species.

"Look at their boats," Ryan said as he placed a hand on the shoulder of the operating lieutenant. "Can you come in tighter on their watercraft?"

The operator brought the drone into a shallow dive toward the towering coral city. The drone leveled out, and the camera zoomed in tight.

"They look like giant abalone shells, or maybe oyster. You can clearly see the inside, and it sure looks like mother-of-pearl."

Ryan was right, and the observation made sense for this waterborne species. With the world lacking in any sustainable wood, at least in this part of their world, material from the seas would be their only source of craftwork. On the screen, the view got even lower. The sails on most of the craft were furled, but the observers could see many of the soft-skinned creatures run to and fro in near panic. They could see that the appearance of the flying machine had upset them to no end.

"Okay, I think we'd better get the drone back. We need her back in the air as an early warning system." Jack pursed his lips in thought. "Captain, can we get a copy of this sent over to Captain Kreshenko without jeopardizing any secrets about Aegis?"

Captain Johnson nodded to the CIC watch commander, and in minutes, a copy was being run off digitally.

"Jack, I would feel much better keeping the ships in motion. Sitting anchored here like this is a little too reminiscent of Pearl Harbor."

Jack nodded in agreement at Carl's fear. "Captain?"

"I agree. It will take some time to coordinate with *Peter the Great* and then time to rig towlines up to *Simbirsk*, but yes, I would feel better in motion."

Jack looked at the digital clock mounted on the bulkhead. "Say two hours?"

"We'll make it less if possible," Johnson said as he picked up the ship-wide communication.

By the looks of the faces manning their electronic gear in CIC, Collins knew the entire crew would feel better on the move. No one liked the aspect of sitting still and getting shot at.

"All right, let's get with Jenks and Charlie and see if they believe we can get that phase shift up and running. I think it's time we try to get our collective asses back to our world."

They all started moving to the hatch, and as the marine guard opened it, it was Ryan as always who placed his mild form of damper on everything.

"Yeah, who wants to get their asses shot off here in Adventureland when we have a chance to do it at home?"

KIROV-CLASS BATTLE CRUISER *PETER THE GREAT*

Colonel Salkukoff watched the command bridge from his place just beneath the forward missile mount. The automatic loading system would burst forth from a rubberized membrane and streak toward its intended target. But after the first two missiles ever fired in anger by *Peter the Great* in the North Atlantic against the Americans, Salkukoff knew she would never fire another. The movement that he could see beyond the thick glass told him that activity had picked up on the cruiser, which indicated that they had collectively made the decision to weigh anchor and be on the move. This was expected, and Salkukoff shook his head. He turned to the large man standing next to him. The commando was former Spetsnaz, the Russian equivalent of a navy SEAL or Delta Force, and very adept in his skills of killing. The man was as dedicated to their cause as Salkukoff himself.

"We can no longer pretend that this mission will not get out to those who can do us harm. We have lost the source, and we must shut down operations on a permanent basis." He shook his head. "It is a shame. We could have recovered far more of the resource material than we have. But alas, we have garnered too much attention. This Colonel Collins, despite what our superiors believe, is no fool. Nor are the people he works for. It wouldn't take them long to add up two plus two."

"Orders?" the black-clad commando asked.

"We will contact *Dolphin* and make arrangements for the destruction of the *Simbirsk*. There will be no recovery. Better to sink her here than take a chance on the Americans or some other NATO member recovering her wreck in the deep waters of home." He smiled as he turned away and looked up into the bridge once more. "At least here it is unrecoverable. Mission complete."

"What will Northstar command say about shutting down the diamond operations?" the commando asked.

Salkukoff lost his smile. "As far as they are concerned, comrade, the mine played out and we lost the cooperation of the Wasakoo. The situation was unavoidable." He faced his specialized killer once more, the very man who had hanged kindly Professor Gervais. "I don't know about you, but I am tired of being a delivery boy. I have other plans, as you do also."

"Yes, Colonel. It's time to make our mark with the Northstar Committee as soon as we get home. We have wasted quite enough time here in this backward world."

Salkukoff held the man's gaze for a full thirty seconds. "The spilling of Russian blood is always, well, let's say, difficult. Necessary, but most difficult."

"Northstar has taught us well, Colonel."

"Yes, yes, they have, Captain. I will try to isolate Captain Kreshenko from the rest of his crew. They cannot be trusted to see the light. They are loyalists to a fault and will follow that man anywhere."

"Dishlakov?" the commando asked as he stood beside Salkukoff.

"I'll leave that to you. Make it as efficient as always, my friend."

The commando chuckled as if the man couldn't be serious. He turned away and left the colonel alone.

Salkukoff watched the bridge once more. He finally turned away and brought up a small device he had on him at all times. The electronic sending unit used low-frequency bandwidths and was virtually undetectable by listening ears. He started typing out his message on the small keyboard: *To Dolphin, Operation Clean Seas has been authorized. Stand by for orders.*

He replaced the device into his pocket, and with a final look at the battle bridge, he moved off for his last few hours on board *Peter the Great*, as he knew by this time tomorrow, the great warship would be sitting on the bottom of this upside-down world. And *Simbirsk* and *Shiloh* would share that same watery grave.

19

TICONDEROGA-CLASS AEGIS MISSILE CRUISER USS *SHILOH*

Jack was dreaming of Sarah and, strangely enough, the small green alien they had lost during the Overlord operation, Matchstick. It was disturbing in the fact that Collins rarely dreamed at all. His mind was so tired that his brain completely ran on in a direction of its own accord. While Sarah said little in the dream, it was the recurring words of the small green alien that kept echoing in his dream over and over again. Matchstick was sitting on Sarah's lap as he did quite often in the long days and nights of debriefing the alien after Arizona. It seemed Matchstick opened up when he was in her lap, as if he were comfortable and trusting of the small geologist far more than any other.

"You are not alone, Colonel Jack; you are not alone. Friends, friends, friends, everywhere." In the dream, Matchstick would look straight at him while repeating the same words over and over. Then he did the strangest thing. As a gift to Matchstick after his debriefing was completed, Jack and the security department had given him a copy of the Beatles' greatest hits. The small alien had fallen in love with "Octopus's Garden." In the dream, he kept singing in his raspy, cotton-filled voice, "I'd like to be, under the sea, in an octopus's garden, in the shade."

The knock on the door woke him. He sat up in the bed and looked around, not knowing exactly where he was. The knock sounded once again. Finally, he knew, and the dream he had been having faded, with the exception of that silly Beatles song.

"Come!" he said louder than he wanted.

A marine opened his door, and Henri Farbeaux stepped inside.

The cabin was small but offered the creature comforts as Henri came in and flipped on the desk lamp. Jack sat up and placed his bare feet on the tiled floor. He looked at his wristwatch and saw that he had been sleeping for six hours, much to his shock. He placed both palms on his eyes and rubbed them. He shook his head until his vision cleared and then saw that the Frenchman was offering him a cup of coffee.

"It's not the seventy-five-year-old coffee from *Simbirsk*, but American dark roast will have to do."

Collins nodded and accepted the offering. "Damn. They let me sleep too long. It's 0220."

"Captain Everett left orders that you not be disturbed for eight, but I needed to see you before I depart *Shiloh*."

"Depart?" he asked when he lowered the coffee cup.

"Yes, we've been under way for five hours. *Simbirsk* is in tow, and *Peter the Great* is bringing up the rear. I couldn't board the cruiser earlier because Salkukoff's commandos were everywhere after dark. I couldn't risk it."

"And boarding a moving ship at sea isn't risky?" Jack asked as he finally stood up. He started dressing.

"Risky, but it will be unexpected."

"We could wait until daylight and find some excuse to get *Peter the Great* to at least slow enough for you to board safely." Collins slipped into his black T-shirt.

"It would be expected. Salkukoff is no fool. My chance of getting to him now is better. I expect the colonel will make his play soon after the sun rises. It's now or never. I have a team of marines that will get me to the stern of *Peter the Great*; I gain egress there and do what was ordered. I only hope Captain Kreshenko appreciates the finer point of my orders and doesn't line me up to be shot."

"I have a feeling the captain won't be too broken up about losing Colonel Salkukoff." Jack put his boots on. "I think it's still too risky, Colonel."

"Why, I didn't think you cared," Henri said as he rose from the desk chair.

"Of course I do, Colonel. I would never deprive Carl of your company. He wouldn't handle it too well if we lost you."

Farbeaux fixed Jack with a look that told him where he could go with his sense of humor. He turned and opened the door to the waiting marine guard who was watching over the sleeping colonel. Farbeaux nodded, and the marine turned and left.

"Henri," Jack said as he zipped up his Nomex vest. He held out his hand. Farbeaux looked at it and then took the offered good-bye. "You watch your ass over there."

"That, Colonel, I intend to do, I assure you."

"Good luck."

Henri let go of Jack's hand and left.

Jack took a deep breath and then sat hard onto the bunk. He started humming that silly tune that Matchstick had been singing in his dream. That and repeating the words about friends everywhere. Then he suddenly stopped and shook his head in wonder.

"Losin' it, Jack."

EVENT GROUP COMPLEX
NELLIS AIR FORCE BASE, NEVADA

Will Mendenhall was sitting at his desk inside the security offices. The four empty cups of coffee sat before him as he stared at the far wall and its bank of dead monitors. He had shut everything down, with the exception of the duty officer's station being manned from the outer offices. He had left orders that he was not to be disturbed.

The information that Virginia and Europa had recovered had been playing on his mind ever since he had heard the theory of a separate Russian government.

The door opened, and it startled Will from his thoughts. The director nodded and then went straight to a chair in front of Mendenhall's desk.

"To ease your mind, Captain Mendenhall, I informed the president on our . . . well . . . our guesswork. It wasn't something he really wanted to hear. So, for now, the ball is in the court of others." Niles Compton slowly stood on aching legs and moved to the door. "All we can do now is our jobs." Niles nodded and started to open the door but stopped. "Captain?"

"Sir?" Will said as he watched the director and his weariness at 12:30 A.M.

"Feel like getting out of here for a few days?"

Will stood and looked at the director, with hope in his eyes.

"I could use some time off, yes, sir."

"If you promise not to inform Sarah, Anya, and Virginia of your leaving, it is my understanding that NATO command has ordered a full-scale search-and-rescue operation in the North Atlantic over some missing ships. I believe we have an F-15 getting ready for departure at Nellis."

"Yes, sir!" Will said as he started making orders for his replacement. He suddenly looked up. "What *do* I say to Sarah and the others?"

Niles paused at the door once again and faced Mendenhall.

"What is that stupid excuse Jack and Carl use whenever they vanish unexpectedly and without orders?" Niles lowered his head in mock thought. "Oh yes—they've gone fishing."

Mendenhall smiled as he knew the old excuse was used no fewer than twenty times when the colonel and captain disappeared without notice.

"Bring back the full legal limit of fish, Captain. Make it six to be exact. I expect nothing less." Niles turned and left.

For Will Mendenhall, he was starting to know the director and liked what he was learning about the smartest man in government service. He especially liked it when Niles knew when not to be that smart.

KIROV-CLASS BATTLE CRUISER *PETER THE GREAT*

The marine sergeant placed the "pop gun" on his knee as he carefully aimed the short-barreled shotgun-like device toward the stern railing sixty feet above the choppy wake being spun by the four giant bronze propellers of *Peter the Great*. Behind him, Henri Farbeaux aimed the night scope up and saw that the stern was as clear as it would ever be. As jumpy as all sailors were, he didn't want to get shot at in this last critical moment. Farbeaux nodded that the fantail was clear of Russian personnel.

The navy motorman manning the Zodiac goosed the throttles on the two 150-horsepower motors, and the Zodiac sprang forward into the shadowy lee of the stern. The marine top sergeant popped off the charge, and the small hook shot up and out of the Zodiac. The rubberized hook caught on the top railing that lined the extreme aft end of the giant cruiser. The rope played out behind as the sergeant pulled on its rubberized coating as hard as he could. He was assisted by another marine, and the rope came taut.

The five-man marine and navy crew assisted Henri to the forward-most position in the large rubber boat. The Zodiac bounced hard as the froth being churned up by *Peter the Great*'s massive propellers almost flipped it, but a quick swerve out of the churning vortex helped in its recovery.

"Good luck, Colonel," the top sergeant said to Henri over the eardrum-breaking charge of the Russian cruiser and the noise of their own motors. Henri just nodded.

He would never have let Colonel Collins know just how out of sorts he was in when it came to remembering his special forces training back in France in what seemed like a hundred years ago. He lowered the goggles and then took a deep breath. The top sergeant held up a remote. He flipped the safety switch off.

"Now remember, this thing will pull your arms out of their sockets if you don't let go at the right time. Just as you reach the topmost railing, let the hell go, or we'll be unspooling your arms from the motor and the pulley at the top for the next month."

Again, Farbeaux only nodded as he adjusted the pack he wore at the small of his back. It had been so long since his training, he felt foolish when the large marine had adjusted the pack from the front—where it would have caught on the railing and flung him back into the sea—to the back, where it wouldn't be in the way. Henri swallowed and then looked at the marine.

"Okay, go!" the sergeant called out as he pushed the illuminated red button on the remote.

Suddenly, the world was split by the sound not unlike an unspooling fishing line as Henri was yanked far harder than the sergeant said he would be. His booted foot was the last to clear the gunwales of the Zodiac as the Frenchman's black-clad body shot from the boat. As soon as he was clear, the Zodiac peeled off and then took up station just to the port side of *Peter the Great*, just in case the Frenchman came crashing back into the sea. The marines knew it was a useless gesture, because if Henri didn't make the slingshot action successful, he would surely die from not only the fall but from the churning and explosive wake of the cruiser that would chew him up.

When the Zodiac slid into the calmer water just outside the wake, they saw that Farbeaux had grabbed the uppermost railing and was dangling. They cringed when it looked as though he slipped and then relaxed when Henri's strength showed through and he vanished over the top rail and onto the deck of *Peter the Great* as she sped along her way. The Zodiac made a sharp and dramatic turn and with throttles full open to their stops and sped away back toward *Shiloh*.

The sergeant handed the pop gun to a corporal and then shook his head.

"That was about the ballsiest thing I've ever seen."

"Just who in the hell are these people, Top?"

"You know what? I don't want to know."

After gaining the coarse steel deck, Henri stayed down as he studied the situation. He quickly stood and then took ahold of the rubber-and-plastic grappling hook and threw it into the sea. He also removed the black knitted cap, and that soon followed. The goggles were next. As he again stooped to his knees, he soon saw that *Peter the Great* was only a quarter awake. Kreshenko must have given his tired crew a break and only went to a lower state of alert so they could get some rest for their journey home tomorrow.

Henri stood and walked as normally as he could past the stern missile launcher and the .50-caliber machine guns lining her deck. If he was seen, he knew that Salkukoff would have the final laugh. Even Kreshenko would not have approved of an assassination on board his ship.

He heard voices, and he stopped and took station behind a tarp-covered lifeboat next to the port railing. He listened as two Russian sailors slowly made their trek toward the stern, where they both lit cigarettes and laughed about something.

"That was close," Henri mumbled to himself. Another minute and that grappling hook would have hit one of those poor fellows right in the head. He smiled and then moved off. He found the steel stairs that led upward into the main superstructure of the cruiser.

Men were seen here and there, but they were too busy concentrating on their tasks at hand to notice the shadowy figure climbing the stairs. Henri quickly found the hatchway he was looking for and then ducked inside. The passage was darkened nearest the door for light discipline reasons. Henri used this darkness to move like an ancient ninja, only at his age, he felt more like a turtle caught in the middle of a road race. Twice he heard voices and moved into another passage to avoid the men. He finally made it to officers' country after narrowly avoiding getting caught no less than seven times on his journey.

He finally saw the captain's quarters and, next to that, the more comfortable guest quarters afforded naval and politburo dignitaries when they came aboard. This was the cabin Salkukoff had been issued. Close to the captain of *Peter the Great* at all times, Second Captain Dishlakov had informed him.

He frowned when he saw that the usual marine guard who was accorded the commanding officer of any warship was missing. The two cabins were unguarded, and that, he knew, was not good.

Farbeaux had that old familiar feeling of danger that had saved his life on numerous occasions in his dealings with shadowy men. He listened but could hear nothing other than the constant drone of *Peter the Great*'s engines as they pushed her through the sea. He stepped quickly toward the wooden door. He placed his head closer to the cabin and listened. He heard nothing. He angrily turned and removed his lightweight bulletproof vest and covered the cage-enclosed light, and then he quickly smashed the cage and bulb with the butt of his nine-millimeter silenced handgun, the vest catching their remains before they shattered onto the deck. He lowered all to the tiled deck, and then without thinking about it too much, he quickly reached out and turned the handle and opened the door to Salkukoff's cabin.

The room was empty. The intel he had received by questioning Second Captain Dishlakov regarding the sleeping arrangements made Henri realize he was in trouble, and he quickly lowered the gun as just then he realized he had been had.

"Step back easily, Colonel," Salkukoff said as his own Makarov silenced pistol jabbed Henri in the back. "And since you have failed in your mission, you won't be needing this." He deftly reached around Farbeaux and pried the pistol from his gloved hand. Henri felt the pressure of the gun barrel ease, and he turned.

"Easy, Colonel. I am no fool."

Farbeaux looked the Russian in the face close up for the first time. He saw a life of privilege in his soft features. A man who had had everything handed to him. One of the chosen of his mysterious organization. Farbeaux knew the type well, as he himself had been one of the chosen as deemed by the French government in his extensive training. But Henri could see this man was a true be-liever in his cause. Whatever end game that was, he didn't know. And if the situation didn't change very soon, he never would.

"If I thought you were a fool, Colonel Salkukoff, I would have killed you in the Ukraine." Henri stepped from the darkened cabin and into the shadowy passageway. Salkukoff watched the Frenchman's hands closely. He gestured with the gun for him to go to Kreshenko's door and enter. He did so.

Kreshenko's body was laid out on his bunk. One leg was on and one off the bed. His uniform blouse was off, and he only wore a white undershirt. Evidently, Salkukoff had murdered the man in his sleep. The bullet hole was clearly visible in his forehead. The Russian clicked on the overhead light and stepped into the captain's cabin and closed the door.

"A tad cowardly," Henri said as he turned away from the still body of Kreshenko to face the Russian killer.

"And you had a different plan of attack for myself?"

"Yes, I was going to wake you before I killed you, Colonel. I wanted you to see who it was that was ending your life."

"You have changed since our last meeting in the Ukraine, Colonel Farbeaux. You seem to have lost your edge. I think the Americans are starting to get to you. Fifteen years ago, could I have caught you in the act?"

Henri said nothing. Salkukoff was right. He had indeed lost his killing edge, and he knew it was Colonel Collins and Sarah who had effected this change the most. Still, he could never admit that and never would.

"Before you kill me, answer one question for me."

"As a professional courtesy, Colonel, why not?" Salkukoff said as he eased his frame onto the captain's bunk only after slinging the captain's stiffening leg away from him. He smiled as he tossed Henri's pistol on the bed next to Kreshenko. "Go ahead," he said as he kept the silenced Makarov pointed at Farbeaux's belly.

"Your organization—is it real, or is it nothing more than I suspected all along when the Americans and the British first brought it up, that you and your mysterious benefactors are nothing more than organized crime thugs pulling strings from behind the wizard's curtain?"

Salkukoff smiled even wider. "Organized, highly. Crime?" He shrugged while the pistol never wavered. "We don't have race wars, Colonel. We don't have internal strife, at least behind the curtain, as you so cavalierly put it. We control certain aspects of government but encourage a more direct approach to the problems of this world. The West has become a serious problem. We are no longer going to play the game, Colonel Farbeaux. And soon, we will make our intentions known to the world. With the market cornered on industrial blue diamonds, we will make military strides the West can only dream of.

The phase shift operation was only the beginning. There are plans in the works that no one in NATO could ever see coming. Never see because the West is blinded by their arrogance in their stance that they are the righteous. I am here to change all of that. The Northstar Committee is changing it."

"Sorry I asked," Henri said as he slowly lowered his hands but raised them again when Salkukoff made a rising gesture with the silenced business end of the Makarov.

"Now, shall we conclude our business, Colonel?" The gun came up toward Farbeaux's head.

On the darkened bridge, the officer of the deck walked the ten steps to his communications console and removed the phone from its cradle after receiving the call.

"Bridge," he said into the handset.

"*Lieutenant Kaninen, we have just received a signal from* Shiloh. *She is slowing to make tight her towline to* Simbirsk. Shiloh *actual is asking for us to take up station aft of* Simbirsk *for rescue operations if needed.*"

"Signal *Shiloh*. We will make the course correction immediately."

"*Aye,*" came the reply.

"Slow to one-third. Helm, bring her hard over. Give *Shiloh* and *Simbirsk* a wide berth. We don't need a collision. Thirty degrees starboard."

"Aye, slow to one-third speed, helm at thirty, aye."

Peter the Great outwardly looked as if she hadn't slowed at all when she started her wide turn. The mighty ship heeled to the port side at nearly twenty-six knots, going heavily onto her side.

Inside the bridge, her crew grabbed handholds as the force of the turn nearly knocked them from their feet.

It was that way throughout the ship.

Henri knew he didn't have the time or the correct distance to make the outcome of the next ten seconds any different from if he didn't move at all. He waited as Salkukoff aimed for the spot right between his eyes.

The sudden roll to starboard at twenty-six knots slammed Henri into the bulkhead as the chair Salkukoff was sitting in nearly tipped over. The speed of the maneuver increased as Henri saw his opening. He quickly rebounded from the steel wall and used that momentum to sling himself into the Russian. The pistol silently discharged as the bullet missed the Frenchman's head by an inch. The next round nearly shot his fingers off as he finally managed to grab the

barrel of the hot weapon. *Peter the Great* straightened as she came perpendicu-
lar to *Shiloh* and *Simbirsk*, and then the cruiser went to full speed. The momentum of the acceleration threw both men from the chair to the deck as they
fought for control of the gun.

Finally, the pistol came free after Henri used one of his elbows and jabbed
the Russian in his face. The weapon flew across the cabin and clattered to the
deck. Farbeaux started smashing his fists into the exposed face of Salkukoff.
With every blow, the Frenchman felt the years of hate sliding away as justice
was finally being meted out to the killer of Ukrainian children.

Peter the Great again made her turn to finally take up station to the aft side
of the towed *Simbirsk*. As the final turn was completed, Henri felt his advantage slip away as, again, the momentum of the turn threw off the colonel's balance and gave Salkukoff leverage. Salkukoff pushed Henri off for all he was
worth. Farbeaux slid into a corner on the tiled deck. His head struck the bulkhead, and he momentarily saw stars. He heard the cabin door open and heard
Salkukoff run. Henri quickly regained his senses and reached for the Makarov
but couldn't find it. He stood on shaky legs and then saw his own weapon on
the bunk next to the dead body of Kreshenko. He grabbed for it and turned
angrily toward the door and then gained the passageway.

The ship was vibrating heavily as *Peter the Great*'s engines went to full power.
Farbeaux stumbled down the passageway until he came to an open door. He
reached for the dogged latches, and then he heard the man behind him.

"The colonel said you were far more formidable a man than what I believed.
I see his concerns were justified."

The Frenchman turned and saw the large Russian commando as he stood
in his black Nomex BDUs. His unsilenced pistol was aimed straight at Henri.
He knew this time no hard maneuvering would avail his limited time here in
this backward world. His eyes went to the Russian's face, and he waited as the
large captain withdrew his radio—the only Russian portables that had been
unaffected by the EMP assault on everyone's electronics.

"The situation has been corrected, Colonel," the man said into the radio.
"You may proceed to the boats, and I will join you shortly."

Henri waited as the Russian placed his radio back onto his belt.

"Good-bye, Colonel Farbeaux," he said as his finger started to pull the
Makarov's trigger.

The blast of weapon's fire made the Frenchman flinch. He actually thought
he could feel the red-hot bullet penetrate his Nomex. Henri felt no pain. As he
looked up, he saw the Makarov slowly slide from the commando's fingers and
fall to the deck. The man himself turned to face the person that had just shot
him in the back. Again, the loud report of a handgun sounded, and the body of

the Russian jerked once more as he slowly slid down to the deck. The large body twitched once and then went still.

Henri looked up and saw Second Captain Dishlakov and two of his marines. The XO was still holding the smoking pistol he had just used to save Henri's life. What was a little disconcerting to Farbeaux was the fact that the smoking Makarov was now pointing at him.

Dishlakov gestured one of the Russian marines forward, and he easily removed the gun from Henri's grasp. The Frenchman watched as the XO angrily looked him over as he handed back the weapon to the second marine.

"Why have you come to my ship, Colonel Farbeaux?"

"To kill the man who's now getting away," he said as he watched the marine to his right. Henri knew that he would never make the move to get his gun back before the Russian made kindling out of his attempt.

"Where can Colonel Salkukoff run to? His only escape from our situation is aboard one of three vessels. And I don't think he will find open arms waiting for him on either the *Simbirsk* or *Shiloh*. He has nowhere to go." Dishlakov reached out and removed Farbeaux's gun from the marine who had taken it from him. He smelled the barrel and then tossed it back to the Frenchman. Henri caught it but could not hide the surprise on his face.

"Captain Kreshenko is—"

"Dead, yes, I know. He is being attended to as we speak."

Again, the Frenchman was taken off guard. He holstered his nine millimeter.

"He was murdered just as this piece of dung tried to murder me in my sleep. I wasn't in my cabin but in the wardroom, writing to my wife and children. When I was finished, I saw this scum"—he kicked at the dead commando—"coming from my cabin. I followed him with company. Then we found you, Colonel."

"I am sorry for the fact I didn't get here on time."

"What were your orders? I assume they came from Colonel Collins?"

"No, the colonel would not have been as stealthy as I. He would have just come across to *Peter the Great* shooting. That's his way. Low threshold for injustice, you see."

"You may find this humorous, Colonel Farbeaux. I assure you, I do not."

"Attention, attention. Unauthorized use of motor launch at station number three. Station number three."

"Damn!" Henri said as he turned and ran from the companionway to the star-filled sky outside. He was soon passed by Dishlakov and his marines. They all ran to the port-side station where the announcement had said the theft was occurring. The dangling lines told Henri all he needed to know. As he peered over the side, he saw two of the large motor launches as they sped away. Both were filled with the remaining Russian commandos and a waving Salkukoff.

A Russian marine stepped to the railing and took aim with an AK-47, but Henri reached out and lowered the weapon's barrel. He shook his head and turned to Second Captain Dishlakov.

"Too late."

They watched as the two boats vanished into the night.

At dawn, the small armada of ships slowed and then came to a stop. Captain Johnson and his officers not on watch joined Jack, Carl, Henri, Ryan, Charlie, and Jenks on board *Peter the Great*. The off-duty personnel gathered at the stern of the cruiser, and the crewmen of *Shiloh* and the riggers on *Simbirsk* watched from a distance. The covered body of Captain Viktor Kreshenko was prayed over, and then the makeshift platform, a table from the ship's galley, tilted forward, and the sheet-wrapped body of their captain slid into the violet-colored sea. They watched until the weighted body vanished below the surface.

The mood of the Russian crew was somber at first, but after the word had spread that their commander had been murdered by one of their own, the morale had changed from one of sorrow to that of vengeance.

Jack saw the mood of the crew as he and the others lowered their offered hand salute. Jenks snorted, and then he and Charlie moved away. Carl, Jack, Ryan, and Henri stayed behind as they studied the sea.

"I think that settles the question of whether Colonel Salkukoff has an emergency out in getting away from this crazy world," Everett said as he leaned on the railing and stared out at the calm ocean.

"I agree," Jack said, but he was otherwise unnaturally silent, as he also was lost in the view.

"After the confession as to this Northstar Committee, he cannot allow us to return to our world alive."

All eyes turned to Henri, who was battered and bruised from his excitement with Salkukoff.

They heard a small disturbance coming from the fantail as several of the crewmen of *Peter the Great* simply tossed the body of the dead commando into the sea as if he were nothing more than garbage.

"The Russians have a hard time expressing their true feelings, don't they?" Ryan said as he turned away from the scene.

"Jack, the master chief and Doc Ellenshaw have a request for you and Captain Johnson," Everett said as he turned and saw the two captains conversing quietly not far away.

"What's that?"

"They want the use of the drone."

Jack finally relented his hold on the calm, violet sea and faced Carl.

"For?"

Carl looked uncomfortable.

"Come on, Swabby, it's a little early in the morning to be hesitant about anything."

"They want to overfly the island's interior to find the remaining villagers who escaped the slaughter. They seem adamant about it."

Everett was sure the colonel would deny the request, as they had operational concerns as far as the drone went.

"If Captain Johnson concurs, I don't see why not. We don't have much time before we make the attempt to return, so get it done."

"The least we can do for those poor bastards is try to get them living again," Henri said as he continued to look out to sea.

Carl was about to say something snappy to Farbeaux, but Jack shook his head. Everett could see that Henri was taking his failure of the mission personally and became silent.

"I see even the master chief is being affected by the loss of the innocence of this world," Jack said.

"Well, then, the least we can do is ease his and Professor Ellenshaw's minds," Farbeaux said, surprising all who heard. "We need some good to come out of this." He walked away with his head bowed and joined Jenks and Charlie as they spoke.

"Henri's beginning to scare the hell out of me, Jack," Everett said as they watched the three men converse.

"Why is that?"

"He's actually morphing into a human being. And gaining respect for that man is the most frightening thing of all."

20

LOS ANGELES—CLASS ATTACK SUBMARINE USS *HOUSTON*

Blankets and other soft materials had been spread out on the deck after the Mark 48 torpedo warhead had been removed. The entire warhead assembly had been taken to the mess to be disassembled by Machinist Mate Ramirez. Captain Thorne and XO Devers watched the kid of nineteen as his white cotton gloves felt for the pin release that would separate the 650-pound charge from its working innards. The entire torpedo, built by Lockheed Martin, weighed in excess of 3,500 pounds when fully assembled, but all Ramirez had was the stainless steel cap. The business end. He pulled the final pin inside the warhead, and his eyes closed momentarily when the warhead's gyroscope released easily. He turned and handed the expensive part to the chief of the boat, who was assisting. The officers in the hatchway watched with sweaty palms as their lives and the life of *Houston* hung in the balance.

Ramirez swallowed and took a deep breath. If the warhead detonated inside the pressure hull, there wouldn't be enough left of them to float to the surface.

"You're doin' fine, kid," the chief said as he too wiped sweat from his dripping brow.

"Now, if I can pull her guidance board without any electrostatic discharge, we may be in business."

The chief looked up and saw Thorne standing silently in the hatchway. He nodded, feeling far less confident than his display to the captain.

Ramirez reached inside past the charge of high explosives. He had his eyes closed as he visually pictured the torpedo from months and months of training. His fingers probed past the metal-encased charge and felt for the panel that had the waterproofed circuitry.

"Oops. That's the trigger. Don't want that," the young machinist mate said as he backed his hand away slowly. He then started over, edging his probing fingers closer to the charge that was strong enough to break a capital ship's back and sink her straight to the bottom.

The chief felt panic at the nonchalant way the kid did things.

"There we are. Now, where is that damn cable?" he asked aloud as his fingers finally found the electronic cable that connected the targeting computer board to the gyroscope. Again, he closed his eyes as he freed the three-inch-wide cable from its motherboard filled with computer chips. "That's it. Now, to pull the board."

Suddenly, *Houston* lurched. The submarine once more lost its grasp on the shelf and started to slide. The chief and Ramirez both lost their footing. The 190-pound nose cap slid free of the table and crashed to the deck, missing Ramirez's head by five inches. He rolled free as the rest of the warhead, including her guidance package, came down next. It smashed into the blue-tiled floor and rolled against a bulkhead, where it came to a stop.

Thorne grabbed for a handhold as *Houston* gained speed. This time it looked as though the boat was going to slide right off the far end and down into a grave they would never rise from.

Suddenly, as men and women sang out prayers for their delivery from the crushing depths, *Houston* rolled to port. Her sail tower dug into the rocky strata, and her periscope and radar mast inside the tower sheared off as *Houston* slid to a stop only six feet from the edge. The grinding halt sounded throughout the boat as her four-story-tall tower had saved them.

Thorne was now at a severe angle as she came to rest almost on her side. He quickly regained his senses and stepped inside the mess. The warhead was lying against the far bulkhead, and its insides were scattered and smashed on the deck. Ramirez was being helped up to the sharply angled deck by the chief. The overhead lighting flickered and then steadied. Thorne reached for the phone and wrested it from its cradle.

"Damage report!" he said much louder than he intended.

"We're still breathing up here. Forward torpedo room and engineering report small leaks, but nothing we can't handle for the time being."

Thorne placed the phone back and struggled forward. He stopped short of entering the mess as he faced Ramirez and waited for the bad news that they would have to wrestle another torpedo from the aft compartment and start over again.

"Well, let's get going and get another Mark 48 taken apart."

Thorne looked around, and then he heard the chief of the boat laughing. He became concerned that the chief had finally lost his mind for the many disappointments they had faced in the past three days.

"Almost blowing ourselves to hell is far funnier than I realized, Chief," Thorne said as he looked from him to Ramirez, who was also smiling. His head dipped down, indicating the object he held. In his hand was the guidance board that had broken free of its screws when the sub jerked to life and started its slide. Thorne smiled himself as he realized that for the first time in three days they had caught a break. He stumbled and walked awkwardly toward the two men across the steeply angled deck.

"If you don't mind, Captain, I think I'd better go change my pants," Ramirez said as he handed Thorne the circuit board. He quickly excused himself and ran awkwardly toward the head.

"Chief?" Thorne asked, concerned over the lifelong navy man's color.

"No, thanks, Captain. It's a little too late for a crap break." Thorne watched the old chief turn and leave, shaking his right leg as he did.

Captain Thorne closed his eyes as he felt the weight of the guidance board he held in his hand. He reached out and touched the cold steel side of *Houston*.

"Thanks for the break, Gray Lady."

TICONDEROGA-CLASS AEGIS MISSILE CRUISER USS *SHILOH*

The CIC was well manned but mostly silent as technicians watched their scopes and screens but kept an ear open for the conversation being conducted by the gruff master chief and Charlie Ellenshaw. While most of the American naval personnel knew about how to take Jenks, they were still confused about crazy Charlie. They all to a man, Russian or American, British or civilian, liked the crazily coiffed Ellenshaw because of his naïveté when confronted with military protocol. They were impressed that the thin scientist wanted to learn everything he could. A million questions were asked by the cryptozoologist that highlighted the fact that the man caught on to everything very quickly. They listened to him and Jenks as they conferred with the young lieutenant flying the remote-controlled aircraft as it went high over Compton's Reef.

"Nothing, Master Chief," the lieutenant said as he banked the drone high over the destroyed village. "There is no one there."

Charlie and Jenks watched the high-definition view of the destruction below the remote-controlled plane. The graves dug by the Russian and American sailors belied the fact that almost every man, woman, and child had been dispatched in the most horrible of ways by a ruthless enemy. Jenks was fuming as row after row of freshly dug graves filled the screen.

"All right, get out of there and head north toward the mountain. That's the only place I think they could have gone."

"The diamond mines?" Charlie asked as he adjusted his glasses.

Jenks didn't answer as he studied the drone as it climbed and headed toward the slopes of the three thousand–foot mountain.

Charlie studied the master chief as he in turn watched the landscape below slide by. Jenks had become obsessed with finding the children and whatever adults of the innocent tribe remained alive.

"I'll bet you your eighteen higher educational degrees, Doc, that those amphibious animal pirate bastards weren't aggressive before the damn Bolsheviks got here." Jenks rubbed a hand through his close-cropped hair and exhaled. "There was no reason for a mutual animosity between two different races to be enemies. One group lives and thrives in the ocean, the other on land."

Charlie looked over at the six men monitoring the CIC's radar and sonar stations. They almost to a man nodded in agreement with the master chief. He knew being a civilian sometimes made you a little slow on the uptake on military fairness. Now he understood it was the sense of justice that was being hurt by what had happened to the innocents of this world.

"Oh, shit," the lieutenant said loudly as he used his joystick to turn the drone sharply away from the mountain. He brought the propeller-driven craft low to the trees.

"What?" Jenks asked.

The technician sitting next to the remote officer pushed a button, and the main monitor flipped pictures and rewound what was recorded.

"Shit!" Jenks hissed below his breath.

"How many?" Charlie asked.

On the screen, there was a long line of the Wasakoo scouring the jungle and sloping land of the mountain. From the high vantage point, it looked as though they were searching for the survivors also. Then the picture went black. The monitor again flared to life with the live feed coming from the drone. It was once more flying very high, and they could no longer see the aquatic species in their effort to find and kill the remaining men, women, and children of the island.

"Bastards," a young seaman said aloud as others nodded in agreement.

"Why are they so intent on killing them all?" Charlie asked. He looked away from the monitor, hoping someone would answer him.

It was Jack who finally did. He had entered the CIC unnoticed. He was standing by the hatchway as the marine guard closed and secured the hatch.

"Because they are under orders."

Charlie turned toward where Jack stood with his arms crossed. He looked tired and angry, but Ellenshaw knew that was the colonel's natural state the past year.

"Orders?" Ellenshaw asked.

"One thing the Russians are good at, their main philosophy when they were being beaten or having to give up land, is to leave nothing behind that their enemy can possibly use; it's called scorched earth. We suspect Salkukoff is getting ready to cut and run—close up shop, if you want to put it that way." Jack uncrossed his arms and strode into the darkness of the control center. "The Wasakoo are exterminating the villagers, and then, I suspect, the blue diamond mines will be collapsed as if they were never dug. Scorched earth."

"There!" the lieutenant said, pointing to the screen. "Recent trail sign."

Jenks looked at the monitor, and there it was. A long line of brush and undergrowth had been etched into the landscape. It had to have been made by many people as they moved northward from the destroyed village.

"That's got to be them. Follow the trail for as long as you can, but don't let those Charlie Tuna sons of bitches see you."

"Aye, Master Chief," the lieutenant said as he drove the drone even higher into the sky.

"There. The trail leads right to the mountain." Charlie leaned in closer. "And it looks like the Wasakoo are looking in the wrong direction."

Jenks stood straight and looked at Jack. In turn, Collins looked at his watch and then back at Jenks. "We are scheduled to leave this world soon, Master Chief. You yourself said the phase shift reactor is too unstable to wait too long, even with it shut down."

Jenks reached into his pocket and gave something to Ellenshaw. Charlie accepted it, and then he looked from the object to Jack.

"There. Give me five hours. If I'm not back, Charlie knows how to start the chain reaction to get the phase shift operational. The frequency is constant. You should be right back where we started in the Atlantic of our world."

"No, I can't take the chance, Jenks. I have too many men depending on your calculations. You can't tell me Charlie can think on his feet on this if something goes wrong. No offense, Doc."

"None taken, Colonel. But I think the master chief is right. We, at least our kind, did this thing to these beautiful people. We have to do something."

"No." Jack sat down in an unoccupied chair and rubbed his hands over his face. He looked up and faced his two people and the interested ears of the sailors around him. "What do we do if we actually find survivors? Uproot the whole species from their world and return them to ours? That would be almost as cruel as what Salkukoff and his superiors have done. We can't return them to their life before this, and we can't bring them back." Jack stood and walked toward the hatch, where it was opened by a marine. He stopped and turned. "I'm sorry, Master Chief, Doc, but no. We have too much riding on this. I am not losing another man under my command for a reason not of our choice. We make the attempt to leave in five hours. I suggest you prepare the reactor on *Simbirsk*, and let's get these boys home before Salkukoff really puts his scorched earth policy into full swing. Because I think we are the final domino he has to push over."

They watched Jack leave, and Jenks looked at Ellenshaw. "I hate officers."

Charlie just pushed his glasses back onto his nose. He saw one of the young seamen looking their way. The kid had to be no more than nineteen years of age. Ellenshaw fixed on the seaman. Jack was right to a point—these boys, along with the Russians and the British, deserved to get home. But still, he was fighting his own conscience and needed to know if he was alone in his confusion.

"What would you do?" Charlie asked.

Every ear in CIC heard the question, and it was if they all wanted to answer. But the young man held Charlie's eyes.

"I think . . ." The boy hesitated momentarily until the lieutenant nodded that he could offer that opinion if he wanted. "I think that we won't make it back anyway. I also don't like running away. What happened to those people isn't right, sir. I mean, what is our duty here? I thought we were here to protect those who can't protect themselves. Does it matter where those innocents live? I say we not only find those people but also that we stay and get the asshole who caused all of this." The boy lowered his eyes. "Sorry, Lieutenant."

No words were spoken. Jenks was proud of what the new navy was currently producing. He could not have said it any better than the young radar tech who had placed everything into such simple terms that he had wished Colonel Collins could have heard it and reminded him of his duty. He knew Jack was killing himself over the losses of his Event Group people the past few years and was compounding his mistake by overprotection. Jenks came to a decision. He looked at the large marine guard and saw that he was watching intently, although silently.

"Lieutenant, feel like giving us heroes an hour without reporting a radar contact heading toward the island?"

The young officer looked around at all the eager faces inside CIC. They were waiting.

"The radar and sonar equipment is still sketchy, Master Chief. Sometimes we lose everything at once. Possibly for at least three hours."

Jenks smiled and popped a cold cigar into his mouth. "Goddamn, I guess the navy is still on the ball when it comes to getting competent men. Thanks, son. Now you keep in contact with the Doc and me. We'll be on secure channel 6. Keep the remote searching but under no circumstances lead those catfish-lookin' bastards to the survivors. Understood?"

"You got it, Master Chief."

Jenks turned and faced Charlie. "Well, Doc, you feel like disobeying the colonel's orders and stealing a boat?"

Charlie looked taken aback at first, and then he came to a quick decision.

"We need more men," he said simply.

The large marine finally stepped from the hatchway and faced the entire CIC.

"That shouldn't be a problem, Master Chief. I have marines just standing around and getting spoiled by these navy boys. I think about fifteen of us. The Brits have the *Simbirsk* covered."

"Thank you, son. I can only guarantee that I'll volunteer to get shot by firing squad first."

"The US Marines appreciate that."

With that simple statement, the rescue of the villagers by Jenks and his team of American pirates was under way.

KIROV-CLASS BATTLE CRUISER *SIMBIRSK*

Jack, Carl, Jason, and Henri examined the small Europa link as supplied by the laptop. Jack pointed out the graph and shook his head.

"Even Europa Jr. is having a hard time keeping this damn thing in check."

"Even with Jenks having removed the main power coupling?" Jason asked as he too saw the graph lines as they spiraled to the top every ten minutes.

"It has to have something to do with the uranium stolen from Chicago in the '40s," Jack said. "Jenks and our late Professor Gervais couldn't get safely into the glassed perimeter surrounding the damn thing without causing a meltdown. They said we would have to wait until we were safely home again to decipher this mess. Until then, Europa will have to siphon off her power to other areas of the phase shift program, as you can see." Jack ran his finger along the graph, and they all saw what he was saying. The graph clearly indicated that the power fluctuations were growing and for longer durations. "She's about to run out of time and space on where to place the added power runoff. Europa?" Jack asked. "Also, in case you hadn't noticed, the weather topside is getting a little dicey. We have storm clouds developing directly overhead."

"*Yes, Colonel Collins,*" the twin sister of Europa replied.

"How long until containment of the power source is lost?"

"*Estimate three hours, forty-seven minutes until phase shift is unstoppable.*"

"Oh, wonderful," Jason said as he turned away from the bad news.

Henri looked at his watch. He grimaced as the pain he was feeling after the fuss late last night showed on his face.

"Regardless, I suggest we get the *Simbirsk, Peter the Great,* and *Shiloh* tied down good and then recall all personnel just in case your little sex symbol computer is off on her estimate."

"I hate to agree with Mr. Optimist here, but he's right, Jack."

Henri looked at Everett but kept his rebuttal at bay.

Jack merely nodded in agreement.

"Where is our esteemed science team?" Henri asked instead.

Jack looked around. "I thought they were right behind us."

The alarms sounded from above deck, and that got everyone's attention.

A Russian-language announcement sounded over the loudspeakers. They heard, even from their low vantage point, many hundreds of feet running across decks far above them.

"They just announced general quarters," Henri said as he started to leave.

Jack removed the radio and called *Shiloh.* "Collins to *Shiloh* actual, over."

He waited as the distant sound of the American warship's alarms could be heard.

"Shiloh *actual to Collins, go, over.*"

"Captain, what's up?"

"We may have an attack brewing thirty miles to the north. They started showing up on radar twenty minutes ago. Thought nothing of it at first, but their forces have built up quite substantially since."

"Anything scary at this point? Over."

"I don't think it's as heavy as their nighttime raid last night, but why take chances?"

"Got it. We'll stay on *Simbirsk.* After this is settled, we must start getting the ships prepped for our attempt to get home, over."

"Hang one, Colonel," Johnson said as the radio went silent. Jack gave Carl and the others a worried look. *"That damn master chief and crazy-haired Mr. Spock just stole one of the Zodiacs."*

"Alone?" Jack asked, forgetting to release the call button. Then he cursed and caught the tail end of Captain Johnson's response.

"—took ten marines with him, over."

Jack lowered the radio briefly and shook his head in wonder.

"Damn fools," Carl offered.

"We have to send someone to help. Ten men and Charlie? Come on, not even the great Jenks can do that. No telling what in the hell they'll run into." Ryan kicked at the steel bulkhead.

"I hate to be the realist here, gentlemen, but what difference do the islanders make? It is not as if we can take them back with us."

"We don't play that damn mythical Prime Directive here, Colonel," Ryan said, but Jack silenced him when he raised the radio.

"Captain, there's not a lot we can do about your stolen boat. We'd better see what this gathering of ships is. Then I'll let you keelhaul Jenks yourself— if you still keelhaul in the navy."

"We do with pride. Now watch yourself over there, Colonel. Johnson out."

Jack turned and nodded as he made for the hatchway and then quickly followed the others to the upper deck.

Men were scrambling everywhere. Russian sailors manned the twenty-millimeter and .50-caliber machine guns. Sailors lined the rails with their smaller close-quarter weapons, the venerable AK-47s. The Royal Marines had joined them, and all eyes looked to the northern seas.

"There," Ryan said, pointing to the horizon.

Collins turned away from examining the readiness of both *Peter the Great* and *Shiloh*. He was relieved to see that, thanks to the overwhelming small-arms stores of the ancient *Simbirsk*, a ship out of time. The old girl had been filled to the brim with American-donated firearms from the days of the old alliance when the Soviet Union had needed everything the United States could ship to her in the earliest days of the war. Now Americans, Russians, and Brits all had either a Colt .45 semiautomatic tucked in their holsters or a weapon that every Axis soldier once feared, the venerable tommy gun—the Thompson submachine gun. One of these was tossed to Jack by Everett, who also slung a holstered .45 over his shoulder. Jack used the binoculars and finally saw what they were facing.

"Count, Mr. Ryan?" Jack asked as he focused on the distant ships.

"Fewer than sixty, no more."

"Maybe we whittled them down a little more than we thought during their night attack," Everett said as he too studied the distant fleet of sail.

Collins lowered the field glasses, and his look carried one of concern.

"You don't have to say it, Colonel," Henri said as he slammed a clip of ammunition into the Thompson. "Something is wrong. Why attack at midday? Why so few of them?"

"Well, since you have all the right questions, got any answers?" Carl asked, lowering his glasses and staring at the Frenchman.

Henri smiled and then charged the machine gun as he stepped to the railing. "In this world, Captain, I suspect that the answer is not going to be to our liking. I feel Salkukoff is out there, close by." He again smiled as he faced the larger Everett. "And that is the man with a plan."

"Yeah, great. I would have never guessed."

Jack cursed when he saw *Peter the Great* casting off all her lines that linked her to the *Simbirsk* and in turn *Shiloh*. He started to raise the radio once more, but this time, Carl held him back. He shook his head and nodded toward the *Shiloh*. Jack turned and saw that Captain Johnson was doing the same thing.

"You can't argue their logic, Jack. A captain is going to protect his ship at all costs. If they need to maneuver, they won't want to be tied down. Without them, the *Simbirsk* doesn't stand a chance anyway."

Collins nodded in understanding. "What the hell. If this damn ship blinks out with all of us on deck, we'll fry for sure, just like those boys on the *Eldridge*. Besides, if we don't return with everyone we can, Niles will have our asses anyway."

"See? No problem at all," Everett said, commiserating with his boss.

"Here they come," Ryan said.

They turned and watched the large sails of the ships unfurl and their outriggers dig into the violet waters of the sea. Some of the larger boats had to hold at least a hundred souls, the smaller, fifty.

An announcement in Russian and then one in English came across the loudspeakers: *"Damage control parties stand by for fire suppression. Reserve units will stand by forward hatchway of turret number one."*

Across the way, Jack heard the now familiar announcement as broadcast by Captain Johnson. *"Stand by to repel borders, port and starboard!"*

The sterns of both missile cruisers churned to life. They sat unmoving, but still the microscopic sea life burst to the surface like a well of rainbow-colored water.

"Damn. This crap is getting real now," Jason said as he watched from the port rail.

On came the fleet of processed wooden, shell, and skinned animal life that made up the Wasakoo seacraft. As all eyes watched, the sails were blown taut as the fast-attack craft came on far faster than anyone could believe. Some cut over the wakes of others, jumping high into the air and then coming down with a splash. The agility of the seamanship on display shocked the modern sailors. Other ships rolled heavily onto their outriggers. Again, the seamanship was astounding as the pilots of these strange and otherworldly ships almost defied the laws of gravity as they hopped over the swells their sisters were creating with their speed.

"Three thousand yards," Ryan said as he finally placed the binoculars down and charged his own weapon.

As the speedy ships came closer, flags of different colors were hoisted by the strange creatures that sailed them. Suddenly, the sound of drums started thumping over the rush of sea and the cacophony of the men watching. The deep bass sound made the sailors of all nations lining the rails uneasy as they watched the attack unfold.

Before anyone realized it, the heavy weapons opened up. Large twenty-millimeter tracer fire lit up the afternoon sky as the missile cruisers opened up simultaneously. Being fed direct targeting from the spotty radar systems of both ships, the fire became deadly accurate as the exploding shells burst among the oncoming ships. Then the sixteen .50-caliber machine guns opened up. The green tracers streaked through the sky and started shredding the lead sails of the tough ships.

"My God, they're chewing them up!" Ryan said, almost feeling sorry for the backward species in the crosshairs of a modern navy.

On the surface, the battle grew closer. The lead ships were either burning from the magnesium in the tracer fire or the explosion of the twenty- and forty-millimeter cannon fire. The din was deafening as the fire continued. A few of the smaller ships virtually disintegrated in front of their eyes as .50-caliber rapid fire tore through the wood, shell, and skin construction. The sickly green bodies started to be hit as many of the Wasakoo attackers chose death in the sea rather than the burning steel-jacketed dismemberment.

The explosion rocked the stern of *Peter the Great*. Even those lining the railings of *Shiloh* and *Simbirsk* ducked as the roar ripped over them. Jack cleared his vision as best he could and then saw the large black cloud as it reached skyward from the stern of the great battle cruiser. As he watched, he saw why as another round object came down on her deck. It rocked the ship once more as it too detonated. The sight was baffling at first, as he thought he was looking at some sort of giant bird. It was Henri who quickly realized what it truly was. He was the first to open fire into the blue of the sky.

A hundred manta-like winged creatures swooped in low. The wings weren't the short, stubby sort you would see on normal manta rays, but long and silky looking. The scales were transparent in nature, making them light but strong. Each of these animals was saddled, and the Wasakoo rode them like stallions in a cavalry charge. They each tossed round balls that hit the decks of both cruisers and exploded. The grenade-like weapons were as deadly as their modern variant. Both *Peter the Great* and *Shiloh* were aflame before they even knew what was hitting them. After delivering their payloads, they drove back into the sea and vanished. Others rose to take their place, and more explosions rocked all three ships.

The volume of defensive fire slowed as each man tried to dodge the death being delivered from an area they never saw coming—the sky. Then the ships finally gained the right distance, and they too opened fire. This attack was far deadlier than the one from the air. The large arrows thumped down and around the men as they tried in vain to dodge both explosives and the sharpened projectiles. They thumped into and penetrated the steel of all three ships. The small platelets of steel-like material attached to the arrows burst to killing life, like a magnesium flare. The steel of the decks and the bulkheads where they struck started to burn and melt. Men ran from conflagration to conflagration, extinguishing as best they could the sun-hot chemical.

The small-arms weapons fire erupted from the railings of all three ships. Jack and the others took aim and started placing a withering fire into the ships as they came close enough to start tossing grappling hooks toward the anchored ships.

Suddenly, *Shiloh* burst to life as her stern dug deeply into the sea as her large propellers churned at full speed. The turbine wash was so severe, it threw seawater high into the air enough so that Jack and his men were inundated with a blinding sea.

"*Peter the Great* is also moving!" Henri shouted as he quickly lashed out with the butt plate of the Thompson, sending one of the climbing Wasakoo flying back into the roiling ocean.

Two hundred yards away, *Peter the Great*, with her engines screaming, exploded into movement. Her bow dug in at first, and then, when her powerful power plant kicked in, the stern went down, and then the giant ship was off. As they watched both the smoldering ships moving off, the men fighting on the desk of *Simbirsk* felt their hearts sink. It was a lonely feeling, seeing all that firepower leaving you behind.

Still, the heavy bombardment from above continued as sailors fired into the sky. Magnesium-fed tracers of green, white, and red filled the air as bullets went in all directions. *Simbirsk* was now fighting for her life.

21

Jack realized that this was not a probe; this was an all-out Wasakoo assault. He leaned over the rail and fired on the closest of the sail-laden ships as they came alongside with the black-emblazoned skull and crossbones flags waving in the increasing winds of a growing storm. Sailors at the rails shot down into them, but still the ropes and grappling hooks kept sailing through the air to attach themselves to *Simbirsk*.

Peter the Great was going out to meet the oncoming fleet. Her main guns of fifty twenty-millimeter and forty-millimeter rounds chewed up the seas as she lay down a withering fire. As Collins managed a look through the din of noise and light, he saw that *Peter the Great* was causing severe damage to the attackers. At the bow of *Simbirsk*, Captain Jackson had placed the Aegis cruiser in between their only ride home and the maniacal Wasakoo as they charged forward. Jack had to admire the determination of this aquatic species as they gave their lives in massive numbers to accomplish their goal, of which Collins and the others had yet to see for themselves.

"Oh, come on!" Ryan said as he dodged one of the large arrows that dug into the steel deck next to his feet, forcing him to hop and jump out of the way. Henri quickly and alertly kicked out at the flaming steel attached to the bone weapon and kicked it over the side. Ryan nodded his thanks but quickly returned to the rail and pointed.

The seas parted, and thirty giant sea turtles rose to the surface. The wakes they created made it seem as though the strange sea life in this even stranger ocean was under some form of high-energy power. On the backs of these enormous turtles that were at minimum thirty-five feet in diameter were the

Wasakoo in all their colored glory, waving swords and spears at the defenders. They shot arrows and spears and even catapulted the deadly extinguisher-resistant steel platelets into the quickly burning ship. Jack and the others started concentrating their fire on this new threat even as more of the flying mantas burst from the sea for a second strike from the sky.

To their front, the *Shiloh* was delivering a brutal defense against this new submerged threat. She rammed three of the turtles just as they broke the surface, forcing the massive bulk of *Shiloh* up and over the creatures, crushing the Wasakoo on their backs. Red blood mixed with the violet-colored sea as the world exploded around them.

The men at the railing ducked as the recently removed Gatling gun of the old and reliable R2-D2 system of Phalanx opened fire manually from the stern of *Shiloh*. Without their radar guidance system operating, the men operating the large cannon had a hard time placing the thousand rounds per minute exactly where they wanted them. Before they knew what was happening, over fifty of the Wasakoo were swept into the sea after the twenty-millimeter rounds bashed their fragile boats and bodies to pieces.

"This doesn't make sense!" Jack yelled at Everett as the captain released a relentless burst of firepower from his Thompson. When that was out, he removed the old Colt .45 and started blasting those he had missed. He faced Jack as he replaced the pistol and then quickly slammed home another clip for the Thompson. "Why are they doing this?"

"Maybe because they are just mean bastards!" Jason offered before Carl could. The captain just shook his head.

"I don't know, Jack—I gave up trying to figure this place out with the purple seas!" He fired again over the railing as a webbed-fingered hand appeared and tried to pull the Wasakoo up and over the rail. Everett's rounds caught the strange creature right in the face and blew most of its head free of its body. Carl grimaced.

"They're running a scam on us!" Jack said as he was pushed out of the way by Farbeaux, who saw the Wasakoo attack from the rear. He quickly shot the scale-covered creature in the chest three times as it crumpled to the deck.

"They covering for something?" Carl asked as he assisted Jack back to his feet.

More small bombs rained down from above as more manta raiders struck from the sea. The sailing ships were now massing around the still bulk of the *Simbirsk*. The attack was now being concentrated on their only way out of this madhouse.

"Well, if they wanted our attention, Colonel, they have gained it," Henri said as he felt his pockets for more clips of .45-caliber ammo.

Just at that moment, a hundred of the Wasakoo burst over the side of

Simbirsk. They came over en masse, and then all hell broke loose as sailors started to fight back at close quarters. Swords of bone and shell started to appear, and it was a terrifying sight as the Russian and British forces charged to meet the threat. Spears of twenty-foot length started sailing through the air and meeting the flesh of the brave men who fought for the ship under their feet.

This time it was Jack who returned the favor for the Frenchman. A Wasakoo had jumped onto the back of Farbeaux and raised a thick, powerful arm up to bring the sharp knife down and into Farbeaux's back. Jack quickly shot the creature in the scaled forehead. The suddenness of his shot made Henri think he was shooting at him. When he realized Collins had just saved his life, all he could do was nod in thanks.

"They have us occupied here, so what is their game?" Jack asked anyone as he emptied his Thompson into a group of three Wasakoo as they had taken down one of the Russian sailors. The men were resisting the boarding of their ship with determined ferocity.

Everett wiped blood from his chin where an arrow had come close to decapitating him. He almost saw the large Wasakoo too late as it plunged a knife into the arm of Ryan, who cursed and dove away just as Everett unloosed a barrage of fire that nearly cut the Wasakoo in half. He assisted the injured Jason to his feet just as four more of the aquatic creatures came at them. Henri sliced through them, sending them all crashing to the deck.

A mile away, *Peter the Great* was taking heavy damage from the air war above them. The mantas were fast and dove quickly away as long lines of tracer fire crisscrossed the skies above. *Shiloh* was faring no better, as her weaponry was even weaker than that of the Russian ship. They were being boarded by the speedy sea turtles as Wasakoo jumped nimbly from sea turtles to the fast-moving *Shiloh*. Men were now fighting close quarter and hand to hand. Her beautiful fantail and bridge areas were awash with the chemically enhanced fireballs striking the great cruiser. Men were fighting from Jack staff to bow as the Aegis cruiser sliced the much slower sailing ships into glass and kindling.

There were over a thousand instances of hand-to-hand combat going on at any one time across the three ships. As much as *Peter the Great* and *Shiloh* were sacrificing for the safety of their ride home, the *Simbirsk*, they found themselves losing by superior numbers that were willing to die in the attack.

"Look!" Farbeaux called out above the din of firing weapons and screaming men and Wasakoo.

On the horizon, even more of the sailing ships came into view. Henri quickly numbered them in the hundreds.

Jack quickly figured this might not be just a ruse.

The Wasakoo were attacking with everything they had.

LOS ANGELES—CLASS ATTACK SUBMARINE USS *HOUSTON*

"You hear what?" Captain Thorne asked as he leaned into the sonar shack.

"Gunfire on the surface—a lot of it, Skipper," the lieutenant said as he offered Thorne his own headset.

Thorne placed the headphones on and listened. It was so strange how one could hear popping noises on the surface of the sea almost a mile above them.

"What in the hell is going on up there?" He closed his eyes and listened, pressing both earpieces harder onto his head. "If it didn't sound so crazy, I would almost have to say that it's small-arms fire." He looked up and watched the startled faces of the men around him. He removed the headphones and then left the sonar room. "Gary, what's the situation with the ballast pumps?"

"Twenty minutes, Skipper," the XO said as he went from station to station checking on his repaired systems. "But I don't know about surfacing into a firefight. Right now, *Houston*'s like an eggshell sitting on the edge of a kitchen counter. I think someone could sink us with a well-placed rock."

"Well, we may not have a choice; someone up there is fighting one hell of a battle, and we are bound to surface right into the middle of it. Weapons, keep the Harpoons warmed and ready, stern tubes seven, eight, nine, and ten loaded for war shot. The last two, I want drones ready to fire. Double-check our decoys. I want to be ready to loose weaps as soon as we break the surface."

"You don't think we'll be able to control our ascent?" Devers asked Thorne quietly as he came to the navigation table.

"Not with a flaky ballast control system. I think once we start our ascent, there may be no stopping her from surfacing. I want to be ready for a fight if and when that happens." Thorne leaned in closer to Devers. "Get the chief of the boat and get to the arms locker and distribute everything we have to the crew. M4s to the watch shift and nine millimeters to the officers. Empty out the locker."

"Jesus, you're expecting some real shit up there, aren't you?"

"You never know—we pop off a torpedo and we may just kill ourselves. And the Harpoons could cook off in their vertical tubes. No, this way we can possibly fight the boat if we have to." Again, his voice lowered. "Depending upon what it is we do meet up there, get the self-destruct sequence entered into the main computer. If this thing goes south and we have a possible boarding situation, I want to blow *Houston* right out from under the bastards."

XO Devers saw the seriousness of his captain and then saw the men around him in the control room. For the first time, like Thorne had days earlier, he saw the bright young faces that were now being asked to do the nearly impossible.

"Chief of the Boat, to the arms locker, please."

Thorne took the 1 MC mic. "Captain to crew, we blow ballast in twenty minutes."

The horn sounded throughout the boat as small-arms weapons were disbursed as far as they could be.

"Make all preparations for getting under way," Thorne said.

All eyes went from their individual consoles to the man standing next to the navigation table. Then the words were said that no submariner ever wants to hear.

"Stand by battle stations surface. Gentlemen, this one we may have to fight up close and personal. It sounds like there's a gunfight going on up there, and guess who is on the fight card? Make all stations battle ready."

The sailors of the USS *Houston* prepared for a surface battle that had not been fought between a submarine and a surface combatant since the end of World War II.

The broken and nearly blind and deaf *Houston* made ready for the fight of her life.

COMPTON'S REEF

The marine lance corporal, a veteran of both Iraq and Afghanistan, deployed the nine men in the makeshift rescue team off the beaten and worn trail that led to the diamond mine high above. It wasn't until the twelve men had climbed to the midway point of the small mountain that they saw as well as heard the battle raging across the sea a few miles away. Most of the marines wanted to turn back at that point, knowing that a fight was taking place that had the ramifications of either staying in this strange world forever or helping in the fight to leave. One look at the determined faces of Charlie Ellenshaw and Master Chief Jenks staid their doubts. The two Event Group men would go it alone if need be.

The PFC at the point position held up a fist, and the others scrambled for cover into the underbrush. Jenks listened as the lance corporal slowly and cautiously moved forward and then knelt beside the point man.

"What is it?" he asked.

"We got six or seven of those squid things up ahead."

"What are they doing?"

"Right now, nothing. Look," he said in a low voice.

Jenks and Ellenshaw joined the two, and their eyes saw the same thing as the marines'.

Six of the Wasakoo were standing and slowly pouring water from large shell-like carriers over their exposed skin. The water seemed to revive the creatures.

"They must rehydrate their skin after so long out of the water. Could be a point we could use if we ever find ourselves stuck here," Charlie said as he adjusted his glasses.

"That's real comforting, Doc," Jenks said, shaking his head.

"Just a point."

"More of them," the point man said as he eased farther back into the bush.

They saw a group of at least sixteen more of the Wasakoo join forces with those already reviving themselves in the clearing ahead. These newcomers did the same as the first group. They doused their exposed, scaly skin with water. Charlie didn't know if it was salt water, but he suspected it was. The entire group was heavily armed with spears and knives. Several had bows made from what looked like the spines, or quills, from some exotic sea life. The arrows were made of the same. The sharkskin pants they wore were reflecting the overhead sun, and it looked as though the heat was dehydrating these creatures at a fast rate.

"Listen," Jenks said.

As the small rescue became still and silent, a hundred of the Wasakoo joined the group. They repeated the same process as the first two sets.

"They must have had a rendezvous set up to refresh themselves," Charlie Ellenshaw offered.

"Too many to take on even with our weapons. They could overwhelm us before we did enough damage," the lance corporal said as he pulled on the arm of the point man. "Come on, we can't sit here and wait them out. Let's find another way."

The twelve men easily moved off to the left to try to make their way around the large group of Wasakoo. As they moved off by at least three hundred yards, they stopped as another group of the sea creatures broke into a clearing ahead of them. This was the largest group thus far. Over two hundred of the aggressive species sat and stood while soaking their bodies with water. Weapons were casually laid at their sides, and the men watched as even these soldiers from a strange world seemed to joke and prod at each other. They were like fighting men from their own dimension as they joked and glad-handed their fellows.

"They have no natural fear," Charlie again said.

"Look, Doc, if you're going to give this *National Geographic* narration all the way in, why don't you just walk over there and get an interview?" Jenks asked in exasperation. "Just stop teaching for an hour or so, will ya?"

"Sorry, Master Chief—hard habit to break."

"One thing is for sure, they are slowly making their way to that mine up there. They're just taking their time in their search. He's right; they have no fear of anyone interfering." The lance corporal turned and faced both Jenks and Ellenshaw. "The doc here may be right; we could use that to our advantage if the need arises."

"I agree," Jenks said. "They have no fear whatsoever and that could be a break for us. They don't know we're here."

"I suspect the natural senses they use in the sea don't translate that well to land. As you can see, these creatures are outright miserable in this environment," Ellenshaw explained.

Jenks was tapped on the shoulder and binoculars thrust into his hand. He was confused at first but saw the marine pointing.

"That must be the mine entrance right up there," he said.

Jenks adjusted the glasses, and then he saw what the marine was seeing. The reinforced mine opening was only a quarter of a mile up. That was where the Wasakoo were heading. As he studied the entrance, he could swear that he saw movement at the mouth of the mine. He cursed as he saw a small child appear and then just as quickly vanish. He lowered the glasses and turned to face the others.

"It looks like the drone told the truth. They're in there."

"Well, we know where we have to go; sitting here isn't going to get the job done," the lance corporal said as he easily stood and then gestured the men farther to take a path that would lead them around the company-sized group of Wasakoo.

If the small rescue team had the use of the drone, they would have seen a far more chilling sight ahead, as over a thousand of the sea creatures were coming up the mountain from the opposite side.

The battle for Compton's Reef was drawing near, and Jenks, Charlie, and the ten US Marines were outnumbered two hundred to one.

KIROV-CLASS BATTLE CRUISER *PETER THE GREAT*

His crew was having a hard time with damage control and the attackers. As men fought to extinguish the chemically enhanced blazes erupting on all decks of the enormous missile cruiser, they were harassed and killed by Wasakoo who had used the speed of their boats to attach themselves to the railings and fight their way onto the main deck. Second Captain Dishlakov had abandoned the bridge and was fighting alongside his men. The battle had been raging as they sped in a wide circle in *Peter the Great*'s battle to protect *Simbirsk*. They were losing.

He was momentarily thrilled to see *Shiloh* as she steamed a closer-in circle around *Simbirsk*. She was also ablaze but seemed to be fighting well.

"Captain, we are running low on forty- and twenty-millimeter ammunition," his new XO said as the man took quick aim and fired his Makarov pistol into the upturned face of a Wasakoo as it sprang over the railing. Dishlakov patted the man's shoulder.

"Then get knives, wrenches, and fuel oil. We fight this ship until she can't fight any longer." He took the young man by the sleeve. "We must give *Simbirsk* all the time we can."

As the officer moved off, Dishlakov looked around and knew his ship couldn't last much longer. The bulk of *Peter the Great* would survive because the Wasakoo had no meaningful way of sinking her, but the attrition upon his crew was growing to a level that they would be expended long before the great battle cruiser gave up the fight.

More of the manta rays burst from the sea and climbed skyward, their long wings crushing the air as they rose. Ten of the ray-like beasts came on, and soon their riders were launching more of the explosive devices that struck and burst open. Their brightly flared results started more intense fires. Dishlakov fired into the sky, as did others. Three of the creatures crashed into the flaming deck, where they and their riders were quickly dispatched by the crazed but lethal defenders.

More of the flying mantas burst from the sea, only this time they were larger and carried more than ten of the Wasakoo on their backs. The rays slammed into the upper deck just aft of the number-three missile launcher. One of the Wasakoo, injured from his jump from the back of the ray, limped over and then slashed at the aluminum cover of the missile hatch. Too late, Dishlakov and others saw the creature as he dropped something into the well where one of the Burn missiles was housed. The Wasakoo was struck down as their bullets ripped into its body, but they all knew it was too late. The Burn missile exploded in its launch tube.

Men were thrown from the deck along with many of the attackers. The Burn missile sent explosive gases up and out of the housing, and suddenly, large parts of the missile cruiser flew into the sky and sea. The entire port side was in flames.

Peter the Great was slowly being bled to death.

TICONDEROGA-CLASS AEGIS MISSILE CRUISER USS *SHILOH*

Captain Johnson was almost knocked from his feet on the battle bridge as the entire port side of *Peter the Great* burst out like an exploding balloon. He adjusted his field glasses and saw the flames being swept backward by the speed of the great warship.

"How in the hell did they know to hit their missile tubes?" Johnson turned away from the horrid scene and then grabbed his second in command. "Get below and place teams on all missile batteries; they'll try the same here."

"Aye," the man said, and then he quickly went to his radio to give out the order.

Johnson hissed as he again sighted *Peter the Great* as she sped along in flames. He could see the crew fought both Wasakoo and the damage that had been done, and it looked as if both efforts were failing. He then turned his glasses onto the *Simbirsk*. Her crew was fighting valiantly, but he knew they wouldn't stand a chance if he moved *Shiloh* from her current close-in station to assist; he knew the *Simbirsk* would be done for. He cursed as he knew that Second Captain Dishlakov was on his own.

"Helm twenty degrees to starboard; get in closer to *Peter the Great*. Fire control, get the fifties and twenty-millimeter weapons to assist the Russians. Sweep some of those bastards off her deck, give her crew a chance to get damage control working."

"Aye, helm answering, twenty degrees to starboard."

As *Shiloh* heeled over sharply, her .50-caliber machine guns and the manually operated Phalanx twenty-millimeter cannon opened fire on *Peter the Great*. Although many holes were punched into her side by the heavy-caliber weaponry, they could see the sudden assault had the desired effect on the attackers. Over two hundred Wasakoo were knocked from their ropes, and some even fell to pieces and then plunged into the sea. *Peter the Great*'s entire starboard side was swept clean of the attackers. *Shiloh* again turned away as her heavy weaponry kept a constant fire in their efforts to assist their one-time enemy.

As Captain Johnson had his mind momentarily eased as Dishlakov and his brave crew once more gained the upper hand in fighting the fires, the announcement from his CIC stunned him. Did one of *Peter the Great*'s missiles cook off? He was frozen in shock as the vision of a missile coming in at sea-top level slammed into *Shiloh* on her bow section.

The warhead's detonation rocked *Shiloh* to her core. Men flew from the decks as a missile slammed into her stern. Flames erupted all along her mainframe and engulfed over fifty men as the fireball expanded. Johnson was thrown from his feet, and with one of his arms nearly broken, he tried to stand. *Shiloh* slowed and then started to immediately list to starboard. She was taking on water.

"All damage control stations shift to decks four, five, and six aft of frame sixteen, all sections!"

The announcement brought Johnson's senses back faster than a face slap. As he stood, he felt hands on him as men tried to gather their wits.

"Conn, CIC, torpedo in the water!"

This time, Johnson felt his heart actually skip a beat.

"Peter the Great is under attack by a submerged source!"

Captain Johnson felt his hopes being dashed as he and his bridge crew were helpless to do anything as the long white wake of a torpedo headed straight toward *Peter the Great*.

LOS ANGELES—CLASS ATTACK SUBMARINE USS *HOUSTON*

Captain Thorne had just made the announcement to seal the boat. All hatches and vents were closed and all stations prepared to trust the last chance they had in getting the ballast tanks to release their hold on the sea.

"Conn, sonar, we have a submerged disturbance twenty miles to the north. Water slug! Submerged missile launch!"

Johnson grabbed the 1 MC mic. "What?"

"Suspected submerged contact has launched a missile."

"Damn," Thorne said as he turned to his XO. "Just what in the hell are we facing here, Gary?"

"Conn, sonar, we have a surface detonation!"

Thorne allowed the mic to lower as his heart skipped a beat. He looked at all the anxious faces watching him. He again raised his mic to his mouth but was suddenly cut off.

"Conn, sonar, we have high-speed screw cavitation—torpedo in the water!"

Thorne closed his eyes as the information refused to break into the clearer thoughts he had been trained in. His eyes went to XO Devers, and both men saw the same look of disaster. Wherever they were, whatever place they found themselves, somehow a shooting war was erupting right above their heads, and they were blind as bats.

They felt the disturbance in the seas even this far down as *Houston* once more rocked and rolled. This time when she started to slide, Thorne knew she wouldn't stop until they went off the almost three-mile ledge she had lodged herself on. Every crewman aboard felt the vibration start anew as *Houston* began to slide. They heard the rush of sand and rock as her massive bulk started her slide into oblivion.

"*Conn, sonar, we have a surface detonation, three-quarters of a mile away from the first.*"

Thorne reached out and took a handhold on the stanchion that helped guide the periscope and felt his heart stop for a moment as the submarine picked up speed in her hurry to slide into the abyss far below. He once more raised the 1 MC mic to his lips, but he stopped when *Houston* once more came to a grinding halt. He closed his eyes in silent thanks.

"Engineering, how are we coming with that repair?" he asked anxiously.

"*Skipper, we're almost there,*" came the call.

Houston slid a few feet and then settled. Thorne again felt the boat move and froze until it stopped.

"Gentlemen, there's a fight going on up there; we don't have the luxury of time here."

For emphasis, every crew member felt the rumble of explosions even from their stranded spot on the side of the submerged mountain ledge.

"Chief of the Boat, stand by to surface!"

22

KIROV-CLASS BATTLE CRUISER *PETER THE GREAT*

Second Captain Dishlakov could not believe what he had just been told. He quickly scanned the waters in the direct path of the giant warship. There it was: a single straight line of a torpedo's wake heading straight at him.

"Hard to starboard!" he shouted as he watched in horror as the wake vanished as the torpedo went deep. The fear of every surface commander ever to take to the modern seas flared into his mind. "All ahead flank!"

Too late. The torpedo dove under the bow of *Peter the Great*, and the magnetic sensors buried deep inside ordered the warhead to detonate. Dishlakov felt the entire front sections of the enormous warship rise free of the sea, and he had the frozen moment in time all soldiers and sailors of the world knew was the pivotal time of an imminent death. The forward sections of the eight-foot-wide keel of *Peter the Great* separated as if they were nothing more than cordwood. The bow flashed brightly as her forward missile battery ignited in a fireball of massive proportions. A hundred feet of bow sheared away as the entire bulk of the battle cruiser came crashing back into the sea. Men, Wasakoo, and steel flew in all directions as the wail and cry of bending and cracking steel sounded even above the din of explosive outgassing.

Dishlakov was thrown into the bulkhead along with every sailor on the battle bridge. Glass shattered, and men screamed as their electronic suites exploded into the frightened faces. Seawater rose to a height of three hundred feet before it came crashing down onto the exposed sailors fighting her fires. Her number-one forward gun mount was tossed into the air as if it were nothing but a toy being kicked by a petulant child. The sea rushed into the now sheared-off bow of the mightiest vessel ever built by the Russians. Her engines kept up their relentless push as they continued to drive *Peter the Great* through the now erupting seas.

Water finally succeeded in doing what the torpedo hadn't. The engine room came to pieces as the sea struck her hot power plant. The stern of the missile cruiser erupted up and out, blasting men and equipment into the opening created by the failing engines.

Peter the Great slowly settled into the water as her remaining forward sections dug deeply into the violet-colored seas. Fire and smoke marked the area where she came to a complete stop. Alarms continued to sound as men started to rise from her decks. They stumbled, assisted others, and watched in abject astonishment as every Wasakoo aboard ran and dove into the sea. The circling mantas and their riders splashed into the water and vanished as if they had never been.

The sea was now littered with large sections and floating bodies of the two most powerful warships in the history of the world. The one remaining vessel was still anchored in the center of an ever-expanding mass of debris and dead men.

The last target left—*Simbirsk*—waited for the final blow to come.

KIROV-CLASS BATTLE CRUISER *SIMBIRSK*

Hand-to-hand battle raged across the expansive deck of the *Simbirsk*. Sailors and marines were running low on ammunition as they fought with the attacking Wasakoo. The war was brutal as men fought this strange enemy on a sea that was unrecognizable. They all, to a man, did not want to die in this world.

Jack had nearly been impaled by a spear as brutal looking as any medieval weapon from humankind's own history. The iron tip penetrated his pant leg and seared his skin as it nicked his upper thigh. He pulled the spear free of the steel and material and then threw it at a charging Wasakoo. The weapon struck the creature and went straight through its chest. The Wasakoo crumpled and then hissed in Jack's direction as it slowly fell and then rolled underneath the railing and fell into the sea.

Henri let loose with the Thompson at a group of Wasakoo as they tried to fight their way up the bridge ladders. He sent five of them crashing down onto the steel deck, but two others were still climbing. He cursed his luck when the bolt of the Thompson slammed open and stayed there. He tossed the weapon away just as Ryan let loose with his Colt .45. The two Wasakoo Henri had missed flew off the ladder and fell to their deaths.

The horns started sounding from the boats that had been tied up next to *Simbirsk*. The seashell call reverberated even over the noise of close-quarter battle.

Collins and the others were stunned as every Wasakoo that had boarded the battle cruiser jumped over the side. The battle had ended just as fast as it had started.

Jack looked around and took stock. The fires that had erupted were still blazing, but he suspected that the attack was not meant to take down the Russian relic. Men were gathering themselves, prodded by Ryan and a few of the marines to start battling the remaining fires that still flamed high into the air. He went to the rail and, after wiping blood from his face, stared at the destruction floating all around them.

Shiloh was dead in the water only fifteen hundred feet away. Her stern section was a mass of twisted steel and flaming debris. She was settling into the water at a rate Jack knew was possibly fatal. He watched as damage control parties scrambled from section to section attempting to save their dying ship. His eyes next went to the mass of flames rising less than a mile away as *Peter the Great* began to slide bow first into the water. Even with the devastation, Collins saw several large Zodiacs as they sped reinforcements toward the stricken *Peter the Great*. Even with his own ship in peril, Captain Johnson was sending assistance over to fellow sailors.

"They're still trying to save her," Everett said as he stepped up to Jack as he searched his bandolier for another clip of .45 rounds for his now useless Thompson, which he tossed to the deck when he found it empty.

"What in the hell hit us?" Farbeaux said as he assisted Ryan in tossing over the side the bodies they had just sent to their doom. He watched as the dead Wasakoo splashed into the water, and then he faced Carl and Jack.

Collins became silent as he angrily watched two great ships fighting for their lives within visual range. He had never felt so helpless in his life. Spitting blood from his mouth, he turned and searched until he found the pack lying on the deck. It was smoldering from some of the chemical accelerant used by the Wasakoo, and he quickly stamped it out. He opened the case and then pulled free the canvas bag they had recovered from the village. He ran his thumb over the Cyrillic lettering as he looked from it to the violet seas.

"I believe the theory of our friend Salkukoff having another ship out there has been confirmed in no uncertain terms, gentlemen," Henri said as he watched Jack study the canvas bag. He felt the shudder of the *Simbirsk* under his feet as the wake from the distant detonations reached the Russian ship. It again settled as Jack looked into Henri's blue eyes.

"Not a *ship*—a *boat*," he said as Ryan joined them. His arm was dangling some, as he had taken one of the elongated arrows to the forearm. It was a simple wound and one he could live with, but it still smarted as he kicked at the remains of a Wasakoo, which he simply nudged under the railing and into the sea. "A submarine," he said as he again read the canvas bag.

"The only boat we had in tow before this mess started was *Houston*," Carl said to Jack. "But she had to have been destroyed or sunk during the transition to the phase shift. If we hadn't heard from her by now, she's had it, Jack. Those boats are like eggshells."

"Not *Houston*," Collins said as he finally looked up and over at the flaming *Peter the Great*. He tossed Henri the bag but faced Everett. "Somewhere out there is the *Rostov-on-Don*. She has to be a Russian sub."

All three men were aghast.

"And this canvas carryall was from the boat's stores," Henri said as he quickly deduced that Collins was right.

"If they have a sub that has phase shift capability, why do they need *Simbirsk*? Why wouldn't they center their attack on us? Why just *Peter the Great* and *Shiloh*?" Ryan asked.

"I don't know," Jack said as he continued to look out to sea.

"I guess we're about to find out," Carl said as he pointed to something a mile away.

The sea erupted in bubbles and foam as the water parted, and the giant black object rose like a mythical sea creature from the depths.

"Back home, Europa, in one of her military intelligence briefings, mentioned a new class of boat out of the Russian shipyards. According to her, this might be the new Russian Yasen-class attack sub. It was only rumored, but there she is." Carl faced Jack. "Good guess on the sub idea, ground pounder."

They watched as the *Rostov-on-Don*, a boat named after the small Russian city in the south, surfaced and then settled onto the calm waters of the violet ocean. She sat unmoving as water cascaded from her blackened hull. The white lettering of her designation was bright against her elongated conning tower. They watched as her antennas and radar dish rose high above that sail. Her menacing bulk just sat there facing the destruction she had just caused. This boat had just fired on one of her own. Even as they watched, they saw the menacing vision of her cruise missile doors opening just aft of that large, sloping conning tower.

"Thirteen thousand–ton displacement weight, top speed of thirty knots, she has a crew of one hundred and twelve officers and men."

All three men turned and faced Henri, who shrugged.

"You are not the only one, Captain, to study and know Russian warfare plans."

"Always full of surprises, Henri," Everett said as he turned to watch the behemoth sitting only a mile away. It was like a predator just waiting for the right time to strike.

"Yes, well, here's a surprise for you, if you like. She also has long-range nuclear-capable cruise missiles whose doors are now open for business, if you had not noticed. Also, I might remind you, we have none of that. I'm afraid our friend Salkukoff has us over what you would call a barrel."

"Some damn surprise, Henri," Ryan said as he watched in wonder at the sub.

"Look, she's signaling," Carl said as he reached for and retrieved his binoculars.

"What does she signal?" Collins asked as he watched the meaningless naval-speak flashing across to them.

Carl watched the flashing strobe from the conning tower of the black submarine.

"Oh, boy, you're going to love this one, Jack."

COMPTON'S REEF

The small team had reached the middle section of the mountain. Only fifty yards from the mine's opening, they waited to see if any survivor of the village massacre appeared. They hadn't in the three minutes they had been watching. Charlie was tempted to spur the marines forward, but he knew when to keep his anxiousness to himself after so many years with Jack and the others. Still, he bit his lower lip as he waited with mounting frustration.

As they waited, they felt the rumble coming from the sea. They did not have the vantage point to see what had happened, but every man feared the worst. Everyone had been around death and destruction their entire professional lives and knew what the war sounds were. Their homes away from home were under attack. Jenks was feeling as frustrated as Charlie was but knew the marines would be cautious, as one disaster did not relate to the other when they were on a mission. They focused on their job and theirs alone.

Before they realized what was happening, they were caught off guard by twenty of the Wasakoo as they broke their cover and ran for the mine opening. They saw them vanish into the darkness beyond, and then they heard the screams emanating from the interior.

"My God!" Charlie said as he mindlessly rushed forward.

"Doc! Doc!" the lance corporal called out after the charging professor. "Damn it!" He waved his men forward. "Let's go!"

The ten marines with Master Chief Jenks in tow ran after Ellenshaw.

The lance corporal never even considered bringing night vision for their little foray and was kicking himself for that minor flaw in their mission planning. Still, they charged silently forward.

They saw Charlie suddenly veer off into the worn trail in front of the mine's opening. Then they watched as ten of the Wasakoo dragged five men and two women out screaming. They were helpless as the villagers were dispatched ruthlessly in front of their children, who ran in panic. Ten more of the Wasakoo broke from the opening, and one of them grabbed a screaming child of no more than ten years of age. Ellenshaw recklessly charged headlong into the creature, knocking it down, along with the crying child. The Wasakoo quickly recovered and then fell on the white-haired madman.

The 5.56-millimeter round caught the scaled attacker in the head, sending it backward as the marines broke into the opening. Expert marksmanship brought down the Wasakoo faster than the marines could site them. They were all feeling the relief at shooting something. The frustration was clear on the young faces as they tried to save as many of the villagers as they could. Ellenshaw quickly recovered and started rounding up all the children he could see. He hustled a group of six off into the trail brush as the United States Marines fought the strangest skirmish in corps history.

It was over in less than thirty seconds from beginning to end.

Ellenshaw was helped by Jenks as they gathered what was left of the innocent human population. Six children, four girls and two boys. One of the parents hung on for three minutes, but her wounds were too great, and she died in the arms of a nineteen-year-old marine.

Six marines checked the interior of the mine until it dipped so low they could go no farther. If any of the survivors escaped the Wasakoo, they were far down into the shaft of the mine. They had no more time to search for them.

"How many?" Charlie asked as he coddled a crying girl of no more than three years of age.

Jenks had two of the children in his thick arms as he turned for the trail and the way back to the Zodiac.

"Six. Six are all that's left," Master Chief Jenks hissed as he pushed by several of the saddened marines. "We failed these people for the second damn time!"

Suddenly, Jenks was pulled from behind by the lance corporal and then roughly pushed to the ground with his armload of children just as several of the elongated arrows came bursting through the air to strike the bush and rocks around them.

"Take cover!"

As the twelve men and six children hit the dirt, they saw the reason why the lance corporal had been so persuasive. On the mountainside a thousand yards away, there were at least a thousand Wasakoo slowly making their way toward the mine.

"Back into the opening! Take cover!" the lance corporal said as he harangued his meager force back into the darkness and safety of the mine's reinforced opening.

"Oh, shit," one of the youngest marines said as he saw the fast-deteriorating situation.

"Yeah," Jenks said as he easily placed the children down next to Ellenshaw. "You took the words right out of my mouth, squid." He pulled a nine-millimeter pistol from its holster and charged the weapon. He looked down at a girl who was hiccupping through her crying. He winked and smiled down at her. Then he started counting the Wasakoo and came to a number he knew would not be advantageous to completing their harried mission. It was the lance corporal who tossed Ellenshaw the radio with the clear indication that he should at least send out a call for help. He knew that from the sound of explosions from the sea that they really couldn't expect a rescue.

"Gentlemen, prepare to defend yourselves!"

KIROV-CLASS BATTLE CRUISER *SIMBIRSK*

Jack knew the truce was at the very least an uneasy one. Russian marines and sailors stared at the four large rubber boats as they approached. Collins saw at least half of the Russian sub's complement riding shotgun for Salkukoff and his black-clad commandos—seventy fresh and heavily armed men against what was left of the *Simbirsk* and her patched-together crew of British, Russian, and American sailors and marines. And as Jack looked them over, he knew the men on board were in no condition to continue a fight that they had no chance of winning. He felt the weight of his personal nine millimeter in its shoulder holster and decided that he would use it in lieu of surrender. He himself would beat Farbeaux in his quest to kill the Russian.

"Do we have a plan, Jack?" Everett said with hope as he continued looking for extra ammunition by checking fallen marines and sailors. The disgusting task was making him angrier by the minute.

Collins continued to watch the boats approach and the arrogant way Salkukoff stood at the bow of the lead boat as if he were George Washington crossing the Delaware. Jack remained silent, and Carl knew that when the colonel went quiet, someone was heading for a heartache. Everett knew that one way or the other, the Russian wasn't going to get away with killing everyone who knew the secrets of phase shift.

"I suspect our colonel is going to attempt the honorable way out," Henri said as he tossed his own empty nine millimeter away.

"Yeah, I'm for that. Any bastard that would shoot at his own people, I think, lacks trust," Ryan said as he joined the men at the rail to watch the triumphant approach of Salkukoff. He saw Collins turn and wink. The action always made Ryan feel good about their impending doom.

Before anyone could speak, Jack's radio crackled to life. His eyes went from the rubber boats now tying up to the gangway to his handheld. He took it and listened. The voice was low and nearly inaudible. He turned up the volume as he and the others moved away from the view of the Russians who were getting ready to board.

"Doc, is that you?"

Again, there was static. Then the faint and distant voice came across again.

"Say again, Charlie," Jack said, and he couldn't help but look over as Salkukoff and his men started the long climb up the gangway.

"Thousands of Wasakoo are nearing our position, over."

"What is your location, Doc?"

"The mine; we have survivors, but we are surrounded by a hostile force. Can we get some support? Over."

Jack lowered the radio and looked from man to man, hoping someone had an idea. Jason shook his head as he anxiously looked around him as if finding a weapon would help Jenks, Charlie, and the marines that were with them. Henri bit his lip as he angrily stewed over Salkukoff's arrival. But he too eventually shook his head. Collins turned away and adjusted his view where he could see Compton's Reef and the mountain at its center fifteen miles away. Too far to even reach them in time even if they had a plan. Jack was frustrated, as his ideas for rescue were rather complicated by their surrender at sea.

When Carl froze, so did the others. He suddenly started looking around, and then his eyes settled on the extreme height of the pagoda-style tower above them. He took the radio from Jack's grasp and then started talking.

"Doc, are the marines close by?"

"They're kind of busy setting up what defense we can mount, which isn't much. There's just too many of them."

"Doc, do you have smoke? Over."

"I don't know what—"

Carl was getting frustrated, and he shook his head as the noise of the men pounding and slowly coming up the gangway was like the sound of a ticking time bomb in his ears.

"Smoke, yes, we have red and green smoke, over."

"Good boy, Doc. Look, I need one of the marines to pop smoke in front of the mine's opening in fifteen minutes exactly. Do you copy?"

"Fifteen, got it."

"Okay, Doc, tell everyone as soon as green smoke has been popped in front of the Wasakoo advance, hunker down inside. You'll know when. Listen to the marines and Jenks; they'll know what's coming. Over."

"Got it—pop green smoke in fifteen. Ellenshaw out."

Carl tossed the radio to Jack and then watched as Salkukoff gained the upper deck only four hundred feet away.

"Jack, you're a ground pounder—what would you estimate the distance to the mine's opening?"

Collins hurriedly opened his bag where he had retrieved the canvas carry-all. He pulled out a small device. "A gift from Sarah—she says my eyes are getting too bad without glasses." He tossed it to Everett, who smiled when he saw what it was.

"A laser range finder. Leave it to little Sarah to cover all your aged short-comings," Henri said as Jack shot him a *be careful* look.

"We may not have a chance, but the Doc and Jenks might," Carl said as he turned and faced Ryan. "Grab four men and get to turret number three; you know what to do."

"Ah, shit, you're kidding!" Jason said as Farbeaux had just caught the drift of what the American naval captain was proposing.

Carl didn't answer as he started for the ladder that led skyward toward the top of the command and control tower of the World War II battle cruiser.

"Hey, where are you going?" Jack asked.

Everett stopped just short of the ladder and pointed up. "Fire control directory. Ryan has to know what in the hell he's shooting at. Jason, secure yourself and your fire team in that turret and fortify it, because it won't take Salkukoff very long to figure out what it is we are up to. I'll pass you fire control readings. I suspect you'll have only three shots—don't waste them."

They watched as Everett started climbing the steel stairs toward the highest point of the *Simbirsk*, the ancient fire control directory once used by every surface ship in the world for directing fire.

"Jack, keep that ass-hat Salkukoff occupied until we make our play."

Henri turned and faced Collins. "And just how are we supposed to do that? I mean before or after he executes us? If he had no particular qualms about killing his fellows, what chance do we have?"

"That's what I like about you, Colonel—forever the optimist."

"And not facing reality is what I so admire about you."

Jack turned as he saw Salkukoff approach, and Everett vanished into the high towerlike structure at the top of the mast.

"I'll make you a deal, Henri. No matter what happens here in the next few minutes, we seriously do that man harm before we die."

Henri Farbeaux watched as the Russian and his commandos approached. They were disarming Russian sailors and marines. The bulk of the Royal British forces vanished with Ryan into the aft number-three turret after they had removed the foul-weather caps from the enormous muzzles of the three fifteen-inch guns.

"That will be a pleasure and, I might add, a worthwhile way to die."

Jack only smiled as Salkukoff stepped up to them.

23

COMPTON'S REEF

For the third time, Jenks sent an angry Charlie back into the deeper part of the mine with the children. After Ellenshaw had passed on the information from Carl to Jenks, he was then placed in charge of getting the children to safety if this plan didn't work. The ten marines and Jenks lined the mine's opening, preparing to fight for the time Everett needed to make whatever happen, happen.

"Twenty grenades and a thousand rounds of ammunition. Four flash bangs, two claymores, which we already laid two hundred yards downhill. One LAWs rocket. That's all we have between us and the fish boys."

Jenks nodded at the marine lance corporal, who delivered the bad news as gracefully and as bravely as any marine could. The master chief managed a look up and over the large rocks they had placed for defense. He saw the Wasakoo as they hesitated only a thousand yards from their position. They were confused as to what these strangers were up to. Many of them threatened to break free of their group, and every time one of them would stand to possibly charge, one of the youngest marines, a private who grew up shooting squirrels in Virginia, took it down with a cleanly placed and long-distance shot. This action, three thus far, had kept the Wasakoo hesitant about charging. But Jenks knew that the situation would soon change as soon as the enemy found out their true numbers.

"Well, that may not be enough firepower to win, but it's enough to make those bastard barracuda-faced pirate fuckers wish they had picked another area for a stroll."

The lance corporal smiled as he went into a prone position next to the master chief.

Jenks felt a tug at his pant leg, and he looked back. It was the same little girl who had hiccupped for thirty minutes through her fear. Jenks grimaced and then snatched the child up. He stuck out his tongue and then winked. She was cautious, but she returned a smile that warmed the gruff old master chief's heart. He thought about losing what was left of the villagers, and he stood with the girl in his arms and then returned her to Charlie, who had been frantically looking for her. Ellenshaw expected a tongue-lashing from Jenks but was relieved when he just handed the girl over. The master chief pulled out a pen that had been given to him by a navy puke a few months before and was one of his possessions he had bragged and showed off to everyone who would listen and admire it. He held it up and then leaned into the girl as he showed her the cheap ink pen he had been given. He turned it up and then down in front of her eyes, and she smiled and clapped her hands, amazed at the magic.

"I don't believe it. They still make those?" Charlie asked as the girl relaxed as she watched the magic before her eyes.

The pen was one of those you might have purchased years ago at a liquor store checkout counter that depicted a slender, beautiful woman on the pen itself, and every time you turned it over, the black dress she wore would slowly vanish. Turn it back and the dress reappeared. The children watched and laughed at the magic coming from the world of the master chief.

"Yeah, well, just don't look too closely at the face of the woman in the pen, Doc, or you'll find me on the short end of the stick that kicks your ass."

Charlie watched him move back to his defensive position. Then he looked closely at the face of the woman, and then his brows rose. The woman's face was the exact twin of Assistant Director Virginia Pollock. A mere coincidence, but it was her all right. Jenks, Charlie knew, had it bad.

Ellenshaw smiled for the first time in days. He soon lost the grin when the noise from the front of the mine froze his blood.

"Here they come!"

KIROV-CLASS BATTLE CRUISER *SIMBIRSK*

Once inside the number-three gun turret, Jason stood momentarily confused as to just how he was going to do this without blowing them and the *Simbirsk* to pieces. Then his eyes fell on the elevator control switches that would allow the silk powder bags to be delivered from the powder stores eight decks beneath him. On the opposite side, he saw the same control system to raise the thousand-pound, fifteen-inch projectile to the turret. Ryan also saw the communications console that would connect him to the projectile and powder bunkers. He hit the switch.

"Hey, is anyone down there?" he asked, hoping beyond hope that the system didn't send his voice out all over the battle cruiser.

"*We're here, Commander,*" said the cockney-tinged voice of the Royal Marine sergeant. "*I don't know what it is we're supposed to do, but we're here.*"

Jason knew his education at the academy had barely touched on surface warfare to the point where he knew how to fire the main guns that were designed right around the turn of the last century, but he quipped to himself that he had seen plenty of movies on the subject. He just hoped they were accurate. He closed his eyes as he tried to remember his instructions.

"Okay, there is an automatic lift near the powder stores on the starboard side of the armory."

"*Yes, we see it.*"

"Now, very carefully go into the vault and, using the elevator, load three bags onto the slide. The switch to raise it up is right next to the aft bulkhead. For God's sake, be careful—we don't know how this powder has been treated the past seventy years."

It seemed like a lifetime until Ryan heard the elevator engage. The noise was tremendous as the automatic doors sprang open, waiting for the delivery.

"*Three shells and six bags of black powder, Commander. I don't know about your end, but we are bloody making a lot of noise down here.*"

In the turret, Ryan heard the motors engage, and he flinched again as the machinery made a tremendous amount of noise as the elevator transferred its heavy load. As he watched, the steel-reinforced door slid up, and before he realized what was happening, the large fifteen-inch shell fell forward, and he closed his eyes as he waited for the detonation that would end them all. Instead, the large thousand-pound shell eased into the steel slide just below it. Jason took a deep breath as a pushrod hydraulically pushed the shell into the breach. He repeated the same motions on the number-two and -three guns. The shells were in. Now if he could only get the most dangerous part over with and see if he could send these shells outward in the right direction.

"Bag elevator has stopped and has delivered your load. We're out of here. We'll take up station in the aft area and wait for orders. I'm sending two men up to you."

Jason didn't answer as he saw the first white-colored powder bag arrive and the auto-loader come into play. He hurriedly moved to the number-one gun of turret three and turned the large stainless steel handle, and he opened the breach. Then he bit his lower lip as he thought about what he had to do next. Then he remembered. He saw another stainless-steel slide and moved it into place. The slide went right to the breach's opening and stopped. The powder bag was now right in front of the breach. Jason kicked at the steel next to the breach in frustration. Then before he could move and think on it, a large piston came free of the bulkhead and then pushed the first silk bag into the breach. Jason was amazed at the sophistication of the Russian design. He knew they were freaks of nature when it came to fully automated systems, and any time the old Soviets could take it out of the soldiers' hands in favor of assurance from automation, they did.

Finally, the last bag was pushed into the gun, and Jason closed the breach. He took a deep breath as the hatch came suddenly open. He quickly pulled his nine millimeter from its holster but stopped when he saw the two hands raised in deference to his threat.

"Scared the hell out of me," Jason said as he shoved the gun back into his shoulder holster.

The two marines came inside and dogged the hatch.

"Now look, even if we pull this off, we're bound to have company."

"The sergeant has that aspect covered, Commander. His four men will lie in wait for any visitors."

Again, Jason took a deep breath and then raised his radio to his lips.

"Ryan to Everett."

There was no answer to his call. He immediately started thinking the worst. Was he caught going up to the directory tower?

"Ryan to Everett," he said once more, looking at the Royal Marines.

"Everett," came the soft return. *"Ready down there?"*

"Yeah, but where in the hell are we going to point these cap pistols?"

"We'll have to wait until our friends pop smoke for a more detailed sighting, but the preliminary coordinates are as follows."

Ryan punched in the numbers on the directory system. It had taken him three full minutes to decipher the Cyrillic language, but he finally saw the small diagram that explained it all.

"Preliminary coordinates entered."

"Okay, now we wait."

Ryan looked at the two marines.

"If we lose our landing party, I think it only fair to warn you gentlemen that I intend to use those shells against the submarine out there."

"Look, Commander," the oldest of the two marines said, "we were shown film once of the old *Missouri* shooting those big bloody guns of hers—they are quite devastating. I don't see why we don't do things the old way."

"What's that?" Ryan asked curiously as he saw the smile on the face of the marine take shape.

"Two of these monstrous things will kill every fish man in that area. The concussion alone would kill them. If that is the case, why don't we save the third shell for our unwanted guest?"

The smile became infectious as Ryan raised the radio to his lips and called Everett and informed him of their new plan.

Someone was going to get shot.

The two men faced each other, and not a word was said between them. Even as Salkukoff's men gathered up the remaining weapons of the ship's defenders, men from both forces became silent and hateful. Jack had been worried that the Russian had seen Carl and the others vanish, but thus far, Salkukoff gave no indication that he had. Thus far, the commandos had rounded up seventy-five men in varying states of injuries and anger. The Russian sailors were particularly having a hard time facing the very countrymen who had stabbed them in the back. One of these came close to being executed as he refused to raise his hands to be searched.

"I may assume your Master Chief Jenks and Professor Ellenshaw are in the phase shift engine spaces?" Salkukoff said as he stepped closer to Jack. "Ask them to secure the space and join us, please."

Jack raised his eyebrows as if he didn't know what Salkukoff was speaking of.

The Russian nodded toward one of his men. The Russian sailor he grabbed could not have been more than nineteen years of age. Collins and Farbeaux knew what was coming, and they also knew they had to talk as the hammer of the Makarov clicked back as the boy was sent to his knees.

"One more time, ask Dr. Ellenshaw and the master chief to join us, please."

Collins allowed his eyes to move from the frightened boy to those of Salkukoff.

"Both men are dead. The engine spaces are empty. We had everyone above decks fighting your creatures."

Salkukoff studied the American for the untruth that would surely be there. He seemed satisfied as he nodded for his men to secure the phase shift engine. The Russian sailor was released.

"Is that what you do now, Colonel—kill all of those in the path of your plans?" Jack asked as he heard sounds coming from the number-three turret and tried his best to cover the noise with his own words.

"The sacrifice of some for the greater good is always acceptable. You know the old tale, Colonel Collins. Or are you that twisted inside that you cannot recognize your own shortcomings?"

"I recognize them and have come to embrace them. But one thing I don't do is turn on my allies—or my own people, for that matter. You, sir, do. A traitor to his country and fellow soldiers is the lowest form of life and always has been."

"Noble speak, that is what I like to call it, and that is the particular reason your nations have always been vulnerable: the illusion that you are the force of good in our world. There is no such force, Colonel. And today it will be explained to you in no uncertain terms." Salkukoff moved away and faced Farbeaux. "Treason, as the old saying goes, is a matter of dates, am I right, Colonel Farbeaux?"

Henri, to his benefit, remained silent.

"Why did you attack our ships?" Jack asked as he again heard more noises coming from the turret and from below, where the carousel and elevator to the armory began to move, transporting powder bags and shells to the turret itself. He knew he needed more time.

"Colonel, it is obvious to those who know how to rule with an iron fist. We cannot have witnesses to our dealings here. Blue diamonds are only a rumor, at least according to you Americans. No one can know how many we have collected. But alas, our mission here has come to an end, and now we have accounts to settle. Even our own people will be forever expendable in the constant endeavor to overcome the failings of our shared Russian history. Yes, they did their duty but will go down as merely missing at sea." He smiled. "Just as yourselves and your brave *Shiloh*. An unfortunate way of doing business, I'm afraid, but a necessary one. My associates are now ready to make our move into the world, and you, sir, stand in the way of that. You and all these men. It was a fluke of science that brought us here, but that is why I will attribute that luck to destiny. It is our destiny to move now against the West."

Jack watched over the Russian's shoulder as both *Peter the Great* and *Shiloh* continued to fight for their lives. Salkukoff saw this, and again he smiled.

"As soon as we conclude our business here, we will sink both ships. A shame, but again, very necessary."

"Why didn't you attack *Simbirsk*?" Farbeaux spoke up for the first time.

Salkukoff laughed as he watched several of the dead defenders of *Simbirsk* unceremoniously jettisoned over the side.

"I think if given the time, your amazing master chief and your small portable computer, of which I must get a copy, would have figured it out. Our Captain Kreshenko was quickly becoming wise to our only vulnerability."

"You can't lock onto this world. You need the constant appearance and disappearance of *Simbirsk* to lock on to. You can't duplicate your own science, just like we Americans couldn't do it in the Philadelphia navy yard in '43. If you tried to go it alone without *Simbirsk*, you would randomly come out wherever the phase shift sent you. You can't duplicate the frequency. USS *Eldridge* had the same frequency, and when you stole the design, you inadvertently dialed the phase shift to the same frequency."

"Your Jenks was getting close when he realized that the frequency of any phase shift engine is completely random. It all has to be precise to be useful; otherwise, you end up in even far more hostile worlds than this one. But since we could only come here with any hope of return, thanks to *Simbirsk*, we had no choice. The blue diamonds were found, and we used the constant phase shifting of *Simbirsk* to hitch a ride, if you will. Why she never powers down is still a mystery, but she's become erratic, just as you saw in the North Atlantic, and that was the reason we are pulling the plug, as you Americans say. We didn't expect her to produce the hurricane the way she did. Something is starting to fail in the phase shift engine. It's deteriorating at an alarming speed. Her power is shifting our very atmospheric conditions. This is why we were caught off guard when she appeared in the North Atlantic. She has now outlived her usefulness. When she is powered up and we hitch our last ride home with her, she will immediately be scuttled in the deepest part of the Atlantic. And then, because of our missions to this world, we will be on an equal footing where blue diamonds are concerned."

"And how many innocent sailors were wasted in your attempts to find other frequencies?" Henri asked.

"Too many to count. Thirteen ships of our navy sacrificed all for the future of their nation. So, we cozied up to *Simbirsk* on one of her magical appearances, and as I said, we followed. We needed a stabler platform because of the dangers of riding the old girl to this world, so we sent in our newest, strongest asset—"

"The *Rostov-on-Don*," Jack answered for him.

"Yes, very good, Colonel. She is strong and very capable as you just learned, and she can submerge to escape the worst of the phase shift forces."

"Why not just use a phase shift engine inside your submarine and copy the frequency of the transfer when *Simbirsk* moved?" Jack asked.

"For the simple reason their sciences couldn't miniaturize the engine— it's too big," Henri said with a small chuckle. "They have no choice but to follow *Simbirsk* wherever she goes. Now that's a plan, a stupid one, but it is a plan. You people will never cease to amaze me with your reach of power, even though that reach will cost lives."

Salkukoff didn't appreciate the Frenchman's humor or point of view. His face was a mask of anger as he nodded at Farbeaux over their failures of science. He gestured, and several of the commandos approached and placed Jack's and Henri's hands behind their backs.

"There, you have successfully exposed our evil plans, Colonel, but there will be no salvation for you or any of the forces you have arrayed against us. You will remain here with these shipwrecked sailors, fighting the Wasakoo for the remainder of your lives, and live a life free of deciding who is evil and who is good in the world. Here, you can be good all you want. With the *Simbirsk* being immediately destroyed upon my return, there will be no going home for you, Colonel."

Salkukoff turned and started toward the hatchway leading down into the phase shift engine spaces.

"Maybe, maybe not," Jack said with a smile, and his voice made Salkukoff stop and turn to face the American and the Frenchman. He tilted his head, not understanding.

Jack moved his hands from behind his back before they could be tied. The Russian commandos seemed amused. Collins tore away part of his shirt, and then that piece was torn into four small strips. Two of these he handed to Henri, who accepted them with a nod. Both men stuffed the torn shirt into their ears and then went to their knees, making the Russians standing around them laugh and smile. Salkukoff was not among them as he realized too late what the American's plan was.

Every man on the upper deck froze as the large number-three gun turret of the Russian battle cruiser started to rotate and the three barrels rose into the air.

The ancient warship had one last surprise in store for her passengers.

LOS ANGELES—CLASS ATTACK SUBMARINE USS *HOUSTON*

The crew strapped themselves down, men ran to their battle stations, and all were armed to the teeth with weapons as *Houston* was prepared to give her all to survive. With the detonations that had sounded through their loudspeakers from the surface of the sea, they knew even if they surfaced alive, there was going to be a possible fight.

"Okay, Rodriguez, warm up those pumps!" Thorne turned and looked at his young crew. They were as ready as he could ever hope; the men at their stations didn't bow their heads in prayer, and there was no panic. They just turned to their duties and prepared for the worst. "All hands, prepare to surface."

The chief of the boat hit the surface alarm, and the beluga call burst from the loudspeakers.

"Chief, blow all tanks, full rise on the planes, stand by for all-ahead flank, surface the boat!"

Every man aboard winced as the announcement was made. They saw the ballast control officer close his eyes as he blindly hit the aft and stern pumps that would activate the forcing of water from her bulk. Just as the ballast control officer turned the switch, they all heard the expansive explosion of water being forced from *Houston*'s open vents. The entire complement all closed their eyes when they heard *Houston* break away from the ledge. But also in accompaniment with the sound of releasing air came the sound they all dreaded. *Houston* started sliding before her tanks emptied enough to get them up and moving. The scraping and outside noise from her crushing bulk ceased almost as suddenly as it started.

USS *Houston* slid off the mountain ledge, and her bow dome dipped. The Gray Lady started a spiraling plummet to her death almost three miles down.

COMPTON'S REEF

At three hundred yards, the defenders inside the mine opened fire. They caught the Wasakoo off guard. The front line of skirmishers was so busy trying to cool themselves with water they never knew what hit them. Thirty-five of the green-tinted creatures went down in the initial volley.

Jenks raised his head and looked. He saw the Wasakoo behind the first line of attackers scramble. However, it didn't take them long to recover. This time, they didn't come on slowly; it was as if they knew they were short of time. They charged. A thousand of the hideous-looking species came on while screaming and shaking long, lethal-looking spears at them.

Three grenades were launched down the mountainside, and they rolled right into the center of the Wasakoo advancing line. They exploded. The bodies flew in all directions, but the grenades didn't have the desired effect of making them think differently about their assault.

Barrels were red hot as the marines kept up their constant fire. But everyone inside the mine's opening knew they would run out of bullets long before the Wasakoo ran out of spears.

"Well, that does it. Cover me!" Jenks burst from the opening, and then with all the strength he could muster, he threw the smoke canister as far downhill as he could.

On the mountainside, the green smoke popped, and the Wasakoo flinched from the strange attack. They avoided even walking into the billowing cloud.

"I hope Toad shoots straight!" Jenks yelled as he burst back into the opening.

Down below them, the Wasakoo made their last charge.

KIROV-CLASS BATTLE CRUISER *SIMBIRSK*

Everett placed his eye to the powerful scope in the fire directory station two hundred feet above the main deck. At first, he couldn't even see the mountain, much less the opening of the mine's entrance. He adjusted the scope, and with one eye closed, he finally saw the green smoke rising from the midway point of the mountain. He made the quick calculation and then entered it into the fire control computer. Computer? He laughed as he thought about it. It was that in name only, as most of the calculations were already made by the operator. He looked down at the wind velocity and saw that it was near zero. The distant target was cross-sectioned, and then the distance was put in.

"God, I hope my math still holds up." Carl went over to the starboard bulkhead and chanced a look down onto the deck where Jack was attempting to buy him the time they needed. It didn't look as if the conversation was going well. He also noticed the crew of the *Simbirsk* was being lined up on their knees. He didn't like the look of that at all. He noticed one other thing also. The bulk of the remaining Royal Marines were nowhere to be seen. That was the little bit of hope he was waiting for. With luck, those marines knew when to attack. He picked up his radio.

"Commander, are you ready?"

"No, I'm never that anxious to blow myself up. Other than that, the tubes are loaded . . . I think."

"Okay, here we go."

On the main deck, the aft number-three turret started to rotate. As it did, the three sixty-foot-long barrels rose into the air. Carl chanced another look as his commands were now automated. It would be up to Ryan to trigger off the first explosive rounds at an enemy by a heavy cruiser since the Korean War.

"Gun number one, fire!"

Jack, Henry, and the Russian commandos were thrown from their feet as gun number one in turret three let loose. The concussion killed two of Salkukoff's men who were directly under the powerful warhead when the two silk-lined powder bags ignited and then in turn pushed the thousand-pound warhead through the tube and out into the blue sky. The recoil on the ship was fantastic. *Simbirsk* groaned against the power of the exploding fifteen-inch weaponry. Her bulk slid ten feet to the port side as the barrel flashed a fifty-foot-long trail of fire from her muzzle. Before anyone could react, another shell exploded from gun mount number two. This time, four of Salkukoff's men were blown over the side, and Salkukoff himself was wrenched from the ladder he had been climbing and was thrown to the hard deck. Henri recovered fast as he tried to get to the downed Russian colonel, but he was hit hard in the back of the head and stilled momentarily.

Jack took a split second to recover. Even with the makeshift earplugs, he was almost knocked senseless. As he raised his head, he saw the Russian commandos were down and the regular crew was fighting with them. It seemed the Russian seamen, no matter how badly bruised they were by the blast of the big guns, were angry enough to shed off that pain and attack the men they blamed for their situation. He then saw a wondrous sight as the third and final gun was turning to the port side and the barrel was lowering. Collins quickly roused a hurt Farbeaux, and they both rolled underneath one of the lifeboats for protection.

"Jesus, Ryan is going for the sub!" Jack said as even in the directory Everett was amazed when the barrel and the turret started transiting on their own with no input from him. He hit the deck as the barrel went to its lowest attitude and the gun exploded outward. Everett quickly stood and saw the submarine. He saw the crew scrambling away in panic as the fifteen-inch shell struck just aft of the conning tower, missing the boat by only eighty feet. The submarine was inundated in violet seawater.

"Damn, Ryan, you missed!" Carl hissed.

Then he saw what no man ever wanted to see: the sub came to life and moved closer to get into position.

None of the Americans thought they would fire on their only way home, but they also knew the submarine captain had been fired on and was reacting instead of thinking. This whole operation may have just gone tits up.

COMPTON'S REEF

The first ranks of the Wasakoo had burst up and over the rock-strewn protection the marines had thrown up. They crashed into men, and the fighting became hand to hand. They knew their time in this life was done when the rest of the thousand enemies burst through.

Jenks emptied his close-in weapon, his nine millimeter, and then grabbed the skin of one of the sickly Wasakoo as it dove into the mine. Jenks started pummeling the creature on the head and neck, but he felt the weight of the large Wasakoo as it drove him into the ground. As the master chief looked into the grinning face of the Wasakoo, it hissed at him as its strong and webbed fingers started to choke the life from him. Then the pressure eased as Charlie appeared in his vision. The white-haired professor held one of the discarded spears in his hand as he brought it down once more into the back of Jenks's attacker.

Suddenly, a freight train sound rent the skies above them. It sounded as if the massive fifteen-inch shell was reaching right out for them and not the advancing Wasakoo. The first explosion blew the marines, Charlie, and Jenks backward as it detonated not fifty feet from the mine's opening. Fire and smoke covered everything. None of the men could even begin to hear the second round as it came crashing down from the almost mile-high arc. Another brutal earth-shattering explosion shook the very rock strata they hid behind. More fire, rock, pieces of Wasakoo, and foliage covered them all.

There was an eerie silence that filled the world. With the exception of men coughing and their painful attempts to rise, the world was gone for them. Dust filled the cave like dense smoke as Jenks shook his head. He saw Charlie move next to him. His spear was broken into two pieces, but he was still tenaciously hanging on to it.

"Come on, Doc, you're all right," Jenks said as he battled to his feet, and in the blinding dust cloud, he assisted Ellenshaw to his feet. Then they started helping the marines who had been closer to the opening than they. Three of them were hard to rouse awake, but they finally opened their eyes and coughed. All was still silent.

Jenks and the lance corporal made it to the opening, and that was when they saw the devastation the ancient Russian weaponry had caused. It looked as if the world had been plowed over. There was not a tree standing within fifty yards of the mine. Wasakoo were lying dead in all directions.

"Look," the lance corporal said, pointing.

Jenks rubbed his eyes, coughed out a mouthful of dirt, and then saw what the marine saw. Out of over a thousand Wasakoo, only fifty or so were heading for the hills. They sprinted downhill at a pace that said they wanted nothing more to do with the intruders to their world.

"Thank God! I didn't want to buy it here," the lance corporal said as he wiped as much of the dirt from his face as he could.

"Hate to tell you this, Lance Corporal Jarhead, but we still have to travel through time and space to get back home."

The marine looked at Jenks as the others, including the six children they had just saved, joined them.

"As long as no one shoots them big damn guns at us, I can live with that danger. That was freakin' brutal!"

The battle for Compton's Reef had ended.

KIROV-CLASS BATTLE CRUISER *SIMBIRSK*

Jack and Henri had lost all sense of time and predicament. The recoil of the large-bore guns had sent everyone to the deck. The gunfire itself had killed at least six men of Salkukoff's command. Still, they held the upper hand. The Russian sailors they had rounded up and disarmed were as helpless as Collins and Farbeaux. They were just rising from the deck, and the commandos, to their credit, recovered far faster than their captives. Henri assisted Jack to his feet. Farbeaux removed the makeshift earplugs and saw that his left eardrum may have been perforated as blood-covered cloth attested to.

"You're bleeding," Jack said as he nodded his thanks at the Frenchman.

Before they realized what was happening, they were both pushed back down onto the deck by three of Salkukoff's men. The man himself was wiping blood from his nose and forehead as he staggered toward them. He angrily kicked out at Jack and caught the colonel in the stomach. When Henri reacted, he was slammed in the back of the head by the foldable stock of an AK-47 and sent to the steel deck next to Collins.

"What did that little display prove?" He kicked at Jack again before he could recover from the first blow. "Two worthless misses at a now uninhabited island, and one toward my boat? Very poor plan, Colonel." He angrily and ruthlessly took an AK-47 from one of his men and aimed it down toward the two men. "Now, here's the rest of my plan," he said as he aimed at the back of Jack's head.

Farbeaux looked up in time to realize that this time around they would not escape that inevitable bullet Collins and men like himself always expected.

In the fire control directory high above, Everett saw what was about to happen but was powerless to stop it.

LOS ANGELES—CLASS ATTACK SUBMARINE USS *HOUSTON*

As *Houston* blew all air from her ballast tanks, it looked as if it would be too late. The submarine flew off the shelf of the mountain and went straight down. The weakened ballast control system was not powerful enough to provide lift to her planes until more water was ejected from her bowels. Every man aboard was thrown into their stations as *Houston* began a descent they would never recover from.

"All back full!" Thorne yelled over the whine of the turbines.

"Answering all back!" the chief of the boat answered. "Reactors at 115 percent!"

Thorne closed his eyes as he hung on in the almost vertical environment. His lips moved as if in prayer, but he was counting internally. He ticked off the depth in his head, knowing where their crush depth was, and his calculations told him they had another hundred feet before *Houston* imploded like an eggshell.

The control room was calm for the circumstances they found themselves in. They hung on, and most of the seamen prayed.

"She's slowing!" XO Devers called out. "Bow's coming up!"

The words yelled over the din of the reversing turbines was God's answer to their prayers.

Thorne looked over at his control board and saw the depth numbers slowing. He again closed his eyes as *Houston* was still nearing her breaking point. The sound of her sail being punched in like a car in an auto accident reverberated throughout the boat. Loud popping started, and each pop of her hull sent fear through the crew. Still, Thorne hoped.

"She's coming back up!" the chief shouted and yipped.

Houston was two hundred feet beyond her crush depth as they felt the forces shift more to the horizontal.

"That's it! We are coming up!" Devers said, agreeing with the chief of the boat.

Houston started to rise at an incredible rate. Hull-popping noises sounded as she started to come to shallower waters. Soon she was heading in the opposite direction, straight up. Every man felt the speed as it increased. Thorne, against his better judgment, fought his way back toward the NAV table. He was hanging on for dear life when an announcement came over the loudspeakers that froze his blood.

"Conn, sonar, we've been hit with a sonar ping!"

Devers looked over at his captain with shock registering on his face.

"Sonar, conn, what are you talking about?"

"Conn, sonar, we have a surface vessel painting us. Torpedo doors opening. Suspected submarine right over our heads!"

"Damn, we're going to be fired on!" Devers finally said.

"Sonar, conn, best guess as to ambient noise?"

"Conn, computer says the profile fits that new Russian sub we were warned about. Her screws are starting to turn. She's Russian, all right!"

Thorne angrily threw the 1 MC mic at Devers, who caught it. "Weapons, open outer doors on aft tubes seven, eight, and nine. Vertical tubes one and two. Are the Harpoons warmed?"

"Weapons, aye, tubes are loaded with war shot, and doors are open. Doors open on vertical tubes one and two."

"Conn, sonar, we have two torpedoes in the water!"

"Ballast control, slow our ascent!"

"Control boards have shorted out, Captain; we have no control."

Thorne knew he would never have the time to get an accurate fix on their target. The firing solution was being scrambled by their faster-than-normal climb toward the sky. He came to a quick decision.

"Vertical tubes one and two, do we have a firing solution?" he asked his weapons station only eight feet away. He knew his torpedoes would be worthless at this high rate of ascent. It would now be up to his vertical launch system to send their Harpoon missile outward to avenge the death they would soon suffer from the hands of the Russian torpedoes. He had decided that *Houston* would kill the sub that killed it.

"Fire solution is constant, Skipper!"

"Torpedoes close aboard!"

Houston was traveling straight up, a position the designers at General Dynamics Electric Boat Division had never intended. Thorne didn't know if the speed of the vertical climb would tear the Harpoons to pieces even before they were fully ejected from their tubes.

"Fire vertical tubes one and two!" Thorne ordered as he waited for the Russian weapons to impact his boat.

"Firing vertical tubes one and two!" Came the answer. "Harpoons have left the tubes, running hot, straight, and normal."

Thorne knew that at least *Houston* would get in her death blow to the enemy just as they were sent to a watery grave themselves.

"*Conn, sonar, torpedoes have locked onto us, impact in five, four, three, two, one!*"
Thorne braced himself for the imminent death coming their way.

Impact. There was a loud bang. Every man flinched, and even a few screamed out. Another hollow-sounding *thung* sounded throughout the boat. *Houston* shook and rattled as she was still speeding full bore toward the surface.

"*Conn, sonar, no warhead detonation,*" came the call in a voice filled with excitement.

Thorne realized what had happened. *Houston* was breaking a speed record in her uncontrolled nose-up ascent. As he looked at the speed on the readout, he saw they were at fifty-five knots and speeding up. They had risen so fast and closed the distance to their enemy at a speed so unheard of that the enemy weapons had not the time to arm themselves. The Russian torpedoes had slammed into *Houston* but disintegrated upon impact. No doubt they would find at least one big hole in her skin when and if they surfaced.

"Oh, shit!" Thorne said as he studied the plot. Thorne looked also.

"Hard right rudder, all back full!"

Houston was heading directly at the enemy sub that had fired upon her, and Captain Thorne and XO Devers saw that their evasive orders would never be input before they surfaced right into their enemy.

Houston was doomed. Her speed and nose-up attitude would send them directly into the bottom hull of the enemy.

KIROV-CLASS BATTLE CRUISER *SIMBIRSK*

Carl took a chance and opened fire from the fire directory two hundred feet up. He missed Salkukoff and cursed his hurried aim.

Suddenly, gunfire erupted from several locations as Her Majesty's Royal Marines came out of hiding.

It was amazing how military men the world over knew exactly when to act. Upon seeing Collins and Farbeaux about to be executed along with the remaining Russian sailors, everyone in hiding broke cover to assist. Bullets were heading in all directions.

Jack reacted without thinking as he leg-whipped the Russian colonel, sending him to the deck. Collins quickly elbowed the colonel and then reached for his fallen weapon. Henri also brought down another of the confused commandos as he ran by. He fell on the man's back and then slammed his head facefirst into the deck, successfully relieving him of his AK-47. The small battle was over in less than thirty seconds.

Jack stood and then started kicking Salkukoff until the man rose to his feet.

He smiled at Jack as he moved his right hand toward the radio and hit the transmit switch three times in quick succession. Collins quickly reached out and took the radio and tossed it overboard.

"Too late, Colonel—we will all be dead in less than thirty seconds."

"What did you do, you maniac?" Henri asked angrily as he unceremoniously popped the Russian in the belly, making him bow from the pain. The Russian started to laugh.

"Thirty seconds is all it takes for a torpedo to cover the short distance to *Simbirsk*." He laughed even harder as he straightened up from Henri's blow to his belly. "If we don't go back home, none of us will."

Jack pulled the laughing Salkukoff toward the railing and shook him. Everett joined them after his hurried climb back to the main deck. The Royal Marines were shepherding the remaining commandos into a small group. They only had six of them left, as the rest had been dispatched nicely by Her Majesty's forces.

"Say good-bye to your friends and the *Simbirsk*, Colonel Collins, as I prepare to greet my own in that other place we all dream about."

Jack cursed their luck as he faced the enemy submarine as it readied to end their lives.

Before anyone realized what was happening, a giant water slug broke the surface of the violet seas. The two Harpoon missiles rose three hundred feet into the darkening skies, and then the large weapons rolled over and dove straight down after shedding their outer protective casings. The impact struck the *Rostov-on-Don* dead center just aft of her sloped conning tower. The large 215-pound warheads of the two UGM-84 Harpoon missiles broke through the heavy steel plate of the submarine and detonated close by the vertical launch tubes with their missiles still inside. Ten other warheads along with the American missiles blew the *Rostov-on-Don* into two pieces. Water, steel, and other debris shot skyward.

Jack and the others were again thrown from their feet as the amazing rescue of their lives decimated the enemy sub. Salkukoff was shocked to see the *Rostov-on-Don* disintegrate right before his eyes. Jack hurriedly stood as the wave created by the two halves of the Russian sub struck them. The *Simbirsk* rolled over, knocking everyone again from their feet. The destruction of Salkukoff's main asset tossed the seas to the extreme.

In the lower spaces of *Simbirsk*, something else was reacting to the roll of the giant ship. Europa Jr. was monitoring the phase shift engine to keep it from ramping back up, but as the giant wave of destruction hit *Simbirsk*, the laptop was thrown from the table and smashed onto the deck. Her lights went out just as the phase shift capacitors began to ramp up. The phase shift engine was once more breathing.

As every man crowded around the railing to see what had just happened, another sight caught their attention. In the middle of the debris-filled spot where the Russian sub had vanished, the ocean shot straight into the air as the seas erupted. The sonar dome of the USS *Houston* broke the surface and rose into the sky. The black-hulled submarine looked as if it had been shot out of a cannon. She shot up until her weight and gravity brought her back. *Houston*'s bow slammed back into the sea, and another large wake slammed into the battle cruiser. The attack boat quickly settled into the remains of the *Rostov-on-Don*. All the world became silent until the eruption of cheers from the Russian sailors and British Marines drowned out the noise of the encroaching storm. Jack looked at Henri and Carl and shook his head.

"I guess we have confirmation on *Houston*'s whereabouts. It looks like she came along for our little excursion."

Cheers erupted again as men saw the crew of *Houston* come into view as they took their stations on the upper conning tower.

Jack smiled as he turned and faced Salkukoff and his look of utter bewilderment.

"Looks like you weren't the only ones to have a navy out here, huh?"

"I . . . I . . . don't understand."

"Welcome to the club, asshole; we never understand our luck either, but there you have it," Carl said as he intentionally slapped Salkukoff on the back as hard as he could, sending the Russian colonel into the top rung of the railing. Then Carl leaned into Jack. "I'll never, ever curse the submarine service again."

"I hear that, brother."

24

Second Captain Dishlakov was the last crewman to be removed from *Peter the Great*. The amazing thing was the fact that he was escorted off and into a rubber Zodiac by none other than Captain Johnson. As Dishlakov dove feetfirst into the churning sea, it was Johnson who gave him his hand and assisted him into the last boat. The two men faced each other and, having no words to say, just shook hands.

A tremendous explosion inside the sinking *Peter the Great* sent debris skyward. The great warship finally broke her back, and the stern section twisted to the right and started heading for the bottom of a sea so far from home that most of the survivors could not begin to fathom it.

The Zodiac carrying the last of the Russian crew to depart watched helplessly as the magnificently raked bow of the missile cruiser rose high into the air just as the stern had done, and then slowly start sliding down to her watery grave. Second Captain Dishlakov watched his life vanish before him. Johnson placed a hand on the man's shoulder as the Zodiac turned and sped away.

As men assisted the survivors aboard the *Simbirsk*, all attention was now focused on saving USS *Shiloh* from suffering the same fate as *Peter the Great*. Her stern was a wreck. The Russian weaponry had managed to punch a hole near her engine spaces, and she was down at the fantail. Her crew was fighting gallantly to save their ship, but from Jack's perspective, she was fighting a losing battle. Even with damage control crewmen from *Houston* assisting, *Shiloh* was going to lose that fight. Collins came to a conclusion that no one was going to like. He turned to Everett.

"Swabby, we can't take a chance that when we make the attempt to get home, *Shiloh* won't break in two during the phase shift. She couldn't stand the pounding. But you know more about what these cruisers are made up of more than I do. What do you think?"

Carl assisted one of the crewmen from *Peter the Great* over the railing and then wiped sweat from his brow. He shook his head.

"I say pile everyone on board *Simbirsk* and *Houston* and we get the hell out of here."

Jack concurred. He didn't look forward to telling Captain Johnson that he was going to have to scuttle his ship. "Get on the horn and inform Captains Dishlakov, Johnson, and Thorne what the plan is."

Everett nodded and then went to deliver the worst news any commander could ever hear: *abandon your efforts to save your ship.*

Jack breathed a sigh of relief when he saw Charlie Ellenshaw as he stepped onto the deck of *Simbirsk*. He watched as Ellenshaw accepted the children saved from the island. Jenks was last to come aboard with the ten marines. He quietly thanked God that none of the landing team was lost. Not that Jenks and Charlie weren't in trouble anyway, but that would wait for a better time. Jack approached, and Charlie held up a hand before the colonel could speak.

"It was my idea, Colonel."

"Bullshit, Chuck. It was me," Jenks countered.

"No, sir, I take full responsibility," said the lance corporal as he saluted Jack.

Collins only shook his head. He then looked at the six frightened children crowded around Jenks. They were holding his legs as if to keep him from running away. Jack's anger evaporated as quickly as it came on.

"We'll discuss this later. Jenks, I need you and Charlie to get below and monitor that phase shift equipment." He looked around and saw the strange weather pattern that was rapidly developing. The heavy clouds were starting to circle in a most unfamiliar pattern. "And take this ass-hat with you," he said as he lightly kicked at the man sitting at his feet. Salkukoff said nothing as he was lifted from his feet by two of the American marines. "Chain him up down there, because if anyone survives this thing, I want it to be him. I'm sure his testimony will be rather informative when we get back home."

"Personally, I think we should leave the bastard here with his fish-faced pirate friends," Jenks said as he unceremoniously lifted Salkukoff from the deck. The children, with their natural instincts, moved away from Salkukoff and went to Charlie for their protection.

"Charlie, get the children to the empty armory; that will provide them with the best protection when and if this thing goes off."

Charlie started herding the children away as Jenks pushed Salkukoff toward the hatchway. The Russian stopped and with manacled wrists shook off Jenks's hold and turned and faced Jack.

"Even if you manage to control the phase shift, do you think bringing me back in chains will do anything to stop our movement?"

Jack smiled as he watched the caged rat before him. "We have some pretty dedicated people from both sides of the Atlantic that will do just that. These men are pretty good at exposing things. I guess we'll just have to see how your countrymen feel about it when this whole thing goes public." Jack turned away and then stopped and faced Salkukoff once more. "That is if your own sailors don't string you up first."

Salkukoff was about to say something when he noticed the men of his own nation's navy were staring at him. They had murderous eyes, and their intent was clear. Salkukoff decided to stay quiet. He was pulled into the hatchway by Jenks.

"You know, someday our luck is going to run for cover the way we push it," Ryan said as he joined Jack.

"Commander, I think our luck ran out when we lost so many during Overlord. I think we're due a break where luck is concerned."

"You have a point."

Farbeaux joined them, and Jack saw the pistol in Henri's right hand. He charged the weapon as he fixed Collins with that glare that was quickly becoming famous. He could see that the Frenchman was ready to fulfill the task he had been given by the American president and the head of MI6.

"I don't know if you gentlemen have noticed, but we seem to have developed a rather strange weather pattern in the last half hour."

Jack and Ryan looked around them and saw that vapor was rising from the sea and going straight up into the air. Before Jack could comment, he got a call on his radio. It was Captain Thorne. Collins lifted his radio and then turned and saw Thorne atop the *Houston*'s conning tower.

"Collins," he said.

"*Colonel, we are picking up a rise in ambient water temperature. Electrostatic discharge is increasing. From your brief, these look like the same readings we got the last time that shipwreck started to speak.*"

Jack looked into the sky and saw that the rate of darkness was increasing. "As of right now, we believe the phase shift engine is disabled. We should know more in the next few minutes. Captain, is *Houston* capable of diving?"

"*Negative. We shot our wad just getting up here.* Houston*'s diving days are done for now.*"

"Captain, we need to get *Houston* tied down to *Simbirsk*. When this thing pops, it could crush your boat with her expanding wave of electromagnetic discharge."

"*That doesn't sound fun. I agree. We can't take another shot like the first one. This time around she'll just buckle.*"

"How many survivors can you take on from *Peter the Great* and *Shiloh*?"

"*Hell, we can fit two hundred if we have to. We're not diving, and our fighting days are done. Too much damage to our systems. We can shove survivors into torpedo tubes if need be.*"

"Good. We'll start transferring men over in the next few minutes. We can't have everyone in one basket. No personnel above decks or near bulkheads when the phase shift happens."

"*Roger, we'll be here. Thorne out.*"

Jack lowered the radio and saw Captain Johnson approach. Everett was shaking his head as he brought up the rear.

"Why did I just have to order my crew off *Shiloh*?" Johnson asked. "We can still save her."

"Captain, I appreciate your position. I know your ship is just as important to you as was *Peter the Great* to Second Captain Dishlakov, but she would never be able to stand the pounding of the shift. You'll lose her. We already have a sub that can't dive that may be blown apart by the power of this engine."

"But—"

"Sorry, Captain, but this is my call. No more is to be risked."

"I have one request, Colonel Collins," Dishlakov said, breaking into the objections by Johnson. Jack waited. "My men and I will take full responsibility, but we cannot allow that man to return with us."

"By 'that man,' I suppose you mean Salkukoff?"

"Yes," came the blunt and angry answer.

"He's needed back home, Captain."

Dishlakov was angered, but his objection was interrupted by Charlie as he broke from the hatchway. He was gesturing wildly as he ran toward the officers.

"Get everyone below!"

"Doc, calm down," Carl said as he took hold of Ellenshaw.

"Europa was smashed during the battle, and she's not in control of the phase shift engine. The master chief says she's about to blow her top. She's getting ready to transition again."

"Damn it," Jack said as he raised the radio and handed it to Johnson. "Order *Shiloh* abandoned, now."

Johnson saw the fear in the colonel's eyes and accepted the radio and started giving orders. Then he handed the radio back, and he and Dishlakov ran to expedite the order themselves.

"Captain Thorne, this thing is about to blast off, and we are nowhere near ready. Do you have a working torpedo?"

"*One and one only. We lost the ability to get air pressure into the tubes on our latest ascent. But yes, we do.*"

"As soon as the all clear is given, put one into *Shiloh*."

The silence from Thorne was long. Jack knew the captain was having a hard time coming to grips with scuttling the proud missile cruiser.

"*I wish you had given me any order but that one.*" Again, silence for thirty seconds. "*Will do. Awaiting signal.*"

A streak of lightning illuminated the darkening skies. As they watched, the clouds began circling at a much faster rate.

"Jesus!" Ryan yelled as he quickly removed his hands from the steel railing. "Electricity is coursing through this ship."

"We don't have the time we need," Jack said as he faced Everett and Henri. "Get everyone belowdecks." He raised the radio. "Plans have changed, Captain. Get your crew belowdecks and into the most protected areas you can. Captain Thorne, abort the plan; *Shiloh* has to ride out the storm."

The wind picked up by forty miles per hour as the still-flaming *Shiloh* started sounding her emergency warning horns. Jack saw the crew of *Shiloh* start to abandon their fire hoses and start belowdecks. There were still over a hundred men aboard her.

"Jenks, where do we stand?" he asked into the radio.

"This thing is ramping up, and there is nothing I can do to stop it. It's like it has a mind of its own. I've pulled every coil I could, but that didn't buy us any time. She's powering up, and there's not a damn thing I can do to stop it short of sinking this relic."

Another deep rumble and the sky above them burst forth with the greatest electrical display anyone had ever seen. The seas became choppy, and the violet-colored water started coming over the side of *Simbirsk* in waves. The sky was swirling in that sickening pattern they had all seen before. It looked as if they could see the mist of ocean rising into the sky as if reinforcing the storm high above. Men above decks were getting shocked as they grasped railings and other steel parts of the exposed ship.

"Get below!" Everett screamed at the men who had assisted the last of *Peter the Great*'s crew aboard.

Henri was pushing and screaming in Russian for the men to protect themselves.

Jack figured they had two hundred survivors aboard *Simbirsk* and over three hundred on the heavily damaged *Shiloh*. Thorne had picked up another hundred and secured them below. They were flat out of time.

"We got to go, Jack!" Everett said as he held the hatchway open. Henri got the last of the Russian personnel below and then turned with Everett and waited for the colonel.

"That's it, Colonel," Ryan said. "We've done all we can!" he said, trying to raise his voice over the power of the rapidly developing storm.

Collins looked up as the heavy rain began, and it was déjà vu all over again. Water was rising into the sky, and electrical discharge raced through the black clouds that expanded into an even wider pattern. He could feel the *Simbirsk* pulsing under his feet. He looked toward *Houston* and saw that Thorne was still up top and was easing *Houston* closer to *Simbirsk*. He pushed Ryan toward the stern of the Russian ship.

"Come on—we have to tie off *Houston* to *Simbirsk*; otherwise, the phase shift forces will rip her apart."

Jack and Ryan fought with the heavy ropes as the deck crew of *Houston* tossed the ropes that would secure her to *Simbirsk*. They were soon joined by several marines and sailors as they disobeyed orders and the team braved the killing elements of the storm as they fought with the heavy lines. Everett was there with Henri, and they finally managed to secure *Houston* for their ride home—hopefully.

With a last look at *Shiloh* and Captain Johnson as he vanished into the bridge section of the still-flaming *Shiloh*, Jack realized that they were as ready as they would ever be. How many more men would they lose with the unstable phase shift? He couldn't calculate the odds that they would all make it back. He raised the radio once last time.

"*Houston*, check in."

"Houston *is ready*," Thorne said as he vanished below the conning tower and into the deepest sections of the submarine.

He looked toward the burning *Shiloh*. "Captain Johnson, are you secure?"

"*I'll never be secure again, but for now, we're as secure as we can get. I hope you don't mind if I place a complaint on your methods of transportation?*"

"You'll have to stand in line for that, Captain. Good luck. Jenks?"

"*Jenks here*," came the hurried reply.

"Abandon the engine spaces and get as far belowdecks as the rest."

"*What about this Ruskie?*"

Jack nodded at Henri. "I have someone coming down to take charge of that."

"*Roger, I am so outta here!*" Jenks said as the radio went dead. Jack shook it, but there was nothing. The electromagnetic pulse was flaring to life.

The skies overhead circled at a speed that was terrifying. Collins took Henri by the arm.

"If it looks like we might not make it, follow your orders. That bastard doesn't deserve the same fate as these men. Put a bullet where it belongs."

Henri only nodded as he, Everett, Ryan, and Jack turned and made for the open hatchway.

Simbirsk, *Shiloh*, and *Houston* started to move in a wide circle as the storm magnified the power of the phase shift.

For twenty miles around the tethered ships, the sea shot straight into the air and then settled once more as the buildup to the shift became unstoppable. The engine was so powerful that it changed the very fabric of the atmosphere.

Jack and the others, with the exception of Farbeaux, went to the battle bridge and made sure to stay away from the solid steel bulkheads. Henri went below with the intention of finishing what it was they were here for.

Once again all three vessels started getting pliable and warped beneath the onslaught of the shift.

The sky exploded overhead, and then the two elements met in an explosion of the magnitude of a detonating nuclear warhead.

Phase shift occurred less than four seconds after.

Jack saw the ship turn almost transparent. This time, his senses had not been caught off guard as they had been on the initial phase shift. He felt the deck beneath his feet grow soft and pliant, but he didn't fight the strange sensation and allowed his feet to remain planted. Everett made the mistake of touching the old helmsman's station, and his hand went completely through it. He lost his balance, but Ryan stopped his fall. Both men felt the nausea running through them. It hit Jack next. He felt his gorge rise, and his brain felt like it had exploded with a massive headache. All around him, the world spun.

Belowdecks, Jenks and Charlie were with the six orphaned children of Compton's Reef as they huddled with the rest of the Russian and British crew of *Simbirsk*. Just before the phase shift started, Jenks had herded everyone he could into the solid steel armory. It was a tight squeeze, but everyone had made it in. Even Second Captain Dishlakov, with pistol out, was standing over a sitting Salkukoff and his remaining three men. Two of the Russian marines from *Peter the Great* also had him covered. As far as Dishlakov was concerned, Salkukoff was going to pay one way or the other for his treachery.

Jenks was watching Henri Farbeaux just as the transition of the phase shift started. The master chief didn't really care for the look in the Frenchman's eyes. He stood, unlike the others, as if he were a burglar waiting for the lights to go out. With his suspicions on Henri's intent, he pulled the children closer to him. Charlie Ellenshaw had the inspiration to place a large rubber mat absconded from the mess facilities of the *Simbirsk* on the steel deck in the hopes it would provide the children with some comfort for the short but miserable ride back.

Then the effects hit with a shock to everyone's senses. The children froze as first the wave of nausea hit them and then the sick feeling of electricity coursed through their small bodies. Jenks was proud as the children hugged him and held on, not making a sound. Then the bulkheads seemed to vanish, and it was like they were sitting on the ocean's surface. It was still violet in color. The illusion was so real, it seemed Jenks could just reach out and place a hand on its cold surface.

"Oh, God," Charlie said as he felt his backside slowly sink into the steel hull.

It was Dishlakov who saved Charlie from becoming a permanent fixture of *Simbirsk*. He reached out, grabbing Charlie's hand and losing his Makarov pistol at the same time. He pulled for all he was worth and caught the professor just as the hull resolidified. Then the armory was filled with all the colors of the rainbow, and every man inside the battle cruiser felt the falling rain from the storm outside the confines of the phase shift. None of them knew it but would later guess that at that very moment they had begun to transition from one world to the next.

When the thunderous sound of static electricity filing the armory, Henri felt his vision go into a tunnel effect as he again lost his balance and fell forward. The pistol he had hidden behind his back flew from his hand as a fast-thinking Russian sailor reached for Farbeaux just after he came into contact with the deck. The young man pulled Henri in and held on for dear life and with a silent prayer to a God that might not even inhabit this bizarre world.

Dishlakov still had his back turned when Salkukoff saw Henri lose his weapon. Thinking quickly and with a murderer's eye for survival, he reached out and with a booted foot slid the pistol toward him. One of his last remaining men saw what he was attempting and assisted by kicking the nine millimeter behind Salkukoff far enough to where he could grasp it with his manacled hand. Before he could congratulate himself, a large hand circled around his wrist, and he felt the bone snap.

A large Russian sailor with a machinist rank embroidered on his sleeve stood above Salkukoff and shook his head as the smaller man held back his scream of anger and pain. Salkukoff looked away when he saw that his fellow countryman would have no qualms of crushing the life right out of him.

Before the large Russian could seat himself again, the world around them flared to white light, and then they and the battle cruiser *Simbirsk* disappeared.

In the battle bridge, Jack felt his legs grow weak as he tried to focus his attention on Ryan and Everett. The bridge suddenly flared to brilliant life and sound. Collins felt his ears pop several times in rapid succession. Multicolored bands of light filled the bridge like an expanding fan, and then the world just vanished.

OPERATION REFORGER IV
NORTH ATLANTIC

Will Mendenhall stood with Dutch Admiral Andersson and Captain McAvoy on the bridge wing of *Nimitz*. The search for the missing ships had found nothing. They discovered wreckage from the destroyer *De Zeven*, but thus far that had been it. F-18 Hornets crisscrossed the skies as the search continued.

Will felt his patience at the slow progress of the search growing thin. He had been aboard for only one full day and thus far had not one good thing to pass on to the Group about their chances of finding their missing ships and their friends. He wiped his face in frustration. His angered disposition was interrupted by a messenger who passed along a message flimsy to Admiral Andersson. He read it and then gave it over to Captain McAvoy.

"How far out are they?" McAvoy asked the messenger.

"Radar places them three hundred miles from our battle group. We also have the Russians asking permission to join the search."

Admiral Andersson turned his attention to the four Russian cruisers and the five helicopters that had joined them the previous day. Needless to say, feelings were running high and tensions even higher.

"Another group?" he asked.

"Yes, sir, this group consists of Russian high brass."

"That's all we need," Andersson said as he looked at Will Mendenhall. "You don't have anything to do with this first group, do you?"

"Look, Admiral, you got a copy of my orders. I'm here to observe, and that's all I know."

The admiral looked at the army officer with skepticism. "And this second group of Russians? Nothing there either?"

"No, sir, I have no idea."

Another runner popped his head into the bridge wing.

"Captain, CIC is reporting a rise in sea temperature, and winds are increasing. They recommend bringing in our CAP and search aircraft."

"Do so, will you, Captain? This is starting to have a familiar ring to it."

Will didn't know exactly what it was they were speaking of. Then lightning lit up the already bright afternoon sky. He ducked as the bolts hit in several locations simultaneously.

Suddenly, *Nimitz* rocked on her keel. Waves began to hit the large warship with punishing blows. Men hurried to secure exposed aircraft, as the weather had turned so suddenly that Andersson and McAvoy became aware that whatever was happening was a familiar scenario as when they had lost ships from both the Russian side and their own.

"Admiral, we have massive activity thirty miles to the north," the announcement came. The admiral looked through his field glasses and saw the large swell of sea and the circling clouds above it. Before he knew what to say or order, the world came crashing inward. The black clouds to the north burst down into the sea.

Will Mendenhall saw what was happening, and his tension ratcheted up with the other officers on board.

Then it happened. They saw the wall of water as it came in from the north. It swelled and then dropped. It rose and then fell. The actions made the *Nimitz* rise and fall with the seas. Mendenhall hung on for everything he was worth. Then the sound of ten thousand exploding bombs erupted around them. The sun was blotted out, and even the Russian ships that had joined them in their search one day ago had to turn their ships into the wind and swells. The sea once more settled, and just when they thought the event was over, the giant carrier rode high on a wave and then came crashing down with steel-wrenching power. Then all was silent.

Andersson was helped to his feet by Mendenhall, who was more confused by what just happened than anyone aboard.

"What in the hell just happened?" Will asked as McAvoy also rose back to his feet. He only shook his head.

"*Captain, CIC, we have three new contacts on radar, thirty-five miles out, bearing three-one-seven degrees.*"

McAvoy picked up the bridge phone. "Speed and course?"

"*Zero speed, zero course; they're just sitting there.*"

"How is my air cover?"

"*Shaken but still in the air.*"

"Get me some eyes on target."

"*Vectoring search aircraft now.*"

"Also order cruisers *Sheffield* and *Saratoga* forward toward the contact. Patch the CAP communications directly to us."

"*Aye, patching through communications.*"

As they waited, Will couldn't help but shake his head. Three contacts for six missing vessels was not a good sign. All he could do was pray for his missing friends. The wait was agonizing.

"*Rough Rider One, this is Ghost Lead, over.*"

"*Ghost Lead, this is Rough Rider, over.*"

The three officers waited as the radio played out their hopeful song.

"*Rough Rider, we have three ships in bad shape. One of them is the* Houston, *one is* Shiloh, *and the third is not identifiable.*"

McAvoy picked up the bridge phone once more. "All rescue elements head to target area, all ahead flank. Bring *Nimitz* into the wind. I want alert one fighters in the air in five. Rescue choppers launch immediately. All medical teams stand by for immediate transport. I want five damage control teams ready to board the damaged ships. All stations, general quarters. Communications, inform the Russian search elements of the situation, but warn them to stay clear, as we have air operations close aboard. Get off a secure communiqué to NATO command; inform them of the situation and ask for instructions in dealing with our Russian friends."

McAvoy relayed the request from Andersson.

"*Rough Rider, this is Ghost Lead, over.*"

"*Go, Ghost Lead, over,*" answered the CIC.

"*We see survivors taking to the open decks, over.*"

Will Mendenhall closed his eyes, hoping that Jack, Carl, Jenks, Charlie, and even Farbeaux were among those survivors.

"Go ahead, son, and grab some flight gear and catch one of the medical choppers. Army officers give me hay fever anyway."

Will smiled and then saluted the Dutch admiral and left the bridge just as the general quarters alarm started flaring to life.

The USS *Nimitz* turned into the wind, and F-18 fighters and Seahawk helicopters started lifting free of her expansive deck.

The search had suddenly turned into rescue operations, and every man aboard was grateful for that.

Over twenty miles away to the south, fifteen Russian warships turned toward the rescue site as well.

The real confrontation was about to start.

Mendenhall was amazed at the scene. Circling helicopters from *Nimitz* and the missile cruiser USS *Ticonderoga* were busy dropping men and firefighting equipment onto the decks of both *Houston* and *Shiloh*. Will saw that none of the assets were headed for the old Russian cruiser, which was currently listing at least ten degrees to her port side.

As the Seahawk circled, he examined the damage to *Shiloh* and figured that she would never face the open sea again. Her stern was completely gone up to the aft missile battery. She was aflame, and before a search for any survivors could begin, they had to take control of her fires.

Finally, they saw the first of *Shiloh*'s seamen emerge from belowdecks. Will stopped counting when he reached a hundred. He whistled and then heard the copilot exclaim that they had movement on *Houston*. Mendenhall saw who he assumed to be *Houston*'s Captain Thorne in the high conning tower gesturing that their damage control efforts should be concentrated on *Shiloh*'s condition.

Mendenhall spoke into the mic on his helmet. "No radio communication?"

The copilot turned in his seat and just shook his head.

"The *Simbirsk*, set me down there."

"No can do, sir—no place to land this thing. We would have to winch you down. Besides, we have orders to stay clear of the Russian vessel by NATO command."

"Damn it, I need to get down there!" Will said as he came close to losing his patience with cautionary orders from NATO brass. He knew if his friends survived, they would have been right in the thick of it. "Look, get me closer for a look-see."

Mendenhall couldn't believe what it was he was contemplating.

The Seahawk swung low over the water and approached *Simbirsk* from the stern. It hovered momentarily as the pilot examined the fantail for a safe landing zone for later. Will saw his opportunity. He unsnapped his harness, and then, tossing the helmet aside, he pushed his way past the naval crew chief.

"Captain, what in the hell are you—"

That was as far as the crew chief got as Will went through the open doorway and fell feetfirst into the choppy sea. With the weather clearing, he knew he stood at least a fifty-fifty chance of surviving.

"What in the hell?" the pilot said as he felt the sudden shift of weight to his bird.

"I can't believe it; that army captain just jumped overboard."

The pilot veered the Seahawk away from *Simbirsk* and rose back into the sky to see if they could get eyes on Mendenhall.

"Damn army's full of nuts these days!" the pilot growled.

Mendenhall found the gangway. It looked as if it had just been laid down for him. He slowly brought himself out of the water and climbed. Remembering the photo from the *Eldridge* file, he removed his nine millimeter from his shoulder holster as he took the steps two at a time.

Will had just made it to the main deck when he saw the blood. It looked as if a major action had taken place not long before, and as he realized this, his heart began to sink. The sun broke free of the cloud cover as the skies rapidly cleared of rain and wind.

Mendenhall almost screamed when a bullhorn sounded from somewhere up above him.

"Who gave you permission to board this ship, mister?"

"Ah!" he said as his eyes went high.

Everett smiled from on high as he was joined by the colonel and Ryan.

"A little late for the prom, aren't you?" Ryan yelled down.

Mendenhall was very tempted to raise the nine millimeter and point it at Jason, but he smiled instead and then holstered his weapon. He closed his eyes in silent thanks for getting his friends back home again.

"If you guys are done yachting, can we go home now?"

Four hours later, the rescue was complete. Admiral Andersson had ordered Shiloh to be taken in tow, and she was mated with her sister Aegis missile cruiser, *Ticonderoga*, and was already sliding lazily through the sea alongside *Nimitz*.

With the assistance of the engineering departments of both *Ticonderoga* and *Nimitz*, *Houston* was able to restore power to her planes and her defensive systems. She couldn't dive, but that didn't faze the crew one bit; they were ready to head for Norfolk and home. She was pacing the battle group as they turned south with the *Simbirsk* in tow by the naval support ship, USS *Hannaford*. The submarine was under guard with the German destroyer *Lutjens* and the Dutch frigate *Vulcan* riding shotgun until she could see her home port once more.

The officers of all combat vessels involved in the incident were safely transported to *Nimitz*. Jack, Carl, Jason, a bruised Henri Farbeaux, and Charlie Ellenshaw joined by Captain Johnson, Second Captain Dishlakov, and Captain Thorne sat tiredly inside a closed-off section of the hangar deck. A manacled Salkukoff sat in a chair in a far corner, having his broken wrist looked after by a navy corpsman. His remaining men were ensconced in *Nimitz*'s rather barren brig, guarded by angry marines.

Coffee and sandwiches were passed around much to the relief of the extremely hungry men.

"Where is Jenks?" Jack asked as he took a heavenly bite of a chicken sandwich.

Charlie, looking haggard and less enthusiastic about joining field teams ever again, sipped coffee and looked at Jack.

"The children wouldn't let him go. He is with them right now in sick bay. He said he would join us as soon as he can." Charlie again took a sip of coffee and then looked back at the colonel. "You know, if I didn't know better, I would think that the master chief actually found something he doesn't despise outside of Virginia." He smiled. "It's kind of creepy seeing him with those kids—it's like he respects them or something."

Collins smiled and patted Ellenshaw on the back.

"Don't worry, Doc. I'm sure he'll be back to his old self once we get home, all miserable and grumpy again."

"Yeah," Charlie said, perking up at the prospect of Jenks becoming nonhuman once again.

"Attention!" one of the marine guards called out.

All but Charlie stood as Admiral Andersson and Captain McAvoy entered the sealed hangar deck.

"At ease, gentlemen, at ease," Andersson said as he went from man to man with the captain of *Nimitz* and shook each man's hand.

"I can't imagine what you have been through. You're back in safe hands now." Andersson nodded at the marine guard, and the two left the hangar deck and sealed it once more. "Gentlemen, please, take a seat." The admiral took an offered chair from McAvoy, and both men sat and faced those who had come back from the grave. "First off, this is not a debrief. That will be conducted at Norfolk. We are here for another reason. We are about to be joined by my counterpart in the Red Banner Northern Fleet and other representatives of the Russian government. We also have NATO representatives arriving in minutes. I just wanted to warn you that the proceedings could get"—he leaned over and whispered into the ear of McAvoy—"as you Americans say, nasty. At the moment, we have three Kirov-class missile cruisers and five destroyers heading our way. They asked permission to board, and on orders from the president of the United States, I have given my permission."

Jack looked over at Salkukoff and saw he was paying attention, and he didn't like the look of relief he saw there. He looked at Henri, who had also noticed the look of satisfaction. He had explained to Jack that Salkukoff was nearing his end when the phase shift hit and he had lost his opportunity.

"*Stand by to recover rotary aircraft*," came the loud announcement from above them.

"I expect that is our guests arriving," Andersson said.

"Admiral, may I ask the condition and disposition of my remaining crew?" Dishlakov asked.

"Second Captain, I assure you they are being well treated and fed."

"Inside your brig, perhaps?" Dishlakov asked with doubt framing the question.

"Your crew is with the remaining marines and sailors of *Shiloh*. As I said, your brave crew is being well treated. I don't think we could separate the crews even if we wanted to."

Dishlakov nodded.

The large panel door opened, and a US Marine stepped inside and allowed four men to enter. Then the large marine approached Admiral Andersson.

"Admiral, your guests have arrived."

Anderson and McAvoy both rose and stood erect as they faced the four civilian-dressed Russians.

"I am Admiral Andersson—"

"Yes, Admiral, we are well aware of who you are, sir. Your commission in the Dutch navy has not gone unnoticed, especially being named to this farce called Operation Reforger IV. It would seem that when it comes to legalities, the Americans would prefer an officer from another country to take the fall; thus, they named you as overall commander. A convenient scapegoat."

Andersson sat instead of remaining standing. He was told to expect that the Russians would be in a position of accusation.

"I am Dr. Leoniv Vassick. My colleagues are General Komsky, General Petrovsky, and Dr. Anton Garlitz." The three other men didn't have the courtesy to nod. They just stood behind the speaker, Vassick.

"I am told you are here to explain why it is you fired on our naval assets three days ago?" Andersson said with a neutral face.

The middle-aged man with silvering hair and the impressive man in the black suit smiled and then took a seat, and the other two Russians quickly followed suit.

"Let us not play games here, Admiral. You know we are here to take back Russian state property. We will not leave this area without the *Simbirsk* in tow. If you refuse our request, we have the naval firepower to assist us in this endeavor." The man looked purposefully over at the line of chairs and then at Jack in particular. His eyes lingered a moment longer than necessary before moving away. "But let us not be militaristic here, Admiral. We need not resort to such horrid conclusions as open warfare. Just surrender our property, and we shall return to our shores, and our friendship will still be intact."

"And what of your man over there who caused the death of over three hundred of my crew aboard *Peter the Great*? He also has to answer for the cold-blooded murder of fellow Russian scientist Gervais and Captain Kreshenko, who this man murdered in his sleep."

All eyes went to Second Captain Dishlakov as he suddenly stood and pointed toward the seated and handcuffed Salkukoff.

"This matter will be taken up upon our return home. Colonel Salkukoff will answer to us and us alone." The words from Leonid Vassick were uttered in a cold and calculated voice, but Jack could see that the coldness was not directed at Salkukoff but was pointedly aimed at Second Captain Dishlakov. Jack figured this whole disaster would be placed squarely on the shoulders of the expendable second captain.

"They're going to hang everything on Dishlakov, Jack," Carl whispered beside him.

Collins merely nodded, as he had become used to he and Everett coming to the same conclusions in roughly the same time frame. In other words, they were both becoming experts at smelling out a rat.

"Now, Admiral, the business at hand is our state property and your willingness to acquiesce to our demand."

To his credit, Admiral Andersson, an old salt at seeing the truth of Russian threats and statements, remained silent and noncommittal. Instead of answering, he nodded toward Second Captain Dishlakov.

"We have the testimony of not only the second captain here but the testimony of your deceased Captain Kreshenko." For emphasis, Admiral Andersson gestured to Captain McAvoy, who held up the logbook of *Peter the Great*. "In these pages, you will find the true culprit of this sordid tale. One of murder and international interference from an unknown entity inside your government. It seems even Captain Kreshenko had his doubts about your Colonel Salkukoff's motives and his disposition to the well-being and safety of his own citizens."

"That logbook is also Russian state property. Second Captain Dishlakov has once again proven his disloyalty. It is a crime to turn this or any Russian naval logbook over to any Western power."

"I gave the logbook to the admiral."

All eyes went to Henri Farbeaux, who stood from his chair. Jack and Everett were caught off guard. Ryan silently whistled under his breath.

"I removed it from the captain's quarters the night he was murdered by this man."

"Once a thief, always a thief. Isn't that right, Colonel Farbeaux? Believe me, your actions in this matter have been discussed at the highest levels of our government," Vassick said as he brushed at nonexistent lint on his pant leg. The other Russians remained silent.

Henri, instead of answering to his charge, merely smiled and half bowed to his Russian accuser.

"Regardless, as the corresponding international agreements on salvage, this logbook is now the property of The Hague, where it will be entered into evidence for our forthcoming fight over the rights of the sea and salvage."

Vassick huffed and smiled. "I gather you have not received information from your outer naval pickets of our intent to regain that which is ours. One of the more powerful Russian fleets in years is sitting on your doorstep with the intention of either escorting *Simbirsk* back home, or, in the failure of that, sinking her and any other vessel that is making the attempt to steal her."

"Threats at this late date, Doctor? Do you think NATO will allow that fleet to get anywhere near this group?"

Jack didn't care for the way this confrontation was heading. The threats of war erupting over this ancient experiment were getting out of hand. He felt powerless to stop it.

"We will retake our property, Admiral," Vassick repeated, reinforcing the standoff.

Again, a US Marine entered the hangar deck and made his way to Captain McAvoy and handed him a message flimsy. The captain read it once and then twice. His brows rose, and then he handed the flimsy to the admiral, who also took his time reading it. He folded the message and then nodded at the marine, who left abruptly. Almost simultaneously, two marines brought in two more folding chairs and placed them directly in front of the Russian contingent.

"Gentlemen, with the exception of Colonel Collins, Captain Everett, Colonel Farbeaux, and Second Captain Dishlakov, would you please excuse us?" The admiral looked taken back for some reason. Jack and Carl exchanged looks that said they were just as confused as Admiral Andersson, who rose with the others and followed Captain McAvoy from the closed-off section of the hangar deck. Overhead, the ominous sound of F-18 Hornets and F-35 fighters being launched into the sky rumbled in the cavernous hangar. Suddenly, it was Jack, Carl, Henri, and Dishlakov sitting alone with the Russians. The room was silent except for what sounded like increased activity on the flight deck high above them.

The hatchway opened once more, and then two marines appeared and, with little effort involved, assisted a wheelchair-bound man over the hatch coming. The small, dark-haired man nodded his thanks and then rolled into the room.

Again, Jack and Carl exchanged looks of confusion as Dr. Xavier Morales rolled to a stop in front of the Russian contingent.

The room was silent as the next two people entered. Jack felt his jaw muscles seize up as he saw his own director, Niles Compton, with cane in hand as he stepped into the hangar. Then he was followed by none other than Virginia Pollock. Both went to the chairs that had been placed for them. All three faced the Russian contingent. The director was dressed in a plain blue suit and Virginia in a pantsuit that held for the viewer nothing but a business impression. Xavier was dressed in simple slacks and even had a tie on. Crooked, Jack saw, but a tie nonetheless.

Vassick smiled and then turned to his companions and said something in Russian. The others nodded. The first marine to have entered returned with a large-screen monitor absconded from the admiral's quarters. He placed it on a steel rolling table and then left the hangar. The room became deathly silent as everyone, including Jack, Carl, Henri, and even the Russians, was confused at this sudden change of personnel onto this politically charged stage. Jack didn't know it, but the three people had flown supersonic over the continental United States and then transferred to four of the navy's newest jump jets, the F-35, and again flew supersonic to get out here to the North Atlantic.

Virginia stunned and silenced the Russians by saying something in their native tongue to their guests. They saw Vassick raise a brow and then nod his head in agreement to something she said. Niles remained silent as he studied his counterpart across from him.

"Yes, Doctor, we can speak English, if that is what you prefer. We know your Drs. Compton and Morales do not speak our language, and we do so need their input in the upcoming matters."

Virginia nodded and then went silent as both groups observed the other. It was Niles who cleared his throat and then placed his small case on the steel deck.

"You seem to know all about us, Dr. Vassick."

"For years, Dr. Compton, it has been my duty to learn such things. Perhaps you have a particular understanding of that?"

Compton said nothing. Instead he looked with his one good eye at the men before him.

"I am here at the authorization of the president of the United States, who has tasked me with the duties we will describe here in a few minutes. May I ask, sir, who you represent?"

Vassick smiled as the game began. "Of course. I am here representing the rights of the Russian people and that of our shared heritage. Thus, we want our property back."

Niles exchanged looks with Xavier, who rolled a few feet closer to the Russian contingent.

"You do, as my director says, know an awful lot about us. But we also have learned quite a lot about you, sir. For instance, we have discovered that you are operating without the knowledge of your highest levels of government. We know that you have been doing so since the fall of 1941. We also know that you and a select group of individuals have committed high treason right under the noses of the Soviet and Russian governments."

"And of course, Dr. Morales, you have indisputable proof of this?"

"Not at all. It is mere conjecture and circumstantial."

"I suspect this comes from that magnificent computing system your group employs. Bravo on your guesswork. This system"—he stopped and leaned over as one of his aids spoke to him in Russian—"ah, yes, Europa. As I was saying, without evidence and actual proof of anything, you cannot harm us. As we"—again the irritating smile—"cannot prove beyond a doubt that your group exists. So here we are, Doctor, both entities standing and shouting to the winds."

Morales smiled in return. "What is your goal?"

"Why, to protect our citizens and our heritage. Just as your group proclaims in its charter."

Niles cleared his throat and then faced down Vassick. Jack leaned forward in his chair. He knew Dr. Compton took the secrecy of the Group very seriously and the knowledge that their secret was now out in the open, at least to these people, and now he was playing a hidden card that Jack himself could not figure out.

"We can sit here and rattle sabers all day long, but that will get us into nothing but open warfare. And that, sir, is one battle you cannot allow to happen. That would take too much explaining to your real government, not this hidden society you claim is running things. As Dr. Morales said a moment ago, sir, we also know quite a bit about you."

"Please continue, Dr. Compton."

"As it stands, your influence with the Russian military is expansive and supported from within your tight circle of confidants. But you still work with a hidden agenda, whereas we do not. We work under the auspices of the United States government, as I'm sure you know."

Jack watched as Xavier wheeled over to the monitor and turned it on. He used a small laptop that looked strangely like the small Europa link lost by them. He hit a few buttons, and the face of an aged man came into focus. Morales nodded at Niles.

"Sir, we now have a guess as to who it is you answer for. This group is called the Northstar Committee."

"A group I am not familiar with," Vassick said as his face remained neutral.

"Well, as I said, everything we have is circumstantial. I'm sure that this fact will be a big relief to the rest of your associates. But we did get evidence that the methods used in your efforts to steal the phase shift information were flawed. You left fingerprints at the scene. The radioactive material from the breeder reactor, as you know, is identifiable and was indeed stolen from the Hanford research facility in 1943."

"Your point in this matter is?"

"That the phase shift engine is the sole property of the United States government, and we wish it returned. It makes no matter that the system is installed inside Russian state property or not. Our science along with your own can find the nuclear fingerprint inside the phase shift engine on board *Simbirsk*. Now, we can make this an issue in the world court, or you can admit to your theft right here and now."

Jack smelled that old familiar odor of rat once more. He didn't know what it was Niles was playing at, but he did suspect that Compton was running one of the biggest bluffs of his life.

"Admit? I am not in one of your courts of law, Doctor. I do say this and always have. Your department is very resourceful at recovery—items of history and items of information. But as I said, this is all hearsay and speculation. The Northstar Committee has always been a rumor, one that has been shot down by most conspiracy theorists within our borders. I will say this: every premier, every president since the days of the old Soviet Union, has investigated these claims, and they have always fallen far short of that rumor. Oh, even now they still suspect, but even if proven, there is nothing that can be done about it. We control the Russian military, and the funny thing is, Doctor, they have no idea."

Niles turned away from the Russian and looked directly at Second Captain Dishlakov. "Sir, on behalf of the president of the United States, we offer you asylum in our country."

Dishlakov stood and nodded. He looked from Compton to Jack and then to Vassick.

"I thank you for the offer," he said in Russian, which was translated by

Virginia to Niles and the others. "But I am not a coward. My people must learn the truth about these arrogant and dangerous men. I cannot accept your gracious offer." He sat back down, and he again looked Jack's way, and he could only nod in understanding. He would do the same thing if it were him.

"Again, you are wasting your time. You will not win this battle. You have"—Vassick looked at his gold wristwatch—"exactly thirty minutes to comply with our request, or we can settle things militarily. This point is up to you."

"As you said, your power is derived from secrecy of your hidden group. That you would control all aspects of your government through your committee members. Well, it may not be that secret any longer. Your little speech has been viewed by a colleague of yours who is now an interested party to your committee's deceit since 1941."

At this point, Xavier Morales rolled his old-fashioned wheelchair over to the monitor and then flipped a switch, and a blank screen came up. Then Xavier typed information into the laptop he had installed on the arm of his chair. He turned in his wheelchair and nodded at Niles.

"Second Captain Dishlakov, your refusal to assist these men and your refusal to seek asylum will not go unnoticed. I assume you will still be alive in the coming months and years as your government figures out what it is they have to do about this rogue element within the sanctity of your national borders. The US government is bowing out of this situation by order of our president."

"That is most wise," Vassick said as his intense gaze fell on the Russian captain.

Jack and the others saw the faintest hint of a smile curl at the director's mouth.

"Mr. President, are you there?" Niles said as he turned to the monitor.

"So, now you think we will bow to your president, Doctor? What makes you think this?" Vassick said with the smile still on his face. "We know that he is powerless to pursue any remedy for my group of patriots."

"Who said anything about *our* president?"

"Uh-oh," Carl said loud enough to be heard. Jack only smiled as the bluff came full circle in a confused mess that Compton would have to explain to simple soldiers like he and Carl.

The color drained from the face of Dr. Vassick as the screen came to full-color life.

The face of Russian president Vladimir Putin was there live for all to see. He was sitting next to a man they all assumed was an English-speaking interpreter. But Jack figured rightly that he hadn't needed one for what it was he had just heard confessed to. The Russian ruler said something in a calm voice, and then the man sitting next to him spoke.

"I am indeed here, Doctor. Your president was very forthright in insisting I join this meeting."

"Did you understand all that was discussed here, sir?" Compton continued, with his one good eye never leaving his counterpart.

Vassick lost that arrogant smile of his as he realized for the first time in his committee's history they had admitted to their treason in full view of Russian authority.

"Yes, I believe we have serious internal discussions we will have to have on state security matters. I have made the appropriate arrangements with your navy, and our response, I understand, has arrived aboard your carrier." The interpreter became silent as Putin, a man despised in the Western circles of government, stared into the screen.

Jack realized that a plan had been formulated between himself and Lord James Durnsford, the bow-tied little Brit who knew more than anyone in the world as far as secret government agencies went. Collins smiled and shook his head as he reminded himself never to allow the best bluffer in the world in the stubby form of one Niles Compton into their weekly poker game. He looked at the seated Russian agent Salkukoff and winked at him. The man turned away angrily, as his plans had been illuminated by the most powerful spotlight in the world.

There was the sound of the hatchway being opened, and the same marine stepped aside to allow men in blue battle camouflage to enter. Jack and Carl knew them to be Russian marines. What was amazing was the fact that the US Marine security detail allowed them to keep their sidearms aboard one of the most protected ships in the entire world—*Nimitz*.

The ten very large Russian naval marines marched straight to the seated Russians. With Vladimir Putin still watching with an intense gaze, the marines took them into custody.

Vassick smiled as he was stood up and handcuffed. He remained silent as he was escorted out.

They saw Salkukoff stand up as if he were the next to be taken, but the marines merely walked past him and out of the hangar deck. It was Second Captain Dishlakov who stopped in front of Salkukoff, and then it was his turn to smile as he simply walked out.

All eyes went to the large screen of the monitor as the interpreter spoke. "My president wishes to express his gratitude for your assistance in this matter and wishes you to pass the same along to your president. This issue will be taken up with trusted members of our politburo, and appropriate measures will be taken. As for the apparatus in your possession, according to official Soviet records, the *Simbirsk* was lost with all hands in the summer of 1945. So, it is our opinion that this ship is not Russian state property, and our government has authorized its destruction if that is the will of your salvage team. We expect a proper outcome to this matter and thus will discuss it no further as long as the appropriate measures are taken immediately. Good day, gentlemen."

The monitor again went blank as the stoic face of the Russian president vanished.

Jack and the others stood and shook hands with Niles, Xavier, and Virginia.

"You are going to have to explain all of this when we get home," Jack said as he smiled and faced the Group.

Niles smiled and looked deeply into Jack's eyes. "That's need to know, Colonel, need to know."

The Russian-made helicopter left the flight deck of the *Nimitz* and sped toward the waiting Russian battle fleet miles away. Vassick was angry as he sat with his fellows and then gestured angrily toward the marines watching them. Second Captain Dishlakov's eyes widened when Vassick held out his cuffed hands and the marine removed not only his but the also the restraints of the other members of his group. Vassick angrily gestured toward a man in civilian dress who had not been aboard the carrier. The black-suited man handed over a laptop.

"Second Captain Dishlakov, you may want to witness this."

Two Russian marines harshly stood the Russian officer and pushed him to the opposite side of the helicopter. Dishlakov watched as a connection was made. The face of Vladimir Putin was there and smiling.

"Are you hearing me, Gregor?" Vassick said into the microphone on the laptop.

"Yes, and I guess you're lucky we were, my old friend. They had me in a television interview for three hours with a silly woman reporter from Germany. I almost didn't make it in time."

"Well, you did good, old friend. You go and finish your interview now."

"Okay, you old Bolshevik, see you when you get home to Siberia."

The laptop went blank.

Vassick smiled at Second Captain Dishlakov as he handed the laptop back to his man.

"Yes, the dawning of knowledge is sometimes rather startling, is it not?"

"I don't understand."

"You and many billions of others around the globe, Second Captain. Let's just say that most people do not know that our great President Putin ever had a brother, much less a twin brother. A twin that our illustrious former KGB operative tried to hide from the rest of the world for over forty-eight years. I would say that he came in handy after we discovered the hiding place our president had buried him under."

"What of the real president?" Dishlakov asked, not believing what it was he was hearing.

"Oh, Vladimir had a chemically induced heart attack seven years ago. Very sad. But he was a stupid man who thought he had the brainpower to take on those far more intelligent than himself. People you may have even met on your little adventure. This is the reason why our old Russian history of acting first without thinking has come to an end."

Two men, also dressed in black suits, sat beside Dishlakov, one on each side.

"I am to be murdered now?" he asked bravely.

"Murdered?" Vassick chuckled. "My friend, you will become one of the true messengers of our new system of government. Very valuable indeed. No, you will make it home alive."

"No matter what you do to me, my crew performed bravely, and they do not deserve to die."

"My dear man, do you think us entirely without empathy or pride in what your crew and the brave Captain Kreshenko executed in the most hostile of worlds? No, your crew will go down in Russian history as the very men who began our new revolution."

"And Captain Kreshenko's legacy is what?"

"The same, my boy. He will be remembered with honor, as you all will. Yes, we have our disagreements with certain military leaders—Kreshenko was one of them." Vassick took a deep breath. "You see, young man, there will be certain . . . citizens and professional military associates who cannot accompany the new Russia to where it is we are going."

Before Second Captain Dishlakov knew what was happening, the man to his right plunged the syringe into the thigh of Dishlakov. As his eyes fluttered shut, his last vision was of the portly man smiling at him.

Vassick took a deep breath and then leaned back against the aluminum body of the helicopter.

"It's a shame we had to lose Salkukoff; he was a very respected member of our society. He will be missed." He again sighed. "But then we all have to make sacrifices for what is to come. Let us go home; we have many things to discuss and plan."

An hour later, the *Simbirsk* was cast free of her towline from *Ticonderoga*, and the USS *Houston* moved away from the *Nimitz* battle group to a safe distance.

Jack, Carl, Charlie Ellenshaw, Jason Ryan, and Will Mendenhall, along with Niles Compton, Virginia Pollock, and Xavier Morales, who was looking around the massive carrier with a child's wonderment, gathered at the fantail of *Nimitz* watching the seas to the north. They were soon joined by Henri Farbeaux, who stood next to them.

"Get it done?" Jack asked.

Henri looked at his wristwatch and nodded. "In exactly one minute, my obligation to you and your president will be fulfilled, Colonel." He looked at Niles, and the director nodded in agreement.

Their attention was drawn to the distant conning tower of the *Houston* as she paced the battle group three miles away. Unable to submerge with the damage she had sustained, she was still able to fulfill this one last task.

Henri tapped his watch as he looked up. "It's time."

In the distance, they saw *Simbirsk* as she bobbed in the calm seas. The Russian relic sat upon the sea proudly as she awaited her fate.

LOS ANGELES—CLASS ATTACK SUBMARINE USS *HOUSTON*

On the conning tower of the *Houston*, Captain Thorne looked through his binoculars and then leaned over and spoke into the intercom.

"Weapons, are you ready?"

"*Aye, Skipper*," came the reply.

"Fire one!"

"*Tube one, weapons release.*"

"Fire two!"

"*Tube two fired electrically. All weaps running hot, straight, and normal.*"

"Conn, run the live feed to all compartments. This is for *Shiloh* and *Peter the Great*. We all deserve this."

"*Aye.*"

Captain Thorne resumed his watch as his torpedoes sped to their intended target.

Three miles away on the battle bridge of the Russian battle cruiser once thought lost to the world, Colonel Salkukoff waited. His handcuffed hands were secured to the wheel of the navigation station, so he had a good view of his fate as the American Mark 48 torpedoes reached the hull. He cursed Henri Farbeaux for his last words to him.

"Remember the Ukraine, for this is the reason why I am sending you straight to hell."

The members of the Event Group watched as the Mark 48s had done what the phase shift and Nazi submarines could not do. The explosions occurred separately. One weapon detonated below her keel and the other directly into the hull below the engine spaces. The resulting fireball could be seen by every ship in the battle group. They watched until the battle cruiser sank in two sections for the three-mile fall to her final resting place.

Jack slapped Henri Farbeaux on the back, as his orders had indeed been fulfilled. It was Virginia of all people who spoke up.

"Now, can I ask where that gruff bastard of mine is?"

"Right behind you," Carl said with the largest smile Virginia or the others had ever seen the captain have.

Stepping onto the covered fantail came Charlie Ellenshaw and Jenks. The master chief was holding two small girls, and the others clung to his pant leg as if it were a maypole.

Virginia lost her own smile very fast.

CHANGING OF THE GUARD

The gathering of the departmental heads and other members of the Event Group, who had never been in one place off complex before, was something that Niles Compton had wanted to do ever since the conclusion of the Overlord operation. The Group needed to be reset, and this was the best way to accomplish that.

The expansive ranch, owned by Compton, was a property that had belonged to his family for generations and placed on display the beauty of Montana. The activity outside the large ranch house was festive as men and women doted over the guests of honor—the six children rescued from Compton's Reef.

The gathering was far more than just a send-off of the children to one of the most expensive private schools in the country, where they would be assimilated into modern society; it was a get-together to celebrate each other and the recent achievements of the Group. To not take for granted the friendships they had developed and to take time to remember those no longer with them but who would forever be on the active rolls of Department 5656.

The large white tent housed the food and drink, and the orphaned children were wide-eyed at the activity. It had been Master Chief Jenks, the brutish bully of a man, who had fallen hard for the children. He was sad to be seeing them leave to start their new lives under the protection of the Group, but it was a necessary one, as explained to him by an eye-rolling Virginia Pollock. He and Virginia were spending the last few hours they had with the kids and looked to be having the time of their lives. The master chief had been transformed by his new charges and would be forever following their progress while they were away.

"Who would have thought, huh?"

Niles Compton turned and saw Alice Hamilton as she strolled up to the small hill that overlooked the expansive backyard of the ranch.

"Thought?" he asked as he sipped his drink.

"That something as small and breakable as children could melt that old, mean bastard's heart."

"The master chief, yes, it is an amazing transformation." Niles took a deep breath and then watched the activity below him. "But you do learn as you get older that the small things are what change you."

She saw the sad look come into Niles's countenance.

"Okay, what's wrong?" Alice said as she stepped closer to the director.

"It's been five days since we returned from the North Atlantic, and there hasn't been one iota of information coming out of Russia. Nothing."

"What does the president say?"

"That's what is so frustrating. The Russians are acting as if the *Simbirsk* incident never happened. No word from Putin on the disposition of his missing crews of three ships." He turned and faced Alice. "The president says it's nothing out of the ordinary when it comes to getting information out of that particular government, but I'm not convinced it's business as usual with our former communist friends."

Alice patted him on the arm. "Go with your instincts. If you think it's not kosher, prove it. You're good at that."

Niles smiled and then faced the party, and the Group down below once more. "I think I'll let it lie for now. The Group needs time to get their heads on straight again. We have to rebuild what it was that was taken from us. I think I'll let the president and the politicians wrestle with this one."

"Well, then, that means you have the time to buy an old woman a drink."

Niles held his arm out, and Alice took it. She smiled, and they both rejoined the party.

Jack, Carl, Charlie, Jason, and Will stood and talked. Jack had never once believed he could become so close to those he served with. After so many years of wars fought and lives lost, he thought he had forced himself to stop caring so much. In the end, he learned that to be a good soldier means to never stop caring. After Operation Overlord had taken so many friends, he found out that these brilliant people needed him; they needed Carl and Will and Jason. These men and women were the best of them, and with Niles leading the Group, he knew that the department, as well as the country, was in the hands of men and women who had one goal—to be the best human beings possible. It was that simple.

Xavier Morales rolled over with a tray of drinks placed in his lap. Jack saw him weaving in and around people, and then he smiled as he ran over Master Jenks's foot with one of his wheels. Xavier sped away before Jenks could yell and blubber. The children around him laughed and thought it was the funniest thing they had ever seen in their young lives as Jenks hopped around on one foot, cursing.

Xavier was relieved of the tray of drinks by Charlie Ellenshaw. Charlie passed out the drinks and then smiled at Collins.

"With your permission, Colonel?" he said to Jack, who accepted his drink, as did the others.

The others went silent as Ellenshaw raised his glass. "For those we left in paradise, Russian, British, and American."

They all nodded as they raised their glasses and drank the toast.

"Good job, Charlie," Jack said as he lowered his glass. "Oh, shit," he said, and the others turned to see what had caught his attention.

Sarah and Anya were heading straight at the group of men, and all wanted to turn and flee.

"I've been expecting this."

"What?" Xavier asked, confused as the women streaked toward them.

"We have both gotten the silent treatment since we came home. I think that grace period is over. They think we go out of our way to get into trouble," Carl said as he set his empty glass down and turned to face the wrath of the former Mossad agent.

Jack's jaw dropped when Will, Jason, Charlie, and even Xavier turned and wandered away.

"Thanks for the backup!" Collins said to their retreating forms.

"We didn't sign on for that kind of danger, Colonel."

Jack and Carl sneered at the four men as they left them high and dry.

"We need to talk," Sarah said as the two women cut off their own retreat.

Most of the Group had left for hotels in town, and the ones remaining said good-bye to the children as the private foundation financed by Niles Compton took the children to their new home in Billings, where they would receive the education and guidance in living in a far more complicated world than the one they had left.

The remaining members stood around the front yard just talking and getting to know each other once more. Sarah, Jack, Carl, and Anya stood by each other with the women laughing and the men staring off into nothingness as Will and Jason watched on laughing at the two cowed men.

"What is this?" Alice asked Niles as she watched the UPS truck enter through the gate.

"I don't know."

Jack walked over with Carl, and they too watched the delivery truck come up the long drive.

"You expecting a package?" Jack asked.

"No," Niles said as the brown truck pulled up and stopped in front of the group of men and women.

The driver popped out of the sliding door with his electronic tracker in his hand.

"Dr. Niles Compton?"

"Yes?" he said as he stepped forward.

"Sign here, please."

Niles took the plastic pen and then signed.

The man smiled and turned to his truck and slid open the back door, and he and his assistant pulled a rather large and heavy box from the back. They struggled with it but managed to get it over to Niles. The director looked at the keypad he had just signed his name to and frowned.

"It doesn't say who it's from."

Jack's hackles rose, as did Carl's. Even the others became curious and turned to see what was being delivered in the large cardboard box. Collins took the keypad and then walked up to the driver and his assistant.

"When did you receive this?"

"It was in the warehouse when we arrived this afternoon. It's the only delivery out this way today, so we made it our last."

"Okay, thank you," Jack said, and he handed the keypad back.

As the driver left, Carl gestured for everyone to step back as Jack and himself approached the large box. Stamped in red on the side was the bold lettering that warned them that the container contained dry ice.

Not only were Jack and Carl worried, Jason and Will also moved everyone away from the box. Xavier and Charlie stayed with Ryan and Mendenhall as Jack cut the straps and then sliced open the front.

"Probably just a gift for the children," Alice said, not really believing her own words.

"Colonel?" Xavier said before Jack could open the box. He rolled over, and

Carl stopped him from getting closer. "This is all I have on me," Morales said as he produced a small sensor that resembled a cell phone. He rolled closer to the box and held out the device. It flashed green, and then he faced the colonel.

"It's not a bomb. At least there are no nitrates of any kind."

"That doesn't mean there is no chemical explosive inside!" Jason called out.

"Why is everyone so suspicious?" Charlie asked in a hushed tone.

"Doc," Will said as he watched on, "who in the hell would know where the director's private compound is? Hell, we didn't even know about this place."

"Oh."

Jack looked at Carl, and then he pulled open the front of the box and then reached in and separated the thick plastic with his bare hands. Fifteen pounds of dry ice spilled out onto the drive, and Collins stepped back.

"Oh, my God," Alice said as she took Niles by the arm.

"Damn them," Jack said as the others drew around him and the gift that had been specially delivered.

All were stunned at the sight before them.

In the box, curled up in a sitting position and in full dress uniform, was Second Captain Dishlakov. The skin was gray in color, and they could see he had been dead for some time. In his arms was a folded newspaper, and Carl reached in and took it. He unfolded it and then stared at the headline. It was in Russian, so he handed the paper over to Alice, who was fluent in the language. She swallowed and looked it over. She lowered the paper and looked at the others.

"It's dated three days ago from the Moscow rag they call a newspaper."

They looked at the paper as Alice passed it around. The one photo on the front page was a black-and-white picture of the missile cruiser *Peter the Great*, seen at her launching three years before.

"It says that the *Peter the Great* was lost with all hands in the North Atlantic due to the effects of Hurricane Tildy. It is sadly reported that two other vessels were lost at the same time."

"How many men on board?" Mendenhall asked.

"We brought home four hundred and twelve survivors," Jason said as his anger at what was just dawning in his mind started to overwhelm him.

"Jesus, Jack, they killed them all. The entire crew." Carl stood aghast as he remembered the Russian sailors who had given the villagers gifts and happiness only a few days before.

Collins said nothing as he reached in and removed a small envelope that was pinned to Dishlakov's uniform jacket. He handed it over to Niles, who stood and stared at the box for the longest time. Instead of reading the message—

because at the moment, he could not trust his voice—he handed the letter to Alice, who didn't want to but tore it open nonetheless.

Dearest Dr. Compton,

Please accept this gift from your new acquaintances across the sea who are endeavoring to end close to six hundred years of injustice to the people of Russia. While we regard your mission to your government worthwhile and meaningful, our hopes are that there is a mutual regard and acquiescence to our goals as well. If not, we have many years to solve our differences. If you desire, you and your president can make this a public matter. If this is the course you choose, we can solve our dilemma sooner, rather than later. We are prepared for this and will be even more so in the near future.

Until we meet again in the fields of endeavor we have both chosen for our life's work, I bid you and your marvelous group farewell. It is a frightening world, is it not?

Vassick

Alice handed the note and envelope to Jack as Jason, Will, and Jenks eased the body of Second Captain Dishlakov from the box. They laid him on the grass by the drive as Sarah, who had slipped inside the house, covered the former naval officer in a bedsheet.

"What do we do now?" Virginia asked, angered at the development coming at the end of such a happy occasion.

Niles looked up at the anxious faces looking his way. "Let's ask the men who had served with Second Captain Dishlakov and his crew. Jack?"

Collins pulled the sheet back and reached down and removed the topmost medal from the breast jacket of the second captain. He looked at the overly large citation and then placed it in his pocket and walked away as the others watched on.

"What was that?" Charlie asked.

Carl turned and started to follow Collins when he heard the question.

"That was the Russian naval commendation awarded by the politburo. It's their version of the medal of honor."

"What's Jack going to do with it?" Xavier asked, not believing what was happening.

Carl Everett looked at the men and women watching Jack enter the house, and then they waited for an answer that all but the naïve already knew.

"It may not be now, next year, or five years down the road, but Jack just promised himself he would pin that medal to Comrade Vassick's liver."

Niles Compton turned also and followed Collins.

"And that man's going to help him do it."

Things had changed for Department 5656, known to a select few as the Event Group. A new element had been silently added to their federal charter, and the world to them and the country would never be the same again.